Shadows of the Past

Trilogy of Flames

Morgan Summers

Published by Morgan Summers

ISBN: 979-8-218-77316-8

Disclaimer:

This novel is a work of fiction. Names, characters, places, and incidents are either the product of the author's imagination or used fictitiously.

Warning:

This novel contains some violence, fear, blood, death, grief, and minor swearing. Please read at your own discretion.

*For those who learned that ruthlessness is a form
of self preservation*

Prologue

They were coming. She could hear them shouting behind her. She couldn't let them catch up.

Couldn't.

Shouldn't.

Wouldn't.

Her mind raced as she sprinted through the foliage. Hair whipped her cheek as she turned her head to see behind her. She stumbled over a root, barely catching herself as she looked forward again.

He was running close by. He would never leave her alone, not when they had left together. Their friends were dead. She had to avenge them.

Avenge.

Revenge.

Vengeance is justice.

Shouts sounded in the distance as they ran. She began to pant, her breaths coming in short gasps as they ran faster than they had ever run before. A rabbit hopped out of her path. A bird cawed in the distance, startled from its perch. She glanced at him. He was staring ahead, his gaze focused intently on the path before him. She leaped over a fallen tree.

The noises of pursuit faded into the background, and she slowed to a stop. He followed. They were both breathing heavily. She glanced behind them, ears straining to hear the yelling.

Yelling.

Shouting.

Screaming.

Death.

She shook her head. Too many words were running through her mind.

She nodded to him. "We need to find somewhere to rest for a while."

"Okay," he replied.

The rushing of a small waterfall sounded in the direction they had been running toward. She made her way over to it and stepped cautiously out of the trees to find an expansive lake with a trickle of water flowing over a cliff, sending out rings of ripples across the shimmering surface. She walked over to the wall of water and began searching.

She praised a god she didn't know if she believed in anymore when she walked into a cave behind the waterfall. A pause in the pattering of water told her that he had followed her in. Giving him a grim smile, she turned back around and walked toward the back of the cave.

Dim light from the moon filtered through the far end of the cave. *Another entrance,* she thought, the words echoing in her head. She carefully walked back to where she had left him.

"It's a tunnel," she told him. "We shouldn't stay here too long, but we need to rest."

"You're right," he said quietly.

They both leaned against the cave wall and slid down. She leaned her head on his shoulder and fell asleep, planning on sleeping for only a short while.

Time had escaped her, but when she woke, he was standing at the waterfall, drinking from cupped hands. Standing, she walked up to the waterfall and mimicked him.

Wiping her mouth, she told him, "We should get moving. They could be here at any moment."

"You're too late on that account."

They spun around to see a man—someone they both knew had come to take them back—standing there, pointing a gun at them. The man motioned for them to get moving.

"I'm taking you back," the man told them.

A swift glance was shared between them before they turned their gazes back to the man and followed him through the tunnel opening at the back. They all walked out of the cave, and the man started leading them back to where the pair had escaped.

She couldn't go back to that place. Nothing they could do would make her return. Leaves crunched under her feet as she came to a halt. The man pressed the gun to her head.

"Keep moving," the man growled.

She took a deep breath before spinning around, knocking the gun from his hand with a practiced move. Grabbing his head, she pulled his face onto her knee, then punched his left eye as he straightened. The man took it in stride, then repaid her with a punch to the gut.

"Stop it!" he shouted.

She glanced at him. The look cost her. When she looked back at the man, he was reaching for his discarded gun. She raced over and kicked it away from him. The man growled at her and grabbed her around the waist. She elbowed him with all her might between his shoulder blades, but the man kept pushing her backward, her feet lifting slightly off the ground.

He made to move toward her, but the man shoved her back. Off the cliff. She screamed.

"Holly!" He shouted her name, over and over, but all she could do was scream until she hit the surface of the water.

Pain exploded down her body as she sank into the liquid depths of the lake by the waterfall. Water filled her open mouth. She needed air. Her mind raced as she tried to move her body, but she couldn't. Her body wouldn't respond. She thrashed in the water, her body convulsing as it tried to get air, but there was only water.

Darkness swept into her vision, and all she could think about was him. He had to escape, even if she couldn't.

Chapter 1

Noise assaulted Holly's ears as she entered the crowded cafeteria, adjusting the straps of her backpack on her shoulders as she scanned the massive room for her friends. She searched the crowd of chattering teenagers for a few seconds before she saw Naomi's hand waving her over to a table near the doors leading outside on the other side of the cafeteria. Holly walked briskly over to the table, stepping out of the path of some giggling sophomore girls in skirts that bordered on skimpy, and sat down next to Jay.

Nathan was noticeably absent from the table—something that had become more and more commonplace in the past few months since they started their senior year of high school. Ever since being made captain of the cheerleading squad, the last person in their friend group had spent less time with them at lunch and more time with his team, and the football team. It sometimes felt like he was avoiding them. Any feelings of abandonment from him were forgotten on those increasingly uncommon occasions when he found the time to hang out with them. His charismatic conversations were enough to keep all of them from the usual dynamics into which they had fallen in his absence. Not that those dynamics were a bad thing, but Holly was getting more irritated every time Naomi and Zac got into one of their debates.

Jay had his head down. He was looking at some homework, not paying any attention to Holly's approach or Zac and Naomi's latest bickering contest. Not wanting to tune into it, Holly pulled out her holopad and started on her chemistry homework. She pressed the end of her digi-pen against her lips as her mind went through the steps of the Lewis structure she was supposed to be drawing. Pulling up an image of the periodic table, she scanned the holographic image before finding the element and began drawing the structure for it.

Moving on to the next section of her assignment, Holly tapped the end of her digi-pen against her temple as she tried to concentrate on her homework. Study hall was always like this, her and Jay trying to do homework while Zac and

Naomi argued back and forth about various topics—though they would never admit to their *conversations* being arguments. It usually ended with Jay disappearing to the computer lab and Holly putting in her earbuds, but today would be different. Holly had forgotten her earbuds at home, which meant that if she had to suffer through their two friends arguing like an old married couple, then so did Jay.

Jay tried to stand up, having finally had his fill of the argument across the table, but Holly put her hand on his shoulder before he could get further than a few inches off his seat and forced him to sit back down. He huffed, shooting her a glance, but didn't say anything before going back to his AP physics homework. After about five more minutes of suffering through their squabble, Holly got tired of listening to them.

She let out a long-suffering sigh. "Don't you two know how to have a civil conversation without it turning into a disagreement?"

Across from her, her two friends snapped their mouths shut. They slid their focus to her. Naomi's honey brown eyes sparkled in the harsh lights of the cafeteria, her black braids swaying in their ponytail as she turned her head. Zac's blue eyes flickered with embarrassment, his cheeks flushing a vibrant red.

Holly had been friends with the four of them, including Nathan, for about five years, so she had learned the hard way how often Zac and Naomi tended to get into one of their arguments. Normally, she would just suck it up, but she had a test in her next class on mythological beings in ancient cultures, and she needed to finish her chemistry homework before she could cram in some extra studying for it. She had stayed up late the night before studying for it, but she didn't feel ready. The test would be a piece of cake if it focused on Ancient Greek or Ancient Native American myths and deities, but Holly had a feeling that Mr. Jeffords would have one of the essay questions be on the presence of Elementals throughout every ancient mythology and the connection between each variation.

"Sorry, Holly," Zac muttered, running his fingers through his dirty blond hair.

"Wuss," Naomi told him, rolling her eyes.

Zac rolled his eyes in return, a soft smile on his lips that was hardly noticeable, but didn't reply. Naomi nudged him with her elbow.

"We will finish our discussion later when Holly isn't studying for a test," she assured him. Despite her tone, Zac didn't seem all that reassured—he must have been letting her win, again.

"You call that a discussion?" Jay chimed in, finally looking up long enough from his homework to enter the conversation. His brown eyes were red underneath the rim of his glasses, indicating that he had likely pulled another all-nighter researching some obscure historical event 'for fun'. "That sounded more like a cat fight. And, shouldn't you be studying too, Naomi? You're in the same class."

"Studying is overrated." Naomi crossed her arms over her chest indignantly. "Besides, what use would knowledge of mythological elementals have in the real world?"

"Didn't you choose this class for your social studies elective?" Zac asked her.

Naomi didn't reply; instead, she changed the subject. "So, any guesses on who will be picked for the representatives this year?"

Zac pressed his lips together, clearly not liking her not-so-smooth change of topic.

"Isn't it obvious?" Jay said, setting down his digi-pen and turning off the screen of his holopad.

Raising her eyebrow at him, Naomi skeptically replied, "Okay, Captain Obvious. If it's so clear to you, why don't you just tell us?"

Jay gave her a flat look but replied nonetheless. "Typically, in the past, the representatives are chosen from the students with the highest potential for positions in military leadership. So, good grades, excellent leadership qualities, the likes."

"Great," Naomi droned sarcastically. "So basically eighty percent of the entire student body."

"We're not a military academy, Naomi," Zac admonished.

She snorted. "Might as well be. All we're missing are the uniforms."

"Well," Jay continued. "At least we know you won't be chosen, Naomi."

"Hey!" Naomi whined playfully, pouting a bit before adding, "That's not nice, it's true, but still."

Holly snorted.

Zac patted Naomi sympathetically on the shoulder as he asked, "What were you saying, Jay?"

Clearing his throat, Jay picked up where he had left off. "Right. Well, like I was saying, it's obvious who they're going to pick. Who do we know that's smart, popular, and athletic?"

"Nathan," Holly offered, turning off the screen to her holopad and sliding both it and her digi-pen into her backpack.

"Right," Jay replied enthusiastically, pointing the end of his digi-pen in her direction.

Naomi tapped her lips with the tip of her finger. "Then that would mean the girl representative has got to be—"

"Izzie Baldwin," Jay interrupted.

A slight frown on her face, Naomi opened her mouth to respond, but was cut off by the bell.

As the bell rang, Holly and Naomi said farewell to the boys and began walking to their next class.

"Are you ready for the test?" Naomi asked, shouldering her way through the crowd of dawdling sophomores.

"Are you?" Holly retorted, raising her eyebrow and shooting her best friend a look from the corner of her eye. "I doubt you have even opened the textbook Mr. Jeffords gave us at the beginning of the year."

Naomi smirked.

"Naomi, we graduate in two months!" Holly exclaimed.

"Holly, how long have we been friends?" she asked, raising a dark eyebrow as she waited for Holly to respond.

"Five years."

Naomi smiled, her white teeth a stark contrast to her dark skin as she said, "Exactly, you should know by now just how much I hate studying."

"I do know that." Holly dodged around a group of girls chatting about the latest celebrity gossip. "I also know that you're going to regret not doing so one of these days."

Rolling her eyes, Naomi adjusted the strap of her backpack on her shoulder. "I have never studied a day in my life, and look how well it's turned out for me."

"Didn't you fail robotics last year?"

A stray football soared through the air above their heads, followed by a surge in the crowd behind them as whoever caught it likely stumbled against the people in front of them, causing a domino effect.

"That's different. I only took that class because I needed to fill in my schedule; besides, that class doesn't have any tests to study for. It's all about how skilled you are with technology." Naomi defended, shooting a murderous glare over her shoulder at the football guy who was prepping to return the throw. It was Holly's turn to roll her eyes.

Naomi was many things, but a good liar was not one of them. Holly knew the real reason her friend had taken the class wasn't because she needed a class to fill the empty slot in her schedule; it was because Zac was also in the class. But Holly let her have this, if only so she didn't have to keep bickering over something so trivial right before a test.

The tardy bell rang as they were sitting in their seats, the entire class reluctantly quieting as Mr. Jeffords stood and told everyone to pull out their holopads and put their phones away. There was some whispering on the other side of the classroom that had Holly glancing over to see Dylan Moros and his group of friends. Dylan was chuckling at something his friend Devin had said when he looked over and made eye contact with

Holly. She shot a disdainful look his way and turned her gaze back to the teacher. In her lap, she absentmindedly rubbed her hands together, the motion soothing her anxiety.

Dylan was one of the smartest kids in the school; he had even won an award their junior year of high school for an essay he had written, but that didn't mean he was necessarily one of the best behaved. He and his friends were some of the most obnoxious kids in the school. They were always chatting at a ridiculously loud volume. It was unclear if their mouths had off switches or if they were stuck on max volume at all times.

Mr. Jeffords finished giving instructions and reminded the class to keep quiet during the test, looking pointedly in the direction of Dylan and his friends. None of the boys noticed the attention, except for Dylan, but he didn't say anything to them.

Taking one glimpse at the test, Holly knew she should have studied more during study hall instead of chatting so much with her friends. All of Dylan's friends were in class that day, which meant that taking the test would be just that much harder. Holly stifled a sigh. Dylan's friends weren't *terrible*; they were just a general pain to deal with, and she didn't typically have the patience to do so.

As Mr. Jeffords left the room, Holly started on the test and tried to block out the not-so-subtle noises coming from the other end of the classroom. Fifteen minutes in, someone tried shushing them, but that just made them louder. Holly was able to make it through a good portion of the test before she couldn't even hear her thoughts. From the corner of her eye, she could see Naomi's agitation at the noise. Her friend's leg was bouncing restlessly beneath her desk, and she kept darting increasingly frustrated glances in their direction. Mr. Jeffords still had yet to return to the classroom, so there was no one with the authority to get the boys to be quiet. That is, until the fuse reached the dynamite.

"Will you all, kindly, *zip it*?" Naomi snapped, her grip on her digi-pen tight enough that her fingernails were likely to leave crescent-shaped imprints in her palm. Her eyes were on the group of boys, who had, in fact, snapped their mouths closed and were tentatively waiting for her to say something more. The eyes of the other students were also on Naomi. Holly had to force down a proud grin as she glanced sidelong at her best friend. When it came to taking tests, Naomi was a ticking time bomb, if even the slightest sound distracted her, she would go off on whoever had made the sound. It was a miracle she hadn't stood up and thrown her chair at the boys for all the racket they were making. Maybe that was a bit of an exaggeration, but Holly knew that however much Naomi hated studying for tests, she had to admit that she was amazingly good at taking them—and getting a good score—so long as the room was basically silent.

Eyes locked on the loudest of the bunch, Naomi narrowed her gaze at him, their honeyed depths daring him to say something more. His lips twitched into a smirk. That was all it took for Naomi to push back her chair as she stood and stalked over to them. Holly stumbled out from behind her desk, her mind replaying all the times she had been sent to detention by proxy of being there when Naomi had gotten into a fight, and hurried over to where Naomi towered over the seated boys, staring down Devin Lewis.

"Naomi," Holly muttered, a warning.

"Something wrong, sweetheart?" Devin asked.

Naomi's nostrils flared. "Call me sweetheart one more time."

The smirk on Devin's face widened.

Holly saw Naomi's hands tighten into fists.

"Leave it, Naomi. He's not worth it," Holly warned, clenching her own hand into a fist to keep herself from putting it on her friend's arm—a move that would definitely end with Naomi starting a fight.

"Let her at him, princess. He could do with a good punch to knock some sense into him," Dylan chimed in, a smug look on his face as he nudged a disgruntled Devin in the arm and leaned back in his chair.

Holly's attention zipped to Dylan. "Back off, *charming* or your pretty face might be the next one hit."

Dylan blinked. "What?"

Ignoring him, Holly firmly gripped Naomi's arm. "Come on, Naomi."

She tugged on her friend's arm. Naomi didn't fight back, but she sent Devin one last warning glance and said, "If I hear one more noise come from any of you before this test is done, I will find a duct tape roll large enough to cover your big fat mouth."

With that, Naomi allowed Holly to lead her back to their desks and sit down. Their other classmates had since turned back to their holopads, pretending not to have witnessed any of the heated conversation.

The rest of the class period went by smoothly after that, with not so much as a peep from the other side of the room. Naomi had clearly gotten to them on some level—even if her reaction was a bit much—but Holly couldn't decide if that was a good thing or not. Mr. Jeffords finally returned with only five minutes left in class.

With a glance around the room, he said, "Well, I can see that everyone has finished their test. Feel free to chat openly or get on your phones for the rest of the period."

Chatter started up slowly around the room, with many of their classmates throwing nervous glances at Naomi as they began talking. Holly laughed under her breath as she slid her holopad into her backpack.

"I think you have officially terrified our entire class," Holly told her.

"Eh, it was bound to happen eventually," Naomi replied nonchalantly. "Honestly, I'm surprised it's taken this long to happen."

Holly laughed. "Me too."

They kept talking as the bell rang and stood up to leave. Holly was stopped at the door by Dylan. She told Naomi to wait for her in the hall.

"What do you want?" she asked warily.

"To apologize," Dylan said. "For earlier."

"Okay, uh, thanks?" Holly said, unsure of how to respond.

It seemed like he wanted to say something more, but he just shook his head and moved aside to let her pass. Holly walked past him without another word, shooting a curious glance back at him before catching up to Naomi.

Chapter 2

The sun was burning brightly as Holly stepped out of the school and looked around for her mom's car. Her own car was still in the shop for the rest of the week, and it was too hot to walk the forty-plus minutes home. Students walked past her as she stood there on the sidewalk searching the line of hover-cars parked along the street. After a few moments of looking, she spotted the little gray hover-car and walked over, sliding her backpack off her shoulder as she slid into the passenger seat.

"How was school today?" her mom asked.

"It was fine," Holly replied. "How was your date with Eddie last night?"

Eddie was her mom's boyfriend of two years. Holly had been skeptical when they had first started dating, but she had grown to like

Eddie. He acted more like a dad than her biological father had.

Holly shut down any thoughts of her father.

Two weeks earlier, Eddie had come to her and asked her for help planning a proposal to her mom. It had been exciting, planning something so monumentally life-changing and keeping it all a secret from everyone—including her younger brothers Dustin and Andrew.

As they turned a corner, the diamond ring sparkled on her mother's hand. "It was wonderful, but I suspect you already know how it was."

A knowing glimmer shone in her brown eyes. Eddie must have told her that Holly was in the bushes of the riverbed snapping pictures of the proposal. It had been magical seeing Eddie kneel on the wood of the bridge and ask her mom to be his wife. The sunset at Holly's back had set the scene perfectly.

"Have you told Dusty or Andrew that Eddie proposed?" Holly asked.

"I haven't had the chance."

"And Adam?" Her voice was tentative, the subject of her older brother just as tense as the day he had moved out after high school. That was the last time she had seen him. She knew things had been difficult for him since the incident with their father, but she didn't think that warranted him to disappear from their lives completely. All of the texts and calls she had sent him over the past couple of years had gone unanswered. He seemed intent on maintaining radio silence.

Her mom sighed. "I tried calling him, I even left a voicemail asking him to call me back, but there's been no response."

Holly slumped back in her seat. She should have known better than to hope Adam would just come back out of the blue after all this time. Things hadn't been the same since he had left. They had all been struggling with moving to a new district, but when Adam had moved out after a heated argument with their mom and then never came back...

Turning her head to peer out the window, Holly watched the buildings flash by as she collected her thoughts and pushed aside her disappointment that Adam wouldn't be there for the wedding.

Shifting back to her mom, she said, "Have you guys picked out a date yet?"

"Holly," her mom laughed. "It hasn't even been twenty-four hours since he proposed."

"And?" Holly urged. "You guys have talked about getting married for like six months now. I bet you spent at least an hour discussing it this morning."

Her mother slid her gaze to her for a moment before turning on the car's autodriver and changing her focus back to the discussion.

"Okay, so maybe we *have* decided on a tentative date," Her mom gave in. "But that doesn't mean it's set in stone."

Holly rolled her eyes. Honestly, she was surprised they hadn't planned most of the wedding prior to their engagement. She couldn't count the number of times she had walked past their bedroom as they discussed the possibility of marriage. One thing she knew for certain, though, was that she wasn't going to let them plan it without her.

"Spill the beans, mom," Holly begged. "When is it?"

"All right, fine. You win. We were thinking about doing April seventeenth," she relented.

Scrunching her brow, Holly asked, "You want to get married the day after the entire country is celebrating the hundredth anniversary of its reconstruction?"

As the hover-car pulled into the garage, Holly's mom turned off the engine. "We know it's not the best timing, but we have waited for this long enough, don't you think?"

The question gave Holly pause. It had *definitely* been long enough. So it made sense that they would want to do it soon, but the centennial was just over a month away. Preparing a wedding in that short of time would be a miracle at best. Not to mention the possibility of Holly being chosen for the Solstice High female representative position. It was a one-in-a-thousand chance of her being chosen, but there was always the possibility.

"I guess you're right," Holly told her. Both of them climbed out of the car and walked into the house. She was about to head to her room when she paused and turned back to her mom. "There was something else you wanted to tell me, wasn't there?"

There was a flicker of surprise in her mother's eyes, but it was quickly overshadowed by excitement. "I haven't told anyone else, not even Eddie. But, I suppose it won't hurt to tell you."

"Tell me what?"

Her mom smiled. "I'm pregnant."

Holly felt her jaw drop, her backpack thudding on the floor as it slipped off her shoulder. *Pregnant.* Her mom was... She squealed with delight and rushed over to her mom, tackling her with a hug. Pulling back, Holly smiled at her mom and took a few steps back.

"I need you to promise not to tell anyone," her mom requested. Holly nodded. She was going to have another sibling!

The excitement of her mom's announcement was almost enough to make Holly want to skip her homework, but she had to finish and turn in an essay for her college resume before midnight.

Her head was throbbing. Writing essays *sucked*. If she never had to write another one in her life, she would be ecstatic. Three months of procrastination had led her to spend a mind-numbing four hours after school writing an essay to get into Stanford. She had already sent in her first application way back in November, but the university was asking her for another writing sample before they would get back to her on whether or not she had been accepted. Tomorrow was the deadline for her to send it in, and she had put it off until the last minute.

A knock on her door pulled Holly from her thoughts. Rubbing her temples, she scooted back her chair and stood. Eddie was at the door, his blue-grey eyes shining and his dirty blond hair tousled from working.

Eddie was a skydiving instructor, so he usually got to choose his hours, which was nice because he was home often and could spend more time with the family. Holly's mom had taken them all skydiving for Dustin's thirteenth birthday two years ago, and Eddie had been their instructor. After their flight and subsequent dive, Eddie had asked her on a date, and one thing had led to another. His clients usually consisted of bored rich people who had nothing better to do with their time, so he had a pretty good salary—or so Holly assumed.

With a soft smile on his lips, Eddie asked, "Holly, could I talk to you and Dustin for a few minutes?"

"Sure." Holly nodded and followed him to the room he shared with her mom.

Dustin was already sitting on the bed, his leg bouncing restlessly as he waited for them to come in. As he saw them, he said," Can we make this quick? My friends and I were in the middle of a round."

Holly rolled her eyes and sat down next to him. When he wasn't off messing around with his friends, Dustin was playing video games with them. It had led to him getting grounded multiple times for not doing his homework.

Eddie leaned against the dresser, crossing his arms across his chest and facing them. "I wanted to talk to you guys about the wedding."

"Can't we do this later?" Dustin whined. "My friends are waiting."

Holly flicked his ear. "This is important, Dusty-bun. Your friends can manage without you."

"Ow!" Dustin's hand went to his ear. "Would you stop calling me that? I'm fifteen, not four."

Sticking her tongue out at him, Holly said, "I will stop calling you that when you get a girlfriend who can do it instead."

"Guys," Eddie said, reminding them that he was still there. "Calm down."

Dustin glared at Holly but didn't say anything else.

Eddie continued, "I know this is short notice, but the date for the wedding is April seventeenth, and we would really appreciate it if you guys could help out with the planning. That also means that you two need to start looking for your outfits."

Holly nodded. "What are the colors?"

"We were thinking of doing crimson for the bridesmaids and navy for the groomsmen."

They were beautiful colors, and they would work well together. Holly's mind raced as she thought of different styles of dresses she would try. Shoving those thoughts into a box for later, Holly brought her mind back to the conversation.

"Next week we will be putting the flower arrangements together, so Holly, your mom would appreciate it if you could help out with that," Eddie continued, going through the things they wanted Holly and Dustin to help out with until they were interrupted by Andrew bursting through the door like a juggernaut.

Andrew's light brown hair had a kaleidoscope of paint streaked through its strands. His dark blue eyes were wide with excitement as he barreled into the room, his face smeared with the same paint evident in his hair and on his hands.

"Mommy says it's time for dinner," Andrew giggled, running up to Eddie and hugging his legs. The action likely left bright red handprints on the back of Eddie's jeans, but he didn't seem to mind. At age six, Andrew was a sweet little boy with more energy than any kid Holly had ever met, but he was also the embodiment of chaos incarnate whenever he happened to get his hands on paint—or vice versa, given the state of his hair and clothes at the moment.

After releasing Eddie from his hug, Andrew scuttled over to the bed. Standing, Holly crouched down to pick him up. She lifted him into the air and kissed his cherub cheeks as he squealed with delight.

"Were you having fun painting?" Holly asked him.

He nodded vigorously. "I painted a forest today. Do you want to see it?"

"Of course I do!" Holly set him down. "But not until we have eaten dinner, okay?"

"Okay!" Andrew left the room in a flash, his bare feet pattering like a penguin's on the wooden floor of the hallway and stairs.

The smell of freshly baked Italian bread permeated Holly's nose as she followed Andrew into the dining room, Dustin and Eddie a few paces behind her. Her mom was placing a bowl of pasta on the table when Andrew pattered past her, slowing only to climb into his chair. Andrew squirmed under their mom's hands as she tried to rub off some of the paint on his face.

"Mom!" he complained, swatting at her hands. "You're removing my war paint!"

"War paint isn't allowed at the dinner table." Their mom took a step back, her hands on her hips as she double-checked her war paint removal.

Andrew huffed, crossing his little arms across his chest, and grumbled, "Fine. I will put it back later."

He sat there staring at his plate as she rubbed the rest of the paint from his face. His cheeks were red by the time she finished and sat down with the rest of them. Once they were all seated, she clasped her hands together and bowed her head to bless the food. The rest of them followed suit, and as Holly's mom finished speaking, they all said "Amen" then began to pile their plates with food.

When most of them were almost finished eating, Andrew was still pushing his vegetables around his plate. Dustin had left a few minutes earlier to get back to his game.

"Andrew, eat your broccoli or you're not getting any ice cream tonight," Holly's mom warned. This conversation would happen at least once a week. Andrew never *wanted* to eat his vegetables, but he would eat them for the most part—unless it was broccoli.

"But it's so gross!" he whined.

"Eat it anyway. It's good for you."

"No, it's not," he mumbled, continuing to stab at the broccoli and swirling it around his plate.

As their mom was finally able to convince him to eat the broccoli, she began helping to clean up dinner. Holly carried the empty dishes over to the sink, setting them on the counter next to it before beginning to put away the clean dishes from the dishwasher. Andrew had wandered off, likely to apply more war paint, but not before their mom squeezed out a promise to take a bath that night before she followed Eddie into the front room.

Plates clinked together as Holly finished stacking them in the cupboard. Brushing her hands on her jeans, she moved on to putting the dirty dishes from dinner into the dishwasher. Quiet conversation drifted over to her from the front room where her mom and Eddie were talking. It was too soft for her to make out what they were saying, but she assumed it was about the wedding, so she finished placing the dishes in the dishwasher and pressed start on the machine.

Her mom and Eddie were still talking as she walked past the room and went back to her bedroom. The rest of her homework called to her from where her holopad sat on her desk, but the exhaustion from writing the essay earlier had her falling onto her bed. She knew sleep would be a long time coming, so she just lay on her stomach, her face half buried in her pillow as she scrolled through social media on her phone.

Chapter 3

The blaring of Holly's alarm was an unwelcome sound that wrested her from the reluctant tranquility of sleep. Letting out a groan, Holly pushed herself up in bed and slammed her hand on the off button to her alarm, rubbing sleep from her eyes as she urged her body to move.

A ding sounded from her phone—which she had apparently fallen asleep on and likely had an imprint of on the side of her face. Probably a *good morning* text from her boyfriend. Her phone was a familiar weight in her hand the moment she picked it up to reply to his text.

Good morning, sweetheart

'*Morning*

You excited for today?

Huh?

Today's the Representative Selection Day, isn't it?

Selection day, right, how could she have forgotten about that? There had been announcements for it at school since the beginning of the year. Today would be the day Domina Garner—along with her assistant, Secretary Selena Garcia, and the top general of the nation, General Hunter Falcon—would announce who would represent their school at the anniversary festival.

The annual anniversary festival entailed a selection of students from the high schools in the district selected for that year giving speeches about the history of the country and the significance of its rebuilding, as well as the country's significance to them personally. Reigning sovereigns from many foreign nations visited Verdona to attend the festival. It was the dream of many kids to be able to represent their school and meet the leaders of various countries across the globe. It looked great on their resumes and college applications as well.

This year, the representatives were coming from the Sunhaven district, and Solstice High was one of the schools within the district that had been chosen.

Oh, that. Holly replied. *I almost forgot about it.*

Her boyfriend sent a laughing emoji.

I thought you might have. Anyways, have fun at school.

Holly returned the heart emoji he had sent, then set her phone back on her nightstand before begrudgingly pushing herself to her feet to get ready for school.

Dustin's door was still closed as she walked past. Banging on it a couple of times on her way down the hall, she heard him groan in protest of getting up. Her mom was already in the kitchen, a mug of freshly brewed coffee steaming in her hands.

Wishing her good morning, Holly reached past her and filled her own mug of coffee. Adding two sugar cubes to the dark liquid, she stirred them in and walked over to the pantry to check out the cereal collection. She blew gently on her steaming coffee before grabbing a box of cereal and returning to the counter to pour herself a bowl.

Blue basketball shorts and a rumpled green t-shirt accompanied the rat's nest that was Dustin's hair as he blearily stomped his way into the kitchen and slumped onto the nearest bar stool. His head fell into his folded arms the moment he stopped moving. Pouring him a bowl of the cereal in her hand, Holly added the milk and a spoon before sliding it over to him. He grunted appreciatively, then lifted his head enough to rest it on his hand as he took a bite.

Finished with her coffee, their mom rubbed Holly's back as she slid out of the kitchen. Patting Dustin lovingly on the head as she walked past, she picked up a recently awakened Andrew before he could start running laps through the kitchen and set him on the stool next to Dustin.

Andrew stared up at his brother and said, "Mommy, when did Dustin become a zombie? I wanna be a zombie."

Dustin flicked a piece of his cereal at his brother. It landed, and stuck, to Andrew's cheek before sliding down and landing on the quartz countertop.

"Mooom," Andrew whined, silver tears beginning to line his eyes, which were on their mom as she prepared him a bowl of oatmeal.

Leaning over her own bowl of cereal, Holly wiped the trail of milk from Andrew's cheek. "Ignore him, he's grumpy 'cause he didn't win his video game last night."

A grunt from her other brother was as much of a confirmation as she needed as she returned to her own bowl of cereal, taking another bite in an effort to hide her smile at Andrew sticking his tongue out at Dustin.

"Dustin," their mom said, placing the oatmeal in front of Andrew. "Be nice."

Another grunt. "Fine. Sorry."

Giving him a kiss on the head, she said, "Thank you. Now go get ready for school, or you will be late."

Fifteen minutes later, Holly was walking into the school, Dustin trudging along behind her, his eyes glued to his phone as he texted his best friend. Everywhere she went, there were conversations about who would be most likely to go. Almost nobody seemed to agree on any one person who would be chosen for the female representative, but Izzy Baldwin's name popped up more often than any of the others. Izzy Baldwin, the captain of the women's football team. Holly had to admit she did seem like a likely candidate. There were, however, more than a few people who speculated that Nathan would be chosen for the male representative.

School went by as it usually did, but there was an underlying current of anticipation running through the building as the end of the day approached and the scheduled post-lunch assembly was soon upon them all. The usual noise of the cafeteria came to an immediate halt as the expected announcement came over the loudspeakers. "Attention students, lunch is officially over, please make your way to the auditorium for the representative selection, thank you."

Conversations once again flooded the hallways, which were bustling with students making their way to the auditorium. Naomi gripped Holly's hand to keep from being separated as they entered the throng.

The hum of dozens of conversations happening at once filled the sprawling room as students filed in and took their seats. Chairs were quickly filled, and friends waved to each other from across the aisles while they all waited for everyone to find a spot to sit. Holly felt the push and pull of the tide of students tugging her forward. She stumbled over her feet as the teens behind her pushed toward the front of the room. Naomi helped steady her a moment before entering the row of seats, taking the last two open chairs, and separating them from Jay and Zac, who had somehow managed to stick close to them up until that moment.

A hologram of the Domina, Secretary Garcia, and General Falcon was already up on the stage, and the buzz of chattering teenagers died once she opened her mouth to speak.

"Thank you all for coming today," Domina Garner began. "I know you have all likely been anticipating this all day, so let's skip the preamble and get straight to it, shall we?"

She paused, waiting as the scattered cheers from the overenthusiastic kids died down. The darkness of her skin gave off a sheen in the lights of the room on her end of the hologram. Despite her actual age, the Domina's complexion made her appear about twenty years younger than she was, but her eyes reflected her experience as they scanned the room of high schoolers, their true hazel color a hazy blue from the holographic technology.

A ripple went through the projection as the Domina continued, "As you all know, in about a month, it will be the centennial anniversary of the reconstruction of our great country, Verdona. Over the past few months, we have looked over the accomplishments of the seniors of this school, trying to find the male and female who we believe will best represent the qualities of this country's future generation. Students who have gone above and beyond to be the best they can be, whether it be in academics, athletics, or civil service."

When she paused to talk to someone out of view of the hologram, the conversations of speculation on who would be chosen rose once more until the room was again filled with a buzz of chatter.

"Students," the Domina interrupted. "We will now announce who will be representing this school. My assistant will read the names. Selena, if you will."

Secretary Garcia stepped forward as the Domina, and General Falcon stepped out of the holographic field.

"Good afternoon, students. Let's get straight to it." Lifting a holopad she had been holding, Secretary Garcia pressed a few buttons on it, then continued, "The male we have chosen to represent this school will be Dylan Moros."

Heads swiveled to where Dylan was sitting with his friends. There was no sign of emotion on his face, not even a smug grin that he was chosen. If anything, he almost looked resigned.

Secretary Garcia scrolled past whatever was on her holopad before saying, "The female we have chosen to represent this school will be Holly Carnell."

Holly blinked. After years of watching graduating seniors having their names called, she never thought she would be chosen for it.

Faces blurred as she processed the information. Her own face was a mixture of shock and disbelief as Naomi gripped her arm excitedly, and the other students around them all politely applauded.

"Congratulations to our fine young teenagers from Solstice High School!" Secretary Garcia announced.

"I knew someone from our group would end up being chosen for the representative," Naomi chattered as they came to a stop in front of the school. "I just never expected it to be you, Holly."

"Thanks for the vote of confidence," Holly deadpanned. Her best friend just smiled and patted her on the shoulder.

It was a week after the selection day, and Holly was about to head over to the airport via limousine to fly to the country's capital, Visceralis, in the district of Aldaria. According to their history textbooks, before the Nuclear World War, or even World War III, it used to be a city called Boise. It wasn't going to be a very long trip from Emerald Bay, but Holly was still a bit nervous to go on a plane for the first time.

"I just can't believe that you have to go with someone like Dylan," Nathan replied, shooting a disapproving look at Dylan.

"I heard that Morrison," Dylan remarked as he walked past, adjusting the strap of his backpack.

Nathan rolled his eyes dismissively. His disdain for Dylan not wholly unwarranted since it was Dylan who had beaten him out of a full-ride athletics scholarship to Stanford.

"I know." Holly sighed, knowing she was likely in for a long flight seated next to him. "Honestly, I would rather be stuck on a plane listening to Jay nerd out about an ancient puzzle called a Rubexit cube or something like that."

"That's not what it's called, and you know it. And, for your information, they used to be popular in the early twenty-first century," Jay retorted, folding his arms across his chest.

"My point exactly," Holly said, gesturing her hand at him.

"Wait," Naomi interrupted. "Isn't that around the time when people ate laundry detergent pods for fun?"

"Why would you remember something like that?"

"Because it's pointless to you."

"I think he meant, why would you *want* to remember something like that?" Zac clarified from his spot next to Nathan.

Naomi smirked. "And yet my answer would still be the same."

"You guys should get going," Holly told them, checking the time on her phone. "Class is starting soon."

The boys each gave her a high five, Zac reminding her to text them after landing, before turning and walking into the school behind them.

Throwing her arms around her, Naomi sighed melodramatically, "I'm going to miss you. Don't have too much fun without me, 'kay? And don't do anything I wouldn't do."

Holly returned the hug, rolling her eyes as she smiled and replied, "And what, exactly, would you not do?"

Pulling back, her best friend smiled and winked at her before waving goodbye, leaving Holly standing alone on the sidewalk next to the sleek black limo. She had said her farewells to her mom and brothers before heading out the door that morning in Naomi's car. Her mom had wanted to drive her, but Dustin had a dentist appointment she had to take him to, so she had reluctantly agreed to let Holly carpool with her friends.

Heaving a sigh, Holly turned to look at the limo. She hadn't gotten more than a couple hours of sleep the night before, and she could already tell her bad mood was not going to get any better. So, she took a deep breath and climbed into the limo. As she did so, Dylan asked, "You finally ready to go, princess?"

"Do you have a mute button? Cause I would love to use it right about now."

Dylan shut his mouth and cleared his throat at her harsh tone. Holly opened her mouth to apologize, but was too late as he had already turned away and put in his earbuds. She winced. No matter how annoying she thought Dylan was, she hadn't meant to be rude. Making a note to apologize to him later, Holly put in her own earbuds and turned to watch the passing scenery out the window.

The drive to the airport was long, but it had beautiful scenery. There were so many beautiful trees and flowers growing on the edge of the road. Towering redwoods overlooked what was left of their once crowded forests. The fields of their burnt trunks now overgrown with white wildflowers and bushes of holly, as well as thickets of creeping barberry. Even the old ruins from long-forgotten cities were stunning. The skeletons of skyscrapers still reaching toward the sky, the remainder of their endless windows that had survived the countless wars, glimmered in the sunlight.

Endless suburban neighborhoods—filled with white-picket fences with chipped paint and yards overgrown with shrubbery—covered the otherwise empty plains, the timeworn roads now covered in bomb pits. Many of the houses were beginning to crumble to ashes after surviving the Chinese-American War.

By the time they got to the airport, Holly thought Dylan would die of motion sickness. His leg kept bouncing restlessly as he stared out the window, his face a greenish color.

As they climbed out of the limo, they saw a couple of others parked next to it. Holly spotted a group of teenagers standing next to the baggage check-in and assumed they were the other representatives. In front of them was a Naval Lieutenant Commander and his entourage, his uniform a stark contrast to the jeans and t-shirts of the teenagers.

Once their luggage was taken care of, Holly followed the group of teenagers onto the plane, Dylan close behind her. The girl in front of her slowed her pace so she could walk next to Holly.

Giving her a warm smile, the blonde girl said, "Hi, my name's Karen. I'm one of the representatives from Drath."

"My name's Holly," Holly replied, returning the smile. "I'm one of the representatives from Solstice.

"It's nice to meet you, Holly," Karen said. She clasped her hands in front of her and added, "Are you nervous? I'm nervous. I have never been to Aldaria before."

"Me neither," Holly told her. "I am a little nervous, I have never been on a plane before."

Karen's smile turned reassuring. "Don't worry about it. There's nothing to be nervous about. At least when it comes to flying."

With that, Karen waved farewell and caught up to the icy blond boy who must have been the male representative from Drath. The boy didn't so much as glance at her as she caught up to him, then passed him to introduce herself to a brown-haired girl who was walking next to a guy who looked to be her twin.

A few minutes later, Holly was walking past the twins in the plane and taking a seat next to Dylan, who had slid past her before boarding to claim the window seat.

Dylan spent the first part of the flight looking out of the window or sleeping. Holly turned on the entertainment screen on the back of

the seat in front of her and turned on a movie—
not that she expected to get very far into it, given
how short the flight was supposed to be, but she
didn't have anything else to do.

Only a few minutes into the movie, there
was a sudden jerk in the plane, and suddenly it
dropped into a steep dive, gravity pulling the
passengers toward the front of the plane.

Screams filled the cabin as the other
passengers clutched their seats and each other.
Holly felt her stomach drop as her headphones fell
off, her voice joining the screams. She looked at
Dylan, who met her gaze, fear in his eyes.

A split second later, Holly realized she
didn't have her seat belt on when she was vaulted
into the air as the plane rotated in its fall. Her
body was slammed into the ceiling, sending sparks
flying across her vision. Then, Dylan was pulling
her back into her seat and strapping on her
seatbelt.

The right wing of the plane billowed smoke
into the air. Wind and gravity tore away the wing,
taking a portion of the cabin wall with it.

Oxygen masks dropped from above them.
Fighting against the centripetal force, Holly
managed to secure hers over her mouth.

Air gushed through the hole, ripping at the metal and taking the Lieutenant Commander with it. Holly stared, wide-eyed, as he was yanked into the open air.

A flight attendant slid down the aisle next to Holly. Wind pulled at her blonde hair as she fought futilely against gravity.

Holly's head smacked into the seat in front of her as the plane crashed into the ground.

Seatbelts snapped like rubber bands.

Other flight attendants were flung across the plane, breaking chairs as they landed, not moving again.

Chapter 4

Light filtered through her lashes as she regained consciousness. Shadows moved along the remnants of the plane's walls. As her mind replayed the events, she was reminded of Dylan pulling her back into her seat, something that had likely saved her life. She shakily pushed herself off the ground, her head spinning faster than a top, to check on him and immediately regretted it as she blacked out again upon seeing him lying in a pool of blood next to her.

Hushed whispers roused Holly from unconsciousness. Her head throbbed too much to hear more than the words 'plane' and 'explosion', but she thought she also heard one of the voices say the word 'bomb'.

Forcing her eyes open, Holly squinted against the brightness of the room. Once her vision had adjusted, she shifted until she was leaning on her elbows and looking around the room. She was in a hospital room. To her right, the curtain was drawn, but to her left, on a bed identical to hers, was Dylan. He was still lying down, but she could tell he was awake.

"Dylan?" she croaked, her voice hoarse.

Turning his head to see her, he replied, "That's me. How are you feeling?"

Scrunching her brow, Holly did a mental scan of her body, taking note of all the aches she felt. Her left arm was in a sling, and her left leg was in a cast resting on top of a couple of pillows, but she couldn't really feel pain from them, only numbness—which meant that whatever pain medication they had given her must be working.

She shrugged, "Been better. You?"

Dylan pressed a button on the side of his bed, the mechanism of the bed lifting him into a seated position. He grimaced at the movement, but then he was saying, "Doc says I got a few fractured ribs, a broken wrist, and a *slight* concussion, but other than that, I'm fine."

As if Dylan's mention of him had summoned him, the doctor came in to check on them. "Good morning, Miss Carnell. Well, good afternoon, I suppose, given the time. How are you feeling?"

"Like I have a rat chewing on my brain," she answered, rolling her neck a bit.

"That would be the trauma to your head, which caused a major concussion, and your broken nose, but it should be gone in a few hours. You also have a dislocated shoulder and a hairline fracture in your left tibia, but those should also be gone in a few hours if you don't overexert yourself and let the argenteral do its job," the doctor replied.

"How long was I out?"

"Three weeks," Dylan called from the other bed, a nurse checking his vitals and writing down the results on a holopad.

"What?!"

"It's only been a few hours," the doctor told her.

Using her uninjured arm, Holly flung an extra pillow at Dylan, who was laughing and clutching his ribs. The pillow landed with a smack right in his face, muffling the laughter and causing the nurse to jump. She sent Holly a disapproving look, which Holly returned with an apologetic smile.

Holly had never seen Dylan act like this with her before. It was unusual. He rarely interacted with her when they went to swim meets, usually preferring to sit and joke around with his friends or do some reading.

"Alright, I deserved that," he said after removing the pillow from his face.

Despite herself, Holly felt a smile pull at her lips. This boy had saved her life, and now he was cracking jokes with her like nothing had happened. That alone was enough to surprise her, and she wasn't sure what to do with that information. If he wasn't the obnoxious chatty boy she had thought he was, then she wasn't sure she knew who he was. Maybe she didn't really know him at all.

As the doctor finished speaking with her and doing a check-up, he moved on to the bed to Holly's right. She could hear a feminine voice responding to his questions, but she wasn't paying enough attention to them to figure out why the voice sounded vaguely familiar. Her head felt like it was swollen with cotton anyway, so she figured it wouldn't be worth the effort to try.

Grabbing the holo-screen remote from where it sat on a bedside table, Holly unmuted the holo-screen she shared with Dylan. On the screen was a person standing in front of an unfamiliar symbol, the outline of a human inside of a circle with the four basic elements—fire and air on either side of the head, water and earth by the feet.

There was a filter over the voice, making it distorted and hard to hear. Turning up the volume, Holly listened carefully to the person as they spoke, "Hello, people of Verdona. We are G.H.O.S.T. As you have no doubt heard from various news sources, a plane on its way to Aldaria made an early, and explosive, landing. I'm sure you're all wondering what could have happened to make that happen. Well, that can stop. It was our doing."

Holly stared at the screen, transfixed by the shocking news. It wasn't an organization she had ever heard of before, and she couldn't help but wonder why they would have shot down the plane she had been on. She made a mental note to search them up later.

The curtain to her right was yanked back to reveal the face of one of the other female representatives. Holly didn't know her name, but she recognized her from watching the broadcast recordings from selection day as the girl from Airfield High—a military training academy in the northern region of Sunhaven. Her features indicated an eastern Asian ancestry—likely Korean or Japanese.

Turning back to the holo-screen, Holly listened as the person continued, her brief distraction lasting no more than a second, "A G.H.O.S.T. operative hid a bomb in the engine of the right wing and remotely detonated it after the plane had taken flight. I'm sure many of you are also wondering *why* we would do this, and to you I say, it is because we needed to wake you up. For too long, we have let the military control this country and call it democracy. Our so-called 'Domina' is nothing more than a tyrant ex-soldier trying to maintain her controlling grip over us. Well, we say no more. No more soldiers patrolling the streets at night. No more educating our children with lies. We need to take back this country, and we need to do it now. Your government is lying to you, and we intend to shine a bright light on all its deepest, darkest secrets. Wake up, Verdona! The revolution is coming!"

An uneasy calm had settled over the hospital in the aftermath of the broadcast. Even the monotonous beeping of the machines seemed dulled after the hostility that had been projected over what Holly could only assume had been every digital device in the country. Everything else was uneventful in comparison.

A few nurses came by to give the four of them, including the boy from Airfield on the other side of the Japanese-Korean girl, another dose of argenteral—a medicine derived from silver, stem cells, and altered amphibian DNA that had miraculously swift healing properties—along with some melatonin for Dylan. Other than that quick visit, the day was spent in almost silence. 'Almost' meaning that Dylan talked in his drug-induced sleep. He kept mumbling something under his breath, but she couldn't decipher any of it.

As she lay in bed with nothing to do other than eavesdrop on anybody who walked down the hallway just outside the door, Holly had overheard some of the nurses chatting about the other patients who had been brought in from the crash. Apparently, it was only the teen representatives and one or two of the flight attendants who had survived. According to one of the nurses, most of the rooms in the hospital had been so full that all of the teenagers had ended up sharing a room. Aside from that, all the chatter had consisted of in-hospital drama—which Holly had tuned out after a while.

The doctor returned after a couple of hours to let her know she could, carefully, start walking around if she needed to. After he left, Holly sat on her bed, staring at the powered-off holo-screen until her boredom was interrupted by a knock on the door.

Looking over, Holly straightened at the sight of General Falcon striding through the door, followed by Secretary Garcia. General Falcon gave her a respectful nod before moving past her bed. Holly followed him with her gaze, watching him stop at the end of the last bed. A moment later, she could hear him speaking in a low tone with the boy there, but she had turned her attention back to Secretary Garcia, who had stopped at the end of her bed.

Secretary Garcia glanced at Dylan, who was still asleep, before moving to take a seat between Holly's bed and the bed of the Japanese-Korean girl Holly still couldn't remember the name of. "How are you ladies doing?"

Holly shrugged. "I'm alright."

She nodded, turning her head to the other girl. "Sora?"

The girl, Sora, looked down at her hands. "Can I call my parents? I tried to do it earlier, but the nurse wouldn't give me back my phone until you guys released it."

Secretary Garcia gave her a sympathetic smile before lifting the bag off her shoulder and digging through it until she pulled out a series of cell phones in plastic evidence bags. "We weren't exactly sure which one belongs to whom, so you're going to have to find it."

Sora took one glimpse at the collection before snatching a phone with a fried egg case. With barely a glance at Secretary Garcia, she tore into the bag and pulled out her phone, turning it on and dialing a number.

Turning her attention to Holly, Secretary Garcia held out the phones to her. It took Holly a few moments to spot the clear case with a printed photo of her and Naomi in the back. Holly thanked her as she stood up and left.

Pressing the power button on the side of her phone, Holly watched the screen light up with the picture of Andrew holding a snail up to the camera, a smile wider than the Cheshire cat's on his face as he showed off his discovery. Seeing the picture brought back the memory. His hair and clothes had been dripping from the storm that had swept through earlier, which their mom had reluctantly let him go play in after much begging. Andrew had spent hours running from bush to tree to various flowers planted in the front yard, crouching next to them as he poked at whatever insect happened to be braving the rain with a stick.

Smiling at the memory, Holly swiped past the lock screen and opened the phone app, clicking on her mom's contact before setting her phone on her lap.

The phone only rang twice before her mom answered, the hologram of the upper half of her body hovering above Holly's phone.

"Hi, Mom," Holly said, putting on what she hoped was a reassuring smile.

"Holly!" Her mom exclaimed, her hand going to her heart, and her shoulders visibly losing tension as she scanned what she could see of Holly on her end of the call. "Are you okay? I tried calling to see if you were okay, but the government people wouldn't give us a straight answer. We were so worried about you."

Holly interrupted before her mom could continue—knowing her mom, she would rant like that without pausing to take a breath until she passed out from lack of oxygen. "Mom, I'm fine, really. I'm in the hospital, but don't worry, the doctors here are taking great care of me."

To her right, she could hear Sora speaking rapidly in Japanese to a woman on her phone who could only be her mother. Holly's mom seemed to overhear part of their conversation, because she asked, "Are you with someone? Did you get released already?"

"No, I haven't gotten released yet," Holly told her. "They didn't have enough room, so I have to share a room with three other people."

Her mom pinched her lips together, but didn't comment on her dislike of Holly having to share a room. "Well, as long as you're getting the care you need, I suppose. Do you know when you're going to be released? Are you still going to perform at the festival?"

"Not for a few days, and yes, I am." Holly could tell her mom wasn't too thrilled with her saying she was still going to perform at the festival, but she didn't feel like she was in any more danger. The crazy rebel group may have shot down her plane, but that didn't mean that she had been the target. She was only a teenager; there was no reason for her to be targeted for something like that. As soon as she had thought that, she vaguely remembered seeing a Naval Lieutenant Commander boarding the same plane. It was way more likely that he had been their target.

Her mom didn't seem very convinced, but she moved on. "I picked up your maid of honor dress from the tailor today. She did a wonderful job of trimming the hem. Have you finished putting together the reception playlist?"

"Yeah, you should be able to find it on the family cloud account in the wedding folder," Holly told her. "Did you and Eddie finally decide where you want the wedding to be? I know you guys were deciding between the church and the beach."

"We decided to go with the church..." Her mom trailed off, her attention snagging on something off-screen. "Andrew! How many times do I have to tell you not to put that in your mouth?"

Holly smiled softly for a moment, then, when her mom's gaze returned to her, she asked, "What about the RSVPs? Have you heard back from Grandma or Adam?"

"Your grandmother is a busy woman, Holly," her mom told her with a flat look. She knew her mom had a complicated relationship with her own mother, but she had hoped that her grandma would at least put aside some time to go to her daughter's wedding.

"And Adam?" Holly prompted. It was a long shot that her older brother would respond, but she hadn't seen him since he had left for college.

"He hasn't responded either," came the reluctant reply. Her mom sighed, seeming like she was going to continue, but was interrupted by a loud crashing sound in the background. "Andrew Bartholemew Carnell, you better not have broken anything! I'm sorry, Holly, but I have to go deal with this. I will talk to you later, hon. I love you."

"Yeah, love you too, Mom," Holly responded just before her mom hung up.

Blowing out a heavy breath, she leaned her head back until it rested on the pillow of her elevated hospital bed. Dylan seemed to be asleep still, and Sora was still speaking to her own mom to Holly's right. If Holly listened carefully, she could hear another hushed conversation on the other end of the room where General Falcon was speaking to the other boy. Her thoughts were swirling with the end of her conversation with her mom. If they were lucky, her grandma would at least send a wedding present—or she would send a reply conveying her 'deepest regrets' that her schedule was too full for her to attend. Adam, on the other hand, hadn't sent so much as a text in the past few years. It was like being around them reminded him too much of their father.

Chapter 5

The next few days went by quickly in spite of how little there was to do. Holly had tried to fill up her recovery time by playing hologram chess with Dylan, but he was infuriatingly good at it, and she did not have the temperament to stop herself from, literally, smacking the smirk off his face after her last loss. Needless to say, that didn't take up very much of their time.

Between rounds of chess with Dylan, Holly had introduced herself to Sora, who had smiled brightly at her and chatted with her for hours while they painted their fingernails with some nail polish Sora had bought in the hospital gift shop. As they were finishing up painting their nails, the boy from the other bed ran over and hopped onto Sora's bed, nearly knocking the bottle of nail polish from her hand.

"Are you two ladies having a sleepover without me?" he asked, a wide grin on his face as he dramatically batted his lashes and leaned on Sora's shoulder.

Sora rolled her eyes and shoved him off of her. "Go back to your own bed, Leo."

Leo pouted. "Aw, Soso, you're such a buzz kill. What if I want to join in on the girl talk?"

Poking him in the forehead, Sora gave him an exasperated look. "You don't even know what *girl talk* is."

"I do too," Leo retorted, crossing his arms over his chest.

"Prove it, then," Holly chimed in, leaning back on her hands.

Leo turned his attention to her, cocking his head to the side. "Hmmm. Nah."

With that, he hopped off the bed and went back to his own side of the room.

Raising an eyebrow, Holly looked to Sora for an explanation. All she got was a shrug as Sora replied, "Don't mind him. Leo just loves to be in the spotlight."

"I can hear you, Soso," Leo called from where he was now doing a handstand against the wall. The olive tone of his face was flushed from the blood that had rushed to his head. His expression shifted from humorous to focused as he bent his arms to a ninety-degree angle for a handstand pushup. Arms shaking, Leo barely completed the full pushup before kicking his feet down one at a time.

Sora hardly blinked at the show of skill.

"Impressive," Dylan said, rolling out his wrist as he stood to do his physical therapy stretches. "He do that often?"

"Any chance he gets," Sora replied, setting the nail polish bottles on her bedside table. "Like I said, he loves the spotlight."

The next day, the four of them were officially released—back to full health thanks to the argenteral. They still had a week before the centennial festival and, in an effort to 'cheer them up,' they would be going to a reservoir that afternoon with the other school representatives as a way to get to know each other before the festival. The doctors gave each of them a warning to be careful and not to strain themselves too much, but they were otherwise given a clean bill of health. Something Holly had a feeling went in one ear and out the other for Leo.

Upon reaching the hotel that they were staying at, Holly and Dylan split up from Sora and Leo on the way to their own rooms to change. Secretary Garcia had informed them that their luggage had been dropped off at their rooms and told them that if there was a mix-up, to contact her directly.

Dylan walked Holly to her room, stopping with her. "Holly, can I ask you something?"

Looking up at him, Holly met his gaze. "Sure."

He smirked. "Are you ready to lose at beach volleyball?"

"Those are fighting words, Moros," Holly told him, a smile growing on her own face. "Are you sure you can back them?"

Dylan said nothing, merely crossed his arms over his chest, and leaned against the doorframe.

"Oh, you are so on," she said, pressing her keycard against the reader and opening the door to her room. "You better hope your bite is bigger than your bark, Dylan, otherwise you are going down."

Closing the door in his face, she looked out the peephole to see him fake a hurt expression, but then he smiled and walked to his room down the hall. Seeing him smile like that, Holly couldn't remember why she had ever disliked him—it was almost like he was a completely different person.

Shaking her head, Holly changed into her swimsuit—a charcoal grey two-piece suit that clung to her beneath the loose white t-shirt she had thrown on as she waited for Dylan in the hotel lobby. She wasn't the only person waiting there. As she set her bag on the seat next to her, she was joined by a blond-haired boy who was cleaning his glasses on his shirt while he walked.

Lifting them up to the light, he squinted through them before putting them on and looking around.

Heaving a sigh, he muttered, "Never on time, I swear."

"Are you waiting for someone?" Holly asked him. As he turned to face her, the boy seemed to do a mental math equation on whether or not he should reply.

After coming to the conclusion that he should, he shrugged. "My girlfriend. We are supposed to be going to a reservoir to meet the rest of the festival representatives, but she still isn't ready."

Patting the seat next to her, Holly smiled. "I am also waiting for someone to go to the reservoir. He's not my boyfriend, but he doesn't seem to have a good concept of time either, so I suppose we have that in common, too."

"Wait, you're also a representative?" the boy asked, taking her up on the offer to sit next to her. "Which school are you from?"

"Solstice. What about you?"

The boy's eyes widened. "Solstice? Isn't that the school designed to look like the Notre Dame Cathedral in Paris that got destroyed during World War three? I heard the architects spent months trying to design it in a way that would do the cathedral justice."

Holly blinked, taken aback by the sudden enthusiasm the boy showed, but nodded.

"So cool." The boy's blue eyes were wide behind the thin rim of his round glasses. "Oh, sorry, right. I'm Kevin, I go to Lakeshore."

Kevin stuck his hand out to her.

Smiling, Holly shook his hand. "I'm Holly."

A moment later, a girl came stumbling down the stairs as she tried to braid the top half of her chin-length hair back while walking. "Sorry, Kevin. I couldn't find my towel. Oh! Kevin, who is this?"

"Kelly, this is Holly. She's one of the festival representatives from Solstice," Kevin said as he stood.

Kelly smiled brightly as Kevin walked over to her. "It is so good to meet you, Holly. Like Kev said, I'm Kelly. Don't be too weirded out if he drills you about the architecture of your school, he's kind of an architecture nerd."

Next to her, Kevin blushed and gently shoved her. "Kelly!"

A look of innocence plastered on her face, Kelly just patted his cheek.

As they spoke, Dylan arrived, walking languidly down the stairs like he wasn't the last person to arrive. Holly caught herself staring at his muscled torso and promptly looked away, her face burning a cherry red. She was being ridiculous; it wasn't like she had never seen him shirtless before. They were both on their high school swim team. Besides, she reminded herself, she had a boyfriend.

Now that they weren't waiting on anyone, they got into the limo that was waiting to take them to the reservoir.

The other representatives were standing around talking by the time the four of them arrived. As they exited the limo, Holly caught sight of Sora talking to a tall, dark-haired girl who could only be described as built like a goddess. Glancing over at them, Sora waved at Holly, inviting her to join the conversation.

Walking over to them, Holly came to a stop next to Sora.

"Hey, Holly," Sora greeted her warmly, shifting the way her large floppy hat rested. "This is Artemis from Washington High. Artemis, this is Holly from Solstice."

Holly smiled and waved awkwardly at the girl, who looked her up and down, her toned arms crossed over her chest.

Artemis returned the smile and extended her hand. "It is nice to meet you, Holly."

Accepting the offered handshake, Holly replied, "Nice to meet you, too, Artemis. That's such a unique name. Is there a story behind it?"

"My mother thought it would be a good idea to name my twin brother and me after Greek gods," Artemis told her, rolling her eyes affectionately as her gaze drifted over to where all of the boys were talking.

Her own gaze drifting over there, Holly could instantly pick out who Artemis' twin was. His tan skin was identical to his sister's, as was his smile as he laughed at something one of the other boys had said.

"I'm going to go get a drink," Artemis said after a moment.

As she walked away, Kelly came up behind Holly and stared after Artemis. "I want to be on her team for volleyball. I mean, do you *see* those back muscles on her? She has got to be a goddess in disguise or something."

Holly laughed.

"Do you not agree?" Kelly asked, taking a sip of a lemonade. "She looks like she could beat up most of the guys here without breaking a sweat."

"She probably could," Sora said, adjusting her sunglasses. She was still admiring the guys' muscles. "She did say something about being an archer."

Reaching her hand out to Sora, Kelly introduced herself. "Hi, I'm Kelly."

"Sora," Sora replied absently, her eyes following a tall, silver blond boy as he went to get himself a drink from a cooler.

"Sora," Holly said, clearing her throat. "Stay focused."

Crimson flushed across Sora's cheeks as she finally looked away from the shirtless boys. Tucking her chin against her chest, she lowered her hat to block out the sight of the boys while she shook Kelly's hand.

Somebody whistled, coming up next to Sora. "Who wants to stay focused when there's eye candy like *that* walking around?"

"*Karen*," Artemis admonished teasingly as she rejoined them, drink in hand. "At least pretend you're not staring."

Karen shared a knowing look with Sora. "You're only saying that because you know they are all too scared to talk to you."

Artemis rolled her eyes. "Please. I'm saying that because we are going to have to beat them in volleyball, and we can't do that if half of us are too busy drooling over our competition to pay attention to the ball coming straight at their face."

Sora sighed reluctantly. "I hate to say it, Karen. But she is right. We must stay focused, ladies. This isn't a game we can afford to lose."

Sighing, Karen dragged her eyes away and nodded. "Alright. But if we win, then none of you are allowed to stop me from admiring from a distance."

"I think you mean *when* we win," Holly told her. "I have a bet to win; there is no way I'm letting us lose this."

Artemis cracked her knuckles, making Holly very glad she was on their team and not the boys. Then again, from the short glimpse she had gotten of Artemis' equally ripped brother, Holly had a feeling things wouldn't be as easy as they hoped.

Together, the girls made their way over to the cooler to drop their things off before meeting the boys at the net. As the two groups faced off, Holly caught a glimpse of Domina Garner, General Falcon, and Secretary Garcia setting some beach chairs in the sand of the man-made beach. To her surprise, they were wearing beach attire—even the General. The adults did not, however, deign to join the teenagers in their game of volleyball.

"First team to eleven points wins," Artemis dictated. "Winning team gets bragging rights."

"And the losing team gets pushed into the lake," Artemis' twin added, a smirk on his lips as he stared his sister down.

The two of them towered over everyone else. Kelly was using Artemis' shadow as shade while the taller girl matched her twin's smirk. "You are so going down, Apollo."

Leaning over to Holly while the others began making their way to their spots, Karen said, "I don't know about you, but I'm not so sure I want to get in the middle of this sibling rivalry."

Patting her arm, Holly started walking. "Me neither. But I'm not going to back out now, are you?"

Chapter 6

Heat bore down on them as the sun arched across the sky. Sweat beaded on Holly's face and arms as she leapt into the air and swatted the ball across the net. On the other side of it, Kevin returned the hit, landing the ball into the empty space between Karen and Kelly and earning the boys the winning point.

Planting her hands on her knees, Holly sucked down some air while the boys cheered and clapped Kevin on the back. In spite of their loss, Holly was kind of looking forward to being thrown into the cool reservoir waters.

No sooner had she thought that than she was being picked up from behind. Grabbing at the hands holding her, Holly yelped.

"A bet's a bet, princess," Dylan said from behind her.

"Let me go." She struggled against his arms, noticing that she wasn't the only one being carried over to the beat-up docks. Each of the guys was carrying their counterpart over to the water.

"Not a chance."

There was no stopping the inevitable, but Holly continued to struggle in his grip as he carried her to the end of the dock and dropped her into the refreshingly chilly water with a splash. Four identical splashes rippled through the water shortly after. The water bubbled above her head as she sank towards the bottom, wishing Dylan could see her glaring at him through the murkiness of the water. The jerk even had the nerve to offer his hand inches above the water. Kicking up to the surface, she grasped his hand hard and yanked him under the waves, giving him a mouthful of water. Releasing his hand, she smirked after him before reaching up and dragging herself up onto the dock. As she pulled her legs away from the edge, she leaned over and stuck her tongue out at him, hoping that he could see it.

Pushing herself to her feet, Holly retreated to the sandy beach, past the other boys, who were laughing and walking to the end of the dock where Dylan was likely resurfacing. As she walked, the other girls ran to catch up with her.

"Did you really pull Dylan into the water?" Karen asked her, shivering and rubbing her hands up and down her arms.

Holly smiled and nodded.

Clapping her on the back, Artemis grinned. "That was genius. I wish I had thought of that."

The sand was turning a light shade of orange as the sun began sinking towards the horizon, a bright, burning rock slowly falling to the bottom of an ocean of sky. Each of the girls was wringing the water from their hair as the boys approached, all of them, aside from Dylan, giving Holly a high five or a fist bump.

All of the representatives rode in the same limo on the return trip to the hotel. Holly sat next to Dylan and Karen, laughing with their new friends. Domina Garner had suggested that they get dinner and head back to their hotel rooms, but Karen had had a better idea. The boys weren't too excited at first about going to the mall, but the girls reminded them that it was either that or follow their recommended curfew. Needless to say, the boys were all for it once it was put that way.

People walked in droves around the mall as the teenagers tried to stay together. None of them bought anything, but just the aspect of going into the stores and trying on horrendous-looking clothes in a competition to see who could find the worst outfit without a care in the world was the best distraction from all the fear and anxiety that the plane crash had piled on them. Even the boys ended up enjoying their makeshift fashion show—though they would likely deny it to anyone who asked.

They stayed out for a couple of hours after the reservoir and were going to get some ice cream when Holly spotted Nathan in the crowd. For a moment, she wondered why he was there, but then she remembered that his family always attended the festival in person. Her feet stumbled over each other as she saw a girl run up to him and wrap her arms around his neck.

Horror froze her body as Holly watched the girl plant a kiss on Nathan's lips. The sight only worsened when she saw his arms wrap around her waist. Every muscle in her body locked up as Holly tried to process what she was seeing.

Her boyfriend.

Kissing another girl.

All the people in the crowd that walked in front of Holly blurred into specters. The only thing she could see was the way Nathan held the girl. A girl Holly *knew*.

Izzy Baldwin.

The captain of the women's football team.

Then Nathan pulled back from Izzy, his fingers gently pulling a small section of her long blonde hair as he smiled at her. His smile dropped when he looked up and saw Holly staring at him.

Mortification wrote itself across his features, killing any joy the kiss had brought him.

Holly's breaths were tight in her chest. He was cheating on her.

Her heart pounded like a warhammer against her ribs as she absently rubbed at her hands.

He *knew* Holly would be there, and yet there he was, his hands wrapped around another girl's waist. His hands were clinging to Izzy Baldwin of all people.

"Holly?" It was Dylan.

Holly had been so wrapped up in her thoughts that she had forgotten she wasn't alone. The other representatives were standing a few feet away from them, laughing and chatting, not yet having noticed that Holly and Dylan had stopped.

Turning to Dylan, her eyes brimmed with unspilled tears, Holly tried not to choke on the emotions welling in her chest.

"What—"

"Nathan's here." Her body was trembling as she rubbed her hands together, viciously trying to rid them of something that wasn't there. She couldn't stop the earthquake of emotions that made her voice shake as she spoke. "Nathan is h-here. He's here and he—"

"Holly, what's wrong?" Concern creased Dylan's brow as Holly cut off. His eyes searched hers for any sign of what it was she was trying to say. He reached for her, but her gaze had slid back to see Nathan walking toward them, Izzy trailing behind him. He stopped a few feet away. Dylan dropped his hands and stepped back.

"Holly, I—" Nathan started.

"Don't. Just... don't. How long have you been cheating on me?" Holly clenched her jaw, swallowing her tears. Her hands tightened into fists at her side, her nails digging into her palms hard enough to leave marks.

"Nathan, who is this?" Izzy asked, her blue eyes looking Holly up and down like she hadn't been in the same classes as Holly for years.

"I'm his girlfriend," Holly snapped. She paused, making up her mind in the split second between that and what she was about to say next. "At least I was. I don't know what I am to him anymore." Then, to Nathan, she said, "Did any of it even mean anything to you?"

"Holly, please." Nathan's eyes were wide, and he was clenching and unclenching his hands, looking desperately between Holly and Izzy as though this were all some nightmare he could wake up from.

Dylan was being uncharacteristically quiet, his head bowed. Holly didn't even notice the other representatives walk up until they were standing just behind them.

"No, Nathan. You know what, I don't want to know how long. Screw this, and screw *you*. We're done. I'm done. Go be with her. You *clearly* love her more anyways. You two are perfect for each other, the football captain dating the cheer captain, what a classic." Holly practically spat the words in his face.

The words were heavy coming off her tongue. She knew she should at least try to fight for their relationship—their friendship. After all, it wasn't just her friendship he was burning to the ground. She had no doubt Naomi would go ballistic once she heard about this. And it stung all the more deeply as Holly took in the way Nathan reached for Izzy's hand for comfort. It cut deeper than a knife to realize that they had likely been together for a long time.

Beside her, Dylan finally moved, punching Nathan in the face with what was the best right hook Holly had ever seen, but at that moment, she couldn't care less. She had to get away. With tears streaming down her cheeks, Holly turned and ran. She pushed through the shellshocked representatives who stood glued to the spot, none of them knowing what was going on or what to do. She didn't see Jacob wrestling Dylan away from Nathan. Didn't hear him telling Dylan to calm down before the military police were called. Didn't see the way Artemis glared at Nathan.

She had to get out of there.

She didn't know where she was going; all she knew was that she was running. Vaguely, she heard Dylan call after her, but she wasn't sure if it was real or a trick of the wind rushing past her as she burst through the doors and into the storm outside.

Holly kept running, not paying attention to the turns she took or how many times her feet nearly slid out from under her as she slipped on the rain-slick pavement. She didn't even pay attention to how far she ran from Nathan until she found herself standing alone on the sidewalk in the pouring rain. Thunder cracked overhead.

Heartbroken and lost, she slumped against the wall of a building and let the tears continue to run down her cheeks in tandem with the rain. She didn't know where she was, but she was too numb to care. Wrapping her arms tightly around herself, she leaned her head against the wall behind her and stared up into the sky. Her eyes blinked against the drops of rain that fell too close to them. Chills raked her body as she heard footsteps rushing toward her. Time had slipped through her fingers as she sat there, long enough that she didn't even know how long it had been since she had left the mall—maybe it had been an hour, maybe only fifteen minutes, it didn't matter. All she knew was that she was cold and tired.

Dylan wrapped his arm around her as he helped her to her feet and led her back to the hotel in silence. He walked her to her room and wrapped a blanket around her shoulders.

"Do you want to talk about it?" he asked gently, sitting next to her on the bed.

"Not particularly."

"Please don't run off like that again," he murmured, staring at his hands in his lap. "You scared the life out of me and the others."

"I'm sorry," she replied numbly. She wanted to feel bad about it, but all she felt was empty. A void of nothingness that swallowed any emotion that tried to breach its endless depths of unfeelingness. Maybe not feeling anything would be better. Better than feeling everything. Better than feeling the knife in her back.

"You need to get some sleep," Dylan told her after a beat of silence.

"Okay," she relented, too exhausted to argue with him.

Holly lay down on the bed after Dylan had left and waited for her mind to fall into oblivion, praying she could avoid the nightmares that often haunted her dreams. She doubted she would be so lucky.

Chapter 7

Birds chirped cheerily outside her window as Holly woke up to a soft knock on her door. Languidly, she crawled out of bed and swayed her way over to the door, stubbing her toe on the corner of a chair and cursing under her breath before opening it to see Dylan wearing a big grin on his face.

Rubbing the sleep from her eyes, Holly blinked away the blurriness in her vision. "Would you see who it is, my knight in shining armor. Have you come to wake the princess? I hate to break it to you, but she doesn't take kindly to solicitors."

Dylan laughed.

"Kelly thought it would be nice to get some coffee and waffles before Secretary Garcia takes us to the opera house to start rehearsals," he told her.

Holly nearly started drooling at the mention of food. She groaned. "Waffles sound divine right about now."

"Come on, waffle girl, let's go get some breakfast."

"In my pajamas?"

"I—"

"Absolutely not," she insisted, giving him a flat look.

"Fine. You may get dressed, your highness," Dylan replied, bowing dramatically before backing away as she rolled her eyes and closed the door.

Moving back into her room, Holly pulled a silver blouse from her suitcase and slipped it on over her head before pulling on a pair of black jeans. As she reached for her small travel backpack, a picture slipped out, fluttering to the ground before she picked it up. It was a picture of her and Nathan. A massive redwood tree reached for the sky behind them as they grinned into the camera. Before she could tear up again, Holly took the picture into the bathroom and ripped it to pieces before tossing it into the trash can.

After French braiding her hair, she grabbed her bag and returned to the door. When she opened it, Dylan was looking at his watch.

"You ready to go, waffle girl?" he said with an enthusiastic wink.

Holly playfully punched him in the arm.

"Yeah, let's go, Lancelot."

He laughed, the sound making her stomach do a flip. Holly mentally slapped herself. Now was not the time. They were just friends.

"Bet I can beat you to the lobby," she told him, paying at the top of the grand spiral staircase.

"Oh really?" Dylan smirked. "I doubt it."

"Try me."

"You're on."

Holly smiled. "On three. One... Two..."

"Three!"

Holly rushed to the stairs, her jaw dropping as Dylan hopped onto the railing and slid to the bottom. By the time she got there, he was sitting on a couch, pretending to be asleep with his arm over his eyes..

"Ha. Ha. Very funny," she said breathlessly, jabbing him in the ribs.

"What? You took too long," he joked, peeking up at her from under his arm.

Rolling her eyes, Holly turned away. "Alright, come on, I need some waffles."

"Did someone mention waffles?" Leo asked, running up behind her and throwing his arms over both her and Dylan's shoulders.

"Yes, care to join us?" Holly asked, trying and failing to duck out from under Leo's arm.

"Miss Waffles here might just fight you for your share, so you might want to be on your guard," Dylan warned Leo.

"I just had an epiphany—" Leo started, dropping his arm from Holly's shoulder to face them.

"Oooh, epiphany, that's a big word, Leo," Dylan joked. "Are you sure you know what it means?"

"Shut up, Moros," Leo scowled playfully. "Anyways, Miss Waffles is a terrible nickname, so shame on you. Lady Waffle is much better."

Dylan rolled his eyes.

"I like it," Holly said. "But seriously, I was promised waffles, and if I don't get them soon, someone is getting slapped."

"Yes, your ladyship," Leo chuckled.

As they arrived at the breakfast area, the alluring scent of freshly made food drifted over to them. Holly's stomach growled, causing a blush to spread across her cheeks. Thankfully, nobody else seemed to notice.

The breakfast table at the far side of the room was blanketed with an assortment of toppings and other various breakfast items. Golden pancakes were stacked in a pile next to the waffles, a platter of crepes beside those. Next was the variety of fruits—strawberries, blueberries, raspberries, bananas, and so much more. Her mouth watered as she took in the sight of all the food available to them and the other hotel residents.

Holly stacked her plate high with waffles, the delectable edibles smothered in chocolate syrup, whipped cream, and a little bit of every berry she could get her hands on. The sight made her mouth water. On a second plate, she had gathered one of each flavor of muffin: blueberry, banana, chocolate chip, and poppy seed. Her plates wobbled as she carried them over to their tables that one of the other teens had pushed together so the whole group could sit together, and took a seat next to Dylan and Karen.

There were only a few other hotel guests in the room with the group of representatives, but they paid the teens no mind as they enjoyed their food. Holly was extremely grateful to the Domina and Secretary Garcia for letting them stay in such a nice hotel with all expenses covered. She hoped she would have time at some point before the festival to check out all the activities the hotel had to offer—she remembered seeing a sign that mentioned paintball, a board game room, bingo, and even a swimming pool.

"Hey, Lady Waffle."

"Yes, Leo?"

"Can I have some of your waffles?"

Holly glanced at the waffles piled sky-high on her plate and skewered one of them on her fork before flinging a syrupy waffle at him. The waffle sailed across the table and smacked him right in the face.

"Sure," she smiled at him, her face the epitome of angelic innocence as she took a bite of her blueberry muffin. `

Leo glared, amusement dancing in his blue eyes as the waffle slowly slid down his face and onto his plate. Chocolate syrup sludged a sluggish trail down after it, some of it sticking to his dark brown hair. Choking on his water, Kevin spewed it all over Apollo, who proceeded to pour his entire cup of orange juice on Kevin's head in return, soaking his dirty blond hair with it. Everyone burst into laughter.

"You are so dead, Lady Waffle," Leo smirked even as he wiped syrup from his face and flicked it off his hand.

"You can try, you little twerp," Holly told him.

"Twerp? That's not even a good nickname," Leo pouted.

"It's not supposed to be," Holly replied.

"I think 'sexy' is better."

This time it was Karen who spewed water all over Apollo.

"Oh, come on!" he yelled, jumping to his feet, water dripping from his brown hair. "Cover your mouths, you *heathens*."

Behind him, Holly noticed Artemis sneaking up with two cups of water. Her sea-blue eyes sparkled with mischief. She put a finger to her lips—careful not to spill—lifted the cups above his head, and dumped their contents on his head. Holly looked away just in time to see Leo standing up to throw a couple of syrup-covered waffles at her. She squealed and ducked for cover behind Dylan.

"Don't hide behind me!" He yelled, bolting to his feet.

As soon as he said it, his face got hit with a double shot of syrupy waffles.

"Oh, you did not just do that," Dylan grumbled at Leo.

"Uh oh. I may have miscalculated this just a bit."

"You think?" Dylan asked rhetorically, wiping the syrup from his black hair with a napkin. "I just showered this morning."

Grabbing any waffle within his reach, Dylan started chucking them at Leo. Pretty soon, the entire breakfast area was a war zone. Any other hotel residents in the room fled for their lives before they could be dragged into the mess—some of them physically dragging their cheering children out the doors behind them. Holly was crawling under the tables to avoid getting hit.

Kevin almost got her once with a pancake, but she managed to dodge behind a chair before it hit her. Looking to her left, she caught a glimpse of Jacob leaning against the doorframe, watching the ensuing chaos. Not a single piece of flying food touched him as he observed the scene.

Moving on from her spot, Holly finally found refuge behind a vending machine in the corner of the room and sat there surveying the mess they had made. Other hotel residents who had yet to eat had taken one glimpse inside the room and had found somewhere else to go for breakfast.

How in the world were they going to explain this to the Domina?

As if she had been summoned, the Domina stepped into the room.

Everybody in the room froze, becoming statues carved from stone. None of them dared to move a muscle, each of them hoping that the more still they stood, the less likely the Domina was to see them—as though t-rex movie logic applied to the woman. Apollo was about to pour a gallon of water on his twin's head—Artemis was clueless to the disaster about to be dumped on her hair. Leo had an entire bottle of syrup in one hand and a plate stacked to the ceiling with waffles in the other. Kelly was holding two cartons of orange juice in each hand above Kevin's head, and Karen was about to dump a bowl of diced watermelon on him in addition to the juice. And Dylan was sitting behind the serving counter—visible only to Holly—hiding from the fight.

Upon seeing the Domina—flanked by Secretary Garcia and General Falcon—everyone immediately dropped everything, literally, causing a catastrophe. Kevin got watermelon and orange juice to the head, and Kelly and Karen hid behind the nearest overturned table. Leo just sat down and started chugging syrup straight from the bottle like a seven-year-old, and Artemis had Apollo in a headlock for dumping the water on her head.

The Domina took one glance at the clutter of food all over the room and said, "You have one hour to finish, clean yourselves up, and be at the opera house." Then she turned on her heel and left.

General Falcon and Secretary Garcia didn't say a word as they followed the Domina out of the room. The representatives stood in stunned silence for a moment before picking up where they left off.

Apollo and Artemis were chucking grapes at each other as only siblings would—with merciless precision. Leo ignored everyone, grabbing Kevin's wrist, he dragged him calmly around the table and out of sight from the others, all while eating strawberries off the floor and tables as he went.

Holly quietly crept to the counter next to Dylan. Reaching up, she pulled down a platter of waffles and set it between them. She ate one, then she and Dylan proceeded to periodically chuck them at their friends over the counter. Everyone else was ducking for cover, trying to avoid the flying waffles and grapes while also attempting to throw them back at whoever had thrown them in the first place. Every once in a while, a hand would reach out from behind the table that hid Kevin and Leo to grab a forgotten piece of food that would never be seen again.

After a few minutes of this, Kelly hopped onto a chair and shouted, "Everybody stop!"

Kevin and Leo's heads popped up from the fort they had made from tables and chairs, the latter eating a muffin that had been on the floor seconds earlier. Kevin stole the muffin and took a bite before handing it back. Leo stared at him in disbelief but continued to eat it nonetheless.

Holly and Dylan peeked up from behind the counter to see Kelly, who was calm as she said, "We're all covered in food and syrup. If we don't shower and clean up now, we are going to be late."

"She's right," Karen told them, then looked pointedly at Leo as she added, "We all need to shower."

"What are you looking at me for? I'm going, I'm going."

Chapter 8

The auditorium in the Saint Michael opera house—where the festival would be held—was like walking into the colosseum. Not that Holly had ever *been* to the colosseum, let alone to the New Roman Republic, but she got the feeling that if she had, it would feel the same.

Holly couldn't take it all in. From the way the others were gawking at the architecture around them—particularly Kevin, who was scribbling down sketches in a sketchbook he had brought with him—she could tell she wasn't the only one who thought so. A large golden chandelier, with dozens of small crystals dangling from its tips, hung from the ceiling. The velvet blood-red curtains were fringed with gold, and there were thousands of seats in the audience. It reminded her of the ancient opera houses rumored to be found all over the European

Empire and the New Roman Republic, with balconies in the walls filled with seats for whichever rich family came to see the show. Holly remembered studying ancient opera houses in her intro to architecture class in eighth grade. But seeing one in person was magnificent.

"Amazing, isn't it?" General Falcon said to her, his hat tucked under his arm as he walked.

"Yes, it is," she breathed, not knowing what else to say. The beauty of it was beyond words, the way the sun was at sunset.

Everyone continued onto the stage, where Secretary Garcia addressed them. "Everybody, please join us on the stage while we tell you the plan for the event. We want all of you to be informed about everything that will be happening in the upcoming days," she announced. The teenagers did as instructed and made their way onto the stage.

"Now, as you all know, this event is very important to our country, and it must go as smoothly as possible. That means no messing around backstage," the Domina said, looking pointedly at Leo and Kevin as she spoke.

"What are you looking at me for?" Kevin whined, pushing up his glasses. "It's Leo you should be worried about."

Leo elbowed him in the side but didn't say anything.

"Moving on," Secretary Garcia continued, tucking her hazelnut hair behind her ear. "We need all of you to be as prepared as possible. In the past, representatives have prepared speeches for the festival on a national historical topic of the student's choosing, but this year we decided to do something different. I do hope you all had a chance to review the email sent to you after your selection because its contents will be critical to this year's festival performance."

Secretary Garcia pulled her ringing phone out of her pocket. "My apologies, but I must take this. General, would you be so kind as to explain in my absence?"

The General nodded and picked up where Secretary Garcia had left off. "This year, the council decided to add cultural dances between each of the historical speeches. Each of these dances was specifically picked from a time period in the country's history and adjusted to be more accommodating to those who may not be as coordinated in dance."

Coming back from her phone call, Secretary Garcia thanked General Falcon and took back over instructing them. "Domina Garner will start the festivities off with her annual speech before the audience joins in on singing the national anthem. Once that has concluded, you will each give your speeches in pairs, then another pair of representatives will do their dance, and so forth until the end of the program, in which General Falcon will give his speech and the festival will end. As the week progresses, we will update you all on the full program, but until that is finalized, we will be coming here every day to rehearse. I expect you all to be refining your speeches in your free time. The entire event will be broadcast to the entire country, as it has in the past, so there will be no redos or second chances. This is a once-in-a-lifetime opportunity, and you will be expected to do your best. This year, there will be a special guest—"

"The queen of Russia?" Leo interjected.

"No. Be quiet, son," General Falcon told him, giving him a cold look.

"Ok, sorry."

Selena continued, "As I was saying, this year, the Emperor of Africa will be visiting. You will each get to meet him, and you will address him with the respect he deserves."

"Secretary Garcia will be helping to teach you your dance routines, but it will be on each individual to write the speeches. Feel free to collaborate with each other to edit and revise the speeches. I look forward to seeing the results at the festival," Domina Garner announced cheerfully, her deep blue eyes shining. "General."

With that, she and General Falcon left without another word, leaving the teens with Secretary Garcia.

The representatives followed Secretary Garcia as she walked over to the piano. It was a remarkable-looking instrument—a Yamaha grand piano that looked to be about a hundred years old. Yamaha was a Japanese brand, so it *had* to be at least that old, since Japan had been sunk during the Nuclear World War, killing hundreds of millions of people, including the president of Venezuela at the time, who had been visiting for a conference with the Japanese president.

That war had left significant damage to every continent. Most of the North American continent had been so badly damaged by the nuclear radiation that anywhere east of the current countries of Verdona and the Republic of

Nova Cana was unlivable. Africa wasn't much better off. After China had officially declared war on the rest of the countries outside of their alliance by sinking Japan, Africa retaliated and lost poorly. China had demolished the southern half of the continent in less than a month with multiple nuclear bombs.

The fact that such a unique relic had survived the disastrous war was incredible.

Secretary Garcia stood next to the piano as she spoke. "To start things off, I have picked the different dances for each pair. Once I have announced which one each partnership will be doing, I will share the reference videos to your phones. As soon as you have received the videos, you are free to go find an empty space on the stage or in the back practice rooms to begin learning the steps. We will start with Drath High, you two will be doing an Argentine Tango."

Karen and Jacob nodded, pulling out their phones as Secretary Garcia sent them the videos for their dance.

As the pair walked away, Secretary Garcia moved on. "Next, Airfield High. You two will be doing a Foxtrot dance."

Leo and Sora checked their phones, then they too went off to find a place to practice.

"For Washington High, you two will be doing a Flamenco." Secretary Garcia barely waited for Artemis and Apollo to see the videos before continuing, "For Solstice High, you two will be doing a Contemporary dance."

Holly felt the buzz of her phone in her pocket, and as she pulled it out to see the collection of videos, she followed Dylan to go find a place to practice. As they walked away, she could hear Secretary Garcia telling Kevin and Kelly that they would be doing an East Coast Swing.

Once they had found a good spot, Holly and Dylan watched the videos Secretary Garcia had sent. Each part of the dance went from a few fast movements that ended in a slower, exaggerated move. The videos all showed the same dance, but from different angles, and as they finished watching each of them, Holly and Dylan began to practice the moves.

After hours of practice—and a half hour break for lunch—Secretary Garcia gathered them all back together. All of them were breathing heavily, sweat beading along their faces as they gathered around her.

"Great job today," Secretary Garcia told them, tucking her short hair behind her ear. "We will stop here today and pick it up again tomorrow morning. I assume you all received the updated itinerary I sent out yesterday. Rehearsals will primarily follow that, but I may make changes to it depending on how well each of your dances and speeches are coming along. Tomorrow's practice will take up most of the day, but I will try to end it an hour before dinner so that you may all work on your speeches. That is all for today. Go get some dinner, and refrain from any more food fights."

The teens nodded slowly, too tired to complain or make jokes about the ban on further food fights. Dylan walked next to Holly as they left the opera house and got into the limo that would take them back to the hotel. When they reached it, not much later, they said goodnight to their friends on the way to their own rooms.

Holly paused outside her room, one hand on the doorknob. Turning her head, she watched Dylan stop at the door to his room and unlock it. With a split-second decision, Holly walked over to him and put her hand on the door, stopping it from closing. The door swung inward, revealing Dylan standing just inside the room.

"Can I talk to you?" Holly asked after knocking gently on the door.

Turning around to face her, Dylan smiled and said, "Of course, come on in."

Closing the door behind her, Holly walked in and followed Dylan to the only place to sit, the bed. There was a chair at the room's desk, but Dylan's backpack had already claimed that seat.

Dylan sat on the edge of the bed, but Holly remained standing. Leaning against the wall behind her, Holly scanned the room—practically identical to her own—and asked, "Do you remember our first swim meet in high school?"

He tilted his head to the side, his eyes on hers. "Yeah. It was the first time my mom let me stay overnight away from home after my dad left."

Holly met his eyes. "Do you remember what happened that night at the hotel?"

"Of course I do," he replied. "Are we talking about what happened before or after Coach busted all of us for sneaking out to get ice cream?"

Holly laughed at the memory. Their coach had been beyond furious when he caught them all sneaking back into the hotel hours after curfew, each of them carrying a carton of ice cream in their hands. He had not only confiscated the ice cream but had sent them all to their rooms with the promise of punishment via push-ups the next morning.

A smile bloomed on Dylan's face as he also recalled the memory. "Those hundred push-ups certainly made us question our decision, but that ice cream was so worth it."

She nodded in agreement, then said, "I never thanked you."

"For what?"

"Not telling him it was my idea."

Dylan laughed. "Why would I do that? You were the best swimmer we had for the women's medley relay in butterfly. Still are. And we both know Coach would have benched you the instant he found out it was you."

Holly smiled and was about to say something more when they heard a knock at the door. While Dylan went to answer it, Holly noticed one of his hoodies lying on the covers of the bed amongst an assortment of shirts. Picking it up, she grinned at the dragon image, and the words that read: *Solstice Swim Team*.

She looked up as Dylan walked back into the room. Noticing the hoodie in her hands, he smiled.

"I can't believe you still have this," Holly said. "Didn't you get this our first year of high school?"

Dylan nodded. "I did. It's probably my favorite hoodie."

"I wish I had gotten one while Coach had the website up," she said, brushing her fingers over the orange scales of the dragon.

"You can have it," Dylan told her.

Holly's eyes shot to his. "You just said this is your favorite hoodie, though."

He shrugged. "I have plenty of others. Besides, it will probably fit you better anyway. It's gotten a little small over the years."

Clearing her throat, Holly hugged the hoodie to her chest and asked, "So, who was at the door?"

"Oh, it was just Kevin asking what time we're supposed to be up tomorrow."

She nodded, lifting the hoodie a bit and saying, "Thanks."

Dylan gave her a smile. "Anytime, princess."

"Are you ever going to let me live that down?" Holly asked, thinking back to the moment that earned her the nickname—the day she wore a tiara to their team's 'anything but a cap' practice. Somehow, Dylan had gotten half the team to start calling her that ever since.

"Not a chance."

Holly opened her mouth to say something more, but was interrupted by another knock at the door. Dylan walked away to answer it, leaving Holly to stare after him, the hoodie he gave her clasped in her hands. After pulling it over her head, she turned to follow him. He was talking to someone in the hall. Dylan's body was tense, and a muscle kept ticking in his jaw.

Walking up next to him, she peeked over his shoulder and caught a glimpse of the person on the other side of the door—Nathan. Dylan's hand fell from where he had previously had it pressed against the doorframe, allowing her to get a better view of her ex-boyfriend.

"You moved on fast," Nathan snapped at her.

"We're just talking, Nathan. Nothing more. Not that it's any of your business," Holly replied coolly, crossing her arms over her chest. "What do you want?"

Nathan looked between her and Dylan before blowing out a breath. "I wanted to apologize. Your friend, Leo, I think, said I would find you here."

"That little rat. Of course he did," she muttered to herself. Then, to Nathan, she said, "What gave you the idea that I would accept it?"

Shifting his feet, Nathan glanced nervously at Dylan before looking back at her. He opened his mouth, then shut it, contemplating. "I just..." Nathan seemed to be regretting knocking on the door. "I don't know why I—"

"I do," Dylan interrupted, the anger in his voice scarcely contained as he spoke. "You came to apologize because you thought it would appease your own guilt. You came because you thought that apologizing would boost your self-confidence about what you probably consider a simple mistake. Obviously, you didn't think through your pathetic attempt at an apology; otherwise, you would have realized that there is no possible chance that you would deserve forgiveness."

Holly blinked. This wasn't something she would have ever expected from Dylan.

"Mind your own business, Moros," Nathan retorted.

"Nathan, stop." Holly didn't know what to do. Here was Nathan, apologizing for cheating even though the odds of him being forgiven are next to zero, and here was Dylan. Defending her. If someone had told her a week ago that Dylan would be protecting her from Nathan, she would have laughed in their face. But after everything that had happened since leaving Emerald Bay, things were different. Everything she had thought she knew about Dylan—about herself and Nathan—was wrong.

"What do you see in him, Holly?" Nathan asked, his blue eyes searching hers. "You have never wanted to be in the same room as him until now. What changed?"

"What *changed*?" Holly scoffed. "Maybe with the fact that you cheated on me, or maybe how Dylan saved my life when our plane got shot down. We almost *died*, and you have the gall to ask me what changed?"

"But you didn't." Nathan glared at her—as if this was all her fault.

Holly glared right back at him.

"No, I didn't. But our relationship did. You made sure of that." Ignoring the pain that flashed in his eyes, Holly said, "A broken bone is more easily healed than a broken heart. You can take your sorry attempt at an apology and shove it."

With that, she pushed Dylan back and slammed the door in Nathan's face.

Sighing, she turned to Dylan. He met her gaze, a smirk on his face.

"What?" she asked.

Dylan shrugged. "Nothing. Just, that had to have felt good."

"You have no idea." Checking the clock, she added, "We should probably get some sleep."

Nodding, Dylan reached around her and grabbed the doorknob. Looking through the peephole, he made sure that Nathan was no longer standing on the other side of the door before opening it for her.

Holly walked out into the hallway, raising her hand above her head in farewell. "See you in the morning."

Chapter 9

Dylan was still asleep when Holly finished getting ready the next morning. She had woken up to the infernal noise of her alarm after only sleeping for maybe two or three hours. Sleeping in a new bed was doing nothing good for her insomnia.

Holly had tried texting Dylan after brushing through the frazzled mess that was her hair, but he hadn't responded, so she decided to go knock on his door if he didn't come down to breakfast. The rest of the representatives were already eating when she joined them in the breakfast room. Dylan still hadn't made his appearance, though. Telling her friends that she was going to go grab Dylan and not to wait up for them, she returned to the floor where their rooms were and made her way over to Dylan's room. It took her two tries of pounding on the wood before Dylan finally answered the door. He was still wearing yesterday's clothes as he opened the door, rubbing sleep from his eyes as he squinted at her through the brightness of the hallway light.

"We're going to be late for rehearsal," Holly told him.

Looking at his watch, Dylan groaned. "Missed breakfast."

Giving him a reassuring smile, she held up an enormous blueberry muffin she had snagged before leaving the breakfast room.

Dylan's eyes widened a moment before he snatched the muffin from her and took a bite out of it.

"How did you sleep?" Holly asked him as he took another bite.

"Fantastic," he replied around a mouthful of food. "That is, until you woke me up. What about you?"

"Like a baby," she lied, shrugging to hide just how tired she felt. It had taken three layers of concealer and foundation to cover up the dark circles under her eyes that morning, and she still hadn't felt like they were completely covered. "You should hurry and get ready. The others have already left, and I might just join them if you're not ready soon."

Lifting the remainder of the muffin to her, he said, "Thanks for breakfast. I'll be out in two minutes."

Shoving the last bite of muffin into his mouth, Dylan closed the door.

Leaning against the wall opposite his room, Holly waited for him to get ready.

True to his word, Dylan opened the door two minutes later. Together they walked down the hallway and made it to the car.

Secretary Garcia was waiting for them in the auditorium along with the rest of the group when they arrived. Looking up from the holopad she had in her lap, she stood to greet them, setting the holopad on the chair as she did. Her short, wavy hair was pinned back from her face. That, paired with cream slacks that she matched with a light blue blouse, gave an open and friendly look.

"Good morning. Now that everyone is here, we can begin," Secretary Garcia told them. "Yesterday, you all watched the videos I sent and started working on the dances I assigned. From here on out, I want you all to just start practicing as soon as you arrive. Each day, I will spend time with one pair for about an hour to help with any questions or parts that may need to be worked on more than others. Go ahead and find a place to practice. I will be over to watch the first pair in a few minutes."

Returning to the same spot as the day prior, Holly and Dylan picked up where they had left off.

A few hours into their practice, Secretary Garcia came over to watch them. She stayed for the next thirty or so minutes but didn't make more than a couple of comments on Holly's posture and Dylan's timing on one of the moves before moving on to the next pair.

By the time they wrapped up, the sun was already starting to dip, casting long shadows across the sidewalks as they exited the opera house. Several of them looked ready to collapse onto their beds. The group hovered just outside the opera house entrance.

"Anybody want to join me at the hotel pool?" Holly asked, glancing at the others.

Artemis groaned. "That sounds delightful right about now."

The others nodded in agreement, the idea of cool water and weightlessness sounding more than perfect after spending the majority of the past two days on their feet.

Each of them split up upon returning to the hotel, going to their rooms to change before meeting up again at the Olympic-sized recreation pool on the roof of the hotel. Fairy lights were strung above the patio, giving the roof a warm glow. Stars twinkled above the lights, creating a mesmerizing view above their heads. Almost everyone was already there by the time Holly and Dylan arrived. The only person missing was Artemis.

Setting her things on one of the lounge chairs, Holly dove into the water without a second thought. A splash to her right told her Dylan wasn't far behind. Brushing her fingers against the bottom of the pool, she maneuvered her feet under her and pushed off. The others had joined her and Dylan in the pool as she broke through the surface of the water.

Kelly sat on the edge of the pool, her feet in the water, as she chatted with Kevin, whose arms were resting on her legs. Further in the pool, Artemis—who had apparently arrived when Holly had been underwater—had Apollo in a grapple, and Leo was cheering her on from a safe distance away. Karen and Sora had swum over to the edge of the pool that doubled as the edge of the roof and were looking out at the city. Dylan had made his way over to Leo and the twins. The four of them spoke briefly before starting a chicken fight with Leo on Dylan's shoulders and Apollo on his sister's.

Jacob came up next to Holly, his eyes on the chicken fighters. "There is no way Leo has a shot at winning."

Holly nodded in agreement. "I doubt he thought that through before agreeing to this."

The two of them watched as, hardly a moment later, Apollo—who towered over Leo and Dylan—easily knocked Leo off of his perch.

"I'm sure Leo is the instigator of the fight," Jacob said, crossing his arms over his chest.

"You're probably right," Holly replied. She watched as Leo popped his head up, flicking water into the faces of Artemis and Dylan as he did so. Then, as the teams switched who the fighters were, Holly turned to Jacob, a smirk on her face. "What do you say we give Leo a little surprise?"

Jacob raised an eyebrow. "What did you have in mind?"

"Do you think we could tug his feet out from under him?" Holly asked, glancing back over at the chicken fighters. Dylan and Artemis were locked in combat.

Chuckling under his breath, Jacob replied, "He has no chance of surviving this."

Holly returned his fist bump, then took a deep breath and dove beneath the surface after him. The pool water stung her eyes as she opened them. Following after Jacob, they made their way over to the chicken fighters and grabbed Leo's ankles before yanking them out from under him. Leo toppled over like a titan, Dylan falling with him and landing in the water with a splash. As Holly and Jacob surfaced, Apollo and Artemis were laughing their heads off at Leo and Dylan, both of whom looked like angry, drowned rats as they resurfaced.

Leo glared at Holly. She smirked at him and motioned for him to come at her. He didn't wait long to take her up on the challenge—in fact, it took him less than a second before he was launching himself at her in a full-body tackle. Holly tried ducking to the side, but the water slowed her down just enough for Leo's tackle to be successful. Water suctioned above her, filling the gap where she had been standing and enclosing itself over her head as she sank through the water under Leo.

Bracing her feet against the bottom of the pool, she shoved him up—he was surprisingly heavier than she had initially anticipated, but the water took some of the load as she shoved him off of her and across the surface of the pool. Leo splashed back into the water a couple of feet away, sinking beneath the waves. Slicking her hair off her forehead, Holly smirked at him as he resurfaced.

Shaking his hair out like a wet dog, Leo said, "Holy superstrength, Lady Waffle. What kind of Wonder Woman strength was that?"

To her right, Dylan laughed.

"What's that for?" Leo asked, turning his attention to Dylan.

Dylan shrugged. "Just remembering the time Holly made a bet with our coach on who would win in an arm wrestle, her or the state record holder for the men's hundred-meter freestyle."

Holly snorted, remembering the expressions on her team's faces when she had beaten the guy. "He really should have come to more morning land practices."

Nodding in agreement, Dylan gave Leo a sympathetic look. "Don't feel too bad about it,

Leo. She could probably give Jacob a run for his money."

Jacob said nothing, just shrugged.

"Ain't no way," Apollo chimed in. "Jacob, aren't you like a three-time national champion for high school football?"

"I'm not *that* strong," Holly told them, rolling her eyes. "Dylan is exaggerating. The only reason I beat our teammate is because he let me win so he could ask me to prom."

Artemis huffed a laugh. "That is such a boy thing to do."

As they spoke, the rest of the group gathered around them to listen in on the conversation.

"What is that supposed to mean?" Leo asked.

"What do you guys say about going to get some ice cream?" Karen interrupted, cutting Artemis off from responding to Leo.

The group shared a look.

"Why not?" Kelly said, her arm looped through Kevin's.

Each of them climbed out of the pool and grabbed the hotel towels to dry off. Once they were all dry enough, they all put on a t-shirt over their suits, then set out to grab some ice cream.

After a quick debate, they decided to walk to the small ice cream shop across the street from the hotel. The sign on the door read *Pierre's Creamery*. As they entered the shop, their hair dripping like trees in a forest after a storm, they walked up to the pale blue painted counter to order. While the others were ordering, Holly glanced around the little shop. It was a decently small shop with thick vertical pink and white lines painted on the walls, and cream-colored hexagonal tiles smattered on the floor to make a honeycomb pattern, giving the little shop a vintage appearance—like it came straight from one of those old photos from the twentieth century. The tables were exactly what would be expected in a little ice cream shop like that, with white tops and shimmery silver stands under the center of each tabletop. Each table had matching bubblegum pink chairs that were just a shade lighter than the pink of the wallpaper that covered the inner perimeter of the shop.

The holo-screens hanging from the ceiling in each corner of the room were showing the ten o'clock news. Holly was about to shift her attention away when a headline snagged her attention.

Rebel attack on local monument...

Rebels. The thought made Holly want to roll her eyes. Plenty of people thought the government was too controlling—that the military shouldn't be ruling the country. They thought the world had become a dystopian future and that the people had been brainwashed by the government. Holly thought it was a load of crap. This wasn't a dystopian world; it was just life moving forward, progressing, and evolving. She knew better than to listen to the nonsense and propaganda that the media tried to sell them, so she pulled her attention away from the holo-screen and back to thinking about what flavor she wanted to order.

Dylan was the only person who had yet to order in the time that Holly had zoned out. It was her turn to order last.

"I would like a double scoop of sour apple, please," she told the cashier. After paying for and receiving her ice cream, Holly walked over to where her friends had seated themselves.

The others were already eating their ice cream as she joined them. Leo and Kevin had dragged some tables together, and the group now sat at one long table. Chatter rose up among the group as they enjoyed their ice cream. Holly savored every bite of hers.

Once they had all finished, they made their way back to the hotel, saying their farewells as they reached their rooms.

The room was pitch black as she walked in, closing the door behind her, and turned on the nearby light switch. Holly gasped, nearly dropping her phone and her room key. Her room was a mess. The chairs had been tossed across the room, a few of them had broken, and there were splintered pieces lying around them. Pillows and blankets were scattered on the floor. Every cabinet and drawer had been flung open, and any breakable object had been smashed to pieces. The walls were covered in graffiti. Pictures of some sort of rebellion symbol—two triangles overlapping each other but in inverted positions from each other were painted all across the walls in a deep scarlet.

She didn't have to enter the bathroom to know it would probably be in a similar state.

Picking her way through the rubble, she noticed a sentence painted on the wall above the bed. She traced her fingers on a drip beneath the first letter and pulled them back, looking at her crimson-coated fingertips. It was still fresh; whoever had been in there had been there recently, probably in the past couple of hours. The sight of that deep red made her vision swim—her stomach churned as she told herself that it was just paint. Nothing else.

Holly forced herself to lift her gaze from her hands before she upended the contents of her stomach. Focusing her eyes, she read the message; *And out of the ashes, the Phoenix was reborn, spreading its wings of fire to remake the world before it returned to whence it came.*

Whatever that meant.

Holly heard a knock on the door. She picked her way back through the mess and cracked the door open to see Dylan standing there. He smiled at her.

Taking in her still standing in her t-shirt and shorts, the smile dropped at the expression on her face. "What's wrong?"

She opened the door wider to show him the state of her room. His jaw dropped, his blue eyes scanning the room. Holly took a step back and let him into the room. The door swung closed, but didn't latch.

Dylan was making his way through the chaos when Holly turned to join him. She followed him across the room until he stopped at the foot of the bed to read the message written above the headboard. He turned to face her, his expression grave.

Holly showed him the paint on her fingers. "It was still wet when I touched it."

Dylan glanced at the paint coating her fingertips, then back up at the messages scrawled on the wall. He ran his hand through his silky black hair before turning his attention back to her.

"We have to tell the Domina," he said.

"I know."

"Do you know what that means?" he asked, gesturing to the message.

She shook her head, ripping her gaze away from the rivulets of red on the wall.

Drips of paint ran down the wall from the letters like blood down the arm. Instinctively,

Holly wiped her paint-covered hand on her t-shirt. Maroon streaks smeared across the white fabric. When the action didn't succeed in removing the paint, Holly started scrubbing it from her skin.

Clean hands covered her frantic rubbing. Looking up, she met Dylan's gaze. His eyes held a question she knew she could never give him an answer to, no matter how badly he may think he wants it. They stood there silently until Holly realized just how close they were. Sucking in a sharp breath, she pulled her hands from his.

"We should go call the Domina," she mumbled under her breath, stepping away from him and making her way over to the door. Holly left the destroyed room along with that unanswerable question.

As she exited the room, Holly pulled her phone from her pocket and dialed the number Secretary Garcia had given them to reach her.

Chapter 10

Holly was sitting on the floor in the hallway with her legs crossed, staring blankly at the wall in front of her. Dylan was talking to General Falcon in her room while Secretary Garcia and the Domina were talking to the rest of the representatives, who had come out of their rooms when the military police arrived—they weren't exactly being very quiet as they did their investigating.

Her room was now cordoned off with yellow tape. A couple of the military police were talking to her friends, but she knew they wouldn't have much to offer.

As she sat there, her eyes stuck, unfocussed, on the greige wall in front of her, she mindlessly rubbed the fingers of her hand, trying to get the feeling of the wet paint to go away. Just as she had six years ago with a thicker crimson that had stained her hands. Her fingers were still stained from the spray paint on her wall. She couldn't stop her mind as it replayed the message over and over and over. Its meaning was lost on her. But she couldn't stop the words as they spun round and round her head like a vinyl record. And as she sat there, her unfocused gaze remaining on the wall, she scraped and scraped her scarlet-stained hands.

A sound to her right startled her enough to glance over at the crowd. Nearly a dozen military police moved through the hall around her friends, but they weren't the only people there. Other hotel guests had gathered. They peered over each other's shoulders, trying to see what was happening, and in the midst of them—

Her heart froze in her chest, a solid block of ice that sapped any heat from her body as she caught a glimpse of a face that shouldn't have been there. A face that was the root of her nightmares—the reason she couldn't stop feeling the sticky red liquid on her hands. She met his eyes—eyes everyone had said hers had looked just like. His face was unreadable, but he met her gaze.

Jumping to her feet, Holly started to shove her way closer to him. She weaved through the crowd, never taking her eyes off the wolf among the sheep. The lights overhead were suddenly too loud and too bright. They drowned out every other sound except for the constant rushing of blood in her ears.

Someone passed in front of her, cutting off her view. By the time they had moved out of her field of vision, he was gone. She stopped moving as she stood exactly where he had been only a moment before. Her breaths were tight in her chest—they were sharp knives scraping her insides as she tried to get some oxygen. They quickened as she spun around. She had to find him. He couldn't get away again, not like he had six years ago when he sent their family spiraling in the aftermath of his bloodbath.

Then she spotted him again, turning back to look at her.

Breath stuck in her throat, Holly pushed through the crowd. He turned away. She had to catch up to him.

Not bothering to apologize as she forged a path through the gathered people, Holly continued after him. He led her through the hall and down the stairs. Her eyes remained glued to the back of his head. He was not going to just disappear again.

Stepping onto the floor of the lobby, she almost lost him, but as she turned, she caught a glimpse of his too fine suit jacket disappearing around a corner and hurried after it. As she rounded the corner, her feet skidded to a halt merely a couple feet away from him. He stood in a secluded spot underneath the grand staircase, his face shadowed.

What she could see of his face was surprisingly well-shaven. His deep blue gaze scanned her as she came to a stop, her chest rising and falling rapidly as she tried to catch her breath.

A million questions pressed on the edge of her lips. She swallowed them down along with the crushing weight of the panic that was one step away from becoming a full-blown panic attack. No matter what she was feeling, she had to know why he was there. And yet, she didn't speak. Neither of them did—not for a good while.

"You look good," he said at last, taking a couple of steps closer to her. Light fell on his features, giving her a better look at him. His dark hair was longer than she remembered. Not by much, but just enough. Those familiar blue eyes held more experiences than the last time she had seen him, and yet they were still the same. Holly could read the memories in them—could remember all the times she had looked up at those eyes and smile.

But that was a long time ago.

He took a deep breath. "It's been a long time, dolphin."

Holly flinched at the nickname.

"Nobody's called me that in a long time," she said, her voice barely audible. And yet he still seemed to hear every word of it.

A soft smile slowly spread across his face. It was far too gentle a look to be coming from him.

Steeling herself for what she was about to ask, Holly forced herself to stand straighter. "What are you doing here?"

He shrugged. "I was in town, thought I would wander around a little and explore the city."

"That's a load of crap and we both know it," Holly said, her voice stronger than she felt. He was hiding something, and she was stalling. She had no idea how she was going to get him to go back upstairs so she could turn him over to the military police, but she had to figure it out. And until then, all she could do was stall.

"Maybe I missed my little girl," he told her, a flicker of warmth in his expression.

Anger boiled in her gut, but she smothered it with the ice that had filled her entire being at the sight of him. "If you missed me so much, you shouldn't have left."

That flicker of warmth shuttered as his expression changed to something harder. "You and I both know I would have been arrested if I had stayed."

Holly snorted. He was right; he would have been arrested, then sent to prison, where he would have been locked away in a cold, damp cell for the next eternity with seven consecutive life sentences to keep him company. But that hadn't happened.

He took a step closer.

She took a step away.

"Holly—"

"Don't come any closer, Harry," she told him, not willing—or able—to use the title he had lost that day. Her mind was screaming at her. Telling her to run as far away from him as possible. Begging her not to let him get his hands on her, because the last time she had let him touch her, her hands had ended up coated in blood. "Now tell me why you're here—and no lies this time."

Harry cocked his head, a different emotion carving a path behind his eyes. "You've changed."

"Why are you here?" Holly repeated, crossing her arms over her chest just to give herself something to do that wouldn't mean taking her eyes off of him.

His expression didn't change as he continued to silently assess this new version of her. It was unsettling.

Opening her mouth to ask him again, Holly paused when he said, "I am not the same person I was when you last saw me—six years on the run will do that to a person, I suppose."

Checking the time on his watch, Harry sighed. "I don't have much time, so I guess we will have to skip over the long-winded explanation and get straight to the point.

"Over the years, I have tried to keep an eye on you—tried to check in on you, your siblings, and your mother as often as I could. You have grown into quite the remarkable young woman, Holly, and I want to ask you to join me and the group I work with. They call themselves

G.H.O.S.T.—a bit on the cheesy side if you ask me, but our interests have recently aligned, so I find myself in need of their resources. I'm sure you have heard of them by now. They recently outed themselves to the public. Recently, they have increased their efforts to recruit new blood, and when I heard this, I couldn't help but think of you."

It took tremendous amounts of effort for Holly not to snap back at him exactly where he could shove his offer, but she found herself too curious about why he would think of her.

Despite her efforts to keep her temper in check, Holly couldn't stop the snark in her tone as she asked, "And what made you think I would *ever* want to join you and your stupid rebellion group?"

"Because you're my daughter," Harry stated matter-of-factly, as though his actions before his disappearance weren't something that should have sent him six feet under. "And I know you could be so much stronger if you would just come with me. We can make up for lost time—make up for past mistakes—"

"You call murdering seven women a *mistake*?" Holly exclaimed, staring at him in disbelief. "You're insane! What made you think I would just forget what you did—what I *watched* you do?"

Taking a step back, Holly felt her resolve dissolving. What had she been thinking, trying to face him alone? She never should have left the hall—never should have left the supervision of the military police.

She took another step away from him, fear tugging at her and screaming at her to run away as fast as her legs could carry her.

On the other side of the stairs, Holly heard someone call her name. That was all it took to get her feet moving—to get her to spin around and run. Rounding the corner of the staircase, she nearly bowled Dylan over.

Catching her before she took them both to the floor, Dylan gripped her arms firmly. Just behind Dylan, Holly could see a soldier with mousy brown hair and pale green eyes. Something about him seemed familiar to her. She couldn't quite place what it was, but her thoughts were racing a mile a minute, so she wasn't sure if it could be trusted at the moment.

"Miss Carnell," The soldier said. "Are you alright?"

Blinking, Holly gathered her thoughts long enough to blurt out, "Harry Carnell was here."

The name had the soldier stiffening, his hand shifting swiftly to draw the gun at his hip. "Where?"

"Behind the staircase," Holly told him, her eyes fixed on his face. She had to know him from somewhere, but she didn't know how. "But he's probably long gone by now."

Not answering, the soldier—whose nametag read *Walker* underneath a Major's pin—brushed past her and Dylan, gun pointed toward the ground as he went to investigate. Turning to follow after him, Holly felt Dylan's hands release their grip and fall, but one of them still held her hand loosely as he too followed the major.

When they rounded the corner where Holly had just spoken to Harry, the major was scanning the empty area, his gun now back in its holster.

"Holly," Dylan said softly. "Harry Carnell, is he..."

"My father?" Holly asked when he trailed off. She didn't look over at him, instead choosing to watch Major Walker inspect the ground Harry had stood on not ten minutes ago. "Yes."

Dylan said nothing in response. Holly could feel his eyes on her, but hers remained on Major Walker. She finally realized where she recognized him. He looked just like his father. Colonel Walker had been the one to show up at her house six years ago, leading a warrant search. It was Colonel Walker who had inspired Holly to sign up for military enrollment post-graduation—something her friends had teased her for relentlessly, claiming she would lose all her hard-earned education by becoming a jarhead.

Standing, Major Walker made his way back over to them. "No sign of him. Are you certain you saw him?"

Holly nodded. "I would recognize him anywhere."

He didn't seem convinced. "How do you know that it was him?"

"Because," Holly said, swallowing back the fear of knowing he had gotten away again. "He's my father."

Major Walker dragged his hand through the military cut of his hair—short and spiked in the front. The action was so casual Holly almost forgot he was a high-ranking officer. Well, that plus the fact that he didn't appear that much older than her—maybe closer to Adam's age, so, early twenties.

Shaking his head, Major Walker said, "I will have to inform the General of this later. For now, Miss Carnell, I would like to ask you a few questions if you are able."

Before Holly could answer, Major Walker glanced over her shoulder.

"Dean," someone behind Holly said. "There you are. This her?"

Major Walker—Dean nodded. "Did the other finish up talking to the rest of the representatives?"

"Yeah," the other soldier replied. "These two are the only ones whose statements haven't been taken yet."

Turning to face him, Holly blinked. He, like Dean, was at least six feet tall, and she could tell they were brothers. They held themselves the same way, and spoke to each other with a certain familiarity that only came with being siblings. Then again, that could just be a military thing. There was a stereotype of soldiers seeing each other as family.

"Are you okay to go with Lieutenant Walker," Major Walker asked, his gaze on Dylan.

Well, that answered that question.

Dylan nodded then followed Shawn around the corner.

Once they were gone, Major Walker shifted his attention back to Holly. "Are you alright if I just ask you a few questions?"

"Sure," Holly replied.

"Was the door unlocked or open before you went in?"

Holly thought back to when she had gotten back to her room. She hadn't noticed anything wrong at first, but that didn't mean much given the fact that she had been—and still was—tired from a long day. "I don't know. I wasn't paying a whole lot of attention."

Writing down a quick note on a holopad Holly hadn't noticed he had, Major Walker continued, "Did you notice anyone suspicious loitering around prior to returning to your room?"

"No," Holly told him, shaking her head.

"Okay. Why don't you walk me through exactly what happened after you arrived?" Major Walker said, making another note on the holopad.

Nodding, Holly went over everything that she remembered—from entering the room to the moment the military police were called. She hesitated at that point, wondering if she should mention the conversation she had had with her father. It didn't seem relevant. Deciding it wasn't worth it—unless he asked—Holly finished her retelling with the call to the military police.

"Okay, that is all. Thank you for your time." Major Walker put away the holopad he had been taking notes on then reached into the breast pocket on his jacket and pulled out what looked like a business card—which he held out to her. "If you have anything else you left out feel free to call me."

Accepting the card, Holly briefly skimmed the information on it before returning her gaze to Major Walker's and saying, "Thanks."

Chapter 11

The military police finally left nearly an hour after Major Walker had taken Holly's statement. They had been reluctant to let her gather her things from her room, but, at Secretary Garcia's insistence, had relented to letting her back in. After she had gotten everything, Holly stood in the hallway waiting for Secretary Garcia to tell her her new sleeping arrangements.

Her backpack was digging into her shoulder as she watched Secretary Garcia speak with Karen. As they finished up, they walked over to Holly.

"Miss Carnell," Secretary Garcia said as she approached. "Due to hotel reservations there aren't any available rooms for you to stay in for the rest of your stay, but Miss Dare has agreed to let you stay in her room with her if you would like."

"Thank you," Holly said, to both of them.

"Now that that is settled. I have things to attend to."

With that, Secretary Garcia turned and left.

Holly followed Karen to her room. It was identical to Holly's room—minus the recent additions of art on the walls—but the location of the furniture and decorations was inverted. Like Holly's room, the bed was king-sized.

On the desk Holly could see a massive collection of skincare and makeup products. They were neatly arranged in sections, leaving an open spot in the center for when the products would be used. There was a variety of eyeshadow palettes and at least two dozen different shades of lipstick, not to mention the various colors of eyeliner and mascara. It was, needless to say, a lot of makeup.

Over at the bed, Karen was piling a bunch of clothes into her arms before unceremoniously dumping them into her open suitcase. The bedsheets were rumpled on one side, the other side still tucked tightly under the mattress the way the hotel staff prepped it after the last guest had checked out.

Gesturing to the bed, Karen said, "Sorry about the mess. I'm going to get ready for bed, feel free to just set your stuff anywhere."

Grabbing what Holly assumed was a pair of pajamas, Karen went into the bathroom, leaving her to get settled with her things. Rolling her suitcase over to the bed, Holly set it beside the frame near the foot of the bed and placed her backpack next to it. She checked the time on her phone. Karen had the right idea getting ready for bed, it was getting late.

Unzipping her suitcase, Holly grabbed out some pajamas and changed into them. A moment after she finished, Karen came out of the bathroom, a toothbrush in her mouth as she tossed the day's outfit onto the pile in her suitcase and snatched a few items from her collection of skincare before returning to the bathroom. This time she left the door open, though.

After rifling through her suitcase for a moment, Holly found her toiletries bag and made her way over to the bathroom. As she entered, Karen was in the middle of rubbing one of her skincare products onto her face. Seeing Holly enter, Karen scooted to the side to give her room. Smiling in appreciation, Holly set her things on the counter and pulled out her toothbrush and toothpaste.

Karen's breaths were slow and even as Holly stared at the door, her back to her friend's sleeping form as she tried to fall asleep. Rolling onto her back for the thousandth time that night, Holly searched the faintly illuminated ceiling for a way to fall asleep in spite of knowing there wouldn't be an answer that could fix the insomnia she had had since she was eleven.

Her mind reeled with the events of the night. All her thoughts came from the same source—her father. She hadn't thought of him as her dad since the day he had disappeared. Not after what he had done that day—and even before that. The fact that he had shown up tonight meant he was desperate for something. There had to be something more to his offer for her to join him, some secret agenda behind his return from being off-grid.

And his offer. She couldn't fathom why he would think that showing his face to her was a good idea. To think that asking her to join him on some insane crusade—which he had neglected to explain—after she had watched him kill someone.

Not even a random stranger, but her aunt. Her mother's sister.

Holly sat up. This line of thinking never ended well. She knew the only way she could try to rid herself from these thoughts—at least for the time being—was to be active. Her therapist had told her to go for a walk whenever the memories were too much.

Throwing off the covers, Holly set her feet on the floor before standing. Taking a glance back at Karen as she stood, she watched her chest rising and falling slowly, grateful she hadn't woken her friend.

She didn't bother grabbing any shoes—she wasn't going to leave the hotel. Putting the spare room key Karen had given her, she slipped out, quiet as a mouse, closing the door behind her with a soft click.

Doors passed by her on either side as she let her feet guide her to wherever they wanted to go. The hallway was deathly silent like the catacombs rumored to run beneath Paris in the east. She walked past the elevator and headed toward the stairs. When she reached them, she started climbing. Her legs were burning pleasantly with the exercise as she opened the door to the roof at the top. A light breeze whispered its secrets through her loose hair, blowing a few strands across her face. Walking to the edge of the roof, she laid her arms on the ledge.

Her gaze drifted out across the city below her. Small gusts of wind continued to blow her hair around her head every so often.

The city was so peaceful at night, the hover-cars rushing down the streets trying to reach their destinations. It was just past midnight so most of the lights in the city were off for the night—including the bright neons of the bioluminescently lit billboards that hung over the middle of the streets—but those few that were still on shone like stars in the night sky.

At the thought, she cast her gaze up at the heavens where the stars blanketed the sky, pollution of the twenty-second and twenty-third centuries a thing of the past. Cities no longer blocked out the view of the stars at night.

When she was younger, she used to stare up at the clouds in the sky and wonder if God was looking back at her with caring eyes the way her mother had taught her. Much to her mother's dismay, she had stopped believing in fairytales a long time ago. Six years to be exact. But she wasn't really counting.

The door to the roof creaked open behind Holly as she stared at those distant stars praying their light could erase the darkness of her darkest memories. She wasn't as religious as her mother, but she still found herself wondering in small moments like this what it must be like to rely solely on some unseen force that was supposed to protect them. There were soft footfalls behind her, then Kevin was standing next to her, mimicking her pose. They stood there for a few minutes, not saying a word.

"Couldn't sleep either, huh?" Kevin asked, finally breaking the stillness of the night as he pushed his glasses up his nose.

"Nope. What's your reason for being up this late?"

"Nothing in particular. What about you?"

Holly could feel his eyes on her. "I haven't been able to sleep well since I was eleven."

Kevin didn't say anything, but Holly could tell he knew she was holding something back. She hadn't told anyone but Dylan and Major Walker about her father's guest appearance on tonight's episode of disaster, but she still felt the urge to speak to someone about it. And maybe it had something to do with how long she had repressed the memories, but she needed to talk about it more than she had.

"I saw my father tonight," she said, keeping her eyes locked on the constellations shining through the blanket of sky. "I haven't seen him in six years and he picked tonight to show up. Even had the gall to ask me to go with him."

"I take it you two don't have the best relationship." Kevin spoke softly, the phrase a gentle prompt to show he was listening.

She snorted. "Harry Carnell didn't exactly earn father of the year after I learned what he is."

Even with her eyes glued to the sky, Holly knew she wouldn't have to elaborate much for Kevin to put the pieces together. Her father was an infamous serial killer, everyone in Verdona had heard his name at least once in their lives, and even if they hadn't heard of Harry Carnell, they had definitely heard of his media-given name. Despite having kept her last name, nobody seemed to connect the dots between Holly and Harry Carnell. Not a single person questioned or even thought about how Holly shared the same last name as the notorious Silverpeak Slasher. There was a reason she usually tried to avoid speaking about him to anyone.

Kevin whispered the name under his breath a couple of times before it seemed to click in his mind. "Holy heavens. Your father is the Silverpeak Slasher?"

Holly nodded, lowering her gaze.. "I have never understood how someone could do something so awful to another person, let alone to multiple people, and I don't want to."

"I know what you mean," Kevin said, looking at his clasped hands. A muscle ticked in his jaw. "It may not be to the same extent, but I know what it's like to have someone so close to you do something so unspeakable that it keeps you up at night."

There was more to his words than he was letting on, but Holly didn't push him to tell her anything, just as he had done for her. Silence fell on them again as the minutes ticked by. The only disturbance was a military plane flying overhead.

As they stood there, Holly's thoughts kept drifting back to her father. He had seen her sitting in the hallway, trying to rub away the bloodstains of the past. Holly remembered the blood pooling on the ground, flowing from her aunt's body. And when she had dropped to the floor she had gotten her too small hands covered in the blood of her mother's only sister, and even after six years she still couldn't wash it away.

Rage flickered in the pit of her stomach. Her father had done this, he was the reason her mom had lost her sister. He was the reason Dustin never went in the kitchen let alone near the knives. *He* was the reason Holly had spent so many nights cradling her younger brother and singing him to sleep after he had been awoken by nightmares of the past.

Burning anger swept through her as she remembered every night that she had burst into Dustin's room, terrified that he was being attacked only to find him tossing in bed, sweat coating his forehead. It burned like a forest fire as she thought of how, for months after it had happened, Holly had seen her father plunge that knife into her aunt's chest every time she dared to close her eyes. She watched as the light in Thea's eyes flickered and died. Holly would never forget the things she had seen that day. And she would never forgive him for what he had taken from them.

A particularly strong wind—almost like a wave of charged energy—blew across the roof as sparks snapped from Holly's clenched fists. She jumped back from the ledge. Kevin was staring at her, his blue eyes wide and focused solely on her hands. Holly lifted them to her face and turned them over. Nothing. She could have sworn that there had been... a tiny flame flickered to life on her palm. Holly stared at it until it disappeared a moment later. *What was that?* She looked back up at Kevin. Surprisingly, he didn't seem frightened. If anything he seemed excited.

"That was awesome!" he said enthusiastically. "How long have you been able to do that? Are you, like, secretly a superhero or something? Can you do anything else?"

"Kevin," Holly cut him off. "Does it *seem* like I expected that to happen?"

"Right, uh, sorry."

Holly continued to inspect her hands, trying to figure out what had happened, and how. A part of her expected her hand to spontaneously burst into flames at any second, but nothing happened so she dropped them to her sides before walking back up to the ledge and resting her arms on it again. Her gaze once again wandered out across the city. Holly embraced the ensuing silence, her thoughts drifting away from what had just happened.

Standing quietly for a while, they watched the crescent moon forge its path across the starlit sky. The air was cool but not cold. Light breezes

continued to fly through the air around them—
none of them as strong as the one that had
preceded the surprise appearance of fire on
Holly's hands. Somewhere in the distance, a clock
struck one—the loud chime echoing through the
buildings. Holly leaned back and turned around to
head back inside. Kevin joined her as she walked
back across the rooftop to the door that stood
open, waiting for them. They walked side by side
down the stairs to the fourth floor where their
rooms were. She bid Kevin goodnight as he
stopped by his door, and continued down the hall,
pausing by the room she now shared with Karen.
Her hand hovered near her pocket where the
room key was, but her gaze had slid to the door
down the hall where she knew Dylan was likely
fast asleep.

Her feet were moving before she had a
chance to think through what she was about to
do—what she was about to say. She had no idea
what it was she was planning on saying, but she
did know that her thoughts were still swarming
her mind in a way that she knew would not allow
her to sleep anytime soon.

The wood of the door was hard against her
knuckles as she knocked softly. After a moment of
silence, she knew she shouldn't have bothered. He

was asleep, there was no way he would answer a knock on his door in the middle of the night.

To her surprise, just as she was about to turn away and return to her room, Dylan opened the door. His black hair was mussed on one side, and he rubbed his face in a way that told Holly he had definitely been asleep before she had knocked on his door.

"Holly?" he asked, his voice husky from sleep. "What are you doing?"

"I–I can't sleep." The skin on her hands burned as she scrubbed at them.

Dylan's eyes held warmth in their pale blue depths as he said, "Come in."

Holly brushed past him as she entered the room. The door clicked shut behind her as she made her way into the room, stopping in the center.

She turned to face him, feeling the tears brimming in her eyes as the emotions she had been shoving down since seeing her father again forced their way to the surface. "I don't know what to do, Dylan. I thought I had moved past what my father had done the last time I saw him, but... seeing him again... What do I do? I can't just go back to pretending I don't see him killing every time I close my eyes. I can't just ignore the fact that I never got the feeling of blood off of my hands. I just—"

"Hey," Dylan crossed the distance between them, wrapping her in his arms as she felt the tears streaming down her face. "It's okay. You don't have to worry about any of that right now. All you have to do is breathe, okay? Just, *breathe*, Holly. Can you do that?"

Holly nodded against his chest, taking a stuttering breath. Then another.

"There you go. Just keep breathing," Dylan said softly, scooping her into his arms and carrying her over to the bed.

Despite the constant reassuring words Dylan kept whispering to her as she stayed curled up on his lap, Holly's mind wouldn't let her move on from the memories. Each image that tore through her was accompanied by a sob. Dylan's hand was so gentle as he rubbed her back soothingly. She couldn't find it in her to feel embarrassed at herself in the moment—not as the slow and methodical movement of Dylan's hand on her back finally brought her hyperventilating breaths back into rhythm and her thoughts of her father finally left her. In their wake, though, they left an empty void that she used to think wouldn't be fillable. But, soft words and a soothing caress were beginning to change her mind on the matter.

Chapter 12

Holly woke up alone, laying on her stomach sprawled across the entirety of the bed. Her left leg was exposed to the air. She pulled it back under the covers and blew out a breath. Cracking her eyes open, she was surprised to see that it was still dark in the room.

"Oh good, you're awake." It was Dylan. What was he doing up at this ungodly hour?

Holly groaned, covering her face with the pillow.

"I want to be asleep right now," she yelled at him, her voice muffled through the fabric of the pillow.

"You can't hide from your problems," he told her as he walked to the bed and pulled the covers off of her. Holly groaned and reached blindly to pull them back over herself. It was far too early to be awake.

"I'm not *hiding* from my problems. Sleeping is the *solution* to my current problems." She managed to succeed in pulling the covers back over her head then curled up into a ball. "Now go away. I would like to go back to sleep, it is too early to be doing anything else."

"What are you talking about? It's almost eleven in the morning."

Holly peeked her head out from under the covers. The only part of her visible being her green eyes and some of her dark hair. She glared at Dylan. He was wearing a navy blue tank top and charcoal gray shorts, accessorized with a necklace that had a pearl tied to the end. Holly had seen him wear it every day since she had met him. She even remembered how he would sometimes wrap it around his wrist like a bracelet, his fingers fidgeting with the pearl charm while he tapped his leg as he mentally prepared for a race. His hair looked silky soft and shone in the dim lighting coming from the window. It was just moonlight though, wasn't it? There was no way it was eleven in the morning.

A moment later, Leo came bursting in through the open door. "There you are. Everyone else is down in the lobby. Sora tried to go find some employees, but it seems like it's only us left in the building. For now, at least. Jacob says that the employees are probably just trying to figure out why the nuclear blast doors got activated."

"What is going on?" Holly asked, pushing herself into a seated position and letting the covers fall into her lap.

Leo snorted as she sat up. "Your hair looks like a pigeon trying to nest in it."

"Leo, I swear if one more word comes out of your mouth I will punch you," Holly warned.

"I doubt it. Not when you're sitting there wrapped up like a frozen burrito."

Holly shifted, trying to stand before ultimately failing and falling to the floor in the process and dragging all of the blankets with her. Her cheek slammed against the carpeted floor.

"Ow," she mumbled.

"She looks like a blanket burrito." A new voice said.

"Who is that? Is that Kevin?" Holly asked, attempting to unravel herself from the tangle of blankets.

"That's me," he answered. "How's the floor? Getting some quality one-on-one time?"

After a moment of struggling, she managed to roll onto her back and leveled a glare at him. She almost expected Dylan to offer a helping hand, but he was too busy laughing with Leo.

Holly sat up. "Ha. Ha. Yes, it's very funny that I fell off the bed and got tangled in the blankets. Hilarious, in fact."

"You need some help there, pigeon head?" Leo asked between bouts of laughter.

Giving him a death glare, she wrestled one of her hands out enough to flip him off. Then she wriggled the rest of herself out of the blankets and stood up. They could spend the next ten minutes laughing—longer if one of them started snorting like a pig—so she decided to change out of the loose shirt and shorts she had worn to bed.

Brushing past them, Holly left the room and made her way over to the room she shared with Karen. The hallway was dark as she pushed open the unlatched door. Her room was empty, the lighting just as dim as Dylan's room had been. Reaching over to the light switch, she flicked it a few times to no avail. Heaving a sigh, she entered the room and grabbed an outfit from her suitcase to change into before going down to the lobby to see what was happening.

In the bathroom, she ran a brush through her hair before pulling it into a messy bun. As she left the room, she tried closing the door, but it wouldn't latch. Something Leo had said came back to her, *'the employees are probably just trying to figure out why the nuclear blast doors got activated'.*

Right, the nuclear blast doors. If they had been activated then any external electricity would have been cut off the instant they had covered the exterior windows and doors. But the building's generator should have kicked in by now.

Leaving the unlatched door behind her, she made her way over to the stairs and headed to the lobby. She heard her friends before she saw them.

"I don't think there's anyone else in the building," Kelly was saying.

"I understand that," Apollo argued. "But why are all the other guests gone?"

"Maybe they all went to that party last night," Karen chimed in.

"And what about the staff? Apollo continued. "It's literally their job to be here. I realize that the night shift is going to be smaller, but where are they? We haven't seen a glimpse of them since waking up to this disaster."

"What's happening?" Holly asked, walking over to them, noticing that Dylan, Leo, and Kevin had already made it to the lobby while she had been changing.

"We were just discussing what's been going on," Sora informed her.

"I was telling them about this weird energy wave I felt this morning," Leo said. "Before I went to check on you and Dylan that is."

"Do you remember when, exactly, it happened?" Holly asked. She wondered if it was the same as that gust of wind she had felt on the rooftop.

"I don't know, maybe around one." Leo shrugged.

That was around the time her hands had started sparking. Normally Holly wouldn't think too much about the timing, but it was too much of a coincidence for it to not be connected. Her eyes shifted to Kevin, but he was listening intently to something Jacob was saying.

"Well, what are we going to do until we can get out of here?" Artemis asked them all, clapping her hands together. "I mean, it's not like we can go to rehearsal, all of the doors and windows are sealed shut behind the nuclear blast doors and it's going to take the military a while to get around to fixing it."

"I have an idea," Leo said with a mischievous glimmer in his eye. "We should—"

"No," Karen interrupted.

"You didn't even let me finish," he whined.

"You were going to suggest trying to smash the windows."

"Nuh uh. I would never suggest something like that," Leo feigned. Dylan raised an eyebrow at him. Leo rolled his eyes, sighing. "Okay, yes. That is exactly what I was going to say. You guys take the fun from everything."

"Well," Holly said. "If the only thing we can do is wait, why not go exploring. The hotel has plenty of activities for the guests, we could check some of those out. Plus, maybe on our way we can find the elusive staff members or any of the other guests. Who's in?"

The others shared a look, but none of them seemed interested.

Karen had mentioned that the adult guests had been out of the building at some kind of pre-festival adult party. This meant that the hotel's soda bar was free game for the teens until somebody came to let them out. They would need to be rescued sooner or later, but as long as they were stuck they might as well find some way to pass the time.

Once they all agreed on what to do—taking Holly up on the offer to check out the soda bar—they found their way to the counter where Jacob showed off some impressive soda mixing abilities. He almost looked like a professional bartender. Holly would have been lying if she didn't say she hadn't noticed the way Sora's eyes sparkled at every move.

Jacob made them all wonderful sodas. Kevin slurped his loudly, drinking it so fast he started to choke. Kelly patted his arm reassuringly.

A few sodas, and many candy bars later, they were all laughing hysterically as they slid down the railing of the grand spiral staircase. Another round of sodas later and they were belting acapella karaoke on the tables in the dining room like they were in a musical. All of them singing at the top of their lungs.

Their singing was cut off abruptly when a tremendous gust of wind knocked each of them off the tables. After a few shocked screams later they were all laughing deliriously on the ground. The floor was sparkling clean as they sat there laughing until their sides ached and they couldn't breathe. Each of them started picking themselves up off the floor with the help of the tables. A few people slipped and fell back to the floor with a thud as they laughed. Eventually, they made it to their feet without falling again. Kevin lay on the ground still, staring at the ceiling like he was having an existential crisis.

"Everyone okay?" Dylan called out.

Most of them nodded. Kevin just gave a thumbs up from his position on the floor.

Breathing heavily, Kevin asked them all the question that had slipped their minds. "Is nobody going to mention the fact that we all got swept off our feet by a gust of wind?"

"Heh, Kevin's in love with the wind," Leo chuckled breathlessly. "Swept off our feet. Pfft."

Brushing his hands off on his pants as he pushed himself to his feet, Kevin said, "I think you've had enough soda for the month, Leo."

"You can say that again," came a voice from above them.

Looking up, Holly saw Artemis swinging on the chandelier above them. How long she had been up there was a mystery—along with how she had gotten up there in the first place.

The rest of the group turned their heads to look pointedly at Apollo. "What? I'm her twin, not her keeper."

"Okay, but seriously guys," Kevin said, rubbing the back of his head with a wince. "Am I the only one who noticed the gust of wind knocking us off the tables while we're stuck *inside a building*?"

A split second later, the lights came on, some of them flickering. Artemis, who had been carefully lowering herself from the chandelier to a nearby table, startled at the sudden brightness and fell. She crashed onto the table below her with a groan. When asked, though, she waved off anyone who offered to help and claimed it was just a flesh wound.

At Kevin's mention of the wind, Holly was reminded of the night before. Her fingers had sparked, almost like the embers of a fire. She lifted them in front of her, inspecting them with renewed curiosity. For the briefest of moments, flames tickled along her fingers, then, in the blink of an eye, they flickered out. The hum of electricity filled the room as the lights stopped flickering—the generator must have finally kicked in.

Holly looked up to see if anyone had noticed her hands momentarily entangled in flames and was relieved to see that they were all too busy checking on Artemis still. She quickly dropped them to her sides. The rest of her friends had moved on to other topics.

"Why can't we just try to break the windows?" Leo was asking again. "I want to see if we can do it."

"How do we know if the air outside is safe to breathe?" Sora retorted.

"How do we know it isn't?" Apollo asked.

"Guys, come see this," Dylan called from another room. "They got the news channel working."

Holly followed the others to the lobby where Dylan was staring at a holo-screen, the remote on the end table in front of him.

"—just received word that there was a powerful shockwave of electric energy that passed through the city causing power fluctuations. The energy wave was filled with chemical compounds that have caused the nuclear blast doors to seal every building in the blast radius. While it seems to be nothing more than a faulty activation in the trigger systems for the nuclear blast doors, the Domina has advised that everyone remain indoors and not risk breaking any windows or trying to force their way through the blast doors until it is deemed safe to leave. Military officials are attempting to use their passcards to access the blast door mainframe, but are so far unsuccessful. In the mean time, military police are compiling a list of possible suspects who may have—"

The holo-screen cut to black.

Standing next to Dylan, Jacob held the remote in his hand.

"What did you do that for?" Kevin asked him.

Jacob shrugged as he set the remote down. "What use is it knowing who *might* have done it?

It's all just speculation at this point. Besides, we should be trying to preserve the building's power for as long as we can. If the energy wave really did mess with the systems, who is to say what kind of damage it could have done to the generator or the solar panels."

"He's got a point," Sora told them, then, to Leo, she added, "Are you glad we didn't try to break any windows now?"

Leo's only response was a noncommittal "yeah."

"Well, I don't know about you guys," Holly said. "But I'm going to go search for something to do while we wait."

"I think I'll join you," Dylan stated. Together they walked out of the room, leaving the rest of the group to theorize about the broadcast.

The hotel was eerily quiet as they wandered down the barren hallways. There was an activities wing they decided to check out first. They didn't run into anybody on their way there.

Every room they passed was empty. With no soul in sight the hotel felt abandoned but for the working electricity.

After nearly fifteen minutes of wandering the main level, Holly and Dylan found themselves in the gear-up room for paintball. There were at least a dozen slots for the paintball guns, seven of which were missing from their spots. An eighth one was in Leo's hands.

"Leo? What are you doing?" Dylan asked him.

Leo jumped, his blue eyes darting to them as he said, "Oop. Pasta la vista!"

Lifting the paintball gun strap over his head to keep it secure, Leo scurried out of the room.

Snatching one of the guns, Holly hurried after him yelling, "You cannot escape from me you little ferret!"

Leo kept running, through the entrance to the activities wing and past the soda bar, then into the lobby. Someone peeked their head through the doorway to the dining room to see what was happening, but Holly didn't get a good enough glimpse to see who it was.

In the lobby were their other friends, firing paintballs at each other haphazardly. Most of the projectiles missed their marks, marring the walls and decorations with vibrant splatters of paint that would likely take a while to clean.

It was no longer a chase, but an attempt at fleeing from the employees who had finally decided to make an appearance. Holly and Leo booked it up the staircase, their friends not far behind them as the shouts of the employees rang after them. Risking a glance behind, Holly watched as Artemis turned back and fired off a shot. The paintball streaked through the air, splattering dead center on one of the employee's chests and covering their maroon uniform in neon green.

Turning back to face the stairs, Holly took them three at a time. As they reached the seventh floor, Leo split away from her. Following him, Holly left the stairs—she didn't bother checking to see if anyone followed them until she had rounded the corner of the hallway. To her surprise, almost all of her friends had taken Leo's lead. The only person missing was Apollo.

Each of them was covered head-to-toe with a rainbow of vibrant paint splattered over their clothes. Her and Leo were the only two who had more clothing showing than paint splotches.

Taking the group in, Leo gestured for them all to split up between the two directions of the intersecting hallway. Before moving, each person who was moving to the other side of the hall checked down the way they had come. Jacob leaned against the far wall. Out of sight of the path back to the stairs, but in good view of what was about to play out. His gun was in his hand, the barrel pointed down. He didn't seem to have any intention of joining in on the ambush.

Leo peered around the corner, his hand raised. They stayed like that for a few minutes without hearing so much as the scuff of a shoe. With no sign of Apollo, Holly wondered if the employees had managed to catch him. Another moment of silence passed before Leo checked around the corner again.

A grin spread across his face as he returned to his position. Then he was motioning for them to go. All at once, the teenagers sprang from their hiding spots, paintball guns raised, and began opening fire.

Through the haze of paintballs, Holly could see it was Apollo, alone, who they were firing at. He remained untouched as their ammo ran out. There was an empty circle of paint spanning a couple inches around him. As she stood there, Holly noticed that not all of the paintballs had been splattered—some of them still hovered in the air before Apollo. A split second later they were sent flying back toward the group. As they did, she could swear she felt a shift in the air around them. Her senses had to be playing tricks on her though.

There was no way Apollo could have changed the trajectory of the paintballs.

Holly was the only one who seemed to realize what was happening in time to duck under the one that had been making a beeline for her face. She wasn't able to dodge the two that subsequently splattered on her leg and shoulder. Casting her gaze around, she tried to see if she was the only one who had noticed the momentary change in the flow of air. Nobody else seemed to have noticed though, they were all too preoccupied with getting splattered with paintballs. She dismissed it with a shake of her head.

All things considered, Holly hadn't been splotched with pain as badly as the rest of them. Most of the redirected paintballs had missed her, only a couple of them having hit her. Dylan and the others weren't so lucky. Only Jacob remained untouched by this last volley of paintballs. Not that anyone would have been able to tell, he was covered in paint splatter just like the rest of them.

Things calmed down a lot after that. They saw no more signs of the employees and assumed they were doing something about their current predicament—that or they were attempting to clean up the paintball mess.

After the ambush on the seventh floor, the group made their way down to their rooms on the fourth floor to change into fresh clothes and clean the paint from their hair. Once they were done, they decided to explore the theater room that took up a large portion of the tenth floor of the hotel.

The day of sealed exits, and no responsibility, had become one of great exercise as the teens made their way up to the tenth floor. They had thought about trying the elevators, but the nuclear protection protocol had shut down all non-essential systems that required electricity. And so here they were climbing a staircase long enough to give Mount Everest a run for its money—at least, that's what Leo had claimed between huffed breaths.

When the group made it to the theater, they heard the muffled sounds of frightened screams being cut off and walked in to find that they were not the only people—aside from the employees— still in the hotel. A small group of young kids had grabbed hold of each other and were huddled in the corner of the room. They gathered closer when the teens walked into the room. The group of teenagers stood there in shock, staring at the kids.

There were two older girls wrapping their arms protectively around the other kids. That was when Holly noticed among the younger kids was a small blonde girl around the age of seven with a familiar set of blue eyes.

She froze, staring at Nathan's younger sister, Amy.

Chapter 13

When Amy saw Holly, she snaked her way out of the arms of the older girls, who reached for her trying to drag her back to them. Their eyes were wide with fear and panic as she slipped from their grasp. Even from the other side of the room it was easy to tell the kids were trembling. Holly wondered how long they had been up here.

"Holly!" The young girl ran up to Holly and wrapped her arms around her waist. Holly crouched down and pried Amy off of her, her hands on the girl's shoulders, so she could look into her eyes.

"Hey, are you okay?" Holly asked, scanning her for any sign of injury.

Amy nodded, then, grabbing one of Holly's hands, she led her over to the group of kids. The others were crowded back at the doorway, the girls trying to peer over the shoulders of the guys to see why they had stopped moving.

As Holly and Amy approached the kids, the older girls of about twelve squeezed their arms tighter around the two little boys between them. Holly knelt in front of them, Amy still clinging to her hand.

"It's okay," Holly told them. "We're not going to hurt you. Where are your parents? Did they go to the party last night?"

One of the older girls nodded. The girls had a color of blue eyes that mirrored each other's, giving the distinct impression that they were twins.

"What are your names?"

After a short hesitation, one of them answered, "I'm Fallon. This is my twin sister, Felicity. This is Garrick and Percy."

"It's nice to meet you. I'm Holly. Those people back there," she said, gesturing to her friends standing awkwardly just inside the room. "Those are my friends. There are quite a few of us, but you can trust us, okay?" We're going to keep an eye on you until we can get you to your parents."

"Will you really help us?" Percy asked, his blue eyes wide as he looked up at her. He reminded her of Andrew, timid yet brave.

"Of course she will," Amy assured him. "She's one of the nicest people I know."

"How *do* you know her?" Felicity asked skeptically, folding her arms protectively over her chest.

"She used to date my dickheaded brother."

"Amy!" Holly scolded.

Amy huffed, looking completely unapologetic as she said, "What? It's true. He was always kissing that other girl while you guys were dating."

Holly's heart twisted in her chest at the comment.

"Where is Nathan, Amy?" Holly asked, changing the subject before the tears came back for an encore.

"Mom said he and his new girlfriend could go to the adult party with them." She sniffed.

"I see. Well, I'm going to go tell my friends what's happening, then we can see if we can get a movie going. How do you guys feel about that?"

The kids all nodded. Fallon and Felicity were visibly more relaxed than they had been moments before. Holly stood and turned to her friends. Amy was still clinging to her while she made her way over and explained the situation.

"Does anyone think they can get a movie started in here?" Holly asked as she finished. She wished Jay were with them, he was amazing with technology. Put him in front of alien tech and he could likely figure out how to replicate it with less than five seconds of looking at it.

Jacob glanced at the projector room. "I might be able to figure it out."

"Do you want any help?" Sora offered.

He looked over at her, his expression as unreadable as ever. "I suppose I could use a second pair of hands."

The pair made their way over to the projector room, leaving the rest of them to find seats and wait for them to, hopefully, get a movie going. Kevin and Leo, who had apparently disappeared around the same time as Jacob and Sora, returned carrying armfuls of candy and soda. They were both wearing wide grins on their faces as the five kids' faces lit up upon the sight of the junk food.

Despite typically feeling like the two were toddlers in teenage bodies, Holly thought it was extremely thoughtful of them to have raided the hotel for candy to give to the scared kids they were collectively babysitting.

While the group shared the treats, they chatted with one another. Holly was deep in conversation with Karen, who had Garrick sitting next to her munching on a chocolate candy bar, when the room started shaking violently.

The younger kids screamed as dust fell from the ceiling.

Karen wrapped her arms around Garrick and pulled him onto the ground.

In the aisle off to the side of the rows of seats, Percy was standing by himself.

Rushing over to him, Holly reached him and shoved him into Apollo's arms. Apollo wrapped his arms tightly around the young boy and helped him get into the relative safety of the space between the rows of seats.

Once he was safe, Holly scanned the room frantically, searching for anyone else. The room was quaking strong enough that large chunks of ceiling were starting to fall. Her feet felt like they were half a second from sliding out from under her.

Stumbling to the side a few steps, Holly almost tripped over an unconscious Leo. Blood was slowly dripping down his forehead where a piece of ceiling had hit him—Amy was holding onto his wrist, trying to pull him to the safety of the chairs.

Grabbing her hand, Holly took over for her.

Leo's brown hair was matted with blood against his skin as she dragged him behind the chairs where she had left Percy with Apollo. Amy followed after her.

Leaving the safety of the chairs, Holly searched the room again, desperately praying that Dylan was unharmed.

As she scanned the room, she caught a glimpse of Artemis, who had blood dripping down her face, being dragged into the rows of seats before passing out of view.

A few rows closer to the back, Holly saw that Fallon had found her way to the chairs with no injuries. She was surprised to see that the young girl had somehow dragged a semi-conscious Dylan with her.

Giving her an appreciative smile, Holly dodged a baseball-sized chunk of ceiling. It seemed like most everyone had made it to safety as she searched the dusty room for anybody else. Hopefully Jacob and Sora were okay.

Taking a step toward the front of the room, Holly tripped over something that felt like a body.

She fell to her knees, coughing as she inhaled some dust.

Raising herself off the floor, she moved closer to what had tripped her. As she approached, she recognized the blonde hair of Felicity. The young girl looked up at her, dust coating her hair as tears streamed down her terror stricken face.

A crack sounded through the room as a large chair from the room above them fell through a hole in the ceiling, shattering to pieces on the floor behind her. Holly looked up just in time to see a table begin to fall directly above Felicity.

In the blink of an eye Holly found herself throwing her body over Felicity's. Pain seared down her spine, spots filling her vision as the table cracked against her back, sliding to the floor with a thud.

Holly collapsed next to Felicity, her arm draped over the girl's quivering form.

Adjusting her position even a fraction sent flares of pain splintering down her back as her muscles seized with the motion. Holly stiffened, releasing a whimper from the pain.

Gritting her teeth, she squeezed her eyes shut and focused on breathing.

Felicity trembled in her arms.

Breathing was laborious as the quaking started to subside, the dust beginning to settle around the room.

Agonizing pain scorched along her spine as she was overtaken by a coughing fit. Her lungs were trying desperately to expel the dust that had filled them.

As the dust continued to dissipate, Holly scanned what she could see of the room. Her friends began to cautiously stand from their various spots between the rows of chairs. Most of them appeared to have missed being hit by any debris.

The room was littered with ceiling debris and furniture from the room above them. Many of the chairs remained unscathed, but a few of them had been hit by falling furniture.

Felicity wormed her way out of Holly's grasp, turning to face her.

"Holly?" she whispered, coughing slightly. "Holly, get up."

"I need you to do something for me," Holly said, forcing a reassuring smile on her face despite the pain. Felicity whimpered, her blue eyes welling up with tears. "Shh. It's okay—I'm alright. I just need you to find Dylan. Can you do that?"

Felicity nodded, smearing tears across her face with the palm of her hand. "Y-yeah. I think–I can d-do that."

She scrambled to her feet and scurried off in the direction of the chairs. Holly watched as the rest of her friends stood from their hiding places, the smile on her face turning to a grimace as soon as Felicity was gone. Percy's trembling body was held tightly in Apollo's arms as he stood next to a pale-faced Leo who was leaning heavily on the chair in front of him. Amy stood next to him, a crease between her blonde brows as she hovered next to him. Karen—holding onto Garrick's hand—slowly stood up a row in front of them, Sora helping Artemis to her feet a few rows behind. Near the back of the room, she saw Fallon standing next to Dylan. In the aisle, Felicity picked up her pace at the sight of her sister, a sob escaping her as she clutched her in a hug.

The room blurred as Felicity reluctantly released her sister and said something urgently to Dylan. Through the haze, Holly could see his eyes widen as the young girl spoke. His gaze darted to the front of the room in the direction Felicity pointed where Holly was trying to lift herself onto her elbows. Dylan called out her name. She swallowed a cry of pain as she reached for the edge of the table. Lifting her head, her gaze locked with Dylan's. Her hand slipped underneath her, causing her to collapse. Exhaustion wore through her bones. With one hand planted on the ground, she closed her eyes and focused on her breathing. The sound of the door at the back of the room opening. Kevin speaking gently to Kelly. Anything but the swelling pain in her back.

Sirens wailed distantly as Holly listened intently to Dylan picking his way through the rubble.

A warm hand brushed her cheek.

Holly opened her eyes to see Dylan kneeling in front of her. She smiled as he cradled her face in his hands.

"You're okay," he muttered. "Right? You're okay?"

His touch was gentle even as he moved one of his hands to her back. Her breath hitched, pain flaring under his touch. Dylan lifted his hand from its place on her mid-back, his eyes leaving her face to scan her for injuries.

"Dylan," she whispered, almost unable to keep herself from vomiting as she spoke. "I can't feel my legs."

Pounding boots in the hall interrupted Dylan's reply, but the terror written in his eyes remained. Seconds later, a soldier entered the room. He scanned the room before signaling to someone just outside. A group of soldiers entered the room, soon after followed by General Falcon. His assessing gaze swept the room until it landed on Leo—he visibly relaxed at the sight of his son.

"Is everyone okay?" The General demanded.

Everyone else nodded as he finished his sweep of the room and landed on Holly and Dylan. With a quick gesture to the soldiers around him, General Falcon walked over to his son and gripped him tightly in a fatherly hug. Two of the soldiers approached the front of the room, stopping next to Holly and Dylan.

One of them knelt next to them and asked, "Are you two okay?"

Dylan nodded, but his gaze returned to Holly. The soldier turned his head to her, a question in his eyes.

"A table fell on my back," she told him, then paused, swallowing a wave of dizziness and trying not to black out. "I can't feel my legs."

The soldier nodded before standing. After a short conversation with his partner, he pulled out a radio and spoke into it. A reply crackled over the antique device. The second soldier nodded then crouched next to Dylan.

Nausea swirled in her stomach as realization and panic started to settle in her gut. There was no sensation from her hips down. Modern medicine was miraculous, but it couldn't always heal paralysis. Is that what this was? Was she *paralyzed*? She couldn't breathe. There were so many things she might never be able to do again—swimming, walking her mother down the aisle, dancing in the centennial anniversary festival. All of it was now beyond her grasp. All of it was quickly slipping away with each pained breath she took.

"The paramedics are on their way up with a stretcher. I need you to come with me. Private Connoway will stay here with your friend."

Dylan nodded but hesitated.

"Go," Holly told him. "I'll be fine."

With one last breath of hesitation, Dylan stood and left with the soldier. True to his word, Private Connoway stayed with Holly as they awaited the arrival of the paramedics.

In moments, the paramedics were rushing into the room, a stretcher held between them. As they set it down next to her, one of them put a brace on her neck before they both carefully shifted her onto her back and onto the stretcher in one move. Her thoughts churned as the paramedics carried her out of the room and headed toward the stairs. Worry for her friends pressed on her attention, but she couldn't stop pressing her fingers against the side of her leg wishing she could feel it. *Praying* that it wasn't permanent. It wasn't even the numbness that came with anesthesia—there was simply nothing there. No sensation aside from the pressure on her fingers as she tried to feel something in her leg.

The possibility of being permanently paralyzed pressed a thousand pounds on the forefront of her mind as they reached the base of the staircase.

Her stretcher was brought over to a temporary medical tent just outside of the hotel and set on a gurney. The paramedics who had carried her talked about overfilled hospitals as they carefully transferred her to a cot inside the tent. Darkness spotted her vision as the motion sent lashes of pain along her back.

Private Connoway, who had followed behind them the entire way, gave a nearby doctor his field analysis and left to attend to his other duties. Before approaching the cot, the doctor turned to Dylan, who had appeared in the spot Private Connoway had just vacated. She pointed to the entrance of the tent, a clear indication of wanting him to leave. Dylan crossed his arms over his chest and said something Holly couldn't quite hear over the rushing of blood in her ears. Frowning, the doctor said something in return. Upon Dylan's response, she pressed her lips into a thin line for a moment before seeming to relent. Together they made their way over to Holly.

"I need to turn you on to your stomach," the doctor told her. Then to Dylan, "Ready?"

He nodded.

Holly braced herself for the burning pain that was about to race down her back. Dylan and the doctor positioned their arms around her before carefully flipping her onto her front. Stars danced in her vision, pain sweeping along her back as the scream she had been holding back since the table had hit her back ripped its way out of her throat.

The last thing she remembered was seeing Dylan's face just before her eyes rolled back in her head and darkness rushed in.

Chapter 14

Darkness met fire and agony as they danced a waltz along the nerves in her back. The dance twirled down through her legs, leaving sparks in its wake. Warmth as comforting as sitting before an embering hearth coated her senses. Then the void dissipated as Holly's eyes fluttered open. She was lying on her stomach in an unfamiliar room. Her body was stiff but she managed to lift her head just enough to turn it to the left. Dylan was sitting in a chair next to the bed. He was staring at the carpet, his gaze unfocused. His hands were clasped between his legs, his body leaning over his knees. He hadn't yet noticed her slight movement.

Holly opened her parched mouth to say something, but had to close it for a second before she could say anything.

"Dylan?" Her voice was quiet and raspy as she spoke.

His head jerked up and he practically fell out of his chair as he stood and moved closer to her, kneeling so he could look her in the eye. There was a crease between his brows. Holly moved her hand to sweep a stray hair from his forehead but froze halfway there. Letting her hand awkwardly drop to the edge of the bed next to her shoulder, she inhaled deeply.

"How do you feel?" he asked, leaning back.

Holly watched him clench and unclench his hands on his thighs. Her mind was sluggish.

Blinking slowly, she tried to remember why she was waking up. "What happened?"

"You passed out. The doctor had to reset your back. The table that hit you dislodged one of your spinal discs, putting pressure on your spinal cord or something. She said that's why you couldn't feel your legs."

Holy looked at him. His face was pale, and he had a bandage above his eye. He still seemed scared though the earthquake was over. Silver lined his eyes—he leaned his forehead against the edge of the bed.

"I was so scared for you," he murmured so softly she almost didn't hear him speak. "The others were all relatively unharmed. Only Artemis needed stitches, but you..." Dylan let out a shaky breath. "I called your mom. She's worried about you—threatened to postpone the wedding to come see you, but I managed to assuage her with a promise not to leave your side until the doctors are sure you're okay."

"Thank you," she replied, wanting to shift her hand to comfort him. Instead, she clutched the sheets of the bed. "Are you okay?"

Dylan huffed out a laugh.

Lifting his head, he said, "I'm not the one whose back got broken."

Pushing himself to his feet, Dylan glanced toward the door. Exhaustion weighed heavily on his shoulders as his eyes returned to hers.

"I'm going to find a doctor or a nurse. You just..." he paused and looked at his phone which had started vibrating. He pressed the decline button and continued, "Don't move. I'll be right back."

"Okay."

He left without another word, phone once again vibrating in his hand.

Holly lay there waiting for only a few minutes when a nurse came in. She was a thin woman, her blonde hair tied back in a ponytail. Her blue eyes glittered in the light as she set her bag on the chair Dylan had left vacant and pulled out a portable heart and breathing monitor. Turning it on, she set the device between Holly's shoulder blades. It started beeping to the rhythm of her heartbeat a few seconds later. The nurse had a name tag pinned to her shirt just above her heart, it read: Melissa Wright LPN.

Melissa started rubbing her gloved hands across Holly's back. "Tell me if you feel any pain."

After a while, she moved out of Holly's peripheral vision and started poking the soles of her feet with a pen. Her feet twitched with each poke. "Can you feel this?"

"Yes." Holly almost cried in relief—she wasn't paralyzed. All those things she had worried about not being able to do, all the things she could have missed out on, they were all within her reach now. She could feel herself reaching for them once more.

Melissa walked back to Holly's side and checked the monitor, writing a few things on a holopad before turning it and the monitor off and putting them both back in her bag.

"You can sit up now, carefully," Melissa told her. As Holly gently rolled over and sat up, the nurse kept speaking. "Your back seems to have healed nicely. I suggest not doing anything too strenuous for the next couple of days. I injected you with some nanobots, as well as some argenteral, to speed the healing process, but you will still feel soreness in your back and legs for a while. The nanobots should be out of your system in about a week."

"Thank you," Holly replied sincerely, nearly choking on the emotions she was trying to swallow.

The nurse gave her a smile before picking up her bag and leaving.

Dylan walked back in, passing the nurse on her way out, sliding his phone into his pocket as he made his way over. Holly swept her feet to the floor but stayed on the bed. Dylan stopped next to her and reclaimed his spot on the chair across from her.

"Now that I've basically gotten a clean bill of health," Holly started, forcing a lightness into her tone that she couldn't feel. "Where are we? I'm not particularly fond of waking up in a strange bed."

"We're on the ground floor of the hotel," Dylan told her. "The military police have set up a makeshift ICU because the hospitals are all overwhelmed and overflowing with an onslaught of patients after the earthquake."

"Oh." Her face flushed. Casting her gaze around the room with a more observant eye, she noticed that, beneath the clear tarp on the floor and walls, the wallpaper and carpet of the room were identical to that of her own room on the fourth floor.

"Do you want to see the others? They've been worried about you."

"Let me guess, Leo begged you to ask me that because he's waiting right outside that door with a plate stacked sky-high with waffles."

Dylan hesitated. *Bingo*. Leo definitely had a plate of waffles for her.

"Yeah, yeah he is."

"Excellent." Holly hopped up from the bed, careful not to strain her back. She *was* still a bit sore—just as Melissa had said she would be—but other than that she was feeling good, if not very hungry at the mention of food.

She walked to the door and opened it. Just as she had suspected, Leo was standing there, a huge grin on his face as he held out a plate stacked with at least seven mega-sized waffles. Holly let out a squeak at the sight of such a delicious offering.

"Your post-almost-dying-or-getting-paralyzed food offering has officially arrived. Prepared just for you, Lady Waffle, by yours truly." Leo's grin widened.

Holly laughed and accepted the plate from him. Too tired to go anywhere else, she sat on the ground and started shoving the heavenly waffles into her mouth. There was no syrup on them, but she took that as a good thing because Leo had conveniently forgotten to give her a fork.

"It's like watching a starving lion devour a zebra," Kevin commented from the other side of Holly's waffle tower.

"Weird metaphor, but one hundred percent accurate," Kelly said, one arm looped around his waist and the other holding the hand of the arm he had draped over her shoulder.

"How does she eat so much?" she heard Sora ask.

"Fast metabolism," Holly replied, swallowing the last bite of her third waffle. "Yes, I can hear you, y'know. And not even the graphic lion line is enough to rid me of my appetite right now. I could probably eat a zebra myself with how hungry I am."

Karen crinkled her nose at that.

Holly finished the waffles in record time. She stood up as Leo grabbed the plate from her and set it on a nearby food cart. Behind him stood the rest of Holly's friends. They had all come to check on her. She walked up to Leo and gave him a tight hug. Her eyes started to water, but she blinked away the tears as she went up to her friends and gave each of the girls a hug—the boys, aside from Leo, she merely accepted a pat on the shoulder from.

When she released Artemis from her embrace, she turned to the person who had just walked up behind the group; Nathan. Amy came out from behind him and ran to Holly, squeezing her waist in a hug. Holly knelt and hugged her back before standing to face her ex-boyfriend. She leveled a glare at him.

"Guys," she said to her friends behind her. "Can I have a moment?"

"Sure," Karen answered for all of them. "Take your time. Come on guys, let's give her some space."

They all walked around Nathan and Holly, who still had Amy clinging to her. Artemis gave Nathan a once-over, her pale blue eyes colder than the arctic as she gave him a look that told him exactly what to expect from her should he try anything. Dylan paused beside her, hesitating.

"You too, Amy," Holly told her.

"But I wanna stay," the little girl whined.

"No, you don't."

"Go find mom, Ames," Nathan said, not even sparing his sister a glance. His electric blue eyes remained on Holly, searching her face for something only he knew he was looking for.

"Fine." Huffing, Amy dragged out the word before trotting off in the direction Holly's friends had gone.

"Holly." Dylan was still hovering next to her as though he felt the need to leave but wanted to stay. She briefly met his gaze, giving him a small smile that told him she could handle this on her own. He nodded, glancing once at Nathan before brushing past him and running a hand through his messy black hair.

"What do you want, Nathan?" Venom coated her tongue like fresh snow on the ground.

"Glare at me all you want, Holly. It doesn't change the past. I cheated on you, I know that, but that doesn't get rid of all the good memories we had. We've been friends since you moved to Emerald Bay, and even before any of this you wouldn't open up to me." He paused, taking a breath before continuing, "I came here to ask you something; after all that time as friends, why wouldn't you talk to me? What scared you so much that you were too afraid, even after years of friendship, to tell your best friend, your boyfriend?"

"What are you hoping to accomplish by asking me that?" Holly retorted, remembering the dark place she had been in for the first couple of years after her father's escape. The paranoia that had settled on her consciousness. Of expecting to see him lurking around every corner, in every shadow, blending into every crowded sidewalk she was on. Nathan knew nothing of that though. He had barely seen the surface-level fears that even her best mask couldn't cover up. The insomnia. The flinching at physical contact. She had never talked about it with anybody other than her therapist, and her actual best friend—Naomi.

Taking a breath, Holly shoved down the memories of the shell she had been after leaving her old life behind. "Is it some desperate attempt to get me back? Find closure?"

"No." He sighed and ran his hands through his golden-blond hair, his fingers interlacing behind his head for a moment before he dropped his hands to his sides. "I don't know. It's just... it's all I've been able to think about since you broke up with me."

"You really want to know, don't you?" she replied. He nodded, disappointment a frantic haze in his eyes. Holly sighed. "You know who my father is, and yet you still ask me what I was scared of. Shouldn't that be enough? I shouldn't need to tell you anything more than that—and I won't. I don't owe you anything, Nathan. We may have had good memories together, but that's all they are now. You threw what we had in the trash the moment you decided I wasn't enough for you. Now leave me alone. I don't want to see you again."

Nathan opened his mouth, but Holly was already moving past him. She wasn't about to stick around to hear another word come from his mouth. He was a liar, a manipulative and selfish liar and she was done with him.

As she rounded the corner, she released a breath she had been holding since she walked away. Dylan was leaning against the wall a few feet away. Straightening her back, she met his gaze. He met hers in return, his expression telling her he had overheard everything. She should be upset with him. Should be mad that he hadn't left when she had asked, but she couldn't bring herself to feel the burning heat of anger.

He looked like he wanted to say something, but Holly stopped him with the raise of her hand.

"Don't say it," she said. "I was harsher than I meant to be, and I know that, but seeing him again, I just... I couldn't stop myself. He broke my heart, and now he's back, asking more from me?"

She sighed, her eyes going to the ceiling as she took in another breath.

"I wasn't going to say any of that," Dylan replied, his voice filling the emptiness of the hall. "What I was going to say, before you so rudely interrupted, was, firstly to profoundly apologize for eavesdropping, and secondly that I thought you put him in his place. You're right. He doesn't deserve your forgiveness." He paused. Her eyes were still on the ceiling, searching it for an answer to why she was so bothered by Nathan's reappearance. By his question. But the beige paint offered no response. Dylan shifted, his clothes rustling slightly with the movement. She half expected him to bring her face down so she would meet his gaze again, but instead he simply said, "Holly, look at me." He waited until she had complied before going on, "You did what you felt was right. It's not easy to forgive someone, but it's also not a requirement—it's a choice. You get to decide who to forgive. And *you* get to decide if and when you do. You made a choice not to forgive him, now move on. There's nothing else he can do to you if you don't let him."

Holly smiled. He was right.

Dylan started walking toward the lobby, leaving Holly to follow him.

"So, how long was I out?" Holly asked as they walked.

"Oh, y'know, it's been about a month. You completely missed the festival—your mom's wedding, too. Everyone thought you were going to die."

Holly punched his arm. "Would you stop that? I know you're messing with me."

"Okay, okay. Stars, you do *not* pull your punches." Dylan rubbed the spot on his arm where she had hit him. "You were only out for two days, Nurse Wright kept you sedated so the nanobots could work quickly through your system without any drawbacks. The festival is tomorrow.

Oh. OH. Holly had gotten so swept away in all the bustle of the past day—well, days, apparently—that she had completely forgotten about how fast the festival was approaching. She had been a little preoccupied with the whole building being sealed by the nuclear blast doors and the freakishly long earthquake. She worried that they wouldn't be prepared for it, but realized that they had nothing to worry about. Everything would be fine. They had been practicing for hours every day, working on every small stumble in their dances and finetuning their speeches near the end of each day. Holly felt ready to perform the next day—and she was sure her friends felt the same confidence. Then, she could leave and still make it to her mom's wedding. It wasn't a long flight, but her mom needed her home as early as possible to help with last minute preparations. Domina Garner had been very accommodating about the situation when Holly had brought it up to her and

Secretary Garcia shortly after her release from the hospital after the plane crash. She hadn't told any of her friends about it, yet, though. Dylan, of course, knew her mom was getting married through the grapevine of gossip at their school—something she could definitely attribute to Naomi's loud exclamation of excitement when she had told her best friend about it a few days before leaving for the festival. She was pretty sure the entire school had overheard Naomi's screeched, '*Your mom is getting remarried?!*' Holly had planned to tell them the day of the earthquake, but her plans had gone a bit awry with all that had happened. She knew she would have to tell them tonight, though, maybe at dinner.

The rest of the day was uneventful and just like the past week. Holly and her friends went to the opera house for some practice before dinner, but none of them seemed to mind the last-minute rehearsal. As she would have expected, the rest of the representatives had been practicing during the two days Holly had been unconscious in the makeshift ICU.

After rehearsal, the group went to a restaurant next to the hotel. It was very expensive, and Holly doubted anyone there would have been able to afford it if the Domina hadn't used government funding for it. Except maybe Leo, knowing his dad was the top general over Verdona's military.

Holly had finally decided how to tell them that she would be leaving right after the festival broadcast for her mom's wedding. She knew they would be disappointed that she was leaving. It wasn't like it was the end of the world, but she knew they were all looking forward to the after party.

When they had all received their food and were beginning to dig in, Holly started to speak up. "Guys, I need to tell you something."

Her friends looked up at her expectantly. Leo had a skeptical expression on his face like he was expecting some sappy toast about them only having one more day together, but seemed curious enough not to risk speaking around his mouthful of barbeque ribs for an interruption.

"I won't be able to join you guys at the after party after the broadcast tomorrow. I'm leaving as soon as we're done." The teens sat there in silence. "Are you going to say anything?"

"What do you want us to say?" Apollo asked, disappointment written on his features.

Kevin was playing with his food, looking like he hadn't even heard what she had said. Kelly nudged him with her arm. He looked up, his eyes meeting Holly's through the reflective surface of his glasses as he said, "I was looking forward to a food war rematch, and you're going to leave us hanging?

Holly smiled. "Kevin, we all know you and Leo hid in your table fort for most of the war. Don't act like you were war heroes or something. Besides, you're acting like we won't ever see each other again." She looked around the table. "Guys, tomorrow doesn't have to be the last time we see each other. We don't live that far apart, and I'm willing to bet we all have cars and know how to drive them."

"She's got a point," Karen spoke up. "Just because we go home in two days doesn't mean we can't still meet up every once in a while, or even video chat."

Artemis grinned. "We can always have a food war rematch after we return home—though, maybe a paintball war would be a better idea. I don't know about you guys, but I have some payback owed after that fight."

Leo and Kevin shared a mischievous grin.

"Can I ask why you're leaving early?" Sora asked from the other end of the table, the chopsticks in her hands empty as they hovered over her bowl of ramen.

"Yeah," Leo whined, wiping his barbeque sauce-covered hands on his napkin. "Why are you ditching us?"

"My mom is getting married," Holly laughed. "I can't exactly ditch her wedding. I'm the maid of honor."

A round of congratulations went around the table. Other customers in the restaurant glanced over at them, more than a few of them pausing as their gazes caught on Sora. Holly could read the distrust in their eyes even though it had been over a century since the Chinese had been a serious issue for the country—not that Sora was even Chinese to begin with, but people were cruel and couldn't care less about the distinction between someone who was Japanese-Korean and someone who was Chinese.

"So, what you're saying is, we should throw one heck of a party tonight before you leave?" Dylan asked, drawing Holly's attention back to the conversation at hand.

Her lips tugged up into a smile as she looked around at her friends. "Yes. That is exactly what I'm saying."

"All right!" Kevin cheered. "As long as Apollo's not in charge of the music."

"Hey!" Apollo punched him in the arm. "I'm sitting right next to you."

"I think that's the point," Jacob told him.

"Let's get this party on the road," Leo shouted, kicking back his chair enthusiastically.

Next to him, Karen caught his chair before it could clatter to the ground. "Woah, take it down a notch, Beast Boy. We're not done eating yet."

"Yeah, I would like to finish eating before we run off to do something else, thank you very much," Artemis said before taking a bite of her pasta.

Leo sat back down with a humph. "Fine, but as soon as everyone is done, we're going straight to that arcade down the street to play laser tag."

Karen kissed him on the cheek. "Alright, but if you scream 'For glory!' when we get there, I'm leaving you in the parking lot."

They finished their food while debating what to do afterward. After much back-and-forth, they ended up going with Leo's idea to hit the arcade for games and laser tag. Once the decision was made, conversation drifted into other topics as they lingered over the rest of the meal.

When they were done, Secretary Garcia came over from her table to tell them they were free to spend the rest of the evening as they wished—so long as they were back at the hotel before curfew at midnight.

They arrived at the arcade shortly after. Without missing a beat, Leo shouted, "For the Holy Roman Empire!"

Karen rolled her eyes, a smile tugging at her lips at his work-around of her request.

The group spent hours at the arcade, playing every game available and going through multiple rounds of laser tag. They were all laughing, enjoying themselves the entire time. Even Jacob could be seen smiling—a rare, once-in-a-blue-moon occurrence with him.

By the time midnight was starting to roll around, they were all losing their enthusiasm for the arcade. Yet, despite their exhaustion, the walk back to the hotel was full of laughter and blissful joy. Everyone was giddy with excitement for the festival the next day, their systems still flush with the adrenaline of their last game of laser tag.

In spite of her exhaustion, Holly had a feeling it would be a long night for her. That is until she remembered the muscle relaxers Nurse Wright had given her for her back—she had informed her that they would also help her fall asleep. Taking a few of them, Holly climbed into the bed next to Karen, who was already fast asleep with her honey-blonde hair splayed across the pillow.

Holly was jolted awake at the sound of something loud outside. Bleary-eyed, she glanced at the digital clock on the nightstand next to the bed. *So early*, she thought. *The sun isn't even fully risen yet.*

After such a late night, she wasn't exactly thrilled about being woken up so early. Knowing she wouldn't be able to fall back asleep, however, she got up and walked to the door. She took half a step out the door and looked up and down the hall. Some of the others were doing the same. They all had bags under their eyes large enough to make Santa jealous.

Kevin yawned widely as he rubbed his eyes, squinting against the harsh lighting of the hallway.

"Does anyone know what is causing all the noise?" Jacob asked, looking like he had gotten a full night's sleep. Holly narrowed her eyes at him, certain he had to be a vampire. Nobody could look that composed after so little sleep. She certainly couldn't. Naomi had teased her for her raccoon mask relentlessly ever since they had met.

"Yeah, what disturbed my beauty sleep," Kevin yawned again. "It takes effort to look somewhat presentable."

He gave Jacob a pointed glare, likely thinking along similar lines as Holly.

There was a muffled sound that reminded Holly of a high school football game, but nobody who valued their sleep would be celebrating that early in the morning.

They all shook their heads, too tired to deal with any of it at that moment. Kelly shrugged her shoulders and went back into her room saying it was probably some people celebrating early. Holly yawned and returned to her own room—she was too tired to discuss it any further. Karen was still fast asleep on the bed, now spread eagle on the mattress as Holly walked over to the minifridge and pulled out an energy drink. There was no better way to start a morning than with caffeine.

She was standing over her suitcase sipping her drink when the mattress shifted and soft footfalls made their way over to the minifridge. Turning to glance over her shoulder, Holly took in Karen's disheveled appearance and couldn't stop herself from snorting.

"What?" Karen asked, snatching an iced coffee from the mini-fridge.

"Nothing." Holly went back to her half-packed suitcase.

"Is there drool on my face?" Karen looked mortified when Holly downed the rest of her drink and turned around to toss it in the trash.

"No. Nothing like that," she reassured her friend. "You should probably check on your hair though. Might have a furry little friend hiding in it."

Karen squeaked in embarrassment, setting her drink on the table before hurrying to the bathroom. Holly chuckled, then went back to packing her suitcase.

After a few minutes, Karen exited the bathroom, her shoulder-length hair brushed out.

As Karen went over to her mound of clothing, Holly set the last piece of her own clothing into her suitcase and checked the clock. They still had plenty of time before they were expected to be at the opera house for introductions to the visiting ambassadors. Each of them was supposed to dress nicely and be on their best behavior when they were introduced to his majesty Emperor Chionesu Lukman of the African empire. Holly and her friends already had their outfits bought and tailored for them days ago. It would probably take her at least an hour just to put on her dress, not to mention she was in desperate need of a shower.

After her hour-long shower, it took her about half that time to dry her hair. Once she was finished, she walked into the bedroom and opened the closet where her dress was stored next to Karen's. The top of the dress was a ruby-red that faded into a brilliant orange edging on yellow at the bottom, almost like a sunrise. The skirts were a little puffier than she had expected, but it wouldn't be too awful to dance in.

Holly carefully took the dress out and returned to the bathroom to change while Karen changed in the bedroom. Locking the door, she hung the hanger on the towel hook attached to the wall. She was meticulous as she put the dress on—which was easier said than done. It took her forever to get it on.

When she had finally managed to get it on, she opened the door and called Karen over. Her friend popped her head around the closet door.

"Yeah?"

"Could you help me to up the back of my dress?" she asked, stepping out of the bathroom. The skirts of the dress swished around her, the light dancing minuets across the silky fabric as she walked.

"Of course," Karen replied. Her eyes sparkled as she took in Holly's dress.

Karen's own dress was a deep scarlet with faux rubies embedded in the blouse. The skirts were asymmetrical, opening down in a triangle to show black fabric underneath.

Holly turned around and pulled her long hair over her neck as she braced herself against the doorframe. She could feel Karen's fingers pulling the fabric tight around her in hard tugs.

"Did you request this evil of a dress?" Karen asked, her melodic voice strained. "I didn't know they even had corset dresses still."

Holly laughed. "Me neither."

"There, all done. You look stunning by the way, just like a princess."

Sweeping her hair off her shoulder, Holly turned back to her. "So do you. That dress really softens your eyes."

Karen smiled. "Thanks. Do you want help with your makeup?"

"Please," Holly begged, grateful her friend was a professional makeup artist. Her own skills were subpar at best. "Let me do my hair first."

"Wonderful." Karen clapped her hands together, then walked into the bathroom to do her own hair and makeup.

Holly walked in after her. The bathroom was, thankfully, spacious enough for the both of them to do their hair.

After curling her hair, Karen pulled out a large makeup kit and set to work on her makeup while Holly curled her own hair. Once she had curled it, she grabbed a hairpin and pulled half of her hair up, sliding the pin through the twisted hair, creating a loose knot at the back of her head.

With her hair done, and only about half an hour before they were expected to be at the opera house, Holly sat patiently on the edge of the bed as Karen did her makeup. Karen's hair had some ruby studded pins holding back the hair on the right side of her head. Silver drops fell from her ears, each one connected to a slim chain leading up to her ear lobe. Her makeup was perfect for the occasion. Her eyelids were dusted with silver sparkles on top of a black base tinted with red on the outside corners of her eyes, and her lipstick was a deep red that glistened in the light.

Holly knew she was in good hands.

Karen made her outfit appear effortless. Of course, Holly knew it wasn't, but she also knew Leo's jaw would hit the ground harder than a comet through the atmosphere when he saw her.

When Karen finished with her makeup, she had Holly check it out in the bathroom mirror. Holly gasped when she saw her reflection. Her eyes were like flames dancing in the sunset. The eyeliner made the golden glitter pop out even more against the red base of the eyeshadow. Her lips were a blood red that would have made a heart jealous. She smiled as she walked back out to Karen.

"It looks amazing! Thank you!"

"My pleasure." Karen smiled sweetly as she packed up her makeup kit.

Holly walked over to her suitcase and pulled out the carefully stored jewelry she had been considering. For earrings, she decided to wear some rubies hanging down from her ears on golden bases. A golden chain hung around her neck with a fire opal embedded in a crescent moon-shaped setting that rested just below her collarbone. The necklace was a gift from Adam for her fifteenth birthday. It was the last time she had seen him before he had left for college, but Holly hoped that he would surprise them all and show up for their mom's wedding. It was a wishful hope, but she held onto it regardless.

The finishing touch for her outfit was a pair of black open-toed heels. Holly didn't much like wearing heels, but she could make an exception.

Karen waited for her by the door, and together they walked down the stairs and got into the limo that would take them to the opera house. Jacob and Dylan were already seated in the limo as the girls climbed in. Upon seeing Holly, Dylan's eyes widened, his lips parting ever so slightly as he seemed to drink in her appearance. He was quick to reign in his expression, though, and offered a compliment on her dress before snapping his jaw shut and adjusting his orange and gray striped tie.

Anticipation nearly drowned out Holly's thoughts as the door closed behind her, but Dylan's reassuring smile calmed her nerves as the car started moving. She had nothing to worry about. The country was about to celebrate its one-hundredth anniversary of reconstruction. Everything would work out just fine.

Chapter 15

Lights were strung on the eaves of the roofs of nearby buildings. The opera house was bedecked with banners and flags. There were flags for the country and a flag for each of the other countries which had sent ambassadors for the festival. Only one ruler was visiting, but delegates and emissaries from all over the world had come to celebrate with them. The banners were those of the school mascots for each high school that would be performing. A panther for Lakeshore, a warrior for Washington, an owl for Drath, a pilot for Airfield, and a dragon for Solstice. The myriad of colors for the schools was reflected in the colors chosen for each of the festival outfits of the representatives.

Holly and Dylan had arrived just after the Amour twins, Karen and Jacob walking in behind them. They had just started up the red carpet that had been laid out when Kevin and Kelly pulled up behind them and climbed out.

All of the boys had identical outfits for the broadcast; black suits with ties the color of their schools. Classic blue with sunshine yellow stripes on Kevin's tie, Kelly's blue chiffon dress a perfect match for Lakeshore.

The six of them walked into the lobby together, trying their best to ignore the hoard of journalists trying to capture their attention. Leo and Sora were standing near the Domina, Secretary Garcia, and General Falcon. Sora reached over to fix Leo's light blue tie striped with white, but Leo smacked her hand away. Rolling her eyes, Sora brushed a nervous hand over the smooth onyx hair she had pulled into a bun on her head. A moment later, she was smacking Leo's hand away as he apparently teased her about the size of the silver hoops hanging from her ears. He was soon distracted, however, as he saw Karen enter just behind Holly and Dylan.

Jacob looked almost bored as he and Karen walked past where Holly and Dylan had stopped next to Leo and Sora. His blond hair was parted in the middle, and his red tie was pristine. Leo's eyes followed Karen as she approached, her and Jacob stopping next to the pair from Airfield just as the Amour siblings arrived.

The twins were arguing about something as they entered the building, the last of the representatives to arrive. Apollo was wearing a gray and green striped tie. The forest green complimenting his brown hair. Beside him, Artemis' dress was made of silver silk that fell just past her ankles. It was sleek and elegant, and very beautiful on her tan skin. She flicked her brother's ear, saying something else before tugging him toward the others.

After the last of them had finally arrived, they all lined up on either side of the doorway to greet the guests who were just starting to pull up in front of the building. Paparazzi lights flashed like exploding stars at the guests—who all ignored them just as Holly and her friends had.

Holly smiled at each of the guests who arrived and shook hands with those who offered her their hand. She even kissed the air on either side of the French ambassador's cheeks, the woman leaning in to do the same. Many people were arriving in their resplendent outfits that probably cost more than Holly's entire house.

Most of the guests were already finding their seats by the time Emperor Lukman arrived. The emperor was a strongly built man with a deep brown skin tone. His black hair was cut close to his scalp, adding to the foreboding aura rolling off him in waves. His eyes were a blue so deep they could have been mistaken for the night sky. His face was stern and looked almost unkind, which only added to the intimidation that seemed to flow from his very soul. As he walked through the doorway he paused, gazing around the lobby. His eyes skimmed over the representatives.

Seeming convinced of something, Emperor Lukman turned to Domina Garner and gave her his hand, which she clasped firmly.

"Thank you for coming today, Your Majesty," the Domina said, the right side of her mouth quirking up a little.

"Anita, how many times do I have to tell you to call me by my name?" His voice was deep and rich with a northern African accent. "It's been fifteen years since you have called me anything but my title. Are you *still* trying to get me back for Italy?"

"Nesu, Italy has nothing to do with it. Can't a woman enjoy annoying her cousin?"

If Kevin had been drinking water, Holly had no doubt he would have spewed it all over the place. As it was, Jacob had a cup in his hand and was choking on a mouthful of water. Holly could have sworn she saw fear in his eyes, but it was gone in the blink of an eye as Karen patted his back in an effort to help.

The teens from Washington and Airfield had just finished greeting another guest and were walking over to them when they heard the last part of the conversation. Holly could tell none of them had seen that coming—it was one thing that had clearly been omitted from their textbooks. Well, everyone except for Leo, who was standing there fidgeting with his tie.

Emperor Lukman appeared to be the last guest to arrive so Holly and the rest of the representatives headed backstage to the practice room just behind the main stage. They all began to warm up their muscles as they waited. Once they had done that, each pair walked through the steps of their dances and each of them did another once-over of their speech. Then, they prepared themselves to go on stage.

A holo-screen in the far corner of the room was showing the broadcast, the audio was muted, but they knew they would be on soon. After a few moments, a stage assistant came backstage, a serious expression on his face.

"I don't like that look," Sora muttered under her breath.

The stage assistant didn't say anything, he just grabbed the remote to the holo-screen and turned up the volume. Where moments before the broadcast had been playing, now there was something else. Everyone in the room froze. The broadcast had been hijacked.

"Hello, people of Verdona." A filter on the voice made the person sound both male and female at the same time—their body was cloaked in shadows on the screen, a familiar symbol could be seen on the backdrop, and Holly could just make out a makeshift bird mask on the person's face. There was something extremely unnerving about them that had Holly and the rest of them tensing. "We are G.H.O.S.T., and we have a message for you. We are declaring war against our tyrannical government. Their military rule can not stay. Our previous messages have been vehemently ignored, but we will not let this one slip through the cracks. We will destroy the government and everything they stand for that has held us back as a nation. For far too long we have allowed them to do as they please—ruling us with an iron fist under their martial law. They have controlled our lives for too long and covered up too much of our history—allowing foreign enemies to remain on our soil in spite of our history with them. Today we make a promise to the people of this country, we will free this country from its oppressive government, and once it's free, this country will be reborn from the ashes.

"To show our commitment, we have planted bombs in seven random buildings in southern Sunhaven. The military police have received fourteen addresses of the possible targets. If you hope to save the ignorant civilians, you better choose wisely." The footage changed from the hazy picture to a tall building in a large city. Her heart froze in her chest as Holly recognized the building. She couldn't breathe as she saw the unsuspecting people through the windows, the camera panned over the gathered crowd and she tried to stop her mind from listing off the RSVPs she had helped her mom go through before she had left. "Let the revolution begin."

Holly heard a buzzing in her ears as she watched the building combust. Debris scattered across the street, slamming into cars and other buildings as the rehearsal dinner she had helped her mom and Eddie plan was blown sky high with her entire family inside.

Her family.

Eddie.

Her mom.

Little Andrew.

Dustin.

Maybe even Adam.

This couldn't be happening.

Holly stood there, her knees locked against the tremors that threatened to send her crashing to her knees. Tears cascaded down her cheeks. Shivers brought unexpected heat to the surface as she held back the scream rising up her throat. Blackness filled her vision until she sucked in a quivering breath. Over the noise in her ears, she heard someone saying her name, her gaze shifted from the holo-screen to Dylan standing in front of her.

She didn't know how long she had stood there before the tears stopped flowing and numbness set it. It couldn't have been that long because when she looked back at the screen, it was still showing the smoldering remains of the wedding reception venue. Inhaling sharply, Holly looked back at Dylan. He took a step toward her.

Holly backed up. "I'm sorry."

Then she turned to the stage assistant.

"I need to leave, *now*," she told him. He nodded, pulled from his stupor, and waved for her to follow him as he spoke into his comms, informing his superior of the change in plans for her early departure.

Dylan grabbed Holly by the wrist. She turned to him, another apology on her lips. Before she could say anything, he was pulling her into a hug.

"Be careful," he whispered. Holly just nodded before letting go and walking out the door behind the stage assistant without so much as a glance back.

A limo was waiting for her when she walked out of the building. Holly climbed into the back.

The ride to the airport was short. Secretary Garcia had made sure a private plane would be ready for Holly so she could leave for her mom's wedding, and it was that very plane that sat waiting for her as she exited the car. Holly's suitcase had already been loaded onto the plane earlier that day, so she didn't have a single worried thought about getting it back. Not that she had anything on her mind but the prayer that someone had somehow miraculously survived the explosion. Her dress swished around her as she hurried onto the plane.

She didn't have a second to panic at the thought of getting on another plane before it was speeding down the runway.

Chapter 16

It was almost sunset by the time she arrived at the edge of the crime scene. It was still surrounded by fire trucks and military police cars when she got there. With her shoes in her hand and her suitcase lugging behind her, Holly ran up as close as she could get to the building. There was a crowd behind the yellow caution tape blocking off the city block. She was panting heavily as she squeezed her way through the crowd to the front where she was stopped by a soldier.

There was rubble everywhere. Large chunks of it laying in the street. The building was little more than charred ruins. Even from this distance she could just make out the rear bumper of her mom's car, the license plate poking out from under a piece of debris. The explosion had caused the entire building to collapse in on itself.

A few tears slipped down Holly's cheek as she took in what was left.

"Did anyone survive?" she asked the soldier in front of her. The soldier turned to her, taking in her outfit—the shoes in her hand and the suitcase beside her.

Her name tag had the name 'Weston' written on it, and her uniform had the marks of a corporal.

When she didn't respond, Holly tried again. "My family was in there. Did anyone survive?"

After another moment of taking in Holly's appearance, Corporal Weston took out a miniature holopad and scrolled through it. Looking up she asked, "Are you Holly Carnell?"

"Yes," Holly replied with a curt nod. "Did anyone make it out? My mom? My brothers?"

The corporal asked for a description for each of her brothers, and after receiving the information from Holly, she asked a nearby paramedic if there had been any survivors.

"They took someone who matched the description of your brother, Dustin, to the hospital about an hour ago," Corporal Weston relayed to Holly. "Would you like a ride there?"

"If it's not too much trouble." Holly swiped at the fresh wave of tears that had started rolling down her cheeks at the news of her brother's survival. Corporal Weston spoke into her radio, asking for a replacement at crowd control.

As soon as another soldier showed up, Corporal Weston led Holly to a nearby military vehicle. The hospital was about fifteen minutes away, but it felt like an eternity. Holly kept replaying the explosion in her mind for the entire ride. One second her family was preparing to celebrate a wedding, the next the building they were in was shattered into a thousand pieces, killing everyone—as far as Holly knew—except for Dustin. That was the only thing keeping her from breaking down again. Just the thought of him being alive was enough for her in that moment.

Corporal Weston parked the car in front of the hospital entrance. "I have to return to the scene. Will you be all right on your own?"

"Yeah, I'll be fine. Thank you, Corporal." Holly's stomach was knotted with anxiety as she clambered out of the car, hauling her suitcase after her, and entered the building before walking up to the front desk. "Excuse me?"

"Yes," the nurse looked up from the holopad she was typing on and smiled. "How may I help you?"

"I'm looking for Dustin Carnell."

"Are you a family member?" The nurse was inspecting Holly's appearance, taking in the wind-blown hair, the sunset dress with light refracting off the skirts, the three-inch heels in one hand, and the suitcase in the other.

Holly knew she looked disheveled, but at the moment she couldn't care less. Right then, all she cared about was getting to Dustin and not what state her hair was in.

"Yes. I'm his sister." Holly told the nurse. The nurse gave her a room number and went back to typing.

Dustin's room was on the third floor down the hall from the elevator. A sign nearby called the floor PICU.

Holly paused in the doorway. She choked on the well of emotions that bubbled up when she saw him lying there unconscious on the bed. She slowly walked up to the side of the bed and set her things down next to the chair stationed there. Rather than sitting down, she just stood there, watching his chest slowly rise and fall. His breathing was so shallow. His blonde hair was streaked with black, just like Adam's. Just like their mom's. Holly forced down the sob that made its way up her throat at the thought.

She pulled off the anklet she had worn since the day Dustin had won it for her at a carnival when she was twelve. He had chosen it to cheer her up. It was the year after their father's disappearance and everything that had preceded it. Those years were some of the hardest of their lives. But Dustin had been a bright spot in that dark emptiness. Holly put the anklet in Dustin's right hand before leaving the room to get something to drink.

There was a vending machine just across the hall from his room where Holly bought herself a bottle of water. She was grabbing it when she heard the faint ringing of her ringtone coming from Dustin's room. Walking back into the room, she almost dropped the water bottle when she saw her brother awake and sitting up, staring at the anklet in his hand.

"Dusty?" Dustin glanced up at her when she murmured his name. Holly was surprised to find she still had tears left to cry as they slid down her face.

Dustin sat up straighter as she walked further into the room and cleared his throat.

"Your phone is ringing." His voice was hoarse as he spoke.

Now that he was sitting up, Holly could see some bandages wrapped around his bare torso, matching the one that was wrapped around his head.

"It can wait. Are you—are you okay?" It was a stupid thing to be asking after what had happened. "I-I saw the explosion. It was on national television. I thought—I thought... I'm so glad you're alive." Her voice cracked on the last word. She took a shaky breath then repeated the question. "Are you okay?"

"I-I don't know. I feel like I got stepped on by an elephant." He was trying to make a joke, but it was clear his heart wasn't in it. His blue eyes were distant.

Holly didn't even notice that her phone had stopped ringing as she walked over to him and set her water on the ground before sitting on the end of the bed. Dustin was still fidgeting with her anklet.

"I didn't know you still had this," he said, twirling it around his bandaged fingers.

"I haven't taken it off since I got it," she replied.

Dustin gave her a small smile that disappeared quicker than it had come.

"Are—am I the only one who made it?" He swallowed. "Mom? Eddie? Andrew? Stars, any of the guests?"

Her eyes ached with tears she couldn't shed anymore. After a moment of silence, she found her voice.

"No, they didn't make it. I'm not sure about any of the guests, but... I think you're the only one." Holly paused, remembering what her mom had told her the same day she had announced her engagement. "She's—she *was* pregnant, you know, mom. She didn't want to tell you guys yet... wanted to surprise you all."

Holly cleared her throat, swallowing the swell of emotions before Dustin could see them. Her heart pattered in her chest, still pumping quickly from the intense emotions shooting through her nerves.

Tears had started sliding down her brother's cheeks as he thought about what she had implied with the statement. Neither of them spoke for a while. Dustin handed her back the anklet and she put it back on.

"You look lovely, Holly. Did you come from the festival?"

She nodded numbly. She had planned on leaving early anyway, just not until *after* the broadcast—not in the middle of it. Her phone started ringing again. Picking it up off the top of her suitcase, she looked at the caller id; Naomi.

"I should take this, will you be alright until I get back?"

Dustin nodded as she stood up and left the room again, answering the phone as she walked out the door.

"Hello?"

"Holly?! Did you see what happened? Wasn't that the reception hall for your mom's—"

"Naomi, please. Calm down. I saw it, just like the rest of the country."

"Are you okay? You sound like you've been crying, like, a lot."

Holly considered how honestly she wanted to answer the question.

"No, no I'm not okay." Any sadness she had felt moments before was replaced with a raging fire of anger. Naomi didn't deserve to be on the receiving end of it, but Holly needed to vent to somebody. Besides, it wasn't like her best friend hadn't experienced anything like it before. "I watched my entire family disappear on national television right before I was supposed to perform for the entire country with my friends. I watched a group of psychopaths kill my family with the press of a single button. Dustin is the only one who made it out alive. The rest of them weren't so lucky. So no, I'm not okay. Not even close."

"Holly, I don't know what to—"

"Please, don't. You don't have to say anything." Holly slid down the wall. It felt impossible, but she was crying again. "I lost so much today, Naomi. How am I supposed to move forward after this?"

Stunned silence came from the other end of the phone, but then Naomi's voice came back strong and resolute as she said, "You keep fighting, Holly. You don't give up. No matter how hard they knock you down, you never give in. We graduate in less than a month. You're preparing to join the military police. And don't say you're not. It's all you've ever wanted to do since the day I met you. You're strong enough to make it, Holly, so don't give up, no matter what happens. And who knows, maybe it'll be you who brings those wannabe rebels to their knees."

Holly suddenly felt frozen. Naomi was right. Colonel Walker had been her role model ever since he had shown up in the wake of her father's escape. She had worked hard for years so she could join the military police, and she wasn't about to stop now.

"Thank you, Naomi. You're a good friend. I hope you know that."

Holly could hear the smile in her voice as Naomi answered, "That's a given. But, let's get on to more important things. Let me guess, you left the festival as soon as you saw what happened, left your friends behind and flew straight home. You're still wearing your fancy expensive dress, your hair is a mess, and you took off your shoes as soon as the plane hit the tarmac."

Holly chuckled, wiping away the remnants of tears that were staining her face. "You know me so well. How'd you guess?"

"I've been your best friend since before I introduced you to the friend group. Hun, I think I know you pretty well. Speaking of, why didn't you *tell* me you broke up with Nathan?! I had to hear it from Dylan of all people that you had broken up with him. I'm not even upset about having to kick him from the friend group now—he rarely talks to us anymore anyways. But I mean seriously, Holly. You've been gone for like two weeks and even amidst the texts you sent, you never *once* mentioned that you broke up with Nathan. I don't even know why you broke up with him. You better explain yourself."

Holly winced. She knew it was bound to happen, but she didn't particularly want to get into the whole thing all over again.

"Okay. Okay. Calm down, you crazy woman. I'll explain everything. Just get Zac and Jay over there so I don't have to repeat myself later." Silence from the other end. "You have got to be kidding me. How long have I been on speakerphone?"

"Would it make you feel better if we said just now?" Jay asked.

"Not after that comment."

"Okay, fine. Now spill, please. You need something else to think about right now," Naomi interjected.

Her best friend was right. She had picked a terrible alternative, but it was certainly better than drowning in the mess that was the aftermath of her family's deaths.

"Fine. He cheated on me, I broke up with him, and Dylan punched him in the face afterward."

Someone on the other line snorted.

"I would have paid to see that," Zac replied. "Please tell me someone recorded it."

Holly rolled her eyes. "I wasn't exactly paying attention to what other people were doing."

Dustin called to Holly from his room. Standing, she walked into the room while adding, "I'm sure Jay could find you some security footage of it if he tried hard enough."

On the bed, Dustin had his room phone against his ear as Holly entered the room and stopped in the middle of the floor. She mouthed *What?* To him as he hung up. He smiled at her and shifted his gaze to the doorway behind her. Holly turned around and gasped, almost dropping her phone.

Dylan was still wearing his suit, his tie loosened slightly. He had his hands in his pockets. Holly opened and closed her mouth, trying to find something to say. Someone behind Dylan cleared their throat.

Moving to the side, Dylan revealed the rest of her friends standing just outside the door. Each of them was still in their festival clothes, and at the front...

"You lying witch," Holly whispered as she saw Naomi standing at the front of the group next to Artemis and Jay, who had almost definitely flirted with Artemis the entire time. Zac was probably talking with Kevin in the hall—she didn't know why she assumed that, but Holly got the sense that those two would get along well together.

Naomi just smiled at her.

"Holly, why are there a bunch of random people in my room?"

Holly turned to face Dustin as he spoke. "That's *so* funny, Dusty. These are my friends."

Dustin surveyed the teens and replied, "You have friends?"

Rolling her eyes, Holly said, "Good to see that a near-death experience hasn't made you lose your sense of humor."

Leo had pushed his way to the front of the group as Holly turned back to her friends. He smiled that mischievous grin.

"Hello, Lady Waffle. You left without saying goodbye."

"Lady Waffle? What happened while you were gone, Holly?" Dustin asked, evidently confused and tired.

"I'll tell you later. Get some sleep, I'm going to talk with my friends for a little while. I'll be right outside if you need me," Holly told him before turning to her friends and motioning for them to go back into the hall.

Dylan was the last to leave, closing the door behind him and putting his hands back into his pockets. Then he leaned against the wall just next to the door.

"Not that I'm not happy to see you, but what are you guys doing here?" Holly asked them, crossing her arms over her chest.

"Well, you sort of just disappeared after the hijacked broadcast," Jacob said, his suit somehow still as pristine as it had been that morning.

"Dylan told us why you left earlier than planned. I'm so sorry about your family," Kelly said, her hair falling further over her eye. She didn't move to brush it aside. That was when Holly noticed how worn out they all were. And when she looked closer, she noticed that they were all covered in small cuts. It had only been a few hours since she had last seen them.

"What happened after I left?" she asked them. All of them avoided her gaze, even Dylan. "What happened?"

"Riots," Sora finally said. Her pale skin was covered in brilliant red lines, and she had a massive red spot on the side of her head.

"As soon as you were gone, a bunch of civilians started rioting. They must have been G.H.O.S.T. supporters. They threw glass bottles, rocks, shoes—anything they could grab at us as we left the opera house and hurried to the hotel," Artemis said from beside Jay.

Karen's hand was wrapped in a bandage as she spoke up, "We barely got all our stuff together before Secretary Garcia was ushering us to the airport and told us to come here."

"Why here?" Zac had been completely still this entire time. Everyone's attention shifted to him. "Why not go home?"

"Because we're targets. As this year's representatives, people see us as something to use as an example. Our parents agreed to let us stay at a safehouse with some appointed military police looking after us," Sora replied, wincing as her finger brushed the bruise on her head as she tried to tuck a strand of hair behind her ear. She forced a smile onto her face. "Besides, Holly's our friend, and she needs us."

Sora's words warmed Holly's heart even as her thoughts turned to what her friends had just told her. They all had targets on their backs now. For no other reason than that they had been chosen for what should have been a celebration. And now none of them could return home on the off chance that someone figured out where any of them lived. But there was no way the Domina would have let her friends just leave the capitol without some form of protection. No sooner had Holly thought this than two men strolled around the corner.

It was the Walker brothers.

"There they are," Dean said to his brother as they spotted the teens.

"Major Walker, Lieutenant Walker," Holly said. "I assume you are the delegated protection detail for my friends?"

"That's one way of putting it. We need to get you guys to a safehouse," Lieutenant Walker told them. "The General has a list of some to choose from nearby if you would like to take a look."

Holly almost sighed with relief. At least they would have a place to stay.

And her... she would be staying in the hospital for the time being, but after that. After that she would be returning to an empty house. An empty house full of memories with people she would never see again.

"What if they stayed at my house?" Holly had hardly considered the possibility of her words before they came tumbling out of her mouth.

"What do you mean?" Major Walker asked, his green eyes meeting hers.

"What if we used my house as the safehouse? It's nearby, and it's not like we would be intruding on anyone's family..." she trailed off, the reality of her situation once again trying to slam its way back to the forefront of her mind.

The brothers shared a look.

Lieutenant Walker shrugged. "I don't see why not. Dean?"

Major Walker folded his arms across his chest as he stared at the floor for a moment. After a beat of silence, he relaxed his posture a tad and said, "I can work with that."

Chapter 17

It took a bit of convincing, but Holly was finally able to send her friends over to her house—after giving them the address and telling them the spare access code to the front door. She managed to wrangle a promise from Leo not to eat all her food, but she had a feeling he would instantly find her hidden stash of crunchy chocolate eggs and devour them like a starved stray cat. Karen had told her she would keep an eye on him. It made her feel a tiny bit better, but only a bit.

After the group of representatives had all left, Holly's other friends remained. It took even more convincing on her part to get them to finally agree to go home. Naomi made her promise to call if she needed anything. And by anything, she meant *anything*—and she made sure Holly knew that.

Watching them disappear behind the closing door of the elevator, Holly released a pent-up breath.

"It's been a long day," Dylan said, nearly making her jump out of her skin. "Sorry, didn't mean to startle you."

Hand over her heart, Holly took a deep breath. "No, no, it's alright. I thought you had left with the others."

She looked over at him.

He seemed very relaxed, with his hair all tussled and his tie loosened while his hands remained in his pockets. His back was still leaning against the wall as she turned to him.

Dylan shook his head. His eyes had a far-off look to them, almost like he was still back at the opera house. She wondered if that's where his mind had taken him.

"How did your mom react when they called her?" Holly asked, her voice too loud in the empty hall.

Bowing his head, Dylan scuffed his shoe against the floor. "She didn't."

"What do you mean?"

He shrugged. "She didn't answer. I'm sure they left her a message, but she's busy working two jobs so I understand why she wouldn't have answered—I suppose."

His voice was soft, blending into the static feeling of the hospital. There was no discernable emotion behind his tone of voice, but Holly had gotten to know him well enough over the years to know his relationship with his mother was rocky at best.

"What do you say we get some food or something?" Dylan asked, abruptly changing the subject with little more than a sniff and the clearing of his throat.

"I-what about Dustin? I shouldn't just leave him." She didn't want to turn down his offer, not when he clearly wanted company, but she also couldn't just leave her brother.

Dylan's expression shuttered momentarily, but he said, "I'm not sure he will notice your absence. Isn't he asleep right now?"

Holly glanced at the door. He was right. Her brother was likely asleep, but that didn't stop her from feeling the need to stay with him. At the same time, though, she knew her friend needed her, and she couldn't abandon him.

She blew out a breath. "Okay. Let's go. I'm going to grab my shoes first. Be right back."

Holly crept back into Dustin's room. Not wanting to rifle through her suitcase for more comfortable shoes, she picked up the discarded heels from beside the chair before quickly putting them on and heading back to the door. She paused, her hand on the doorknob, and peeked back at her brother, sound asleep on the hospital bed. His breaths were still shallow, too shallow, but he was alive. She hesitated—she should stay with him, but she needed some time to take her mind off of things. Besides, there was nothing she could do for him while he was asleep. Her teeth bit her lower lip as she stood there. He would be fine. She wouldn't be gone for long.

Opening the door, she stepped out and closed it behind her with a soft click. Dylan was waiting for her. With one last glance at the door, Holly blew out a breath before following Dylan to the elevator.

As they exited the hospital, they walked around the corner of the block to a small restaurant. It was a cozy little place, with soft music playing from speakers in the ceiling. They ate in comfortable silence for a while, listening to the music. The two of them were the only people there, which was to be expected that late at night when it was so close to curfew, but still a bit unsettling.

After they had finished eating, they threw away their trash and made their way toward the nature reserve down the street from the hospital. It was small for a nature reserve, but still big enough to house its own small forest on either side of the walking path they were on. The city had built it on the ruins of an old mall decades ago, and in that time the flora and fauna had flourished.

The cobblestone path made it hard to balance in heels so Holly once again removed her shoes and held them as they walked. Tree boughs covered portions of the sky above them. Distant stars peered through their leaves down on the pair, lighting their path as they left behind the city lights that were now all set to night mode to prevent light pollution.

"Do you remember when I joined the swim team?" Dylan asked, his voice drowning out the soft chirping of crickets. He was looking up at those stars through the overlapping branches.

"Yeah," she replied calmly, following his gaze to search the sky for any of the constellations she had learned in school. There were too many leaves covering the sky for her to distinguish any, but she still stared at the small dots in the sky, in awe at the power to shine so brightly from so far away.

"We were what, thirteen at the time?"

"Something like that." They were quiet for a moment, Holly looking at the tree boughs looming over their heads like their intertwining branches were reading a fate she couldn't understand.

"I wish I could go back, Holly. I wish I could go back and slap myself for not telling you how awful those pink swimsuits looked on you."

"Excuse me?" Holly scoffed. "If I remember correctly, you're the one who started calling me *princess* because of them. You had the entire team calling me that for two years."

"You heard me. Those neon pink swimsuits you always wore—the ones with the little ruffles on the sleeves. They looked terrible on you. Just because I started calling you princess doesn't mean they weren't horrendous."

Holly shoved him away as he laughed. It was a phase she completely blamed Andrew for. While he was too young to understand it, he could tell she was sad all the time, so he had told her that wearing brighter colors would make her happy again. So she had asked her mom to buy a bunch of bright pink swimsuits. She had hated them, but had worn them anyway. Dylan knew she hated them, too.

She was just about to tell him off for laughing at her expense when she stepped on something that felt a lot like a bug. Screaming, she leaped on Dylan, dropping her shoes in the process. Dylan, surprisingly, didn't fall over when she jumped on his back.

Peeking over his shoulder to see what she had stepped on, she felt her face go red. It was a cherry. From the tree she had just walked under.

Dylan took one look at the smushed cherry and burst out laughing. Holly smacked the side of his head.

"Don't laugh at me! I thought it was a spider!"

That only made him laugh harder.

Hopping off his back, Holly grabbed her shoes before storming off in the direction of the water fountain in the clearing ahead of them, making sure not to step on any more cherries. Setting her shoes on the ground, she sat on the edge of the fountain—hiking the skirts of her dress up so it wouldn't get wet as she put her feet in the water to clean off the remains of the cherry on the bottom of her foot. She heard Dylan walk up to the fountain and stop next to her.

"I hope you're here to apologize. Otherwise, I am not speaking to you," she said stiffly.

"What would be the fun in that?"

Holly didn't reply as she continued trying to rub the scarlet residue from her foot while holding onto her skirts. It wasn't working very well. Every time she reached down to rub her foot, her dress shifted to cover her vision or started to slip from her grasp.

"Okay, I'm sorry," Dylan relented, taking a seat next to her.

Taking off his shoes and socks, Dylan removed his jacket and rolled up his pants. After rolling up his sleeves too, he swung around, putting one foot in the water before taking her foot and rubbing the last resistant piece of cherry residue from it and setting her foot back in the water. He then brought his other leg over the edge of the fountain and set it in the water, sending ripples out through the fountain.

"Are you going to talk to me now?" he asked her, his head tilted as he tried to read her expression.

"Maybe." She winked at him, reaching her hand down into the fountain before bringing it back up and flicking water in his face.

He let the droplets slide down his face like tears, his eyes closing briefly upon impact. Shaking his head, he wiped the water from his face, flicking it back at her.

"You're lucky I'm too much of a gentleman to splash you while you're wearing that dress," he told her.

The smile she gave him in return was half-hearted. She wanted to stay in this moment, relish in the carelessness of it, but she couldn't stop thinking about what would have happened if she hadn't been chosen for the festival. Maybe she would have been there when the bomb went off. If she had then she wouldn't have had to lose her entire family. Or maybe, in that other world, there wouldn't have been a bomb. Her mom would have married Eddie and months from that they would have welcomed their baby into the world. She imagined the happiness on her mom's face as she held her child. She imagined the tears of joy her mom would have shed at her graduation. Imagined years down the road at a family Christmas, coming home for the holidays in her military uniform and lifting her sibling onto her shoulder to put the star on the tree.

It felt real enough to reach for, but it wasn't real. Her fingers merely grazed the water around her ankles like it was that unattainable future.

In the distance, a clock chimed and an automated message went over the speakers reminding them that curfew was approaching. They both climbed out of the fountain, sitting on the edge in silence as they stared at the stars and let the wind dry off their feet. After a long while, Dylan stood and offered her his hand.

Holly accepted it, letting him pull her to her feet, her shoes held loosely in her other hand. He didn't release her hand immediately, but when he did, she felt a rush of cool air replace the warmth of his touch. Dylan grabbed his shoes and jacket, putting on his shoes and slinging his jacket over his shoulder.

They walked in silence back to the hospital and up to Dustin's room.

Pausing just outside, Holly turned to face him. "Thank you."

Dylan gave her a soft smile. "You're welcome, princess. I'll see you later."

Holly watched him turn and head back for the elevator. Emotions she didn't know if she could express stuck in her throat as she waited until the elevator doors had closed before going into her brother's room and setting her shoes next to her suitcase and slumping in the chair with a sigh. She was exhausted. Every second of the day weighed heavily on her chest and she knew she should move to the couch up against the wall to sleep, but she couldn't bring herself to move. Instead, she sat there watching her brother breathe. With the rest of their family gone, he was all she had left, and she didn't know what she would do if she lost him too.

Wandering through the empty halls of the hospital, Holly screamed herself hoarse calling for her brother. Where was he? He should have been there. He had always been there before. She called out for him again, begging him to come back, but the only sound that came out was a rasp of air that turned into a soundless sob. Her body shook with emotions she couldn't contain any longer. He was her older brother, he was supposed to be there when she needed him—he was supposed to protect her as he had in the past. So where was he? She needed him to support her, needed him to tell her what to do. She needed him to be there in case Dustin didn't make it, but he was nowhere to be found.

A thud sounded through the desolate hallway as she fell to her knees. Mist surrounded her until it was choking down her throat...

Holly woke with a start, sitting up straight in her chair and bringing a hand to her pounding head. The remnants of the nightmare were soon smothered under the sound of blood rushing through her head. Taking a deep breath, she checked her phone for notifications, praying that maybe, just maybe, Adam would have seen the footage and tried to call her—text her, anything. All she was met with was disappointment and a phone empty of notifications.

Dustin was still asleep, thankfully, as she grabbed her wallet and walked out the door. The hallway outside the room was empty as she walked to the espresso machine and bought herself a cup of coffee. She didn't particularly like the drink, but she needed something to wake her up—and help her to brush aside the last pieces of the nightmare.

The coffee was hot and bitter as she took a sip of it. She would need to get some breakfast before Dustin woke up. Making her way down the stairs with her coffee, Holly walked down the block to a breakfast diner, throwing out the empty coffee cup on her way in.

Holly strolled up to the counter and sat on one of the stools. A waitress ambled over to her after a few moments.

"What can I get for you, hun?" the lady asked, smiling brightly. Her light blue uniform accented the caramel color of her hair.

"I'll take the pancake special with a cup of chocolate milk, please," Holly told her.

The waitress wrote Holly's order on a notepad and walked away, but not before she did a subtle double-take of Holly's outfit and appearance. She wasn't the only one. Holly could feel the other customers in the diner staring at her. *She* would have been staring at her in their shoes. The thought had her internally groaning—she had left her shoes in Dustin's room. *Fantastic.*

A man—probably in his late thirties— walked up and sat down next to her. *Great, just what I need.* Holly thought, trying to pretend that she hadn't noticed his presence.

Unfortunately, just as she had expected, the man started speaking to her, "What's a pretty little thing like you doin' here all alone?"

"That's none of your business," Holly told him. She could feel his eyes inspecting her from head to toe, but she kept her focus on the silverware the waitress had left for her. Her fingers fidgeted with the utensils.

Holly tried to shy away as he reached for a lock of her hair. She had half a mind to get up and leave—this was not something she wanted to deal with right now. When she didn't feel him touch her, she risked a glance. His hand was still raised toward her, but someone had grabbed his wrist, effectively stopping him in his tracks.

"I don't think she wants you to do that." Holly looked at the person who had spoken. It was Major Walker. "Now, why don't you scamper off to whatever damp hole you crawled out of and sleep off that hangover."

"Why should I listen to you?" The guy asked, turning to face the Major.

Major Walker waited patiently for the man to recognize his military uniform. As soon as he saw who had stopped him, the man's face lost all its color—the blood draining from it in less than a heartbeat. He apologized swiftly before scrambling away and out the door.

The waitress returned a moment later with Holly's food as Major Walker claimed the recently vacated seat next to her. Holly started shoveling food in her mouth as he asked the waitress for a cup of coffee.

"You're still wearing the dress," Dean said, blowing on his cup of coffee before taking a sip.

Holly swallowed the bite of food in her mouth before answering with, "I haven't bothered to change out of it yet, and I got hungry. Is there something wrong with thinking of food before anything else?"

"Not at all," he laughed, taking another sip of his coffee. "Shawn is always getting mad at me for not thinking about work before breakfast."

"Is that so? Hmm, Major Walker, I didn't take you for a foodie," Holly teased, drinking some of her chocolate milk to wash down the latest bite of her pancakes.

"I guess you learn something new every day, right? And you can call me Dean, I'm not that much older than you."

"I don't know about that. How old are you, exactly?"

"I'm twenty, and you?"

"Don't you know it's not polite to ask a girl her age?" Holly scoffed jokingly. This earned her a laugh from him, but he also seemed a bit flustered by the comment.

"I'm kidding! I turn nineteen in July."

"Well there's your answer," Dean replied before giving the waitress his order. "We're only two years apart, so, you may call me Dean."

It felt strange for her to be calling a soldier by his first name, but he kept insisting, so she gave in, "Okay, fine. You win, *Dean*."

His smile was brief, there and gone again the way a solar eclipse came and went in the blink of an eye. "So, how's your brother doing?"

"He seems to be doing okay, but I can tell he's hiding a lot of pain. I can't really blame him—we lost *everything*, and he watched it all happen. He won't tell me what he experienced and I don't plan on asking him to, I couldn't imagine being in his place when it happened."

"It's not easy," Dean told her. "Losing a loved one never is, let alone your entire family."

"Have you ever lost someone?"

Dean was silent for a moment, only breaking that silence to thank the waitress as she set a plate in front of him. "Yeah, my dad. He died a couple of years ago."

Holly nodded solemnly, not quite sure how to answer at first. "You must miss him. But, hey, you still have your brother, right?"

"Yeah, I still have Shawn—pain in the rear that he is." Dean paused for a second, taking a bite of his food. "You know, just out of curiosity, have you ever learned how to fight? Like, a self-defense class or anything?"

"No, I haven't. Why do you ask?"

Dean took a bite of his food, a knowing gleam in his eye like he had a secret he was keeping from her. "Would you like to learn? I get the feeling you might need it—you seem to be a magnet for dangerous situations."

"First off, rude I do *not* attract dangerous situations—as you put it. And secondly, yes, I would love to take you up on your offer." A hesitant smile pulled at the corners of her mouth. Growing up she had begged her mom to let her learn hand-to-hand combat—for self-defense purposes—but her mom had never let her. It felt wrong to be so excited about something so soon after what she had just lost, but Naomi was right—she needed a distraction or her feelings would eat her up inside as they had done after her father's escape.

Guilt swirled in her gut as she thought about leaving Dustin alone again. She would have to talk to him before she left—or wait until he was released from the hospital before taking Dean up on his offer. Then again, she didn't want her brother to feel like she was being overbearing. He had already called her a mother hen once in her lifetime, she didn't need a repeat of that.

They chatted a little as they finished their food and Dean walked her back to the hospital. Then he waited in the hallway for her.

After changing into a fresh pair of clothes, Holly went into the bathroom and gaped at the way her makeup had smeared all over her face. Mascara was streaked down her cheeks in translucent lines of tears and the once-vibrant colors were now cracked and fading. She couldn't *believe* nobody had said a word about it. No wonder she was getting so many odd looks from the patrons in the diner.

Wiping off the remnants of her festival makeup, Holly plaited her hair before exiting the bathroom to check on her brother. Dustin had finally woken up and was sitting up in bed.

"Where ya goin'?" he asked between mouthfuls of hospital food.

"Gym. I'll be back later. Get some rest, okay?"

"Okay." He waved her off. "See ya."

Holly hesitated, her earlier worries returning. "Are you going to be okay with me gone?"

Dustin rolled his eyes. "I'll be fine. Quit your mother-henning, my nurse brought in a gaming system for me to play. There's nothing for you to worry about."

Pressing her lips into a thin line, Holly said, "I'll call you at lunch to check up on you, okay?"

His eyes shifted to hers and he gave her a reassuring smile. "I'll be fine. You don't have to worry so much."

"I'm your big sister," Holly told him as she tied her sneakers. "It's kind of in the job description."

Holly stood, testing her shoes before joining Dean in the hall. They hopped into his hover-car and drove south. It wasn't a long drive, and eventually, Dean pulled up to a warehouse parking lot and turned off the car.

"You ready?" he asked, turning to meet her gaze.

"Yes. Let's go."

Dean opened his door and climbed out. Holly followed behind him as he walked toward the warehouse.

"What is this place?" Holly asked, her fingers fidgeting with the hair in her braid.

"It's an old military training gym. Hasn't been used in years so nobody will be interrupting us. It'll be just you and me."

Holly nodded and followed him through the doors. For being unused, the gym looked amazing. It had so much training and workout equipment. She was surveying it all as Dean led her to a sparring mat.

He stopped next to the mat, taking off his officer's jacket along with the dark dress shirt he wore over a black undershirt.

Dean tossed his things to the side and stepped onto the mat, waiting for her to join him. When she did, she stood across from him.

"We're going to start easy, okay? I want you to try and hit me." Dean motioned for her to start. When she hesitated, unsure of how to proceed, he said, "Punch me. Don't be afraid of hurting me, you won't be able to. Now come on."

Taking a breath, Holly threw a punch at him, and failed. Dean knocked her feet out from under her before she could blink. He gave her a hand up and told her to try again. She did and was on the floor again in seconds.

"I don't see how this is helping me learn to fight." Holly crossed her arms, refusing to throw another punch. "All I'm doing is getting knocked on my butt over and over again."

"And you're going to keep getting knocked on your butt if you don't learn," Dean replied. *Great, cause that's* super *helpful*. He walked over to her, stopping a few feet away. "Anytime you get into a situation where you need to fight, always assume the other person knows how to fight. It's safe to bet that they're also better than you. That's why you need to focus on becoming the best fighter you can be, and you can start by perfecting your technique. Good technique will save you from avoidable injuries."

Holly nodded. "So the point of you knocking me on my butt was what? Your way of showing off? Of proving just how much better you are than me at fighting?"

"That's one way of putting it—though I wouldn't exactly say I was showing off. I would have said it was me getting a perspective on how bad your technique was while showing you what it's like to lose to someone better than you, but that works too."

She rolled her eyes. "Great. Lesson learned. What now?"

"Now, we fix your punch," he told her. "I want you to throw a punch, but keep your arm extended."

Holly did as instructed.

"Good, now take note of your foot placement. What feels wrong about it?"

She shrugged. "I don't know. They feel fine."

Dean shook his head. "They're too close to each other. If someone were to push you, you would fall over."

As he spoke, he shoved her shoulder hard, causing her to stumble sideways as she tried to regain her balance. Just as he had said, she fell over, landing, once again, on her butt. Brushing off her pants, she pushed herself to her feet.

"Plant your feet shoulder-width apart, putting one foot a few inches in front of the other," Dean instructed, showing her how to do it.

Walking back to her spot, she tried to copy his position. This time she was prepared when he tried to push her over, her wider stance allowing her to stay upright and, mostly, in the same spot as she pushed his hand aside.

"Better. Now throw a few punches. I want you to notice how your upper body rotates with each punch. Be sure to inhale between punches—you should be exhaling with each blow." As he spoke, he demonstrated in slow motion a few punches.

When he finished, Holly threw a few more punches at the air, her feet planted as she focused on the way her body twisted with each throw, her breath puffing out as she pummeled the empty space before her.

"Okay, stop. That was good," Dean said, moving back to his position across from her. "Let's put it into action now. I want you to try and hit me again. Remember what you just worked on, and use it."

"Are you going to knock me on my butt again if I mess up?" she asked, raising an eyebrow.

He smirked but didn't answer.

Smug prick.

Shaking her arms out, she planted her feet again and swung at him; just as he had before, he reached up to block, but he didn't see her knee coming up to his side. He grunted as her knee connected with his side. She hopped back lightly as he recoiled.

"That was good," he said, sounding winded. "Not exactly what I asked for, but great utilization of the element of surprise."

"Oh, you definitely asked for it," she told him, her hands on her hips as she paced a few steps.

His eyes shone with laughter as he met her gaze.

Holly stopped moving. *Unbelievable.* "You *wanted* me to do that?"

"Well, I didn't exactly expect you to land a hit," Dean admitted. "But I was hoping if I gave you the right motivation you would use more than just your fists."

"You goaded me into kicking you."

He shrugged, wincing as the motion pulled on the bruise that was likely forming on his side. "Maybe I did."

"Let me guess, another object lesson?"

"Something like that." Dean ran his fingers through his hair. "Alright, let's go again."

Rolling her eyes, Holly returned to her position across from him.

They kept practicing for at least another hour before taking a break. Holly was panting hard, sweating more than she had in her entire life.

Dean wiped sweat from his brow before taking a swig of water from a bottle he had brought.

"How long have you known how to fight?" Holly asked him, curious.

"Since I was a kid. My dad was in the military, so, naturally, Shawn and I constantly begged him to teach us. Eventually he gave in, but he made us promise only to fight when necessary. He would always tell us that talking things out should be the first thing you try before you even think about starting a fight." Dean trailed off, his expression going distant for a moment before he cleared his throat. "I want to have you try one more thing, and then we can be done for today," he told her. "Go ahead and wait for me on the mat, I'll be right back."

Holly nodded and walked over to the sparring mat as Dean strolled over to a box of training equipment and grabbed something from it. As he strode back to the mat, she caught a glimpse of the gun in his hand. Her heart picked up its pace as he stopped a few feet from her.

"This is a training gun," Dean told her, lifting it so she could see the orange tip of the barrel that indicated a fake gun. "It has no actual shooting capability, it doesn't even have a magazine to remove. The purpose of this is to emulate the real weight and feel of a handgun. There are a few exercises you can use this for, but I want to teach you how to disarm someone who is holding a gun to your head, like this."

Lifting the gun, Dean aimed it at her head, the barrel little more than a few inches from her face. Blood rushed in her ears as she forced herself to take a deep breath to calm her racing heart. *It's not real,* she reminded herself. Not real. Just a training gun.

"Holly," he said, his voice gentle as she met his gaze behind the gun. When she did, she saw the reassurance in his green eyes telling her he wouldn't hurt her. Somehow it made all the difference to her. The tension in her shoulders eased a fraction as Dean went on, "Take the gun."

She had no idea how to even start. Taking half a step forward, she stopped as she tried to think of what to do. Her mind raced a thousand miles a second. Should she try to close the distance first? Shove the hand holding the gun away?

"Don't think about it," Dean interrupted her racing thoughts. "Just move."

She nodded, moving quickly. Her right hand pushed against the inside of his wrist as she reached for the gun with her spare hand.

Chapter 18

Dustin was still resting on his bed when she walked into his room after a trip to the hospital's cafeteria for lunch. He was playing a game on the console one of the nurses had brought him a couple of days prior. She knew he was putting on a brave face for her, but she still worried about him, especially when he stood and walked toward the bathroom. His body was covered in bandages. He had to use a crutch to get anywhere, his leg still healing from being crushed underneath a large piece of debris.

Sitting down in the chair, Holly rested her head against her hand. The training with Dean over the past two days had been a good distraction for her, but every time he dropped her back at the hospital, she could feel all the thoughts and feelings she had shoved aside rush back to her.

Holly had spent most of her time outside of the training sitting in the chair next to Dustin's bed—and when she wasn't doing that, she was pacing the room. Her brother would complain every time she did that, saying she was going to wear a hole into the floor. He might have a point. She was restless. But there was nothing for her to do other than wait—for Dustin to be released. For *something* to happen.

G.H.O.S.T. had been surprisingly silent ever since the day of the multiple mass bombings. There had been no news coverage on them since then either. It was almost like they had disappeared. Either that or the government was keeping their movements to themselves while they came up with a strategy on how to deal with them. It was infuriating. Not knowing if they were still out there hurting people, killing them. Not being able to *do* anything about it.

Dustin had tried to convince Holly to go back to school now that the festival break was over, but she couldn't bring herself to leave him for longer than was necessary. Jay had stopped by a couple of times to share his notes and go over the homework with her. He had told her he mentioned her situation to her teachers, and said that they were willing to do a livestream of their classes for her to watch while she was gone. She had promised to think on it.

Three days after she had started training with Dean, she was sitting in the chair, Dustin asleep on the bed, staring at her school holopad—which Jay had brought over on his first visit. Her vision blurred as she looked blankly at the differential equation. Why she had decided to take another math class was beyond her, it wasn't like she was really going to need that high of math skills after joining the military police. She was almost tempted to switch the tabs back to her registration form, but she knew she had to focus on passing this ridiculous math class so she continued to stare at the equation.

Holly didn't realize she was drifting off until her phone started ringing, startling her. Picking up the phone, she saw Naomi's contact on the screen. Yawning, she answered the call.

"Hey, Naomi, what's up?"

"Holly!"

Holly pulled the phone a few inches from her ear. "Can you please not yell i my ear?"

"Ah, sorry. Anyway, I need your help with something. Are you busy?"

Without so much as a moment's hesitation, Holly turned off her holopad and set it aside. "No. What is it?"

"I don't want to say over the phone. Can you come over?"

Holly checked the time before answering. "I should stay with Dustin."

Glancing at the bed, she watched her brother's breathing. As though feeling her gaze, he said, "If that's Naomi asking for you to hand out, go." When she opened her mouth to object—and accuse him of faking sleep—he added, "Quit your helicopter mothering, Holly. Your anxious pacing is more obnoxious than your restless leg syndrome. Go to Naomi's. I'll see you later."

Rolling her eyes, she lifted her phone back to her ear and said, "I'll be there in a few minutes."

"Okay, see ya soon." Naomi hung up quickly.

Holly got up and opened the door. A glance back at her brother showed him now sitting up in bed, controller in hand as he focused on the holo-screen.

"I'll see you later," she said before turning and walking out the door.

As she exited the hospital, she hailed a taxi and gave the driver directions to Naomi's house. Her own car was still parked at her house. She supposed she could ask her friends to bring it over, but that could wait until Dustin got released—which she hoped would be any day now. The doctors were being aggravatingly vague about when he would be released, merely giving her a *'he's recovering well and should be able to be released in a couple of days'* anytime she asked.

Fifteen minutes later, she was knocking on Naomi's door as the taxi drove away. Naomi was quick to answer the door. She had a grin on her face and she was wearing a princess dress that was much too small for her over a t-shirt and jeans, some fairy wings peeking over her shoulders, and in her hand was a fairy-princess wand. The corners of Holly's mouth twitched, wanting to smile but unable to quite make it all the way there.

"You're playing fairy kingdom with Sarah again, aren't you?" Holly quirked an eyebrow. Sarah was Naomi's five-year-old sister who always wanted to play some kind of princess game with Naomi and Holly, and they could never seem to turn her down.

"What gave it away?" Naomi asked, moving aside for Holly to walk in. "Was it the wand or the dress?"

"Definitely the dress," Holly told her.

Remi—Naomi's twelve-year-old sister—was standing at the top of the stairs to their left wearing a similar outfit. Sarah must be having a field day with *both* of her sisters playing with her.

Naomi closed the door behind them and followed Holly and Remi downstairs. Sarah was wearing a light blue princess dress with orange fairy wings on her back. Her black hair was pulled up into pigtail buns and she had a little golden tiara resting on her head between them. She grinned when she saw Holly walking down the hall to the playroom she was in. Rushing down the hall, she tackled, Holly's legs with a hug. Holly bent down and squeezed her back.

Sarah pulled back and grabbed her hand. She pulled Holly into the playroom saying, "It's about time you got here. I got a new dress I want you to wear."

The smile fighting for a place on her face finally won out at the little girl's enthusiasm. Holly gave Naomi an appreciative look. Her best friend always knew what she needed when she was stressed out—though she had a sneaking feeling Dustin had called Naomi and begged her to get Holly out of the hospital.

Letting go of her hand as they reached a miniature wardrobe filled with colorful dresses, Sarah rifled through them before pulling out a red one that was slightly larger than the others.

"This one's a little big for me so I can't wear it yet, but I bet it will fit you good." Sarah handed Holly the dress and motioned for her to put it on, so she did.

The skirts of the dress reached just past her hips—which is more than could be said for the pale pink dress Naomi was wearing. Sarah had grabbed a pair of yellow fairy wings for Holly, along with a plastic fairy wand that had a little star-shaped top and a yellow ribbon tied around the handle. Holly shrugged on the wings and accepted the wand from Sarah.

"So, what's the story today, highness?" Holly made her voice sound regal and princess-like.

"We were jsut planning an escape from the pirateses," Sarah squeaked. "They want to steal our wands to make themselves powerfuller than everyone else."

For the next couple of hours, the girls ran around the playroom fighting off imaginary pirates, waving their wands and giggling. They stopped only once for some snacks Naomi's mom brought them, but they were soon fending off the pirates again—Naomi with a sandwich still in one hand as she furiously waved her plastic wand in the air before her.

About half an hour after their snack break, Sarah decided she had had enough of fairy princesses and pirates for the day and told them she wanted to '*wead a book wif mommy*." So, they all took off their costumes and went their separate ways.

Holly and Naomi decided to go for a walk through the forest in the backyard. Birds chirped their songs as they silently made their way through the trees to a nearby clearing. It was a large clearing that brought back memories of the first few years of Holly's childhood in Emerald Bay; running barefoot through the forest, each of them racing to the clearing. Jay was always slowing to take a couple of puffs from his on-hand inhaler while Nathan and Zac sprinted ahead to see who could jump from tree to tree the fastest— leaving the girls leaping over fallen logs and rocks until one of them ultimately tripped and got their hands and knees smeared with dirt.

There was a big boulder in the center of the glade with a tree growing out of one side and a long flat surface that was exposed to the sun. Holly and Naomi started climbing up the side of the boulder until they reached the top and lay down on their backs, the late afternoon sun bright on their skin.

Naomi heaved a big breath of air. "Do you ever miss those moments here as kids?"

"All the time," Holly replied softly. There were very few clouds in the sky and she could see a flock of birds flying overhead.

"I wish we could make more memories like those. Do you remember when Zac climbed too high in that tree causing a branch to snap—"

"Before falling and breaking his arm?" Holly laughed lightly. "Yeah. Your mom was not happy about having to drive him to the emergency room."

Naomi laughed softly for a moment. In the lull, they lay there in the stillness of the forest, letting the sounds of it fall over them.

"How long does Dustin have to stay in the hospital for?" Naomi finally said, breaking the silence.

"I don't know. The doctors haven't said anything definitive yet. I hope it's not for too much longer, but," she paused. "But I don't know what we're going to do after that. I'm living day by day, and the only future I can focus on is the day he gets released, but past that... I don't think I'm ready to become his sole guardian. I guess there's my grandma in LA, but she wasn't exactly the greatest parental figure for my mom."

"And what about graduation? You haven't been back to school yet and I'm sure the teachers would prefer it if you came back to finish."

Holly sighed. She was right. Graduation was in a little less than a month and she was procrastinating her schoolwork more than she should.

"I know. I just don't have the mind to think about it right now."

Naomi just nodded and fell silent again. The only sound was, once again, the occasional rustle of leaves and a bird chirping in the distance.

"Did you watch the broadcast last night?" Naomi asked.

"No. What was it about?"

Her best friend stared up at the darkening sky. "The Domina was addressing the riots. They didn't just happen in the capitol that day but in almost every major city across the country—and they're only getting worse. It's gotten to the point that the media has stopped reporting them in the hopes that the lack of coverage will make the riots stop. Anyways, the broadcast was a bunch of reassurances that the government wouldn't let anything like it happen again, and Domina Garner said that starting tonight the curfew is now at nine o'clock."

Holly lay in stunned silence next to her, then sat up leaning back on her hands, and glanced at Naomi. She had come here to get away from all the problems she was dealing with, and she had the perfect idea of how to do that. Naomi sat up too, concerned curiosity splayed on her face until Holly started speaking.

"What do you say we go climb the tree?" Holly said, pointing to the tree growing out of the rock.

"Didn't we *just* talk about how Zac fell out of that tree?"

"Yeah, but that was years ago, and when has Zac ever been cautious while showing off to his crush." Naomi blushed. "I knew it! You like him too!"

"Oh, shut up, would you? He doesn't see me that way anymore. It was nothing more than a childhood crush." Naomi turned her face away and stood up, brushing her hands on her jeans. She held her hand out to Holly and helped her stand.

Swiping her hands on her pants, Holly said, "That's not true and you know it."

Naomi rolled her eyes and replied, "Says the girl who didn't realize Nathan was in love with her for years."

Now it was Holly's turn to roll her eyes, if only to hide her flinch. It took more self-control than she would have been willing to admit not to say, *yeah, and look how well that turned out*. She rolled her shoulders and shoved down any more thoughts about *that*.

"Let's go. We're going to climb to the top and brag about it to Zac later." Holly smirked.

Naomi returned the look and nodded. Together they walked over to the base of the trunk. Naomi was much better at climbing than Holly, but whenever she got too far ahead, she would pause and wait for her to catch up.

The girls stopped when the branches started to get too thin to hold their weight. Huffing, Holly sat down on a branch close to Naomi. The branches they sat on formed a wide 'V' shape. Holly smiled at her friend and they both started laughing. They were both out of breath from the climb, causing Holly's vision to start spotting while she laughed.

"Okay," Holly wheezed. "Okay, that's enough."

They both took a breather, calming their breaths. Holly leaned her head against the trunk of the tree to her right and sighed. She looked out across the expanse of trees beneath them. A few birds soared into the air, breaking through the canopy of leaves with distant chirps.

"I've missed this," Naomi spoke suddenly, startling a nearby squirrel.

"Missed what?" Holly replied softly.

"Us. Recklessly climbing trees and racing through the forest without a care in the world." Naomi paused. Something was weighing on her. Holly opened her mouth to ask, but Naomi continued speaking. "You know, when that weird energy wave thing shut down the capitol, activating all the nuclear blast doors in a hundred-mile radius, I freaked out. I knew you were there, right in the center of it all, and I didn't know what to do, Holly." Tears welled up in Naomi's deep blue eyes as she spoke. "I don't know what I would do if I lost you. You've been such a big part of my life since my dad had that heart attack, and, well I just don't know what I would do if I lost you too. I can't go to another funeral like that."

Holly breached the gap between them and clasped Naomi's hands between hers. "You won't lose me. Look, I know I'm reckless sometimes, and I know I make more than my fair share of stupid decisions—many of which can be blamed on Zac—but never, will I let one of those choices stop me from coming back to my best friend. It's us against the world, remember?"

Naomi smiled and pulled her hands back to wipe the tears off her cheeks. "Yeah. Us against the world. How do you always know what to say?" She laughed. "Sometimes I think you might be psychic."

Holly laughed. "I appreciate the sentiment, but, while I am many things, psychic is not one of them."

"Darn, I was hoping for a palm reading next."

Snorting, Holly shifted her position on the branch, causing the leaves to rustle. With her back now to the trunk, she looked out over the treetops. The sun was continuing its descent before them, casting an orange glow over the trees. Holly smiled, it was delightful to just sit here and forget about everything that had happened over the last week.

"We should get going," Naomi stated. "We'll need to be back before it gets too dark."

Holly nodded and followed Naomi's lead. They were a lot more careful as they climbed down the tree than they had been on the way up. The sun had sunk further beneath the horizon by the time they reached the base of the tree. They put their shoes back on and scaled down the boulder. The walk back to the house was filled with laughter and a lot of racing each other until one of them tripped—which led to even more laughter.

It was completely dark by the time they made it back to Naomi's house. They both assumed her siblings were asleep so they quietly snuck into the garage and got into Naomi's car for the drive back to the hospital.

Once they arrived at the hospital, Holly paused, her hand on the door handle. "Thanks for calling. I needed this."

"No problem. Just, don't do anything stupid without me, okay?"

"How can I you've got all the stupid with you."

Naomi shook her head smiling. "Yeah, whatever. Just go inside. And tell Dusty I said hi."

Holly returned the smile and replied, "All right. I'll see you later."

She climbed out of the car as Naomi put it back in drive. Holly waved goodbye to her friend as she peeled away and sped off before turning around to enter the hospital.

As usual, the building was quiet when she walked in, but something felt different as she strolled over to the elevator and pressed the button to Dustin's floor—the nurse at the front desk was absent. Immediately as the doors began to open, she heard yelling and a stampede of feet rushing down the hallway. She stepped onto the floor to see what all the commotion was and nearly got trampled by a nurse. The nurse caught her before she face-planted on the floor, his grip on her arms tight.

"Thanks," Holly breathed. "What's going on?"

"I'm sorry miss, I have to go," the nurse said, not answering her question.

He rushed off in the same direction as Dustin's room, leaving Holly standing there in the middle of the hallway. It took a moment of her staring after him before panic set in. Then she was rushing after him, her heart pounding.

The door to Dustin's room was open when she skidded to a halt in the doorway. Nurses were crowding the bed. There were so many of them that she couldn't see her brother. They were shouting, but the noise turned to buzzing in her ears.

Over the din, she focused on the doctor, who was standing near the head of the bed. "What do you mean his heart gave out?! There was nothing wrong with it!"

No no no no no.

This couldn't be happening.

He was supposed to be released soon.

Holly was shoved to the side as a nurse pushed past her, wheeling in a defibrillator. She paled when the group shifted to make space for the cart, giving Holly a glimpse of her brother. His face was whiter than paper and drenched in sweat. It didn't look like he was breathing.

She stopped breathing.

No.

She couldn't lose him too.

The doctor looked up and—noticing Holly standing immobile in the doorway—said, "Morris! Get her out of here. *Now!*"

The tall nurse she had run into turned and walked swiftly over to her. Tears had started sliding down her cheeks as she watched them trying to revive her brother.

She sucked in a sharp breath.

"No!" Holly screamed. "No, no, no. Please, he's my brother!"

The nurse gripped her arms tightly. "I'm sorry, miss, but you have to stay in the hall. Let the doctor do her job."

Holly struggled against his grip a moment longer until she realized any effort she made was futile. Standing in that doorway wasn't going to help. But she had to do *something*. She couldn't just let him die. Not the way she had let the rest of them die. She had to find a way to save him. Had to.

She stopped resisting as the nurse guided her into a chair in the hallway. He asked her something, but she couldn't hear anything over the noise in her head. She just sat there. Sat there and stared blankly at the wall.

He's not dead, she told herself over and over again. *He's not. He's going to be fine.*

He's fine.

Holly didn't move when the nurse left her there, her expression just as blank as the wall she was staring at. Emptiness filled her head as a void widened in her chest, ready to swallow her whole. She was more than willing to let it, too.

People walked past her as she sat in silence—silent but for the constant buzzing in her mind. The tears had long since dried, but she could feel the salty tracks they had made on her face. The noise in her head was a constant companion. She didn't register anything around her. Not the nurse returning with a cup of water. Not someone exiting the elevator and walking over to her. None of it. All she could do was sit there staring at nothing and pray.

She couldn't have said why she was praying, she wasn't sure anyone was listening anymore. Wasn't sure if it was just something she had picked up for her mother or if she was just desperate for something good to happen after all the bad she had experienced recently.

Praying for a miracle was all she had left to do.

Her family was gone.

All of them.

And she didn't know what she was going to do without them. She didn't know how to move on. This wasn't something she could just wish away like a dandelion in the wind. She couldn't save them.

Over the chaos in her mind, she could almost hear someone saying her name, but she didn't have the energy to focus on them, let alone respond. She finally moved when the doctor approached, solemnity following in her wake. Holly looked up at her. Any shred of hope or faith disintegrating as she took in the doctor's expression. She knew what that look meant. Knew what was coming. An empty ache pressed on her lungs in place of tears as the doctor began speaking.

"I'm sorry, miss. There was nothing we could do. His heart just wasn't strong enough. I'm very sorry." The cup in Holly's hands slipped to the floor, spilling water as the doctor spoke.

The doctor seemed prepared for Holly to get in her face and scream for her to try again. And she very well might have, but she had to see for herself that he was really gone. She had to know that there was no chance of Dustin coming back—had to know if she had really failed him.

Slowly, she stood and trudged into her brother's room. He was lying on the bed, eyes closed, skin pale. He looked peaceful—he had no right to look so serene like that.

In that moment all she could feel was anger, pure anger. At her brother for leaving her. At the doctors for not bringing him back. At the world for taking her family from her. At herself. But at the top of that list sat the people responsible for all of it in the first place.

Someone's hand gently rested on her shoulder. Holly hadn't realized she had been shaking until she felt the sudden steadiness of their touch. She shrugged off their hand and stalked from the room, not seeing who it was. She didn't care, she wanted to be alone—needed to. So she left, walking calmly through the lobby until she reached the front doors.

Then she bolted.

She didn't know where she was going, but she had the faint distinction that she was heading to the nature reserve down the street.

When she finally slowed, she found herself on the path she had walked with Dylan on that first night after the festival fell apart—though now she had gone farther into the reserve than the water fountain, the sound of water a distant memory to her ears. She was surrounded by trees, and she was alone. Blessedly alone. She slowed to a stop, breathing hard, and wailed. It didn't matter to her if anyone heard her, not as she let out all of her frustration, anger, and grief into it. Her scream turned into a sob as her voice cracked.

Dustin's body would join the rest of her family's bodies in the morgue down the street from the hospital until Holly finished planning a funeral. She hadn't yet dared to see their bodies, what little remained of them.

She fell silent, her throat raw as the trees echoed her cry, startling a couple of birds from their perches. Leaning her forehead against a nearby tree, she punched the trunk. The bark dug into her knuckles as she pushed against it. She turned around and sank to the ground, leaning against the tree as she did so.

Holly sat silently staring into the empty space before her. The buzzing in her head had finally silenced. She took a shaky breath, trying to keep the aching in her chest at bay.

Footsteps thudded on the cobblestone path as someone came running down the path to her right. "Holly!"

Her eyes slid toward the sound. Lieutenant Walker—Shawn was running toward her. His pace slowed as he got closer.

"Lieutenant." She greeted him.

Shawn stooped down in front of her. His brow was scrunched, and worry lined his features.

"Don't look so concerned, Lieutenant. I'm fine." Holly told him, her voice hoarse. "I just needed some air."

"Holly, we've been looking for you for over an hour. We have a right to be a little worried," he replied.

Holly shrugged and shifted her gaze to her hands. Instinctively she wanted to apologize, but no words made it out of her mouth so she remained silent.

Shawn's face softened. "I'm going to call Dean, let him know I found you."

He stood and pulled his phone from his pocket, walking a few steps away. She could hear him mumbling something over the phone, but her ears were filled with that insistent buzzing again.

After a few minutes, someone came walking toward them. Holly's eyes drifted over to them. It took all of her remaining energy to keep from breaking down again at the sight of Dylan rushing toward her. Dylan came to a stop next to her, kneeling down next to her.

"Holly," he started.

"I'm fine. I just wanted to be alone for a while."

Dean showed up soon after Dylan, making his way over to the tree Holly was sitting against.

Crouching in front of her, Dean met her gaze. "Holly, I doubt you're up for it, but I promised the hospital chaplain that I would give you the offer anyway. They want to know if you want your brother's body cremated." He paused and she could read the raw grief behind his green eyes that he tried to cover up. Holly kept her face impassive—whatever he was feeling wasn't anything she cared about. "I'm sorry, Holly, but they want your answer tonight. As well as your decision for the funeral of the rest of your family."

"Okay." Holly stood, brushing grass and dirt off her shorts. "I'll take care of it."

"Would you like someone to go with you?" Dean asked her gently.

Holly glanced at Dylan, his head bent as he twirled a strand of grass in his hand.

"Dylan." His name was nothing more than a whisper on her lips, but he heard it all the same.

Dropping the blade of grass, he stood and said, "Whatever you need, princess. Just say the word."

"Do you want a ride to the hospital?" Dean asked, clearing his throat and backing up a step.

Holly opened her mouth to decline, but Dylan beat her to it. "We would appreciate it."

"Okay. Let's go." Dean turned and started back toward the path, motioning to his brother as he walked away from the tree. The pair muttered a few words before Lieutenant Walker left.

Dylan followed her as she walked over to Dean.

"Shawn is going to meet us at your house. Are you two ready?" Dean turned to them.

Holly averted her gaze at the compassion in his eyes and nodded.

The short drive back to the hospital was like being in a graveyard at midnight—uncomfortably quiet. It was well past the new curfew, but Holly assumed they would be fine as they were with a military police officer.

Dean stayed in the car as Holly and Dylan got out and made their way inside. They went straight to Dustin's room. There was only one person in the room—judging by the all black attire, he must be the chaplain—standing at the end of the bed scribbling notes on a holopad when they entered. Noticing them, he gave Holly a grim expression.

"Miss Carnell, I'm glad you decided to come back. How would you like to proceed?"

"I-I want to bury him." Holly swallowed, the words were thick coming out. Dustin was her baby brother, she didn't know how to say goodbye to him like this. She took a steadying breath. "I want to bury him with the rest of my family."

"All right. As it is, he didn't come in with many personal effects, but he did have this on him when he was brought in," the chaplain told her.

He handed her a necklace with a shark tooth on it. Holly expected tears to fall again as she stared at the necklace she had bought him for his birthday only a few months ago, but they didn't come. Numbly, she took the necklace from the doctor, clasped it behind her neck before nodding her thanks to the chaplain and hoping he couldn't read in her eyes the memory of her mom telling Dustin not to wear the necklace to the wedding. She had been insistent on everyone looking nice. Dustin had argued that nobody would see it under his shirt—apparently he had gotten away with hiding it from her.

Holly gathered her things from the room and followed the chaplain as he handed her off to a nurse. She said her final goodbyes to Dustin's body as it was loaded into a transport that would take it to the funeral home. Her hand clutched Dylan's as she watched the doors close on her brother.

The light of the stars danced in her eyes as she watched the transport pull away from the building. She played with the shark's tooth until it was out of sight, extremely grateful for Dylan's quietly reassuring presence and was soon back in the car with him and Dean on their way to Holly's house. Her mind whirled. The funeral would be later the next day. It would be a private event, just her, her friends from home, and the Walker brothers. She didn't bother even considering inviting her grandmother. It wasn't like she would show up anyway, she was too busy running a multi-billion dollar business. Besides, Holly didn't want to drag it out. She wanted to get it over with as soon as she could. Her family deserved to be put to rest.

Her hands were clasped tightly in her lap the entire duration of the ride, Dustin's pale face seared into her memory as she watched the buildings outside zip past in a blur. The doctor's words spun across her thoughts. '*What do you mean his heart gave out?! There was nothing wrong with it!*'

Nothing wrong with it.

So what had happened?

A perfectly good heart doesn't just stop working like that.

Then again, Holly was sure hers had stopped the same time her brother's had.

What an odd coincidence.

Chapter 19

Echoes of memories blurred the haunting emptiness of her house. *Her* house. It belonged to her now.

The memories overlapped with reality as she stood motionless before the walkway up to the front door. Dylan had already made his way inside at her insistence, but she could feel Dean hovering behind her. His presence was both soothing and unsettling at the same time.

Heat from his gaze burned the back of her head—he didn't move though. Didn't speak or try to convince her to move. All he did was wait. For her.

Taking a deep breath, Holly forced herself to walk the familiar path up to the house. She didn't have to look behind her to know that Dean was following her, his proximity to her warding off the ghosts that waited for her just inside the door.

The white paint on the door was a stark contrast to the darkness of the night as she reached for the handle. Her hand hovered over it, shaking slightly. She knew the moment she stepped inside she would have to confront her friends and their sympathetic pity. And that was something she wanted to delay for as long as she could—even if it was only for a few moments more.

"I want you to train me harder," she said to Dean, breaking the silence between them. She was done being helpless. G.H.O.S.T. needed to be taken down, which meant that she needed to get stronger, fast, and the only way she could do that was to train with Dean. In just the short amount of time that she had been training with him, she had already seen more improvement than she ever had doing it on her own—without her mom's knowledge of course. She *had* to defeat G.H.O.S.T. They had taken everything from her. It was their fault her family was dead. Them, and her father. She didn't know how, exactly, he fit into the equation, but his offer to join him—to join *them*—rang through her head. He was a part of this, and she wasn't about to let him get away with ruining her life for a second time.

Dean remained silent for a moment. When she looked over her shoulder at him, he didn't seem surprised to hear her say that, but as she met his gaze, he sighed and dragged a hand down his face before speaking. "Okay. Just... Holly, don't shove down your grief. It will build up and cause irreparable damage to the relationships you still have. Don't push away your friends, they care about you. If you need someone to talk to, I'm willing to bet any one of the people beyond that door is willing to listen. Don't be afraid to let them."

"I understand."

"Good. I will train you as much as I can, but right now you need to go inside and get some rest." Dean gave her a look as she averted her gaze. "You just lost the last of your family other than your father—"

"Don't call him that," she interrupted.

"He may not have been a dad to you for years, but that doesn't change the fact that he is your father. I understand that you have a lot of anger toward him, and I'm not saying you're not entitled to those feelings, but just because you don't see him as your father doesn't mean he doesn't see you as his daughter."

"I know."

"Holly," Dean said, waiting until she looked him in the eye before continuing. "Blood doesn't make someone family. You get to choose your family, you just need to know where to look."

Holly snorted. "Thanks, old man."

"You make it sound like I'm ancient. Haven't we already established that I'm not that much older than you?"

Her eyes shifted back to the door and the faded streak of red from when Andrew had gotten into the permanent markers. "I guess some wisdom doesn't come from years of experience."

Dean didn't say anything. After another moment's hesitation, Holly opened the door. The silence that had blanketed the end of her conversation with Dean was replaced by the chattering of teenagers floating up through the house. Their voices seemed to be emanating from the basement so that's where she felt her feet taking her.

Standing at the end of the hallway leading into the makeshift theater room, Holly watched her friends chatting like they didn't have targets put on their backs by a group of psychotic wannabe rebels. They had pushed the furniture to the edges of the room, dividing blankets and pillows from the futon amongst themselves. Each of them had their own little area on the floor where they had apparently been sleeping over the past few days.

At the moment, Kevin and Kelly were cuddling on the couch next to Dylan—who looked like he was regretting his choice of seating— watching the Amour twins wrestling on the ground. Jacob was leaning against the wall, his icy blue eyes tracking Sora and Leo as they held plastic dinosaur toys like microphones up to their mouths, narrating the siblings' fight on the ground. Karen sat on the other couch, laughing as Leo made a joke into his makeshift microphone.

Heavy bootsteps sounded on the wood floor behind Holly as Dean approached. The group in the room fell silent as they turned their attention to where she stood in the hallway. Dean came to a stop beside her.

Her eyes were glued to the plastic dinosaurs. *Andrew's* dinosaurs.

"Holly," Sora started, any laughter in her expression gone as she lowered the dinosaur in her hand to her side. "You're home."

"I just wanted to make sure you guys had settled in okay," Holly said softly. Tearing her gaze away from the toys in her friends' hands, she added, "I'm glad you all found a place to sleep."

With that done, she turned to leave, brushing past Dean as she did. He didn't move to follow her, but she could feel his eyes trailing her as she went up the stairs.

The second floor of the house was blissfully quiet as Holly hovered in the doorway to her mom's room. She found herself moving deeper into the room until she came to a stop next to the neatly made bed.

Crawling onto it, she grabbed a pillow and curled up into a ball with it clutched against her chest. What she wouldn't give to return to being a kid. When she had nothing more to worry about than the fickle nightmares of monsters under her bed. When, on restless nights, she could climb inside her parents' bed and be comforted in their presence.

She didn't want to feel this need for justice carving deeper into her heart with every beat. Didn't want to feel like she had failed everyone who had ever placed their trust in her. Things were so simple as a kid. Before everything she knew came crashing down around her. But she was stuck with this feeling—this need to get justice for her family's deaths.

And maybe it wasn't as bad as she was making it out to be.

But for right now, she just wanted to feel like a kid again, crawling into her mom's bed after a bad dream.

Early morning light filtered through the window hours later. Holly was still curled up on the bed, wide awake as she had been all night breathing in the quickly fading scent of lilac that was embedded in her mom's pillow. For a moment she could imagine that she was in her own bed. She could almost hear Andrew's little feet pattering around the kitchen downstairs as he squealed with joy while their mom chased him down. The fantasy vanished just as quick as it had come as a flood of memories rushed into the empty space of her mind where the restfulness of the sleep she hadn't gotten should have been.

Holly rolled onto her back.

Birds chirped outside her window as she pulled her buzzing phone out of her pocket. It was a text from Dean.

If you still want that extra training, text me. I'll be free for a few hours today.

Holly sent a quick reply.

I'd like to do it soon. Is fifteen minutes good?

That's fine, he sent. *I'll meet you in front of your house.*

Leaving the comfort of her mother's bed, Holly made her way downstairs. As she entered the kitchen, she saw Jacob pouring himself a cup of coffee, dark circles under his eyes as though he had also been up all night. Her green eyes met his ice-blue gaze. He nodded a greeting to her and made his way out the back door to sit on the porch chair.

After finishing off her own cup of coffee, Holly went down the hall to her bedroom to change into something better for training. She got dressed and pulled her hair into a ponytail. The house was still quiet with lazy wakefulness as she exited the front door.

Dean was leaning on the hood of his car when she closed the door behind her. Upon seeing her, he stood and opened the door for her. Once he had gotten into the driver's side, he started the car. They didn't speak as Dean drove them back to the warehouse they had spent every morning for the past few days.

Killing the engine, Dean climbed out of the car. Holly followed suit. She entered the building behind him. Just like they had every other morning, Dean guided her through some exercises—starting where they had left off. They practiced for almost an hour before Dean called for a break. Holly drank some water, trying—and failing—to avoid thinking about her family.

After a few minutes, Dean led her back to the mat for some sparring. Despite her best efforts, her thoughts kept returning to her family, bringing with them the feelings she had been ignoring since the festival. Anger and frustration swelled in her stomach, spreading through her entire body like a forest fire. It coursed through her veins, down her arms, and into her hands, until it was practically visible around her fists as she sparred. Dean grunted, hissing as he stumbled away from her as she landed a hit to his side and tore his smoldering shirt off before tossing it aside to reveal a very muscled torso.

Holly dropped her stance, her brow scrunching even as she couldn't stop staring at his muscles.

Heat flared around her hands. Lifting one in front of her, her jaw dropped as she realized both of her hands were ablaze with a brilliant orange flame. The heat enveloped her hands but didn't burn her. Flames flickered over her palms, their tendrils rippling across her skin, leaving a soft tingling sensation in their place.

Holly stared at her hands, watching as the fire winked out in the blink of an eye. She looked up at Dean. He was tenderly pressing around the fist-sized burn on his lower ribcage. It wasn't a particularly bad burn—it would most likely disappear after a while if it got treated—but she had burned him. *She* had done that to him. Moving quickly, Holly grabbed a first aid kit from the wall, telling Dean to sit on a bench. He did as she asked, wincing at the movement. As he sat, Holly knelt next to the bench and rummaged through the first aid supplies. Once she found what she was looking for, she turned her attention back to Dean.

The spot where she had burned him was an angry pink, almost like a bad sunburn. Her touch was gentle as she applied the burn cream, forcing herself to focus on that and not the fact that Dean was shirtless.

After applying the cream, she put a bandage over the burn and cleaned up the rest of the first aid supplies while Dean put his black dress shirt on and picked up his ruined undershirt, a look of dismay on his face. Tossing the ruined shirt into the trash can at the edge of the room, he rolled up his sleeves over his toned forearms while Holly returned the kit to its spot on the wall before going back to the mat.

"Is that new?" Dean asked her as she stopped near the center of the mat.

"What?" Holly flicked her eyes to his as the question pulled her from her thoughts.

"The flames."

"Oh, sort of." Her heart pounded in her chest. Of all the powers she could have had, it had to be these. She would be lying if she said she wasn't scared of what she could do—especially after what she had just done.

"You don't need to tell me anything, but I would appreciate it if you wouldn't use it in the future. It stings a bit." He added a bittersweet laugh to the end of his sentence, a hand hovering over his side.

"I'll try."

"I suppose that will have to be enough, for now." Dean shrugged. "Are you ready to get back to training? Or would you rather we stop now? I still have another two hours before I have to go—three if we really need the time."

Holly almost protested, concerned about his burn, but her desire for training stopped her. If he was still willing to train with his injury then she would take advantage of that.

She nodded to him.

He picked up where they had left off. Her focus never strayed once as she paid attention to each move he showed her, and didn't see even one more spark of fire from her hands.

They kept training for another two hours. Dean seemed to be fine, it was as though he hadn't been burned in the first place but for the fact that Holly could tell he was moving slower than he had before. After the initial break, Dean tried telling her to take some more, but she would just shake her head and tell him to keep going. By the time they had to stop, she was panting and coated in sweat. It was worth it, she reminded herself. She wouldn't let G.H.O.S.T. win. Couldn't.

The sun was getting closer to its peak in the sky as Dean drove her back to her house. Holly bid him farewell as she got out of the car and made her way up those haunted steps before going straight to the kitchen to raid the freezer.

Chapter 20

The next three days passed in a blur. They were all the same. Get up early in the morning, train, spend the rest of the day gorging on freezer food, avoiding her friends, and failing to get more than three hours' sleep—repeat. There was only one exception, on the second day after returning to the house, she had buried her family. The funeral was small, and she had gone back to the house and eaten her weight in her mom's emergency emotional support ice cream. It was a miracle there was any food left for her to eat. Though, she was pretty sure she saw Sora and Karen carrying groceries into the house one day as she was lugging a plate of dinosaur chicken nuggets up to her mom's room. That was the extent to which she had seen any of her friends— from a distance as she locked herself in her mom's room and ate food while reading the journal her mom had kept. It didn't bother her, if anything she was grateful for how busy she was—how scattered her mind was. In her mind, it was only a matter of time before G.H.O.S.T. did something and she had to be ready.

Despite her determination to be prepared, she continued to get lost in her mom's words, reading each passage in the journal with fervent attention. Her mother had been so confident in everything she did, it was comforting to read her insecurities—to see that she had struggles she had kept hidden from her children. Reading the entries only hardened Holly's resolve. This is what was taken from her. She never got to really know her mom, only knew what she had been shown, and now she never would. Not really.

It was early in the morning on the fourth day after she had accidentally burned Dean. The day was starting just as the past three. She got up with the sun—after scarcely sleeping—dressing swiftly before eating breakfast and going out to meet Dean in front of her house.

He was late.

Holly paced the sidewalk, waiting for his car to pull up. When it did, she wordlessly climbed into the passenger seat. Dean had an unreadable expression on his face as he drove, and he didn't try to start a conversation as he had on previous days.

There hadn't been any sign of her powers since that first day of training. Holly inspected her hands once again as Dean drove. It puzzled her that she couldn't understand how she had gotten the ability—not to mention her lack of control over it. If she could learn to harness it, maybe she could actually be able to stand a chance against G.H.O.S.T. There wasn't enough time to worry about that though. At least, she didn't think so. With each passing day, she could feel this impending doom looming over the country—and it only seemed to be getting closer. The nine o'clock curfew remained firmly in place, and there were more military police patrolling the streets of major cities all across the country. Everyone was on edge. But it felt strangely calm at the same time. Maybe it was the calm before the storm, maybe not. That wasn't something Holly needed to concern herself with at the moment. What she needed to focus on was continuing her training— and somehow managing to graduate high school in the next couple of weeks. Her teachers had been more than willing to work with her not showing up to school, but they required more work from her if she was going to switch to online work for the last stretch.

As they pulled up to the gym, Dean finally broke the silence. "I have some work to do today so I'm going to give you some exercises to do, okay? I'll be here to supervise and advise on anything you need, but I won't be able to be as hands on."

Holly nodded. "That's fine."

She followed him into the building, the steps to get there as familiar to her as if she were going to school, and listened intently to his directions. He gave her some combos to use on the punching bag and reminded her to rotate with each punch—something she continually struggled with.

While she steadied herself and prepared her stance, Dean walked back to where he had dropped his things near the door and pulled out a holopad as he sat down with his back to the wall.

Holly ran through each drill again and again until her muscles burned. Each time she looked over at Dean he was hunched over his holopad, his brows furrowed as he swiped back and forth on the device. At one point he had removed his jacket and started pacing before returning to his spot on the floor.

After nearly an hour of this, Holly stopped mid-drill and strolled over to him, stopping a little less than a foot away. It took him a moment to realize she was standing there. When he did he lifted his head, his pale green eyes meeting hers.

"Did you finish?" he asked, dragging his hand through his hair in a show of exhaustion and frustration.

"No. But you seem like you could use a break." Dean started to shake his head, but she stopped him. "Stand up."

Dean sighed and gave in, setting aside the holopad. Holly caught a glimpse of someone wearing what looked to be a mask made to look like a merlin falcon and the logo of G.H.O.S.T.—the outline of a human inside of a circle with the four basic elements, only this one was more simple than the ones she had previously seen. It only had the circle with the four elements. The image as a whole piqued her curiosity, but Dean needed a distraction, not a curious teenager focused on justice—she would do her own research on G.H.O.S.T. later.

Holly led Dean to the mat, tossing him a bo staff. He caught it with ease, eyeing the wood with a critical expression before giving it a couple of twirls.

"Do you even know how to use one of these things?" he asked her, lowering the staff and meeting her gaze.

Holly balanced her own staff between her hands, weighing either end. "It can't be that hard, right?"

Dean quirked an eyebrow. She winked—when she had turned twelve she had begged her mom to let her take a combat class offered by the city, of course, her mom had refused and instead signed her up for a summer swim team, but in her free time Holly had taught herself how to handle a bo staff. It took her many, many internet videos and dozens of bruises blamed on racing her friends through the woods behind Naomi's house, but eventually, Holly had taught herself how to use a bo staff. Unfortunately, it wasn't a very useful skill for a teenage girl so she didn't assume she would be as good as she had been during the years she had spent training with it. Not that she was particularly great in the first place, but, she reminded herself, this was meant to be a distraction for Dean. Something to help him clear his head.

Holly adjusted her stance and raised her staff as Dean leapt toward her.

Sweat dripped down the side of her face as she and Dean circled each other on the mat. A sheen of sweat coated Dean's face across from her. His chest rose and fell in rapid succession. He had ditched his dress shirt a while ago, and sweat was making his black undershirt stick to his skin.

"I thought you said you've never used one of these before?" Dean huffed.

Holly smiled. "No, I said it can't be that hard."

Dean grunted, taking another step to the side before lunging into a swing. His staff met hers in a dull clack as she blocked the hit. Rolling out of the attack, Holly swung her staff. Another clack of wood as Dean blocked the hit. The sound was followed by a thud and a groan as Holly swept her leg behind his, knocking him to the ground.

Laying there on the mat, Dean closed his eyes for a moment until a ding sounded from his phone on the other side of the room. He sat up, wiping sweat from his brow before standing and walking slowly over to his things. Holly took the staff from him and returned both of them to the rack where she had gotten them. When she turned back to Dean, he was staring intently at the message on his phone, his brow once again furrowed as he read until he shut off the device and shoved it in his pocket. He rapidly gathered his things from off the floor.

"We have to end early today," he told her. "Something came up."

"Something to do with G.H.O.S.T.?" she asked.

Dean gave her a hard look. "I know what you're thinking, Holly, and I don't want you to look into these people. They're dangerous."

"And what exactly am I thinking?" she retorted.

"This organization—this *rebel* group killed your family, taking them from you. I've seen that look in your eyes plenty of times before. It never ends well."

It was her turn to give him a hard look.

"You don't know me, Dean."

He sighed, dragging his hand through his hair before replying. "I know you want justice, Holly. If you want to know more about this group I can't stop you, but... just be sure that it is justice you're looking for and not revenge. There's a fine line between the two and I don't want to see you end up on the wrong side of it."

Holly opened her mouth, but whatever she had been planning to say slipped away like an evening tide.

She nodded.

"Let's go." Dean held the door open for her as they left the building.

On the drive back to her house, the only thing she could think about was the symbol on Dean's holopad—G.H.O.S.T.'s symbol. It was the same symbol her father had carved into every single person he had killed.

Chapter 21

The house was quiet when Holly walked through the front door. That didn't mean much though as her friends could be outback enjoying the warming weather.

Flicking on the light to her mom's room—where she had been spending most of her time when she was home—Holly turned on the holo-screen, if only to have some background noise. A news channel came on, the anchors midconversation about the events at the festival broadcast—again. It was all that the media seemed to be talking about these days. She could still hear the chattering voices as she went into the bathroom and washed her face before changing into more comfortable clothes—she had all but transferred her entire closet into the room over the past couple of days, but she sometimes found herself putting on some of her mom's clothes just to feel something other than anger or grief.

"Last night the Domina's office released an announcement of a nationwide address that will be taking place in the next few minutes on every device across the nation," the anchor stated, her auburn hair kept pristinely out of her face as she spoke. "The public is warned that any person who does not watch this broadcast will be arrested on grounds of treason."

Holly turned her attention fully to the holo-screen as an image of the Domina replaced that of the anchor. Domina Garner's light brown skin shimmered in the light of her office. Her face was set in a grim expression as she stared into the camera.

"Citizens of Verdona. I know you have been troubled by the terrifying events of what was supposed to be our country's largest festival since the end of the Nuclear World War. But I want to assure you all that we are doing our best to find these so-called rebels and put an end to their streak of terror." The Domina paused, her expression stern and unyielding as she looked into the camera. "In light of recent events, it has been decided that the evening curfew needs to be adjusted yet again. It will now be required for all citizens without a night worker's permit to be returning to their homes by seven o'clock—any citizen outside of their homes past this new curfew who does not have a night worker permit will be arrested on sight and charged with treason."

The image of the Domina flicked back to the news anchor, who immediately began chatting about it with her co-anchor. Holly tuned the two anchors out as she grabbed her laptop from where she had set it on her mom's nightstand the day prior after doing her homework. Sitting on the bed, she placed her laptop on her lap. Her fingers clicked against the keys as she typed in her password and began searching the internet for anything related to G.H.O.S.T.

A majority of the results were news articles written about the recent broadcast made on live television the day of the festival. Once she dug a little deeper she found some older articles dating back about ten years, but they were little things— a graffiti symbol here, a small protest there— nothing that amounted to anything until about five or six years later when the body of a high ranking lieutenant general was found mutilated just inside the nuclear containment wall with a G.H.O.S.T. symbol carved into her cheek. The symbol was exactly the same as what she had seen on Dean's laptop at the gym, the outline of a human inside of a circle with the four basic elements giving the design an almost three-dimensional feel to it despite its simplicity. It was hard to distinguish some of the lines in the skin. There was a paper with the full crest held up next to the carved symbol—likely for reference. This one was in far more detail. The words Genetic Human Observation and Statistical Taskforce formed a secondary ring around the circle. *That's what the acronym stands for?* Holly asked herself. She was about to delve deeper into the history of the group when her research was interrupted.

A sudden knock on her door jolted her from her thoughts and the crude carving on the lieutenant general's face. Holly slid off the bed and strolled over to the door. Opening the door, she found Dylan standing on the other side. His face lit up when she opened the door, and his mouth twitched like he wanted to smile but wasn't sure it was appropriate.

Holly made the decision for him, a small smile spreading across her face as she opened the door wider.

"Dylan," she said. "What's up?"

"I came to check on you," he told her. "I also wanted to see if you were doing anything fun."

Holly huffed a laugh as Dylan brushed past her and entered the room. She didn't try to stop him, instead just watched as he brushed his fingers along the dresser, inspecting the room with a curious gaze.

"You must be really bored if you've come to me looking for something fun," she teased. Leo had texted her a couple days ago asking for permission to use the gaming consoles downstairs. She had given him permission, shoving down the guilt she felt at letting someone other than Dustin use them.

Dylan rolled his eyes. "Since when have you not been fun, don't you remember our first high school swim meet?"

It was Holly's turn to roll her eyes.

"If I remember correctly, you said, and I quote, 'sounds boring' when Olivia asked you to join us." Holly raised an eyebrow, watching as he processed what she had said.

"And yet I still joined you." He smirked.

"Only because Jordan bribed you."

He looked away. "I would never stoop so low."

Holly smiled. "Keep telling yourself that."

Her eyes widened when she noticed her still-open laptop sitting on the bed a mere foot away from where Dylan was looking out the window. Closing the gap between her and the bed, she closed it just before he turned around, his gaze finding hers.

"Maybe I was wrong, you're more boring than Jay when he talks about computers," Dylan complained.

"That is what I was trying to tell you," Holly said, grabbing her laptop and setting it on the nightstand.

Dylan's reply was interrupted by a knock on the half open door. As Holly turned to see who it was, she heard him say, "Somebody's popular today."

"Hey guys!" Karen stood just outside the room, Apollo and Jacob a few feet down the hall. "We were thinking about getting out of the house to go check out the old playground down the street, did you guys want to join us?"

Holly glanced at Dylan, his eyes lit with a spark of excitement. He definitely wanted to go, but as he met her gaze she got the sense that he would only go if she went as well. She recognized the intervention for what it was. Maybe she had been a little harsh by ignoring them all since the festival.

"Of course. That sounds like more fun than just hanging around here all day," Holly answered, and she knew without looking that Dylan had just done a fist pump. "Is anyone else coming?"

"We tried asking Leo and Kevin, but they were busy playing games on the console with Artemis. Kelly and Sora were both asleep so we didn't want to wake them," Apollo told them.

"Alright then," Dylan said, practically bouncing on the balls of his feet with the need to do something other than standing around. "I guess it's just the five of us. Let's get going."

They all nodded and followed Dylan as he all but skipped down the hall. Holly rolled her eyes, holding back a laugh at his childish excitement. He had to be bored out of his mind. It reminded her of all the swim meets they had gone to over the years.

Holly was mostly quiet on the walk to the park, as was Jacob, offering a comment here and there as the other three debated on who would be the first to climb to the top of the large pyramid. She smiled to herself, she had gotten so busy training with Dean that she hadn't realized how much she had missed hanging out with her friends. Jacob slowed his pace to match hers and walked with her at the back of the group.

"It's crazy isn't it?" he said. "How close we've all gotten since we met."

"Yeah." Holly nodded.

As they arrived at the park, the group walked to the water feature—a small fountain with a gray wolf statue on top. It was at the center of the park, past the playground and the pavilion. Holly was the first to take off her shoes, sitting on the edge of the fountain with her feet in the water. Her friends followed suit.

"Who wants to race to the top of the pyramid?" Apollo asked after a few minutes.

Jacob looked at him incredulously. Dylan grinned, his eyes flicking to Holly's for a brief moment. The corner of her mouth lifted slightly. Before anyone said another word, Karen was climbing out of the fountain.

"Last one there has to pay for ice cream after," she shouted as she ran in the direction of the pyramid.

"Hey!" Apollo yelled after her. "Wait up, that's cheating!"

Dylan and Holly scrambled out of the fountain after him and started running. Jacob followed closely behind them. By the time the three of them reached the base, Apollo and Karen were already a few feet above their heads, moving quickly. Her hands gripped the ropes of the structure as she pulled herself up. To her left, Dylan was a little ahead of her.

The ropes were hot beneath her hands and bare feet, the dark material having sat in the sun for a couple of hours before they got there. Glancing down at her feet as she momentarily lost her footing, Holly noticed Jacob a few feet below her and to her right.

As she glanced back up, she heard a loud snap accompanied by dual screams. Her eyes darted to the mostly hollowed out center of the pyramid where Karen and Apollo were falling.

Holly's hands tightened their grip on the ropes as she felt the structure shake and from the ground rose a large formation of dirt. The rising tower broke through any ropes in its way before stopping as Karen landed on it with a thud and a groan. A few feet above her, Apollo braced for an impact that didn't come, his arms covering his face. Before he could splat on top of Karen, a large gust of wind burst through the air, slowing his fall to a halt and sending Dylan flying backward. His foot was caught in the rope, stopping him from being flung off the structure. He groaned as he fell backward.

"Are you guys okay?" Holly called out to them.

Karen gave her a thumbs up, coughing as she rolled onto her back. Her face scrunched up in a grimace as she tried to roll out her shoulder—which was jutting out at an odd angle. "I think I'm okay. Just lost my grip is all."

"I think my bones are all intact," Apollo said, floating a few feet above the dirt tower.

Twisting, Dylan managed to pull himself upright. His ankle looked swollen as Holly glanced over to check on him.

"What in the..." Dylan gaped at Apollo, hovering in the air like he was floating in a pool.

Apollo, realizing this, gripped the nearest rope before he suddenly lost his flotation. "I-what just happened?"

"Dude," Dylan said, trying to hide his grimace behind a grin as he tentatively rubbed his bruised ankle. "You can *fly*."

"And Karen can control dirt," Jacob said as he came to a stop a few feet from Holly. "Yeah, this is a totally ordinary thing for teenagers to be able to do. Not abnormal at all."

"I can fly," Apollo muttered under his breath. He repeated the statement again before saying, "I don't think I can control it."

Karen shrugged, wincing at the movement. "Well, you can always practice it."

Glancing at the somewhat distant ground, Apollo gulped. "Yeah. I don't think I want to test that out at the moment."

"Don't tell me you're scared of heights," Dylan teased. Apollo shot him a glare. Blinking, Dylan said, "I was just joking. I didn't know you're actually scared of heights?"

"You're like seven feet tall," Karen said. "How can you be scared of heights?"

"First off, I'm only six two," Apollo retorted. "And secondly, my height has nothing to do with it."

Karen snorted but didn't say anything more on the topic. "So, can someone come help me down? I think I dislocated my shoulder."

"Me too," Dylan said, gently rolling out his ankle. "I think I sprained my ankle."

Chapter 22

After helping Karen and Dylan down to the ground, Jacob said something about calling one of the Walker brothers. The rest of them returned to the water fountain where they had left their shoes—Apollo helping Dylan walk. By the time they got there, though, their shoes were gone. All of them. They were all exhausted so they didn't bother worrying about it and instead just collapsed next to each other on the rim. Holly put her feet into the cool water, cleaning dirt off. Her mind whirled with thoughts of the abilities her friends had exhibited. She remembered the strange warped air around Apollo that day back at the hotel. It made her think of the day she had burned Dean, her hands engulfed in flames. That had only happened once before, on the roof of the hotel with Kevin.

They sat there for a few moments before Apollo got up and told them he was going for a walk. Karen got up and said she would go with him, holding her injured arm to her chest as she stood.

"Are you serious?" Jacob asked them as he walked over. "Karen, you're injured. We should stay right here and wait for either the Lieutenant or the Major to get here. Not to mention someone could have seen either of your displays of elemental power."

Apollo rolled his eyes. "If someone had seen us, do you really think we should be staying in one spot? Besides, we won't go very far. It's not *that* big of a park."

"Fine. I'm staying here with the cripple, though," Jacob said as he took a seat on the edge of the fountain next to Dylan.

"Hey!" Dylan whined. "I'm not a cripple. Maybe I want to go with them."

"You're staying here," Holly told him. "You sprained your ankle, you're not walking around on it unnecessarily."

Dylan huffed and crossed his arms.

"I didn't want to go anyway."

"Whatever, we'll be back in a few minutes," Apollo told them before going off toward a hill.

Jacob shrugged and laid on his back, one arm under his head, the other resting on his stomach, and closed his eyes. Dylan carefully maneuvered his feet over the lip of the fountain and slid his feet into the water next to Holly's. His ankle was more swollen than it had been earlier, but at least the cold water would help. They sat there in silence for a while, listening to the water walling from the spouts of the fountain.

Dylan started swirling the water with his hand. Holly turned to glance at the path behind them, looking for either of the Walker brothers. They should be there soon. As she turned back to the fountain, Dylan was lifting his hand out of the water, a stream floating up with his hand almost as though he were pulling it. Holly stared at the water as it now hovered in a ball above Dylan's hand. She was again reminded of the flames that had enveloped her hands, both on the roof at the hotel and when she had burned Dean. It brought her back to the lessons on mythological beings in ancient cultures from her mythology class. In some cultures, there were legends of people who had the ability to manipulate and control the natural elements of fire, air, water, and earth. They were real, she realized, the mythological elementals. Naomi had been wrong. Knowledge about them would actually be useful in the real world.

The water moved around in mesmerizing patterns above Dylan's hand, following the movements of his fingers. After a moment or two, he let the water slip back into the fountain, staring in awe at his hands. Holly felt a pang of jealousy in her chest—her ability to control fire was shaky at best, at worst... she hurt people. Her powers were more a curse than a blessing, and she had rarely used them. But what good could she even do with them—fire was an unstable force and using it would only bring pain. Looking up at Holly, Dylan's eyes glimmered with excitement—his mind no doubt filling with pranks he could pull on Leo and Kevin. He grinned at her, and she allowed the corners of her mouth to lift slightly at the childish joy that lit his face.

Jacob stirred and sat up, casting his eyes in the direction Apollo and Karen had gone.

"What's wrong?" Dylan asked, his smile disappearing.

"It's nothing," Jacob replied softly, his gaze still on the hill that hid their friends. "I'm going to go find Karen and Apollo."

With that, he got up and walked off in the direction of their friends. As soon as he had disappeared over the crest of the hill, Holly heard shouts coming from that same direction. Dylan followed her gaze, his eyes widening.

"Stay here," Holly told him, standing abruptly. Dylan opened his mouth to protest, but she gave him a hard look and said, "Don't even think about it. You are staying here. You'd be more of a hindrance than a help on that ankle of yours anyway."

Dylan shut his mouth, but then he said, "Fine. Just, be careful. I'll call Major Walker."

"Good idea. I'm sure it's nothing, though," she replied. He grabbed her wrist before she could walk away. "Okay, I'll be careful. I promise. Just stay here. I'll be right back."

Holly climbed out of the fountain and took off running toward the shouting, her heart a rapid drumbeat in her chest. Her bare feet slipped slightly on the grass as she ran to the noise. She could hear Jacob shouting, "Let them go!" over and over. Pushing herself harder, she sprinted over the hill toward the other side of the park until she saw them.

Masked men were dragging a bound Karen and Apollo into a van. Jacob hadn't yet noticed her presence, but neither had any of the men who were holding him down. The four men weren't doing a particularly good job of it, which wasn't altogether surprising since Jacob was a nationally ranked quarterback. All the same, Holly had to help. Her feet pounded against the ground as she approached, her sudden arrival shocking the men just long enough for her to tackle the nearest one to the ground.

They rolled across the grass, away from Jacob. As her momentum slowed, she got to her feet and kicked the man in the face—miraculously knocking him out cold. There were still three men trying to hold Jacob down. Despite her having knocked one of them unconscious, they didn't seem to see her as anything more than an annoying pest. None of them moved to stop her as she charged at them and leaped onto one of their backs, putting him in a chokehold.

The man released his hold on Jacob and reached up to pry at her arms. She clenched her teeth and tightened her grip as he got a hold of her wrist and was trying to pull her arm away from his neck. His hand was bruisingly tight on her forearm, but she didn't release her hold until he had collapsed on the ground. As soon as his body hit the ground, she bounced to her feet. Jacob had gotten free and was sprinting toward their friends.

Only one of the men who had been holding him chased after him. The other turned to Holly, glaring at her from behind one of those stupid bird masks G.H.O.S.T. was known to wear.

Holly returned the glare and settled herself into one of the fighting stances Dean had taught her. The man stalked closer to her, and as soon as he got in range, she threw a right hook directly at his face.

Shock lit up his eyes as her fist connected with his head.

He stumbled backward long enough for her to land in a good kick.

Before she could return her foot to the ground, however, the man was grabbing her ankle and pulling it, causing her to lose her balance and fall.

As he bent down to grab her, she rolled away and sprung to her feet.

He growled, prowling closer.

Holly dodged the punch he threw at her head and countered with a punch to his kidney.

Her fist barely connected as he danced back, just out of reach.

She adjusted her position as he threw another punch. His fist hit empty air as she ducked.

Black spots appeared in her vision as the man's knee connected with her face. She narrowly knocked aside his next punch, her vision splotchy as she blinked away the darkness.

He tripped on a small rock, and Holly took advantage of the stumble, grabbing his head and pulling it down on her knee with as much force as she could muster. Blood started gushing from his nose. He reached his hands up to stop the bleeding.

While he was distracted, Holly kicked him in the balls, effectively taking him out of commission.

Her head spun as she realized the fourth man who had been holding Jacob had not gone after him. He had gone in the opposite direction. The direction Holly had come from.

The direction of the fountain.

Holly's heart thumped loudly. *Dylan!*

She scanned the area around her, her eyes searching for Jacob. He was struggling to get to their friends when she spotted him. Karen's abductor had already thrown her in the van and was stalking over to where Jacob was fighting another man. Holly took a step toward him, but hesitated, her attention straying to the direction she had come from as the man who had gotten away was dragging a struggling Dylan across the grass.

Her hesitation broke as she dashed toward the man. Jacob would have to handle things himself.

Holly was almost there.

She was so close.

Dylan was only a few feet away from her when something hard collided with the back of her skull.

Holly stumbled, falling to her knees.

"Holly!" Dylan yelled, kicking at the man dragging him by his ankle.

"Dylan." Holly's voice came out in a whisper. She reached her hand in the direction of his voice. Darkness swallowed her vision momentarily as she collapsed. She rolled onto her side to see the men throwing Dylan and an unconscious Jacob into the van with their friends. That was the last thing she saw before blacking out, the sound of an engine starting ringing in her ears along with the sound of Dylan's voice.

When Holly regained consciousness, she was still lying on the ground. She groaned. Her head pounded loudly against her skull, and her entire body felt sore as she cracked open her eyes. Someone was leaning over her, concern glinting in their eyes. Holly blinked away her blurry vision as the woman's face came into focus.

The woman was saying something, her lips moving in rapid succession. Her pale blue eyes scanned Holly's before shifting to a second person Holly hadn't initially noticed.

"Are you alright?" the woman asked, her voice at last registering over the sound of drums in Holly's head.

Holly squeezed her eyes shut for a moment. When she opened them again, a man had crouched next to the woman, his blue-gray eyes soft as he looked into hers.

"It's okay," he said. "No need to be scared. Can you tell us what happened? Why are you out here unconscious?"

Scooting away from them, Holly carefully stood up, stumbling a bit at the sudden motion.

"I-I'm fine," she told the couple. She scanned the area around her. "I'm fine. I think. I just tripped and must have hit my head."

She rubbed the back of her head, her eyes staring at the side of the road where her friends had been tossed into the van. Turning back to the couple, Holly gave them a smile, the sort of smile a clumsy child would give a parent.

"Do you need us to call someone?" the woman asked, brushing grass off her knees as she stood. Strands of her long blonde hair fell around her face.

Holly eyed the couple, trying not to seem like a doe in the headlights. They seemed nice, but something about them was off. She shook her head—immediately regretting it as her vision began swimming—keeping the smile plastered on her face.

"No. Thank you, though," she told the woman. "I have a friend coming."

The woman smiled sweetly. "Okay, if you insist, sweetie."

"Holly!" Holly turned at the sound of her name. Dean was running over the hill, his brother at his side.

Glancing back at the couple, Holly was relieved to realize that they were already gone. She blinked, they weren't walking away, they were just... gone. Shaking her head—again regretting it as she swayed on her feet—she looked back at Dean.

Her body ached, but all she could think about was her friends. G.H.O.S.T. had them. She knew it was them. They had been wearing those ridiculous bird masks, just like in all their stupid videos.

Taking a step toward Dean, she lurched forward, trying and failing to stay upright. Dean reached her just in time to catch her before she collapsed. Lifting her into his arms, he called to his brother. His voice was muffled in her ears. When had she gotten water in them—everything sounded like she was underwater. Her vision blurred, colors mixing with each other as she walked—no, Dean was walking.

Now he wasn't.

Where was she?

What happened?

Holly, what happened?

More movement.

The sun was beautiful this late in the day.

She couldn't tell if it was rising or falling.

She was falling.

Falling.

Falling.

Laying on a bed.

The words of the man sitting on the edge of the bed next to her floated around her head, dancing along the ceiling of her mom's bedroom. She was home.

"Holly?"

Her vision wouldn't focus on his features. All she could see was a blur of colors.

Tan.

Brown.

Green. Such bright green orbs.

Wait, she had to tell this being something. What was it again? Something about her friends?

Names slammed into her mind.

Karen.

Apollo.

Jacob.

Dylan.

Each one was a punch to the gut until she was leaning over the side of the bed vomiting into a garbage can, a comforting hand on her shoulder as she trembled.

Someone gave her a cup of tasteless blue liquid to drink. She gulped it down, grateful to have something in her stomach.

As the shaking subsided, Holly felt the words tumbling out of her mouth. "They took them. They're gone. My friends. I need—"

Her rambling cut off with another wave of nausea.

Salty tears streamed down her cheeks, further blurring her vision and mixing with the taste of bile, but nothing came up.

Leaning back on the bed, Holly waited for her mind to clear. The world finally began to reshape itself around her, revealing two very concerned military police staring at her.

"How do you feel?" Shawn asked, leaning against the wall.

Holly grunted.

"Are you sure you gave her enough?" Dean asked, his eyes going to his brother.

Shawn rolled his eyes. "Yes. She'll be fine, just give it a bit longer to kick in. Head injuries take longer to heal."

Holly's eyes fluttered then she squeezed them shut for a moment—her head throbbed. The cuts and bruises on the rest of her body were mere annoyances compared to the pounding in her head—but even that was beginning to subside just a fraction. She heard the brothers talking to each other, but couldn't discern what they were saying. Her thoughts were drowned by the constant thumping in her head. She didn't realize Shawn had left until suddenly he was walking back into the room and handing something to his brother.

Dean opened whatever it was and dumped something into his hand before closing it. Then, he brought it to Holly's mouth. She saw his lips moving, but his words mixed with the cacophony of noise in her ears. The pounding in her head lessened enough for one thought to come through. *Dylan.* They had Dylan. She had to get to him.

Holly sat up, trying to get off the bed, but was stopped by a hand on her shoulder.

"Holly, you need to lay down," Dean was saying. "Take this, it will help with the pain."

Help with the pain.

Pain.

The throbbing in her head.

Holly allowed Dean to give her the small red pill and help her drink some water. She sat there, feeling the pain finally easing enough that she was no longer seeing double and the pulsing in her head subsiding to a dull ache.

She looked over at Dean.

"They took my friends."

Tears rolled slowly down her cheeks. She blinked hard, trying to make them stop. "They took them. Why did they take them?"

The tears didn't last long. They were replaced with an empty numbness. Holly didn't know what to do. She could barely breathe.

Why take them and not her?

"Holly," Shawn said softly, hesitantly. "There's nothing we can do at the moment, but we can figure something out in the morning."

"He's right," Dean interjected. "You need to get some rest."

Holly nodded. She didn't know what else to do. Dean and Shawn would think of something, they had to.

"The rest of your friends are downstairs," Dean told her. "I told them to give you your space, but they'll be here if you need anything. So will I."

She nodded again, not knowing what to say.

Shawn pushed off the wall, leaning over to whisper something in Dean's ear before leaving the room.

Pushing himself to his feet, Dean asked, "Would you like some tea?"

"Sure," she replied. "There should be some chamomile in the cabinets somewhere."

Dean nodded then left the room.

Alone with her thoughts, Holly pulled her knees up to her chest and tried to think of something, *anything* other than what had just happened. But all she could think was why they hadn't taken her, too. Her father had said he wanted her to join them—to join *him*. So why take her friends? Unless they somehow knew about their powers, but then why was she the one left behind? She had powers too. Maybe they didn't know about them.

Dean returned a few minutes later, a cup of tea in his hand. Thanking him for it as he handed it to her, Holly sipped the hot liquid gently. The pain in her head ebbed bit by bit with each passing moment. Dean nodded, and said something about being downstairs if she needed him before leaving her alone again.

After finishing her tea, Holly set her empty cup on the nightstand and, grabbing some clean clothes, went into the bathroom to shower.

She didn't take long, but by the time she was done, she could hear a jumbled conversation floating up to her as she combed her fingers through her wet hair.

Her feet carried her to the top of the stairs where she had a good view of the living room where Artemis was talking to the Walker brothers, her arms crossed over her chest. From her position, Holly could hear the conversation in more than fragmented pieces.

"You were supposed to protect us, and then something like this happens," Artemis said accusingly. "What is the point of you two being here if you're never there when we need you? Those psychopaths have my brother and you two want to do *nothing*."

"Artemis," Shawn said, his tone placating as he spoke like he was approaching a rabid animal. "That's not what we said. We have no idea where G.H.O.S.T. may have taken your brother and the others, but that doesn't mean we're just going to stand around doing nothing."

Artemis sneered at them before brushing angrily past them. As she did, her wrathful gaze landed on Holly, hovering at the top of the stairs. The rage in her blue eyes staggered and then she was climbing the steps and, in a very unusual show of affection, wrapped her arms around Holly.

Holly felt her body stiffen beneath her friend's embrace, but then Artemis was whispering in her ear. "They sent me a message. Meet in the basement in ten minutes. The Walkers are not invited."

Nodding against her chest, Holly took a step back. She met her friend's fiery gaze and, under her breath, promised, "We'll get them back. With or without the help of the military police standing in my living room."

Her friend gave her an appreciative nod before turning and walking back down the steps—not without shooting a glare at Shawn though.

Shawn blew out a breath. "I need a drink."

"Not tonight," Dean told him, patting his brother on the shoulder. "Come on, we need to call the General."

Holly watched the brothers go out back, shutting the door behind them. Then she was moving again, going to the basement where the rest of her friends were sitting somberly on the couches—all of them except for Artemis. She was standing in front of the large holo-screen attached to the wall, her phone held in her tan hand.

"You made it," Artemis said, tapping the phone against her other hand.

"The Walkers?" Sora asked tentatively.

"Out back making a call to General Falcon," Holly responded as she sat between Sora and Kelly on the couch. "We have maybe fifteen minutes before they're done—twenty before they come to check on us."

Artemis nodded, her eyes shifting to the phone in her hand. "I got a message from G.H.O.S.T., claiming to have Apollo, Dylan, Karen, and Jacob."

Her gaze went to Holly, who nodded in confirmation.

"They want to trade them."

"For what?" Leo asked, his usual smile missing as he tapped a digi-pen restlessly on his thigh.

"Holly," Artemis replied. "They want Holly."

Holly blinked. "What?"

Shrugging, Artemis slid her phone into her pocket and crossed her arms over her chest. "They didn't really elaborate, just said they would return the others in exchange for you."

"They had ample opportunity to take me back at the park—they knocked me out for crying out loud." Holly barely managed to keep herself from shouting. She could feel heat rising to the surface of her skin and instantly tampered down on the rage boiling just underneath—she would not let her powers take over. Wouldn't let Sora or Kelly get burned by her temperament.

"They knocked you out?" Kevin asked, his blue eyes scanning her from behind his glasses.

Sora placed a comforting hand on Holly's arm.

Kelly tapped her finger on her opposite arm. "What exactly happened, Holly?"

Knowing they didn't have much time, Holly quickly relayed everything that had happened at the park. When she finished, the group sat in silence, letting it all sink in. She didn't know whether or not to tell them about her father's offer to join him so she left it out—no use telling them something that may or may not be relevant.

"If they wanted you all along," Kevin started, his blue eyes distant as the gears in his mind whirled. "Why not take you in the first place?"

"What if they got scared off?" Kelly suggested. "Was there anything that would have made it too risky for them to stay and take you too?"

Holly shrugged. "I mean, there was a couple there asking me if I was okay when I woke up, and the Walker brothers were on their way, but that raises the question; if G.H.O.S.T. wants all of us, why would they trade all of them for just me?"

"You raise a good point," Kevin said, tilting his head back. His eyes scanned the ceiling above him in search of an answer.

"Did the message say anything else?" Sora asked Artemis.

Artemis nodded. "They gave me a time and address; tonight, an hour after curfew in the warehouse district."

"This is definitely a trap," Leo said, stating the obvious. "I mean, come on, the *warehouse* district? That location just screams trap."

"We have to go. I'm not leaving my brother *or* our friends with these people." Artemis insisted.

"It's a trap," Leo repeated, his blue eyes slid to Artemis. "Does it tell you to go alone?"

Artemis hesitated then pulled out her phone and scanned the message. "No. It doesn't."

"It's a trap," Leo reminded them yet again.

"Yes, Leo. It's a trap," Holly snapped at him. "But what other choice do we have? I would love nothing more than to go upstairs and tell the Walker brothers to deal with this, but I'm not going to because we all know they would just lock us in this house while they call their commanding officer who will likely just tell them to sit back and wait for further instructions. So if you're too scared to go, then you can stay here and be just like them—sitting back and doing nothing."

Leo stared at her, mouth hanging open.

She knew she should feel at least a little bit of remorse for her harsh words, but she didn't. All she could think about was how these people had killed her family—how they had taken her friends. They took and they took and they took, leaving them with no other choice. Holly was determined to get justice for everything G.H.O.S.T. had taken from her, and right now that meant rescuing her friends.

"Okay," Leo finally said. "So what's the plan, then?"

"We can't just go in there guns-a-blazing," Kevin said, sitting up straight. "Even if we had access to guns."

"I have an idea," Artemis told them. "It's not a perfect plan, but it might just be crazy enough to work."

"I think I speak for all of us when I say, I'm in. Whatever it is," Kevin replied, leaning forward. "But first, we should probably figure out how we're going to get there. Does anyone have a car?"

Holly nodded. "I do. It's in the garage."

Her friends gaped at her as she pulled out the keys to her black Cadillac. It was a sixteenth birthday gift from her mom and Eddie. Cadillac had been one of the only car brands that had upgraded to the hover system when the United Nations had started the ban on gasoline-powered cars, most of the others hadn't been able to make the change and had gone bankrupt when people stopped buying and using gasoline cars. Holly had been ecstatic when they had given it to her. With everything that had happened recently, Holly had almost forgotten about it until her lawyer had dropped off a list of all her mom's assets the day after the funeral. She had subconsciously been carrying the keys with her since then—moving them into the pockets of her pants each day.

"Well, okay, then," Leo said, still eyeing the keyfob. "I suppose that settles, that, then."

"Send me the address," Holly said to Artemis. "We're leaving as soon as we can get away from the Walker brothers. You can fill us in on the plan on the way there."

Pushing herself to her feet, Holly made her way upstairs, the image of her friends' faces—so full of determination and hope—burned into her retinas as she put another tether on the fire raging under the surface.

What had she gotten them into?

Chapter 23

Her car was filled with silence as Holly pulled up to the warehouse with her friends. Nobody had spoken a word on the long drive after Artemis had explained the plan. They arrived at the warehouse only a few minutes earlier than the note had requested, but it had taken them longer than expected to grab the baseball bats in the garage—as well as Holly's bo staff—and sneak away without the Walker brothers noticing.

Holly killed the engine as they all climbed out. Opening the trunk to her car, Holly pulled out her bo staff. Her friends each grabbed a metal baseball bat—she tried not to think about how each of them had belonged to one of her family members as she did a test spin of her bo staff. It wasn't much, but it would have to do. They knew they were going in severely underprepared, and they were aware that what they were doing was insanely idiotic, but they had to do something.

She could tell her friends were nervous—all of them were shifting on their feet, casting anxious glances around them.

Artemis rested the bat that had belonged to Adam on her shoulder. "Everyone remember the plan?"

They all nodded.

"Good. Let's go kick these psychos into next week."

All of them gathered together and walked into the warehouse. Holly and Artemis were at the front of the group, with the others keeping to the shadows as much as possible. The warehouse was dimly lit with old lightbulbs hanging overhead.

It took all of her self-control not to dash to Dylan's side when she saw him standing not even a hundred feet from her. Of course, he wasn't alone, but neither was she. Holly forced herself to walk calmly beside Artemis until they stopped a good distance from the two rebels holding Dylan and Apollo by the arm. Both of them had their hands bound and their mouths covered with duct tape—no sign of Karen or Jacob. Not a good sign.

"You didn't come alone, I see," the man gripping Apollo's arm said.

"You didn't specify not to," Artemis retorted. "Where are Karen and Jacob?"

Despite her calm exterior, Holly could feel Artemis shaking beside her, her friend's grip on the bat tight enough to choke. Holly was tempted to grasp her hand, but thought better of it—she barely had a handle on her powers, it wouldn't do her any good if she lost control of them. Besides, they had to be able to move at a moment's notice.

"You're right," he said, blatantly ignoring Artemis' question. "We didn't, did we Osprey?"

"No, we didn't, Starling." Osprey sneered at them. He was a large, heavily muscled man with brown hair cut in a military hairstyle. Blue eyes peered out from behind the mask he wore—likely styled after an osprey as his code-name suggested. His stocky stature was offset by the man next to him.

The other man, Starling, had a regal standing about him, his black hair was peppered with streaks of gray to match the blue-gray eyes. Eerily familiar eyes that studied them behind a silver mask shaped like the bird of his namesake. The white dress shirt he wore was as immaculate as his posture. His shirt was matched with finely pressed dress pants that were much too nice for such circumstances.

"Clever," Holly quipped. "Using birds as code names. Ridiculous, but clever. I'll give you that."

Osprey scoffed.

"Ridiculous as it may be, it's like you said, clever," Starling remarked. Holly narrowed her eyes, the cadence of his voice was familiar to her, but she couldn't quite place it at first. Her eyes widened. The man at the park. *Starling* had been at the park when she had woken up. His presence only deepened the confusion slowly blending into the anger she felt.

Starling smirked at her. He knew she recognized him.

"Well, what do you say we move this along?" Starling asked, adjusting the lapel of his suit jacket.

Holly opened her mouth to reply, a snarky remark on the tip of her tongue, but was cut off as someone emerged from the shadows to her right. "She's not going anywhere with you, Starling."

Dean.

He had followed them.

Behind him, Shawn stepped into the light, gun in hand as his blue eyes assessed the scene. Dean's gun was raised and aimed at Starling.

"I've been looking for you," Dean snarled, his green eyes drilling holes into the rebel.

Starling raised an eyebrow. "Are you sure it's me you've been looking for?"

"Well," a new voice chimed in. "If it isn't the brothers Walker. I haven't seen you two since, well... since I put a bullet in dear old Luke Walker's head."

Someone walked out of the darkness behind Starling and Osprey, pointing a gun at each of the Walker brothers, who swiftly swung their guns to the new arrival. They both paused, their faces paling in recognition. This newcomer didn't wear a mask.

"Welcom back, Merlin," Starling said. "We didn't expect you in the city until tomorrow."

"The meeting with Eagle and Hawk went smoother than expected," the newcomer— Merlin—replied. His voice was gruff, Holly wouldn't have expected it to have been so deep had she seen him on the street. It surprised her, and yet it fit him somehow. His black combat boots thudded softly against the ground. Unlike either of his companions, Merlin was wearing clothes typically seen in an apocalypse film— forest green cargo pants, a beige shirt with rolled-up sleeves, and a gun holster pulled taut across his muscled back. Merlin's intimidating aura spread behind him like a wake of water behind a boat. "Why haven't you secured the dolphin yet?"

"She only just arrived, sir," Osprey replied.

Dean looked like he was about to interrupt the conversation when Merlin made a bird call. If he hadn't helped abduct her friends and been responsible for killing multiple people, Holly would have almost called the sound lovely. As it was, Holly didn't like this man. His pale blue eyes were dull, and his graying brown hair made him seem older than he probably was.

Merlin's bird call had been a signal for an attack. Holly tried to get to Dylan, but someone jumped from the rafters, landing in front of her and blocking her path. She glanced around the rebel and saw Starling dragging Dylan from the fight. Dylan struggled against his bonds, his gaze clashing momentarily with hers.

Holly's temporary distraction cost her. She gasped as the guy in front of her kneed her in the gut, knocking the air from her lungs. Stumbling back a few steps, she tried to get air back into her system.

Oxygen filled her lungs just in time to dodge the next punch the rebel threw at her.

She had to get to Dylan.

With a split-second move, she switched to the offensive, swinging her bo staff at the man blocking her path to her friends. After a few moments of their fight, she managed to hit him hard enough on the head to send him to the ground, unconscious.

Lifting her eyes, Holly surveyed the space around her, searching for any sign of Dylan or Apollo.

A few feet away she saw Dean locked in combat with Merlin and almost went to help him when she heard a scream. Spinning around, Holly spotted Sora, her onyx hair matted with blood. Holly bolted for her friend. She had to reach her, had to get to her before—Holly screamed as the woman Sora was struggling with shot Sora in the chest, once—twice. The woman spun as Holly screamed, and *smiled* at her before running away.

Holly skidded to a halt next to where Sora had fallen to the ground, blood pooling around her. Hands shaking, Holly fell to her knees, dropping her bo staff, and tried to stop the bleeding. Blood filled the gaps between her fingers. Sora's breathing had gone shallow, her pale skin more ghostly white than it should have been. Sweet, gentle Sora who couldn't hurt a fly and who could cook better than any world-renowned chef Holly had ever heard of. She couldn't let her die.

"No no no... Sora?" Holly whispered. "You can't die. You can't. Just... hold on, okay? Keep breathing."

"Hol-ly?" Sora rasped. "I'm... I-I'm so-sorry."

"Shh. Don't say that." Tears had started forming in Holly's eyes, steaming as her grip on her powers slipped. "You have nothing to be sorry for. Just hold on, okay? We can get you to a hospital, they can help you." Holly was rambling, words tumbling out of her mouth before she could process what they were. "You need to stay conscious, though. Keep talking. Sora, *please.*"

Holly trailed off. She didn't know what else to do. The bleeding had slowed, but she knew that wasn't a good sign in this case. Her throat tightened, and all she wanted to do was call out for help.

Salty tears mixed with the blood on her hands as they overwhelmed the heat of her skin.

Sora's breathing was labored and gargled as her lungs filled with blood. Then it stopped.

Time.

The bleeding.

Sora's breathing.

All of it.

And Holly felt herself go numb.

She could see the fight in her peripheral vision still going on, but she was stuck in the timeless bubble Sora's death had created.

Closing Sora's still-open eyes, Holly cast her own gaze around the room. Her other friends were standing their ground, all except—except... Kevin. She couldn't see Kevin. Couldn't find him.

Not him too.

Then she saw him—his body.

Kevin's glassy blue eyes stared in the direction of his girlfriend. Kelly had blood dripping down her arm as she held her ground against the rebel in front of her. She hadn't noticed yet that her boyfriend was gone.

First Sora, and now Kevin.

Holly clenched her fists at her sides, her heart clenching as Kelly threw the rebel off of her and glanced to the side.

Kelly let out a wail, her feet stumbling underneath her as she left the fight and rushed over to Kevin. Cradling his face in her hands, her cry turned into a sob.

Air felt constricted in her lungs as Holly tried to force herself to take a breath, but she couldn't seem to get enough air. Pins and needles pricked her fingers as she started taking faster breaths. It had all been for nothing. They had *failed.*

She had failed them.

Her friends.

Her friends were dead because of her.

Kelly's body shook with the force of her sobbing.

Seeing her friend like that, Holly felt the last fragile hold she had on her powers slip from her grasp. Fire, burning and raging, exploded out of her. She could feel its heat, but it was a comfort to her—it couldn't hurt her. If she was going to have any chance of saving the rest of her friends, she had to give in to the destructive nature of her powers.

The other people in the warehouse froze at the sudden blaze of light and heat. Rage burned hotter than a forest fire through Holly's blood, singing a battle cry as her flames encircled the rebels with adrenaline fueled precision. Her friends backed away from their fights.

She saw Leo finding his way to where Kelly knelt over Kevin's body. Leo fell to his knees on the other side of his best friend's body.

The rest of her friends froze as they too noticed the corpse. They were all covered in cuts and bruises—some worse than others. Leo had a nasty gash on the side of his head, but he didn't seem to notice. Artemis was cradling a dislocated shoulder, and Shawn had blood dripping from a cut above his eye.

Dean's eyes were on her though. Watching the way the fire flowed through her hair like water. All the emotions she had bottled up fueling the flames as she stalked through the trapped rebels before coming to a stop in front of the woman who had killed Sora.

The woman met her gaze with unabashed pride.

"You killed my friend," Holly said, her voice low.

The ring of fire around the woman tightened like a noose. She had the good sense to look scared, but she hid it under a sneer.

"Orders are orders, kid. I did what I was told."

"You're lying," Holly snapped, her flames jumping at the words. "You *liked* it."

The woman started shaking, sweat beading on her exposed skin. She deserved everything coming for her. And more. So much more.

Holly's fists were enveloped in the fire that burned through her veins as she took another step closer and, reaching through the fire, wrapped her hand around the woman's throat. Her grip was loose, but the woman screamed as the flames licked her skin. She passed out quickly and Holly let her fall, forcing herself not to look at the handprint seared into the woman's flesh.

She had half a thought to end her where she lay, but the two slowly cooling bodies of her friends behind her stayed her hand. Holly wouldn't kill the woman. Wouldn't let herself stoop to the rebel's level. She had to be better than them—she couldn't become a monster.

Instead, she took a few steps back. These people were taking everyone she had loved and they were destroying them. All that pain. All that grief. It was enough to bring a grown man to his knees, never to rise again. But Holly didn't have that luxury—no, she still had people she cared about. Not everyone she loved was dead, and she would sooner burn than let her grief stop her from getting them back alive. Not even the Major, who had walked up to her—the only one not afraid of the flames entwined in her hair.

Smoke and fire flooded the air, and Holly stood above the woman's unconscious body as she met Dean's gaze. Her hands and clothes were soaked with the blood of her friend. Her head flooded with the images of her friends' bodies. And yet he was standing there, unafraid.

It was too much for her. The grief—the anger. All of it was too much.

Stepping away from Dean, she felt the sobs building up in her chest. They were swallowed in the inferno in her blood.

It was too much.

Too much rage.

Too much raw emotions.

Too much *power*.

She had to release it.

Now at a safe distance from Dean—from her remaining friends, Holly shoved all the trapped emotions out of her in a scream.

Spots danced in her vision but she kept screaming, the power pouring out of her in a tornado of scorching flames. She hadn't gone far enough.

Stumbling away from her friends, she felt the dizziness setting in as she continued to scream under the unrelenting pressure. It just kept coming, threatening to crush her under its weight.

Her fire winked out around her in a sudden blast of cool air, and she felt a warm trail of blood leak down her upper lip.

Bringing her hands to her temples, Holly knew what was about to happen. Just before she collapsed, she saw her friends reluctantly retreating from the advancing rebels. Nobody caught her as she collapsed onto the concrete, the world going black around her.

Holly woke up to complete silence, her head pounding with the steady drumbeat of a headache. She had no idea where she was—only that she wasn't at the warehouse anymore—and as she opened her eyes and sat up, she felt the weight of strange metal cuffs on her wrists, a blue light emitting from them. It took her a moment to remember what had happened.

The meeting with G.H.O.S.T.

The warehouse.

Sora.

Kevin.

Her powers.

Her eyes scanned the room she was in. She was sitting on a cot in a completely white room, bare but for the cot, a sink, and a toilet—a cell. With no windows, the only source of light was a bright headlight built into the ceiling with a white luminescent glow emanating from it. Panic started to seep in as she studied the door. It was made from a heavy-looking metal with a small slit at the bottom—possibly for food trays—and a small rectangle higher on the door where she suspected people from the outside could open it and look in.

It looked sturdy enough to withstand a nuclear blast. She had to force herself to take a few deep breaths in an attempt to stave off a panic attack. There were no cameras that Holly could spot, but she had no doubt there was at least one hidden somewhere in there.

Finished surveilling the room, Holly inspected the cuffs that had been put on her wrists. They weren't connected, but they each had a thin glowing blue ring that lit the cuffs with an underglow, giving her the inclination that she had them for a reason. A reason that wasn't to restrict her movement. But what that reason could be, she didn't know.

Her hand flew to her throat, tears rising to the surface as she felt the absence of Dustin's necklace—which she had worn since the day he died, even through her training with Dean.

Holly jerked her head to the door—swallowing her tears—as she heard footsteps pounding down the hallway outside. She strained her ears, guessing there were at least two—maybe three—people dragging something heavy down the hall.

Scrambling off her cot—and fighting the wave of lightheadedness—she pancaked herself on the ground next to the door and looked through the hole in the bottom. She held her breath as she waited for them to walk past. Her initial guess had been right, there were two people—guards most likely—dragging something heavy between them—a person. The slit beneath the door didn't offer her a good vantage point. All she could see was the boots of the guards and the bare feet of the person held between them.

Whoever was between the two guards dropped their arms to their side. Holly swallowed a gasp when she saw the pearl necklace wrapped like a bracelet around his wrist. She would never forget whose necklace that was.

Blue-gray eyes and black hair became visible as the guards dropped Dylan on the ground. Holly stayed quiet as Dylan saw her, his eyes widening with recognition. She covered her mouth with a hand, stifling a cry as she saw blood drip from his nose onto the white tiled floor.

Dylan was pulled to his feet as one of the guards opened the cell door across from Holly's and shoved him in. Holly caught a glimpse of him on the floor just before the guards slammed the door closed. She scurried off the floor and back onto her cot when she saw the boots turn toward her cell, barely getting on it before her door opened to reveal Starling standing there in his finely pressed clothes next to someone Holly didn't recognize. Both of them wore their signature bird masks.

"Well, well, well," the stranger remarked with a grin. "Sleeping beauty's awake."

Holly scowled at him, not deigning to respond. His grin turned into a scowl to match hers, hit light blue eyes glaring into hers. He was a large man, who clearly ate his weight in foon, with a smattering of thinning ginger hair on his head.

"You won't be so quiet in a few minutes, girl," he growled at her.

Starling rolled his eyes, straightening the cuffs of his jacket. "Just grab her Kestrel. Don't make an incident like you did with the other girl."

Holly whipped her gaze to him. Other girl? *Karen.* Kestrel grabbed her arm while she was distracted. She flinched.

"Let go of me!" she shouted at him.

His grip tightened.

She tried to wrench her arm out of his grip, but couldn't get him to release her. He started pulling her toward the door. She fought against his viselike grip.

"Stop! Let me go!" she yelled, trying in vain to pry his hand off her arm.

Her bare feet slid against the smooth tiles.

They were out of her cell now, Starling grabbing her other arm after closing the door. She dug the heels of her feet into the floor and kept struggling until she felt the muscles in her side contract in pain—she felt her body convulse. After a sharp intake of air, Holly went limp and breathless. Then she gasped, sucking in as much air as her lungs could take at once. She lifted her head and saw the taser in Starling's hand.

A loud bang echoed in the hall, coming from one of the cell doors behind her. Holly offered no further resistance as Kestrel yanked her further down the hall and Starling pocketed the taser.

Holly was dragged down hall after hall, through door after door. Finally, they stopped outside a set of metal sliding doors. Starling released his grip on her arm and punched in a code to open the doors. From the corner of her eye, she watched him input the code, tucking the numbers into the back of her mind.

Starling took a step back and took hold of her arm again as the doors slid open. He and Kestrel dragged her into the poorly lit room and placed her on a cold metal chair. They put her hands and feet in the restraints on the chair and clicked them closed. She tested the restraints to no avail. They were cinched tight. The men left, leaving her alone in the darkness.

She pulled at her restraints as she surveyed what she could of the room. Her back was to the only entrance. Eventually, she stopped moving and slumped in the chair. Escaping from the room would not only be impossible, but foolish—for various reasons. The room was chilly, and she could hear the soft whooshing of air flowing through a vent nearby.

Holly jolted as she heard the doors behind her slide open and squeezed her eyes shut, blinking furiously as a bright light was turned on above her head. Once her eyes had adjusted to the light, she scanned the room again. In front of her was a large mirrored wall—most likely one-sided glass. There were probably people standing on the other side of the wall. Twisting her hands in the restraints, she had just enough room to flip off whoever was watching.

The man who had just walked in stopped a few feet away to her right where he stood and sized her up. Finished with his initial impression, he strode closer to her. She tried to pull away from him, but all she did was bruise the skin under the restraints.

"Stay away from me," she hissed. His face was mere inches from hers, his electric blue eyes seeming to see right to her soul.

"Nothing has to happen to you, so long as you answer all of my questions," the man told her, backing away from her just enough to be within arms' reach. His rough voice gave Holly the distinct impression that he was from a slavic country—maybe the German Empire.

Her breaths quickened, her eyes firmly planted on the man in front of her. She didn't know what it was about him, but she wanted him far away from her. Her eyes trailed the movement of his hands as he took off his jacket and pushed up the sleeves of his shirt. She swallowed, noting the burn scar on his forearm. Tossing aside his jacket, he moved closer again and grabbed the back of her hair right before slicing a thin line across her cheek. Hissing in pain, her eyes went to the knife she hadn't seen him pull out. Tears pricked her eyes as he brought the blade within a few centimeters of her left eye.

"Now, let us begin. Shall we?" Inspecting the blade, he tsked and wiped the thin line of blood on her arm. He didn't wait for her to respond before he asked her, "Are you pleased with what you did?"

"I don't know what you're talking about," Holly told him truthfully.

"Does it bring you... joy, knowing that you burned her throat so badly she will never be able to speak again?" he asked, trailing the tip of the blade down her throat until it rested just above her collarbone.

"Wh-what are you—" Holly cut off with a gasp as he pressed the tip into her skin until it drew blood.

Leaning closer until his lips were next to her ear, the man whispered, "My *wife* will forever bear the mark of your hand on her neck."

Holly paled as the image of Sora's killer laying unconscious with her handprint branded into her flesh seared across her mind.

"Ah," the man said, yanking her head back and exposing her neck to his knife. "So you *do* remember her."

"Yeah, I remember her," Holly replied softly. "She killed my friend."

"So you *maimed* her?" he snarled, pressing the blade harder into her skin.

Her breaths were quick and shallow. Fear pulsed through her veins, she could feel it beating against the edge of his knife.

"You will know what it's like," he told her. "To bear a scar for all to see."

Pain seared through her chest as he sank the blade deeper into her flesh—slow enough to be sure it was painful. Tears streamed down her face as she forced herself to keep from crying out—afraid even the slightest twitch could end with her artery slashed.

"What do you think you're doing, Goshawk," a woman's voice all but shouted through a speaker. "This is not your assignment."

The man, Goshawk, huffed, but released his grip on her hair—his knife slid out of her skin covered in deep red blood.

Behind her, the doors slid open and Starling entered with Kestrel. Starling took one glance at the bloodied knife in Goshawk's hand and glanced briefly at the one-sided mirror before turning his gaze to Goshawk.

"You disobeyed orders," Starling stated. "You know what happens when someone disobeys."

Goshawk held his head high but didn't respond.

"Take her to the medbay," the woman's voice commanded, fury still underlying her tone. "Songbird will be in to care for her shortly."

Starling and Kestrel moved to the chair, unlocking the restraints and pulling Holly to her feet. The throbbing pain above her collarbone was matched by the pounding headache building as they forced her to stand. Blood oozed from the wound, dripping down the white scrub-like outfit she had apparently been put into while unconscious, staining the material red.

All she could hear now was her hollow breaths and the thumping of her heartbeat as they half-carried her from the room. Her head spun with the pain and the quick loss of blood.

They dragged her through the maze of halls in complete silence. The rapid blood loss was making her dizzy as they pulled her like a rag dog to a sterile room filled with medical equipment. Starling opened the door and Kestrel unceremoniously dropped her on the floor inside. Holly slumped to the ground, grateful for the coolness of the white tiles on the heat of her wound.

The slamming of her door resounded down the empty hallway. Kestrel and Starling walked away, pieces of their hushed conversation floating through the air only to be indistinguishable from inside the empty room.

Holly laid there, listening to the click of the door at the end of the hall that signaled the rebels' departure. There was scarcely a moment of silence before a new set of footsteps came from the opposite direction of the hallway. They were much lighter than any Holly had previously heard. A set of what she assumed were women's feet stopped just outside her cell. Holly managed to roll onto her side as a woman opened the door. The woman held a holo-pad in her hands—hands which had near identical cuffs to the ones on Holly's wrists, except hers had a red glow to them rather than blue. Closing the door, she knelt before Holly.

"We're gonna need to get you on the table, darling." Her voice was flat and emotionless as she spoke.

Nodding, Holly accepted the woman's help onto the exam table.

The woman did a preliminary scan of her, brushing aside the fabric of her shirt to see the injury.

Tsking, the woman set aside her holo-pad and told Holly to lift her arms. Holly didn't try to stop her as she lifted her shirt over her head and tossed it into a medical waste bin. As she wandered the room gathering supplies, Holly took in the details of the room. It was filled with strange equipment she had never seen before. There were papers scattered around the countertops, with half filled beakers acting as paper weights on a few of them.

The woman returned to the exam table with her arms full of supplies. Glancing again at the wound, she cursed under her breath and shot a glare at the corner of the room where the distinct red light of a security camera could be seen. Turning her attention back to Holly, she handed her a strip of leather, telling her to bite down on it before pouring an antiseptic on the wound. Holly's scream was muffled beneath the leather strip as the antiseptic seeped into her wound like acid. The woman was quick in placing gauze over the wound and wrapping Holly's torso with bandages.

When she was finished, she helped Holly put on a new shirt—identical to the one now sitting in the medical waste bin next to the door. She put a bandage over the thin cut on Holly's cheek, and, after injecting her with a vial of argenteral, went over to the door and knocked twice, paused, then knocked two more times.

Stepping back, the woman waited as the lock on the door clicked and Starling and Kestrel reentered the room to take Holly back to her cell.

Once back in her cell, Holly waited for the door at the end of the hall to close before taking a step toward her cot.

She paused when she thought she heard someone whisper her name.

When she heard it again, she carefully laid on the ground by the door and peered out of the slot.

"Holly?" Dylan's voice sounded hoarse.

"Dylan," she breathed.

"Welcome to Hell," he joked. "I have a feeling you won't enjoy your stay."

"I couldn't save you," Holly whispered, rolling onto her back to stare at the ceiling. "I couldn't save anyone."

"Hey, don't do that to yourself," he told her, putting all jokes aside. "These people knew what they were doing. You did the best you could, and that's all I could ask for."

Tears started rolling down her face, dripping into her hair as she turned her head to meet his gaze. "It wasn't enough, though. They got what they wanted—and they killed Sora and Kevin in the process." She took a shaky breath. "Our friends died trying to save you and the others, and it was all for nothing. I couldn't save you, and I couldn't save them."

Dylan's eyes held hers. She had the urge to turn her head away, but something made her hold that gaze.

"We'll get through this, Holly. Together."

"Together."

Dylan gave her his celebrity-worthy smile. "Are you okay?"

"I..." she paused, mulling it over. She wanted so badly to put on a brave face and say she was fine—that nothing was wrong. But she didn't want to be strong. "I feel like crap. What about you—are *you* okay?"

"I've been better," he replied.

They both fell silent as footsteps echoed through the hall. Holly didn't move as she heard a door at the end of the hall creak as it was opened. She shared a look with Dylan.

"Why did Merlin want them moved here with the other two?" Holly recognized Osprey's nasally voice right away.

She didn't recognize the other person's though. "Don't question our orders. Merlin told you what Crow's orders were."

"I hate taking orders from a kid," Osprey mumbled. "Why does Raven keep him around again?"

A third man sighed. "Because he's her brother you dunce."

That was when Holly noticed that the partners of the two speakers were each pulling someone with them.

"You're all going to pay for this." Karen's strong voice shook as she spoke, but she was as brave as ever.

"Shut up girl," she heard Kestrel say. Holly heard a slap, her stomach churned bitterly at the sound.

Standing, she banged loudly on the door and shouted, "Leave her alone!"

She knew she should have stayed quiet, but she couldn't just stand there and let some prick slap her friend.

Her words hit their mark. Kestrel growled on the other side of the door. She couldn't see him, but she had a feeling he was scowling at her door.

Holly had no doubt that if she were to look through the slot at the base of the door Dylan's eyes would be filled with warning. It had been a risk, bringing attention to herself, one she was probably about to pay for, but it was too late to take it back now. Besides, she wasn't about to let a pig like Kestrel get away with hurting her friend.

She could hear Kestrel having a whispered argument with one of the other rebels. They argued quietly until Osprey finally said, "Fine. Do what you want, but if you get in trouble for it, I will not be there to back you up this time."

There was a beat of silence, then two cells were opened. Karen and, who Holly assumed was Apollo, grunted as they were tossed in their cells. The doors creaked slightly as they were closed, and Holly heard three sets of footsteps walk away. Her shoulders tensed. Only three sets had left.

Her thoughts returned to what she had overheard Starling say to Kestrel—panic quickly set in as she remembered what he had said and she found herself taking a few steps away from the door until she was a few feet away near the center of the cell.

Forcing herself to keep breathing, she watched as the door was opened and Kestrel strolled in, closing it behind him. Kestrel was wearing a gray suit with a plain red tie loosely strung around his neck as though he had just come from an important meeting. She tried backing away from him, but the cell was only so big, and her back was soon pressed against the wall. Her heart beat rapidly in her chest as she watched him loosen the tie around his neck. He moved slowly, methodically, as if he had all the time in the world—which, he probably did.

"Are you scared?" he asked her absently.

She didn't answer.

"You look scared."

Holly just stared at him as he spoke, her mind racing.

Faster than she would have expected for someone his size, Kestrel grabbed her by the arm and pulled her away from the wall. She couldn't stop him as he pressed some buttons on the cuffs she had on her wrists, clicking them together. Holly tried pulling her wrists apart, but they were locked in place.

Kestrel dropped her onto her back, driving the air out of her lungs as he planted a knee on her chest. The pressure on her chest was enough to bring spots to her vision. As he pressed his knee harder, she felt something crack in her chest. The bloodcurdling scream she released echoed through the cell and into the hall. Tears left salty paths down the sides of her face as she tried to sob, each tremor that rippled through her body coming to a halt at the point of pressure on her chest.

"You shouldn't have spoken up," Kestrel told her, placing his meaty hands over her throat. "You should have stayed quiet like the little pet you are."

Holly grasped at his hands, vainly trying to pry them off her neck but he only pressed harder. Her lungs ached for relief that wasn't coming. It felt like she was drowning from the inside out and there was nothing she could do to stop it.

Stars flickered above her, dotting in and around Kestrel's head as he finally released the grip he had on her neck to check his watch. Heaving a sigh of annoyance, Kestrel stood and left—not bothering to unlock her cuffs.

She couldn't move as he left her lying there suffocating on her own blood. Her body flared with pain as she coughed against the tightness in her chest and tasted copper at the back of her throat. Each breath she took felt like gasping for air—like she had accidentally inhaled water rather than drank it.

In an attempt to stave off the growing panic, Holly found herself picturing how much she would enjoy making Kestrel feel the painful slap of karma, and for some reason, that didn't bother her as much as it should have.

Chapter 24

As Holly drifted in and out of consciousness, she could have sworn she heard someone yelling to her telling her to respond. Maybe it was more than one person. She couldn't be sure. She was barely conscious for a few seconds at a time so their voices meshed together in a harmony of fear.

Loud banging outside her cell startled her back into consciousness and caused her to fall into another coughing fit. Bright red liquid sprayed into the air with each cough. She could feel the loss of sensation in her hands and feet spreading slowly up her limbs. It didn't seem all that important to her. Nothing did. She tried to focus on the moments of silence so she could get some sleep, but that banging outside kept jolting her back to wakefulness.

After an eternity of this, she heard rushed footsteps coming from the end of the hall. Someone slammed open the door and was storming down the cell block.

"Osprey, if what you told me is true I will have to tell Raven what your cousin did," Merlin was all but yelling as he stalked down the hall.

The banging sound finally stopped, allowing Holly sweet relief from its torment.

Merlin's words registered slowly in her pain-addled mind before quickly flowing away into the fog hanging over her.

"I understand, sir, and I will stand by whatever decision she makes. He may be my cousin sir, but I know we need these kids for whatever reason Hawk has. I would rather betray him than go against Owl or Hawk," Osprey replied, his nasally voice firm in his statement.

Merlin came to a stop outside Holly's cell and ordered, "Open it."

Her door swung open, revealing Merlin standing there in a pristine black tuxedo. Merlin swore when he saw her. Starling and Osprey, who were standing behind him both cursed vehemently.

"Take her to the med bay. But be careful, we can't let it get worse," Merlin told Starling, then to Osprey he said, "Come with me. We are going to inform Raven what that idiot did."

Holly groaned softly as Starling slid his arms under her and lifted her off the ground. The others disappeared down the hall. As they left, Starling carried her into the hall where another person was waiting.

The woman cursed under her breath. "That moron deserves everything coming for him. After all the work we have put into this project, he deserves worse."

Starling gave her a hard look but didn't reproach her.

He was surprisingly gentle as he carried Holly back to the med bay.

The woman who had dressed her earlier wounds was in the room when Starling brought her in. Mallard closed the door but stayed in the hall. The doctor looked up from what she was doing and swore.

"What exactly did you do to this girl?" the doctor demanded, motioning for Starling to bring Holly over to the far end of the room.

Starling didn't reply right away. "I didn't do anything. It was Kestrel."

"Of course it was. That man is going to be our downfall if he's not dealt with. All our efforts to activate the elementals' powers early would have been for nothing." The doctor motioned for Starling to set Holly in what looked like a healing pod. Holly had heard of the pods saving people's lives, but she had never seen one before, let alone used one. They were extremely expensive. The fact that G.H.O.S.T. had at least one spoke measures about their financials.

"Watch what you say, Songbird," Starling warned, his voice dropping as he laid Holly in the pod and unlatched her cuffs from each other. "Don't worry about Kestrel, Merlin is taking care of it."

Songbird tsked but didn't respond as she closed the lid over Holly's head and pressed a few buttons. The pod was snug enough that if Holly were to move either of her hands they would brush the cool material of the pod, but not tight enough to invoke a sense of claustrophobia.

The glass lid above her fogged as a sedative gas filled the chamber. A few seconds after the gas was released, an aqua-tinted liquid poured quickly into the pod. Holly didn't have the chance to feel panic as the sedative kicked in and pulled her into a deep and dreamless sleep.

Holly woke with a start, finding herself back in her cell. She sat up and was pleased to find herself completely healed. Her chest no longer felt like it was collapsing in on itself, and the bruising on her throat was gone. As she felt around the area where Goshawk had stabbed her, she could feel the scar tissue—it was like the wound had been healed for months.

As she sat there, she heard footsteps walking down the hallway. Holly tensed when they stopped outside her cell, but they didn't open hers, they opened Dylan's. She listened as they shoved him back into his cell. Climbing off her cot, she laid on the ground and watched as they closed his door, managing to catch a glimpse of him before the door was shut. She choked back a gasp. Sweat drenched his hair, dripping from his forehead. His breaths were all but gasps of air. That was all Holly was able to discern before the door was closed and the two pairs of feet were moving away.

She was tempted to try talking to Dylan, but decided to let him rest. Whatever the rebels had done to him seemed to have left him exhausted, she wouldn't keep him from resting. Holly climbed back onto her rigid, low-lying cot and laid on her back. She lay there staring at the ceiling, listening to the silence of her cell. After a while, she got bored and started pacing.

Four steps from her bed to the opposite wall. Seven steps from the door to the back wall between the sink and toilet. Almost eight steps from one corner to the one diagonally across from it. Four steps. Seven. Eight.

Four.

Seven.

Eight.

And on and on she went.

Tracing her steps until she was sure she would wear a path into the tiles beneath her bare feet. All she could hear was her heartbeat as she traced the steps again and again.

Again.

Four.

Seven.

Eight.

Until something outside her cell had her stopping.

Footsteps.

She was standing in the center of her cell when a tray of food slid under her door through the open slot. Three identical scraping sounds followed. Whoever had given them food walked away without saying a word.

Waiting for the click of the door at the end of the hall, Holly picked up her tray of food and set it on her cot. There wasn't much food to speak of on the tray—a bowl of what looked like oatmeal, a banana, and a cup of water—but it was the first meal she had had since before her doomed fight with G.H.O.S.T. in the warehouse and she could feel the tempered pangs of hunger pulling at her stomach.

Holly wolfed down the food and drained the cup of water. When she was finished, she set the tray under her cot and sat near the head of it with her back pressed against the corner of the cell. She began counting the tiles that made up the wall across from her, making it to seven twice before she lost count again and gave up. Her eyes scanned the room. As she surveyed the barren room, her eyes started to drift closed.

Her eyes drifted open groggily to the sound of someone opening her door. As soon as the sound registered, she bolted upright and stood in the center of the cell, her muscles screaming in protest—she hadn't exactly fallen asleep in a comfortable position. Behind the rebel who stood in the doorway, Holly could see Dylan's door was also open.

"Come," the rebel said to her. "Raven has requested your presence."

Holly followed the man into the hall and found herself walking next to Dylan. Karen and Apollo were walking in front of them. Two rebels were walking in front of and behind the four teenagers.

In the narrow hallway, Holly found her hand reaching for Dylan's—he grasped it in return, clinging tightly to her like a lifeline. If the rebels behind them noticed, they didn't say anything. A sliver of relief wedged its way into her chest as she held onto his hand for dear life. That small connection was a reminder that despite the nightmarish circumstances, at least they weren't alone.

The walk was long, but they finally reached their destination after passing through a labyrinth of hallways and staircases. The room they entered was large enough to comfortably fit two dozen people, and it was currently past its max occupancy. All four of the rebels who had accompanied them stopped once inside the room and stood waiting—for something, likely this Raven person.

Holly stared at the floor and listened as the clicking of heels announced Raven's arrival. Her gaze flicked up as a tall woman walked into the room, her heels tapped against the concrete floor with each step. Holly's eyes widened as she recognized Raven as the woman from the forest. Not only had Starling been there, but his woman, Raven, too. She schooled her features as Raven swept her gaze over her and her friends.

Raven stopped and watched as two rebels dragged a barely conscious Kestrel into the center of the room and forced him to his knees. Stepping forward, Raven ripped off the mask covering Kestrel's eyes. Raven's silver-blonde, waist-length hair swished in its ponytail with the action.

"You might be wondering why I wanted you all here." Raven didn't shift her deep blue gaze from Kestrel, but Holly knew who she was addressing. "I want you here to witness what happens to those who don't follow orders. My brother was very specific when he ordered that you four not be unnecessarily harmed. We were lenient once, but a second chance is not granted easily and Kestrel ignored direct orders—again.

"Theodore Hopkins, as of this moment, I strip you of your title of Kestrel and hereby give you your punishment." Something about Raven's icy white hair gave Holly a feeling of familiarity, but she couldn't quite figure out what—she was a bit preoccupied with the scene playing out in front of her. "As the highest ranking member of G.H.O.S.T. present, I decree your punishment to be execution—for putting your selfish desires above that of the cause."

Holly jolted but didn't say anything. Not as images of a body on a hospital flashed behind her eyes, followed by the unseeing eyes of two friends and the charred, cold and lifeless bodies of two adults and a small child. The images burned the back of her eyes but were gone in an instant.

Nobody said a word.

They all stood silently, watching as Raven pulled out a gun from the back of her waistband, aimed its barrel at Kestrel's head, and pulled the trigger. Holly flinched and squeezed her eyes shut as the sound reached her ears. Two faces flashed through her mind—she shoved them away and forced herself to open her eyes.

She immediately regretted it as the room started spinning around her. Kestrel's body had fallen to the floor with a dull thud, blood spilling around him as his lifeless eyes stared out at nothing. Bile rose in the back of her throat as she forced herself to look away before the sight could bring back any more unwanted memories.

Silence echoed through the room.

"Take them back to their cells," Raven ordered the guards. She dismissed them all with a wave of her hand and walked out of the room the way she had entered.

Chapter 25

Her cell was silent as she sat there in the days following Kestrel's execution. At least, she assumed it had been a few days. She couldn't be sure, though. Her only way of judging the passing of time was the trays of food and the occasional visit from Songbird. The woman was always accompanied by another rebel who stayed on the outside of the cell while Songbird took a blood sample. Holly didn't want to ask why. She couldn't imagine it was for anything good—not when Songbird didn't seem to want to do it.

To pass the time between visits from Songbird, Holly found herself humming a lullaby under her breath. She didn't know why she did it. Maybe it was just a distraction, something to remind herself that hope wasn't gone. The Walker brothers would search for them. She had to believe that.

At the very least, the soft lilt of her voice bouncing gently off the walls around her kept the memories at bay. They sank back into the depths of her mind leaving her with nothing but the near-unbearable silence of the cell as the last notes of the lullaby dissipated.

Every once in a while she would stretch out her muscles, trying to keep them from atrophying in the enclosed room. She would continue to hum while she did this, feeling the deep ache in her chest from losing her family ease just enough to allow her to breathe. The song had been one of the few that her mother would sing to them as kids before Harry's disappearance. Grief flooded her heart as she realized how much she missed her mom's strength. The strength to move forward despite the cards she had been dealt. How would her mom have reacted if she had been alive when Holly had been taken? *She would have likely come knocking down the door on day one,* Holly thought. The words almost made her want to laugh.

Songbird had left only a few minutes before, and Holly found herself absently rubbing the spot on her arm where the blood had been drawn. Whatever they were hoping to get from taking her blood, she hoped it would prove to be pointless. Songbird had instructed her to rest after each visit, and Holly tried to acquiesce, but, laying on her cot, Holly stared at the ceiling until she was restless enough to scream. Her feet barely registered the cold of the concrete floor as she began pacing.

Four steps.

Seven.

Eight.

Four.

Seven.

Frustration boiled the blood in her veins.

Eight.

Sitting around doing nothing was not something she could deal with.

Crossing the distance of the cell back to the cot, she sat on the edge and stared at the opposite wall. The visits from Songbird always came with at least a dozen meals in between them. By Holly's best guess, each sample of blood taken was at least a few days or more apart—something that didn't settle well with her. If they had been gone as long as Holly was estimating, then it had been weeks since the fight in the warehouse—which meant that they had missed graduation. It had been fast-approaching before they had been taken, but they had missed it. Classes had ended and they were all finished with the end of year tests, but that still left the actual day of graduation.

As relieved as she should have been at the thought of being done with high school, it was nothing worth celebrating when she was still stuck in this facility. Thoughts and ideas rushed through her mind as she tried to think of an escape from this nightmare, but every time she tried to reach out and grab one it slipped through her fingers the way a mouse slips under the crack of a door to escape a cat.

The metal frame of the cot groaned as she shifted positions. She scooted to the head of the cot, leaning her back against the corner of the room, and started anew on her counting of the tiles on the wall across from her.

Holly didn't know how long she sat there, counting and recounting the tiles in the walls, the ceiling, the floor, but eventually she laid down on the cot and continued staring at the wall from a different angle.

How exciting, she thought sarcastically.

She knew she wouldn't be able to fall asleep any time soon, so she began to quietly sing the lullaby again while her fingers fidgeted with the fabric of her shirt.

After a while, a yawn stopped her mid-verse. Her eyelids fluttered shut as she continued to hum the song until she drifted off. The sweet, but brief, oblivion of sleep was torn from her grasp at the sound of a door slamming shut down the hall. She sat up, bleary-eyed, and stared at the far wall of the cell.

Someone was walking down the hall.

They stopped outside her cell and opened the door. Glancing at it, Holly saw Starling walk over to her. She didn't resist as he pulled her to her feet and tugged her down the hall. Forcing down a yawn, she tried to memorize the route they took as he dragged her through a series of halls, but her sleep-addled mind was too foggy to remember anything more than to keep her feet moving.

Starling was the only rebel with her. They were the only people in any of the hallways they took. It must have been early in the morning—or late at night, she couldn't be sure.

Holly stumbled as she was pulled up a flight of stairs. Starling yanked her to her feet—more harsh with her today than he had been after the incident with Kestrel. She reminded herself that these people had killed her friends and were holding her captive, there was no expectation of hospitality.

Her eyes blinked rapidly at the sudden brightness of the early morning sun. in the distance, she could make out what looked like a forest, but her vision blurred as she tried to focus her vision in the natural light after so long trapped in a room with artificial light. Starling removed the cuffs from her wrists. She almost expected something to feel different, but nothing noticeable changed with their absence.

She scanned her surroundings. Starling had brought her to the edge of a forest full of towering trees—redwoods. The massive trees scraped the pale sky with the might of a giant. Turning to Starling, Holly waited for him to tell her what he expected of her.

Starling nodded at a tree. "Set that tree on fire."

Holly raised an eyebrow. He wanted her to set a tree on fire.

"How?" she asked, stalling.

"You know how."

She did, and she knew it wasn't with a flint and steel the way Adam had taught her when she was younger. But her powers were temperamental. There was no telling what would happen if she tried to use them. Not to mention she had hardly been able to feel their warmth in her veins since the warehouse. Her gaze shifted to the tree Starling had indicated to, briefly snagging on the cuffs he was holding in his hands.

In spite of her fear on the matter, she had seen what these people would do to people who disobeyed them and knew she wouldn't be an exception. Lifting her hand before her, she concentrated on the flames that lived in her blood. A small flame flickered to life, hovering an inch above her palm. Holly crushed the flowering fire in her fist and returned her attention to the tree.

This could end very badly.

But she had to try.

Focusing on that living ember inside of her, she imagined its hunger devouring the tree, pictured the orange flames burning through the bark. She stood there for a moment, waiting for something to happen.

When nothing happened, she frowned. Whatever precision control she had had over her powers in the warehouse was not instinctual.

As she stood there, an idea sparked in her mind as she shifted on her feet. Raising her hand palm up in front of her, she brought to life a small sphere of fire above the palm of her hand, a tingle of energy dancing down her arm. Her brows drew closer together as the ball wavered in its formation. Once she got it to keep its shape, Holly drew her arm back and tossed the ball of fire in the direction of the tree. A triumphant smile crept over her face, only to be dimmed as her fireball hit the wrong tree.

Oops.

Holly turned to Starling. His face showed no emotion under his mask, but Holly saw the glimmer of victory in his eyes.

"Again," he told her.

A sigh escaped her lips as she turned back to the forest, her eyes locking onto her target. Sweat gathered on her forehead as she concentrated on forming a new flaming sphere. The most she got was a half-hearted spark. Irritation flooded her mind. Shoving it aside, she wiped the sweat from her forehead on her pants and tried again.

Pushing her concentration to its limit, Holly focused on the whirlpool of energy swirling in her and tried to draw her power from it to no avail. The tree she had initially hit had stopped burning, the small lick of flame flickering to smoke in the air. After a few more seconds of unbearable silence, she felt the tell-tale tingling sensation flow down her arm and watched as a small fire grew above her hand, forming a ball. Before it could dissipate, she threw it at her intended target, her eyes locked onto the tree as she felt the pull of her fireball and directed it at the tree. Her focus wavered as a wave of nausea swarmed her senses, sending the sphere on a collision course with a different tree.

Holly doubled over, vomiting into the grass. When she had upended the entirety of her stomach's contents, she wiped her mouth with the back of her hand and straightened. She glanced at Starling, praying he wouldn't make her do it again. Her hope shattered as he gave her a nod to do it again.

She turned back to the line of trees.

Taking a step backward, she raised her hand before her once more. Her face scrunched in concentration. Sweat slid down her temple as she pinned all her focus on her target, a ball of fire burning above her hand, the power heeding her call quicker than it had in her previous attempts. Her focus was unwavering this time as she launched the ball of fire at the tree and pulled its aim toward the target tree, colliding with it in a shower of fire.

Something warm slid down her upper lip. Her arms refused to cooperate as she tried to wipe it away. She dropped to her knees in the grass, but Starling was soon yanking her back to her feet. He returned the cuffs to her wrists before pulling her back inside the building, leaving the trees to burn.

The world was spinning like a top as she was taken back to her cell.

Starling left soon after locking her in.

Holly slumped to the floor, any remaining energy sapped from her by the cold floor as she blacked out.

Chapter 26

A puddle of blood greeted Holly as she regained consciousness. She managed to push herself up into a sitting position on shaky arms, lifting a hand to her face and pulling it back when she felt a thick, sticky residue. Half of her face was covered in a thin layer of blood.

There was a tray of food underneath her door. She pulled it to her and slowly ate the oatmeal and grapes. The water tasted amazing as she drank it. Sliding the tray into the hallway, she pushed her back up against the wall behind her. Exhaustion pulled at her limbs as she rested her head against the tiles. There was no way for her to know how long she had been unconscious, and yet she still felt the urge to lay back down and sleep.

Bracing herself, Holly used the wall to stand. She walked the perimeter of the room—

using the wall as her support—until she reached the cot. Sighing softly, she flopped onto it and closed her eyes hoping for the quiet void of sleep, but it eluded her. Despite her inability to fall asleep, Holly was perfectly content to lay there with her eyes closed for as long as she could.

Sleep was just around the corner when she heard approaching footsteps. Her body tensed as she forced herself to sit up as her door opened.

Had it been a day already? Longer?

Starling was not the one to escort her this time. Instead, it was someone she hadn't seen before. Craning her neck, she looked up at him for a brief moment before standing and following him into the hall. His blue eyes were covered with the usual bird mask—though, as she looked closer she thought she could see holographic contact lenses—and his blond hair was cut close to his head. He was like a walking tree.

The newcomer walked a lot faster than Starling had, leaving Holly scrambling to keep up with him. They passed way more people than she had ever encountered before in this place, but the walking tree didn't stop to chat with any of the others until they reached the top of the stairs.

"Evening Pelican," Mallard greeted. Holly vaguely remembered meeting her shortly after Kestrel's *visit*.

"Evening Mallard," Pelican replied, peering down his nose at her. Mallard was about the same height as Adam had been the last time Holly had seen him, with pale blue eyes that were so cold they could turn a man to stone. "Debriefing today?" Pelican asked Mallard, nodding to someone behind her.

Holly couldn't tell who it was at first, but as Mallard shifted, she caught sight of Karen. Pelican and Mallard continued chatting, their words blurring into background noise as Holly subtly tried to get Karen to look at her. Her friend's gaze remained blank, leaving her unable to snag her attention before the two rebels finished speaking and Pelican was pulling Holly down the hall opposite the one Karen and Mallard had been coming from. Something about her was different.

Pelican entered the code to the door and led Holly into a large concrete room with a vaulted ceiling.

"I have been informed of your... progress," Pelican said as he removed her cuffs. "Today will be simpler. Form a flame above your hand and see how long you can hold it there."

Holly nodded, once again shoving down that instinctive fear that threatened to overwhelm her and, lifting one of her hands before her, brought forth a quivering fire. She stared at the glow, mesmerized by its beauty. The flames licked her skin gently, unable to harm her as she touched it with her other hand, twirling it into different shapes. After a moment, the fire winked out, but Holly quickly brought it back.

Time flowed slowly as she stood in the room with Pelican, testing the size and shape of the flames in her hands—sweat beading on her temples as she concentrated on her task. The fire continuously went out, but she kept trying.

Again and again, and she kept pushing through in spite of how dizzy she started feeling.

The fire between her hands took the shape of a fiery bird for the briefest of moments before sizzling to ash. She stumbled, falling to the ground. Planting her hands on the concrete on either side of her, she took a deep breath. Pelican crouched next to her and replaced the cuffs.

Days passed in a blur of repetitive visits to either the forest or that concrete room. It was always Pelican who took her, but he rarely pushed her as hard as Starling had that first day. She spent every day—or what she assumed was every day—training her powers. In the beginning, she had tried to count how many times she was taken from her cell, but lost track after she breached day thirty. Her powers no longer terrified her. If anything she was beginning to love watching them flourish. But even after all that time training her powers, they had yet to be as powerful as they had been in the warehouse.

During the time between training, she barely caught a few glimpses of her friends, but when she did she wished using her powers didn't make her feel so good—so powerful. Karen had stopped looking at her when she passed her in the hall, and Apollo, he looked one step away from passing out and not waking up. It had been a long time since Holly had been able to see Dylan, the last time being when Pelican brought her into the training room right after him. Puddles of water had littered the floor of the room, drops of blood mixing into one of them as she had watched the rebel escorting Dylan drag his unconscious body from the room.

When she wasn't training she spent her empty time pacing her cell and humming to herself while repeating every route she had taken in this building and every door code she had been through, all while hoping she wasn't wasting her time trying to figure out an escape route. It had been weeks since she had stopped praying, her already fragile faith whittled to nothing in the face of all she had lost. If there was a God watching over her, he had long since abandoned her.

Her routine was interrupted one day—weeks after she had lost count of the days—when she heard a familiar set of footsteps coming toward her cell. Holly stood in the center of her cell as Pelican swung open the door and took a hesitant step toward him. When he didn't stop her, she followed him into the hallway.

As they reached the stairs where they would either continue straight for the forest or turn left to the concrete training room, shouts and thundering footsteps could be heard coming from the hallway to their right. Pelican didn't halt their trek until they made it outside. The small clearing before the edge of the forest was in complete chaos. Dozens of people crowded around something, and there were dirt formations scattered everywhere the eye could see. Pelican's grip was firm on her arm as he pulled Holly to the side as Songbird came bursting through the door behind them, followed by Merlin. He was yelling his head off at Mallard, who walked beside him.

"How could you let this happen?!" Merlin shouted.

"I-we're sorry, sir. He overpowered us—"

"Overpowered you?! I don't care if we need him, you have a stun gun for a reason!" Merlin growled, taking a deep breath. "Show me where they are."

Holly watched them walk away. Her heart pounded in her chest, hoping they hadn't been talking about Dylan—by the tone of their voices something bad had happened and she didn't want to know if she could handle the death of another friend. The crowd of people parted like the Red Sea to let them pass, but Holly didn't get a glimpse of what they were surrounding before they shifted back. Merlin and Mallard weren't there for long before Songbird pushed her way out and strolled calmly toward the door, her arms coated in blood. The crowd bustled uncertainly, their bird masks reflecting the midday sunlight as they shared uncertain glances with the people around them.

Moments later, Holly heard Raven shouting at Songbird before barging through the door.

"What do you mean dead? What happened?" Raven yelled, the fair skin of her face bright red with anger.

She forced her way to the center of the crowd, Songbird close behind her. Holly heard Raven let out a slew of curses before she yelled for everyone to clear the area. As the crowd dispersed, Holly managed to sneak a glimpse at what had caused them to gather in the first place. Laying in the middle of the clearing—covered in blood—were the bodies of Karen and Apollo. Holly's stomach churned, nausea clouding her senses as she saw her friends lying there in the field, covered in blood—both their own and each other's. Karen's face was turned away from her, but Holly knew she would be forever haunted by the blank look on Apollo's face as he stared accusingly toward the door.

Holly choked on a scream and didn't resist Pelican as he shoved her back through the door and back to her cell. Her legs gave out as she was thrown into the small room, collapsing to the ground. She only just made it to the toilet in time to empty her meager meal into it. When she stopped heaving, she flushed it away and slumped to the floor.

Not caring who heard her, Holly stood on shaking legs and screamed, throwing all her anger and grief into the sound as it morphed into a sob. If there had been anything to throw across her small cell, she would have done so already. As it was, she threw punch after punch at the tiled wall—tears streaming down her cheeks sizzled and turned to steam as she cried, screaming all the while. Some of the tiles cracked under her knuckles, but she didn't stop, even as her fist left bloody smears on the wall. Her voice cracked as she fell to her knees, leaning her forehead against the wall.

She sat there, staring numbly at her bloodied hand. Distantly, she could hear faint footsteps getting closer, but she didn't move as her door creaked open. Someone sighed, the sound barely audible over the ringing in Holly's ears, but she didn't resist when Songbird pulled her hand toward her and started wrapping it in bandages. Starling was standing in the hall outside Holly's cell.

"Trying to escape always has a cost," Songbird whispered to her as she worked. "Don't make the same mistake as your friend, someone is always watching through the eyes of others."

Finished wrapping Holly's hand, Songbird stood and exited the cell. Once they were gone, Holly stood and walked over to her cot. The metal frame groaned as she climbed on and leaned against the corner of her cell. She sat there for a long while, thinking Songbird's words over in her head until they became a jumbled mess.

Someone is always watching through the eyes of others.

Through the eyes of others.

Holly blinked, the holographic contact lenses. She had glimpsed them in Pelican's eyes. The other rebels must have them as well. Which meant... *someone is always watching*.

A plan began forming in her mind. She had to get herself, and Dylan, out of the nightmare they were stuck in. G.H.O.S.T. seemed to have taken every precaution to keep them there, but they had made one vital mistake, they hadn't changed the door passcodes since she had gotten there, and she had memorized all seven of the codes from her cell to the forest. They could have been changed after the... incident today, but, if she bided her time, she could just try again. Her confidence grew as she visualized the path they would have to take to get outside. She made a mental map of what she knew about the facility— which was far too little. Still, she knew enough to create a plan.

In the past few weeks, she had overheard some rebels whispering about military raids on other locations. Holly knew they had to be looking for her and her friends, all she had to do was get to a place where she could safely contact Major Walker.

As she finished her plan, something tugged at the back of her mind—where was Jacob? The rebels had taken him too, but he didn't have any powers that she knew about, and she hadn't seen him once since the abduction—hadn't so much as heard anything about him since then. She shook her head, her hand scratching absently at the edge of the bandage on her hand. There was nothing she could do for him if she didn't know where he was, let alone if he was even still alive. For all she knew, he could be dead.

As far as she could tell, the forest Pelican took her to was not enclosed within any walls. It would give her sufficient cover to hide as she and Dylan made their escape. Holly sighed, she wanted to tell him every part of her plan, but it was too risky and she didn't know when she would see him again. Their opposing training times threw a wrench in her planning. They would have to make a break for it the next time they were both in their cells at the same time.

For the time being, Holly had to bide her time and wait for things with G.H.O.S.T. to calm down before she did anything.

She let days pass, reserving as much energy as she could. Her fingers twitched with the excess energy as she heard Pelican's footsteps coming down the cell block about a week after the incident in the clearing, or what she guessed had been a week. She had no sense of time locked in her cell outside of meals, visits from Songbird, and training, which was varied enough to never be consistently lit by the sun or moon on the occasions she was outside.

Holly stood and walked to the center of her cell as the door was opened. He didn't see it coming as Holly pulled back her arm and struck him in the throat with all her might. Pelican stumbled sideways, one hand going to the stun gun at his hip, but Holly grabbed the back of his head and slammed his face into the wall repeatedly until his body went limp.

Not waiting another second, she took a set of keys from his belt and took off her cuffs. She figured they were designed to block her powers, but in the hours spent alone in her cell over the past few days, she had sparked to life a flame in spite of them.

Dragging Pelican into the center of the cell, Holly put the cuffs on him and clicked them together as Kestrel had done to her. She quickly and quietly left her cell and closed it behind her. Her heart pounded in her chest as she turned and opened Dylan's cell. The rebel assigned to him hadn't taken him out that day, so he was sitting on his cot when she opened the door. Dylan jumped to his feet, his mouth opening when he saw her.

She raised a finger to her lips to quiet him and walked over to him. The cuffs clicked softly as she removed them and set them on his cot before motioning for him to follow her. Once they were out of his cell, she closed the door behind them.

"Holly," Dylan whispered. "What are you doing?"

"Getting us out of here," she breathed as they walked down the hallway, past the vacant cells Apollo and Karen had occupied.

Dylan followed her quietly for a while as they made their way to the end of the hall and she punched in the password, hoping it hadn't changed.

The lock clicked open.

Holly paused as Dylan grabbed her arm and muttered, "What about Karen and Apollo?"

Her heart was in her throat as she avoided looking into his eyes. "They're dead, Dylan. They've been dead for days."

Dylan swallowed, not looking wholly surprised at the news as his grip on her arm went slack.

"We need to leave," Holly said softly. "Right now. We're not dying here, too."

He nodded and walked beside her as she followed the path she had mapped in her mind. They stopped once as two rebels walked past, slipping into an unlocked door to wait them out.

Opening the door a crack, Holly peered out, and, upon seeing nothing, motioned for Dylan to follow her as they continued toward the door to the forest.

It was beginning to get dark when Holly opened the door to the clearing, the sun sending up the last rays of light before falling below the horizon. An alarm went up from the building behind them. Holly shared a panicked look with Dylan before they both took off in the direction of the forest. Her legs burned as she sprinted as fast as they could carry her through the foliage.

After a while, Holly came to a halt, breaths tight in her chest.

Dylan walked up next to her. "We shouldn't stay long."

"I know. I just, need a moment to catch my breath," Holly replied. A moment later, she said, "Okay. Let's go."

They moved quickly, only taking a break when absolutely necessary. Each time they stopped, they made sure it wasn't for long. During one of their few breaks, shouts began echoing through the late-night air.

"I think they figured out where we went," Dylan muttered.

"Yup," Holly responded, her voice soft. "Let's keep moving. Hopefully we're far enough away to be long gone before they can catch up to us."

Dylan nodded. "Let's go."

Without another word, they moved on. The shouts became more distant as they kept moving, but they didn't slow down. The trees stretched on, seeming to go on into eternity. After a while, both of them were breathing heavily, exhaustion slowing their steps. Holly knew it was a huge risk, but they needed to find a safe place to rest.

Holly slowed the pace and started searching for any signs of a cave they could rest in. She was about to give up and tell Dylan they should keep moving when she heard the soft tumbling of water and stepped out of the trees, stumbling onto a lake. Her feet came to a stop as she stared out across the rippling expanse of water. Dylan came out of the forest behind her. The lake was magnificent, but not particularly large—and yet, the water seemed to be made out of moonlight. To their left, a waterfall flowed over a cliff into the lake, sending large ripples into its wake. The dark sky was reflected in the lake's surface as they took in the scene. Stars flickered in the soft movement of the water, the gentle glow of moonlight glistening in the waves.

The ground was soft as Holly started toward the waterfall, curious to see if it hid a cave. She climbed over rocks and, behind the veil of water, found a small cave with no end visible in the darkness. Dylan came to a stop beside her as she entered the cave.

There was a steep incline at the back as she walked up until she saw the dim light of the moon at the end. It wasn't just a cave, it was a tunnel.

Walking back to Dylan at the base of the incline, she said, "It's a tunnel. We can rest here for a while, but we'll need to leave before long."

"You're right," Dylan replied. "We should rest up while we can."

Holly nodded, then covered her face with a hand. "I completely forgot about food. I thought about everything else, but I forgot about food."

Dylan gave a humorless chuckle. "It'll be fine. There's bound to be something in the forest we can eat."

"You're probably right."

Dylan moved to the wall of the cave and sat down. Holly walked over and joined him on the ground. Leaning her head against the dirt wall behind her, she closed her eyes, not planning on sleeping long, but she needed to get some rest before they started moving again. It would only be a matter of time before someone caught up to them and they needed to get out of there while they could.

Chapter 27

Holly woke up alone. Sitting up, she looked around. Dylan was standing by the waterfall, scrapes and bruises covering his arms from their escape. His black hair was mussed and tangled as he brought handfuls of water to his lips. Holly stood and joined him, the scrapes on her own skin stinging with her movement. A breeze flowed through the cave, bringing with it the scents of the forest. Birds chirped harmoniously in the distance as she drank.

"How long was I asleep?" she asked, wiping excess water from her mouth.

"Maybe an hour or two," Dylan replied.

"We should get moving," Holly said, taking note of the early morning light filtering through the waterfall.

"You should have done that a long time ago." Holly and Dylan spun to see Merlin standing behind them. They stared at him, not daring to breathe.

"The tunnel," Dylan whispered.

Holly didn't say anything, her gaze fixed on Merlin, waiting for him to move. Her breaths came shallowly as she forced herself not to move a muscle. The sound of her pounding heart filled her head with each beat. Holly swallowed, her mind racing. Her fingers clenched at her side. She felt the rush of fire eager to burn, but she couldn't use it with Dylan a mere foot from her, her control was not that good.

"I came here alone," Merlin admitted, taking a step closer. "But the others aren't far behind. Now, come with me before this gets worse, and I will ensure you receive a less severe punishment."

"We're not going back." Holly's voice was firm as she spoke, hiding the fear that left her nearly breathless.

Merlin sighed, his blue eyes narrowing. Holly heard Dylan take a step back. There were two exits to the cave they were in, and Merlin blocked one of them. Holly subtly backed up a step. Merlin reached for the gun in his holster and aimed it at Dylan. Holly froze. He waved them closer, keeping his gun aimed at Dylan.

Holly knew how fast a life could end when the trigger of a gun was pulled. She couldn't stop picturing the way the rebel woman had smiled as she shot Sora—she would not let anyone else die that way.

Slowly, the two moved closer to where Merlin was standing. "That wasn't so hard, now was it?"

Holly's gaze remained trained on the gun in his hand, her mind repeating to her that he wouldn't kill them. G.H.O.S.T. needed them alive. Despite trying to reassure herself that they would be fine, Holly couldn't stop the fear building in her chest. But fear was a persistent thing, it would never ease up once it got its claws into you.

Once they were out of the cave, Merlin turned them back in the direction of the compound. Her heart pounded in her chest. She wouldn't go back. Couldn't let him take them back.

The moon was still high in the sky, casting the world in shades of gray as Holly frantically scanned the area around them as they walked, trying to figure out what to do. Panic thrummed in her chest, but it faltered as she remembered she had another weapon in her arsenal. G.H.O.S.T. had been training her for weeks to use her powers, and even with her fickle control over them, she could still use them as a distraction.

Her eyes locked with Dylan's when she glanced at him and mouthed for him to run. He gave her a confused look. It disappeared when she lifted a hand in front of her and sparked a tiny fire on her palm. Understanding lit up his gaze, quickly shifting to concern, but he had to know that whatever she was planning might be their only chance to escape because he gave her a subtle nod before turning his attention back to the path in front of them.

They both stopped walking, Dylan's gaze finding her again. She waited until she heard the cocking of the gun behind her.

"Keep walking," Merlin ordered, pressing the cool metal of the gun against the back of her head.

Closing her eyes, Holly took a deep breath. She thought back to Dean's training, remembering how it felt to take the gun from his hand again and again, then opened her eyes. Moving quickly, she reached up and shoved the gun away from her head. She didn't give Merlin a chance to lift it again as she grabbed his shirt. Pulling him toward her, she lifted her knee and pulled him onto it. He groaned in pain, dropping the gun as she shoved him backward and set a circle of fire around him before stepping over the burning line. It was nowhere near as powerful as the rings had been at the warehouse, but it should be enough to contain one man—especially given the fact that, once set, she didn't have to remain concentrated on the fire as it became self-reliant on the foliage littering the ground. Brilliant orange flames danced as a breeze brushed past, the fire crackly harshly. Merlin's eyes blazed brightly with fury behind the wall of fire.

Turning on her heel, Holly started walking away, scanning the nearby forest for Dylan. She spotted him a few feet away, coming out from behind a tree.

As she started toward him, Dylan shouted, "Behind you!"

Holly spun around too late as Merlin leapt through her ring of fire and charged her. Her reflexes were too slow to react as he tackled her right over the edge of a cliff. Expecting ground to be beneath her, Holly screamed as she realized she was falling through open air.

Dylan called out her name, but she couldn't do anything but scream as she fell through the air.

Merlin clung to the edge of the cliff above her as she fell. Surprise flashed briefly in his eyes, but it was overshadowed by triumph. A smirk spread across his face before he pulled himself onto the top of the cliff.

Water filled her mouth as her body slammed into the surface of the lake and sank. All of the air in her lungs evacuated as the momentum of her fall caused her to sink deeper into the murky water. She tried to claw her way to the surface, but her body wouldn't respond to her commands.

Her body was shutting down.

Something heavy splashed in the water. Holly couldn't even turn her head to see what it was. Her body convulsed as it tried to get oxygen into her system. Darkness blotted at the edge of her vision, her eyelids growing increasingly heavy.

Arms wrapped around her body.

Someone was pulling her to the surface.

Holly was barely conscious as they reached the cool air above the water. Every limb of her body felt like it was made of lead. Her lungs refused to take in the plentiful air above the water.

The last thing she remembered before the darkness claimed her was the sensation of being dragged onto the shore.

Holly's chest felt bruised—like someone had performed chest compressions on her—as she coughed up lake water onto the shore. Someone beside her sighed in relief as her lungs expelled more water. Holly turned her head in their direction.

"Don't you ever... do that to me again," Dylan huffed, his dark hair plastered to his forehead.

He sounded exhausted. Holly inspected him for injuries, but he seemed alright to her, aside from being sopping wet. There was a small cut on his upper arm, but it didn't seem to be bothering him.

"I'm sorry," Holly coughed. "What—what happened?"

"As soon as you fell, I saw Merlin climb back up and I-I couldn't stop myself." Guilt and remorse flooded his eyes. "I could *feel* the water in his blood. And I knew I could manipulate it if I tried, and I... froze it."

Holly blinked. Dylan had... frozen Merlin's blood. There was no way he survived that— Merlin was dead. She wanted to ask but thought better of it.

"After that, I dove in after you and dragged you to shore, but you weren't breathing, and I couldn't feel a pulse. So I did chest compressions."

Tears trickled down his face.

Holly rubbed her aching chest.

"I was worried you wouldn't—" Dylan's voice cracked. "We've already lost so many friends and I just couldn't lose you too. I—"

Grabbing either side of his face, Holly pulled his lips to hers, hoping the action would be enough to keep him from spiraling any further. His breath hitched. Then she felt his hands grab her wrists, but he didn't push her away. The rushing of the waterfall and the ambient sounds of the forest faded to nothing as Holly kissed him. After everything with Nathan, she almost expected to feel something akin to guilt, but it was noticeably absent as Dylan returned the kiss. His jaw was coated in a small layer of stubble under her fingers. It created a prickling sensation that wasn't altogether unpleasant even as her hands moved to his hair. His hair, which was feather soft as she tangled her fingers in it, rivulets of water trailing down her arm. The tension in Dylan's body eased as his hands slid down her arms and wrapped around her waist. He tugged her closer, deepening the kiss.

She hadn't planned on kissing Dylan, but she found she couldn't bring herself to regret it. Besides, it was working, and, as she pulled away, she could feel the way they both seemed to hesitate breaking it off.

"I'm right here," she told him, her voice breathless. "I'm okay. We're okay."

Dylan nodded.

Holly forced herself to lean back, their situation slamming back into her like a truck. Her gaze shifted toward the direction they had run from. "We should get moving."

Dylan stood, offering her his hand. She took it, her legs protesting as she stood. Water dripped from her hair, making her shiver. Raising her powers to the surface of her skin, she heard the water evaporating as the heat of her skin turned it to steam. Dylan gave her a look of dismay and shook his head, spraying her with water. The drops hissed as they met her skin.

Finished acting like a wet dog, he looked around and asked, "Which way? We don't exactly have a predetermined destination."

A mirthless laugh bubbled up her throat before she said, "Whichever direction will take us as far away from that place as possible."

Huffing a laugh, Dylan picked a direction and started walking. "Sounds good to me."

They weren't walking for long when they heard the sounds of pursuit. They shared a look, they were in no shape to start running. Dylan had brought her back from the brink of death not too long ago, but it seemed as though they had no choice.

Adrenaline surged through her system as the sounds got closer. Knowing Dylan would follow her lead, she took off through the forest, leaving the soft rumbling of the waterfall far behind them. Fallen branches and sharp rocks stung her bare feet as they sprinted through the forest, needles from the trees softened the sound of their footsteps as they ran.

As the trees started to thin, Holly careened to a stop at the edge of a road. There was no sign of cars on it, but she had no idea which direction to go.

Dylan skidded to a halt beside her.

"Which way do we go?" Holly asked him.

"I don't know. Let's just do what we did before—pick a direction and run," Dylan replied. He paused then pointed to the left. "That way. But we should cross the road first and follow it from the other side."

Holly nodded and checked both ways before charging across the road after Dylan. Once on the other side, they walked a bit further into the brush before they began running again. The sounds of pursuit grew distant the further they ran.

No cars passed them as they ran. Both of them panted heavily, exhaustion wearing on their bones. They slowed to a walk to stretch out their remaining energy. It was a wonder neither of them had tripped over anything in their haste to get away. After another few minutes of walking, they decided to stop and rest. Dylan wandered off in search of food as Holly settled next to a tree and rested her head against the trunk. She didn't let herself drift off to sleep—not after what had happened at the lake.

Dylan returned a few minutes later with some apples. Holly raised a skeptical eyebrow.

"I didn't steal them if that's what you're wondering," Dylan told her.

"I believe you." Holly shrugged. She wasn't sure there would be anybody living this far into the redwood forest.

He sat next to her and handed her an apple. She took a bite and groaned in delight. Dylan chuckled softly beside her and took a bite of his own apple. They finished eating in silence. Starlight fell in streams through the needles of the trees above them. The forest was peaceful and quiet in the evening hours.

They rested there for another moment before deciding to keep moving. As they were walking, Holly heard the sudden sound of a snapping branch behind them. Dylan froze, sharing a swift glance with her. She turned her head but didn't see anything, and was about to turn back when she heard the cocking of a gun. Panicked, she grabbed Dylan's wrist and yanked him down as the stun gun went off. Electric sparks bounced off the tree in the place where Dylan had been seconds before.

Holly searched for the shooter, spotting him after a moment and throwing a ball of fire the size of a baseball at the bush he was hiding behind. The flames came to life instantly, licking the air with their hunger for oxygen. The man shouted, jumping away from the burning bush—his shout no doubt alerting others to their location, not to mention the sudden light of her fire.

Not waiting for them to arrive, Dylan grabbed her hand as they darted out of the forest and onto the road. Throwing caution to the wind, Holly followed Dylan as he sprinted their feet pounding against the hot asphalt. Luck was on their side as there were no cars on the road as they ran, and yet it eluded them for that same reason. Holly was surprised to see the first rays of sunlight bringing life back to the world.

People chased after them on either side of the road, but they didn't stop running even as stun guns were fired after them—the shots leaving sparkling lightning in their wake. The sound of multiple car engines hummed around a bend in the road. Dylan pulled her closer to the right side of the road without breaking pace. Her hair flew in her face, still a bit damp from her ill-fated swim in the lake, as the first car sped past them, followed closely by a long line of military deployment trucks.

Holly almost stopped to flag down one of the drivers, but caught sight of movement in the trees to her right and pushed herself to run faster. In the distance, she heard the squealing of car tires. Shouts sounded behind her, but she didn't want to stop—couldn't. Dylan spared a glance behind them, his eyes widening at whatever he saw before he pulled her to a stop next to him. Holly looked at him, opening her mouth to tell him they shouldn't stop, but no sound came out as her mind recognized the voices shouting after them.

She spun around and stared at the men shouting their names. Her eyes met Dylan's then shifted back at the two men who had to have been the ones leading the military raids on the G.H.O.S.T. safehouses. The Walker brothers stood next to General Falcon. A laugh burst from her lips a moment before Holly was racing toward them and tackling Dean in a hug.

"You found us!" She pulled back, lightly smacking his arm as Dylan came to a halt next to her. "Took you long enough."

Dean grasped Dylan's hand, pulling him into a hug just as Shawn said, "We have company."

Chapter 28

Dozens of G.H.O.S.T. rebels had surrounded them, walking out of the woods on every side of the group. Holly spotted Pelican, Mallard, Osprey, and Starling among them. Raven stepped out onto the road ahead of them all.

"Well, if it isn't General Falcon," Raven smirked, her hands hanging loosely at her sides.

"Raven," the General growled.

"You have something of mine," she told him.

"I don't see anything of yours here."

At some point during the exchange, Dean and Shawn had positioned themselves between the rebels and the teenagers. From the corner of her eye, she noticed Dylan's hands clenched tightly at his side. In her head, she replayed the day Raven had mercilessly shot Kestrel in the head. Blood had spread over the concrete floor, staining it as much as it had her memory.

Raven snarled, bringing Holly back to the present, and replied, "Give me the boy and the girl, and I'll consider letting you and your men leave here alive."

General Falcon didn't so much as blink, her words bouncing off him like rain on an umbrella. "These kids aren't going anywhere with you. They're coming back with us."

"You and what army?" Raven scoffed, a smirk firmly pressed on her face as she barked out a laugh. "There's no one here for you to order around, Hunter. You're outnumbered."

As she spoke, Holly watched as all the soldiers from the deployment trucks surrounded the rebels—effectively turning the odds in their favor. Raven looked around her, the smirk ever persistently stuck to her face.

"Is that the best you've got?" Raven was completely unfazed as she signaled to her rebels.

The surrounded rebels replaced their stun guns for regular ones and turned to attack the soldiers around them. General Falcon unholstered a gun of his own, a knife appearing in his hand as he stalked toward Raven. Holly shifted her attention as a few of the rebels charged at the Walker brothers. Shawn drew his gun and shot them down in rapid succession. They went down quickly, some of them shouting in pain, but were soon replaced by others.

"You two stay out of the fight as best you can," Dean ordered.

The brothers joined in the frenzy. Dylan seemed content following Dean's order, and Holly couldn't have agreed more—she was exhausted—but she had to give them something to remember her by. Had to get even for what they had put her and her friends through.

Scanning the nearby forest, Holly searched for a stick large enough to use as a makeshift bo staff. After finding one, she ran to grab it before returning to the battle.

During her training, Holly had gotten remarkably good at aiming for a specific target. So, as she scanned the mass of rebels and soldiers, she picked out a few targets and sent a couple of blazing fireballs their way. At first it seemed that nobody but her victims cared, until Pelican was charging at her from amongst his peers. He didn't get within ten feet of her before blood spurted from his thigh.

"I thought I told you to stay out of it," Dean yelled at her.

He didn't get to hear a response as Osprey came up behind him, the knife in his hand aimed at Dean's neck. But then Shawn was stepping between Dean and the knife. Dean turned around just as the knife sunk into Shawn's shoulder and fired multiple shots at Osprey. Shawn cried out in pain. One of Dean's bullets struck Osprey in the arm as he pulled the knife out and backed away.

Holly turned her attention away and threw a fireball at a rebel who had taken that moment to aim her gun at Dean's back. Dean had taken a handkerchief from his pocket and tied it as best he could around Shawn's wound as Holly used her impromptu bo staff and powers to keep rebels from attacking the brothers. Dylan had picked up Shawn's discarded gun and was firing shots off at any rebel who Holly couldn't get to with surprising accuracy.

Sweat began to dampen her brow when she heard someone shout, "General Falcon is down! Retreat!"

"Down? What does that mean?" Holly looked to Dean for an answer.

Dean looked up from caring for his brother and caught Holly's eye. Concern filled his gaze as he briskly lifted Shawn to his feet and started helping him back to the military convoy. Holly didn't want to think about what that meant.

The men at the back of the retreat held off the rebels as the group made their way to where they had parked the trucks. Dean helped Shawn into the backseat of the car, his hand leaving a smear of blood on the door.

"Holly," Dean called to her over his shoulder. Her gaze met his as he tossed her the keys to the car, slid in next to his brother, and said, "You're driving."

Holly blinked, then nodded. Dylan climbed into the backseat to help Dean with Shawn—who was looking pale from the blood loss. As he did, Holly took one more look behind them. Through the movement of soldiers, she saw the rebels disappearing into the forest. Turning back to the task at hand, Holly opened the driver's side door and got in, pressing the key against the start panel and listened to the electric engine thrum to life and the car lift off the road enough to hover nearly six inches above the asphalt, the sound echoed by the trucks behind them. In one fluid motion, she strapped on her seatbelt and put the car in drive, cranking the wheel as far as it could go to the left. Once the u-turn was complete, she was speeding down the road. The rebels were gone when they reached the sight of the battle, but the bodies weren't.

"Slow down, Holly," Dean told her, a second after she pressed her foot against the break.

Putting the car into park, Holly climbed out and surveyed the scene. Her breath caught in her throat at the gruesome sight. Bloodied corpses littered the ground, the viscous liquid oozing out in small streams that absorbed the sunlight of dawn. Dylan stayed in the car with the Walker brothers while Holly stood silent like a solemn statue, one foot still in the car as she watched soldiers carry the bodies to one of the trucks and load them on. As she stood there, she caught a glimpse of General Falcon's body being loaded onto a truck. Holly shook her head in disbelief. General Falcon couldn't be dead. He couldn't be— what about Leo, he had to be waiting for his dad to return. Once the road had cleared, Holly settled back into the driver's seat and switched gears, pulling away from the battle sight.

"How long was it?" Dylan broke the thick silence that filled the car.

"Too long," Dean replied. "It's been three months."

Holly cast a glance at him in the rearview mirror, clenching her jaw to keep it from dropping. Their nineteenth birthdays had come and gone, and they hadn't even known.

The rest of the drive was spent in a tense silence, filled only with Shawn's rasping, shallow breaths. Before she knew it, she was pulling up to the emergency room. Dean sent Dylan inside to get help while he and Holly helped Shawn out of the car. It was nearly impossible for her to help him keep his brother standing upright with how heavy he was. It didn't help that they both had several inches on her. Some nurses and doctors came out soon after their arrival, taking the weight from her shoulders.

Dean told a nurse that he wanted both Holly and Dylan checked out as well. Holly protested, but Dean didn't give her any room to object so she allowed a nurse to lead her away for some tests.

Holly sat patiently on the hospital bed, waiting for the results of her tests. They weren't anything special, just a standard patient assessment. After a few minutes of waiting, a doctor came in to give her a check-up. Dean walked in behind him, taking a seat next to the door.

"Miss Carnell," the doctor started. "You seem to be in almost perfect health. There's some bruising on your chest and ribs, and you're a bit malnourished, but it's nothing a few good meals and plenty of water can't help. We're going to keep you here for the time being just to be sure and give you some fluids and ice for the bruises, but after that, you're home-free. Be sure to continue putting ice on the bruises once you get home."

"Thank you, doctor," Holly said.

The doctor smiled at her and left, passing a nurse on his way out of the room. The nurse came in and attached an IV line to Holly's arm.

"You're free to walk around," the nurse told her as she then strapped an ice pack over her chest. "When the bag gets empty click the green button on your admittance band and I'll come remove the IV."

Holly nodded her thanks as the nurse left then followed Dean into the hallway, her bag of fluids hanging from a rolling stand that she rolled out the door behind her. Almost immediately she got tackled, her vision filled with a mass of curly black hair. Through the mess of curls, she saw Zac and Jay standing a few feet away. Dean stood a few feet from them. The smile on his face told Holly all she needed to know about how her friends knew she was there. Holly extracted herself from Naomi's hug, nodding her thanks to the Major.

"Holly, I'm so glad you're back. We missed you so much," Naomi said, her typically braided hair bouncing around her head in a halo of curls. She said it so fast that Holly could barely keep up with the words.

"You took out your braids," she said.

Naomi reached up to touch her curls. "Oh, this? I'll tell you about it later when we get some alone time."

Holly smiled as her best friend winked at her, her sea blue eyes darting in Zac's direction before returning. "So, how have you guys been?"

"How have we been?" Jay asked, his blue eyes filled with exasperation.

"The real question is how are *you*, Holly?" Zac said, shooting Jay a look.

"You were gone for way too long," Naomi stated, bouncing on the balls of her feet as though restraining herself from crushing Holly in another hug.

"We didn't know where you were, and Major Walker wouldn't tell us anything other than 'we're working on it,'," Jay told her, his Dean imitation scarily accurate.

"I'm fine guys," Holly insisted. "Seriously."

Her friends looked skeptical—Jay eyed the IV line connected to her arm, but they didn't push her.

"Holly," Dean spoke from behind her. She turned to face him.

"Yeah?" She paused, taking in the look on his face. "You want to debrief me."

Dean nodded. Bidding farewell to her friends, Holly told them to wait for her and followed Dean into a room where Dylan was sitting on the bed with his arm also hooked up to an IV. Dean motioned for Holly to sit. She sat on the end of the bed and waited as he closed the door.

"Okay," Dean said at last. "Tell me everything that happened."

Dean leaned back in his chair and sighed. Holly could see thoughts racing through his mind as they sat there in silence for a moment or two. She let Dylan tell Dean most of what they had gone through, her mind kept going back to their escape. It did that often, every time she wanted to move forward, her memories wouldn't let her. They wouldn't let her forget. Wouldn't let her move on.

Holly was dragged back from her thoughts as Dylan stopped talking. Dean shifted his position, with his elbows resting on his knees, his churning thoughts visible in his green eyes.

"That's a lot of information," Dean told them. "Was there anything you left out?"

"I don't think so," Dylan replied.

Dean went silent again, his mind still seeming to try and catch up with his racing thoughts.

"Dean?" Holly asked quietly.

"Hmm?" Dean looked up at her.

"Has someone called Leo yet? He needs to know."

"No, not yet."

"I can do it," she offered, the words out of her mouth before she could stop them. She did not want to be the one to break the news, but she felt like it was her fault the General had died. He had been there to rescue her after all.

Dean gave her an appreciative look as he pushed himself to his feet. Holly watched him go, not wanting to figure out how to call Leo quite yet.

As the door closed behind Dean, she said, "How am I supposed to tell him? I saw Karen's body, Dylan. His dad died protecting us, and we couldn't do anything. He already lost his best friend, and now I have to tell him that because of me he's lost his girlfriend and his dad too?"

What have I done? She didn't say. Didn't want to bring the words to life by putting them out into the world.

Holly squeezed her eyes shut and sighed.

"You'll just have to tell him, princess. It might take you a while to get him to realize you're serious, but it'll be alright."

"You're right." She blew out another breath. "Of course, you're right."

She glanced over at him as he gave her an encouraging smile.

Rather than trying to return the smile—knowing she wouldn't be able to even if she tried—she stood and left the room, the wheels of her IV stand rattling against the floor. Walking over to the hospital phone, Holly reached for the phone and paused, unsure what number to put in. It wasn't like she could look up his number, and she didn't have it memorized either.

"Yo, Lady Waffles!" came a shout from down the hall. "You're alive!"

Holly's gaze darted to where Leo was walking down the hall.

"Leo? What are you doing here?" she asked as he walked up to her.

He shrugged. "Dunno. Major Walker called and said to come here. He didn't say anything about getting you back, though."

"Yeah, they found Dylan and I a few hours ago," Holly responded, her throat tight. This was going to be so much harder than she expected. She wasn't sure if she could do it.

Leo tilted his head. "You and Dylan? What about the others? Apollo, Jacob, and... Karen."

"Leo—" Her voice cut off, as she choked on the words. Clearing her throat, she decided to just blurt it out. "She's dead, Apollo too."

"Oh." Leo's face fell. Any joy he had felt at seeing her again gone in an instant. His eyes went unfocused as he seemed to be processing the information.

"There's one more thing," she told him, not wanting to let this drag out any longer than it was. "Your father, he—when he came to rescue us he..."

Leo swayed on his feet, stumbling backward until his back hit the wall and he slid to the floor. His blue eyes were rimmed with red despite the lack of tears staining his cheeks. Those blue eyes, the same shade as his father's. The only notion Holly got that told her he was still alive was a slow blink.

"He's dead too, isn't he?" Leo said numbly, dragging his eyes to her face to gauge her reaction.

She nodded.

Shifting his eyes to the wall across from him, Leo's gaze went blank once again. He didn't move for a while after that. It was as though he had been turned to stone but for the occasional blink. Holly sat down next to him and, drawing her legs up to her chest, rested her head on her knees. Leo stood abruptly a moment later and chucked something at the wall. Startled, Holly looked up. Her eyes darted between Leo and the object he had thrown. She stood and walked over to them, kneeling so she could pick up the dog tags she had seen him wearing more often than not. As she inspected them, she saw the name *Hunter Falcon* inscribed on one and *Leo Falcon* on the other.

Holly peered over at her friend. He was breathing heavily and staring at the floor, his fists clenched tightly at his sides. Standing, Holly put herself in front of him. Grabbing his hand, she peeled his fingers back and planted the tags in his palm before curling his fingers around them. Her hands clasped over his.

"I'm sorry, Leo. This was my fault. They would both still be alive if it weren't for me," Holly whispered to him, her hands dropping to her sides. "I'm sorry."

As she moved to leave, Leo's other hand grasped hers. She turned to him, green eyes meeting hazel—no... blue. Leo's eyes were blue as he met her gaze. Tears streamed from his angry eyes.

"Don't," he murmured. "I've lost enough today. Don't make me lose another friend. None of this is your fault, Holly. G.H.O.S.T. They're the ones who killed them. Those *rebels* are the ones responsible for Karen's death—my dad's death. Kevin's death. Don't let them take you too."

A tear escaped Holly's eye as she stood there looking at her friend. She squeezed his hand.

"I'm right here, Leo, and I'm not going anywhere."

Leo gave her a grim smile and released her hand, then he turned and walked over to the elevator, waving farewell to her over his shoulder.

Chapter 29

Dean was sitting next to Shawn's bed when Holly finally found him. Shaw was still out cold from the sedatives, his face still pale from blood loss. He was lucky the knife hadn't penetrated his heart. Holly walked in and took a seat next to Dean.

"Any word on Jacob?" Holly implored, her fingers toying with the bandage wrapped over the spot her IV had been removed from moments earlier.

"We've tried putting out word that we want to talk with G.H.O.S.T., but their only response was vague," Dean replied solemnly. Dark circles hung heavily under his eyes.

"Can I hear it?"

He sighed, dragging a hand through his already tussled hair. "Sure. It wasn't very long, only one line. '*The crow caws at noon.*'"

"Cryptic," Holly said bitterly. "Why would they even respond to you anyway?"

Dean shrugged. "To taunt us maybe."

His eyes glazed over as his thoughts moved elsewhere. Holly joined him in the silence, listening to the steady beeping from the heart monitor.

When it became too much, she broke the silence and asked, "How's he doing?"

"It's not his best day," Dean answered. "But he'll live. The doctor said it might take a while for him to fully recover, but he'll be back on his feet in no time. The knife only just missed the nearby artery, he's lucky he didn't bleed out before we got here."

Holly nodded and stood. She examined the door when she heard a commotion in the hall. People were shouting and she could hear the sound of many pairs of shoes running. They had only been there for a few hours and something was already going wrong. Then again, they were at a hospital, it could be completely unrelated to her presence there. At least, that's what she kept telling herself, but she couldn't shake the uneasy feeling in her gut that something was wrong.

Rushing out the door, she followed the source of the commotion. Nurses crowded around someone on the floor. Blood was pooling around them as Holly got closer. She caught a glimpse of an eerily familiar white sneaker, but her view was obstructed almost immediately after she noticed it.

Dylan was kneeling on the ground nearby, leaning close to the person's face, but she still couldn't catch a glimpse of whoever it was. Her heart pounded anxiously as she raised herself to her tiptoes trying to see who it was. Finally, someone moved out of the way and she caught sight of Jay's face just before his eyes glazed over. Holly stared at his brown eyes, waiting for them to close, to shift over to her as he told her one of his stupid historic facts or ask her when their next math test was. But he didn't move. His eyes continued to stare unblinkingly at nothing.

Buzzing filled Holly's ears as she once again watched one of her loved ones lose their lives. She didn't hear anything over the sound in her head, but she stared blankly as one of the doctors gathered around Jay shook his head and called a time of death.

Holly took a step backward. That decayed spot in her heart grew as her mind started to fully understand that Jay wasn't coming back. That he wasn't going to crack a joke with Zac or argue with Naomi again. He wasn't going to spout off random facts about history that nobody cared to learn about on their own. He was gone.

Her breaths were getting increasingly fast. She took another step backward and bumped into someone. Stopping, she turned to peer up at Dean. He had a grim expression on his face. She watched as he walked over and helped Dylan to his feet. Dean guided him away and into an empty room.

Breaking from her trance, Holly followed behind them, leaving the nurses to take care of Jay's body. Dylan had a haunted look on his face when she entered the room.

Dean looked over at her as she walked in.

"Holly," he said calmly. "I'm going to go get a nurse. Will you help him clean up?"

"Yeah," she replied.

Nodding, Dean walked out of the room, leaving her to make her way over to Dylan. He was covered in blood, but she wasn't sure if any of it was his or if it was all Jay's. She scanned the room until she spotted a washrag by the sink in the bathroom. Gentle as a cloud, she guided him over to the sink and turned on the faucet. She grabbed the rag and soaked it in the warm water.

Holly had Dylan sit on the edge of the bathtub while she scrubbed at the blood caked on his face. Dylan didn't say a word as she washed it away. She tried being as gentle as she could but pulled back when he winced. Leaning closer, she inspected a cut on his collarbone. Holly carefully dabbed the area around the cut with the cloth.

He didn't resist as she pulled his blood-soaked shirt over his head so she could continue washing away the blood. Dylan leaned his head against her shoulder. She pulled his head closer to her, her fingers buried in his hair. Looking down, she gasped as she caught a glimpse of scars criss crossed over the entirety of his back. She reached out and tenderly touched one of them, pulling back when a muscle in his back twitched under her touch. Some of the scars were the vibrant pink of newly healed wounds, the vivid color contrasting the pale white scars that told of older injuries.

Hesitantly, she pulled out of the embrace and crouched in front of him to continue cleaning the blood from his chest. She wanted to ask about the scars, but didn't dare. He would tell her when he was ready—if he even wanted to talk about them.

Dean came back with a nurse just as Holly had finished wiping off the blood. The washrag dripped red droplets into the bathtub as she set it down. She led Dylan over to the bed and helped him settle onto it. Walking over to where Dean stood, she leaned against the wall next to him while the nurse dressed and bandaged the gash on Dylan's collarbone.

"Did he say anything?" Dean asked her in a hushed tone.

"Nothing." She didn't say anything else until the nurse left. "Did anyone see what happened?"

"No," Dean replied, then nodded his head in Dylan's direction. "Talk to him. He needs you right now."

Holly straightened and slowly walked over to the bed. Dylan's gaze was distant when he looked up at her. Her heart twisted as she took in how broken he seemed in that moment. She couldn't even offer him a comforting smile.

The door clicked shut as Dean left.

Standing in front of Dylan, she reached for one of his hands and squeezed it.

"Dylan?"

When he didn't respond, she squeezed again before releasing his hand and cupping his face in her hands. His eyes closed as tears dripped from their depths and rolled slowly over her thumbs. One of his hands reached up and grabbed her wrist, tugging her toward the bed in a silent request for her to sit—one she acquiesced to.

Opening his eyes, Dylan stared at the hand he held, tracing lines on her palm as he started speaking. "I was in my room, lying on the bed. The doctor told me to get some sleep before a nurse would come to take out the IV. Someone came in, but I didn't hear them at first. I only noticed their presence when I felt something sharp pressing against my collarbone." He rubbed the spot next to the bandage on his chest. "When I opened my eyes, I saw one of the rebels standing over my bed, wearing one of those ridiculous bird masks. His hand was shaking as she tried to push the knife down, but something was stopping him."

His voice cut off and he squeezed his eyes shut.

Holly felt her chest tighten.

Clearing his throat, he continued, "I sat up and saw Jay gripping the rebel's wrist, stopping him from… finishing what he had come to do. The rebel twisted out of his grip and ran out of the room. Jay didn't even hesitate to run after him."

Dylan took a shaky breath, about to go on when Holly said, "And the rebel killed him."

He nodded.

"Jay saw who it was, didn't he?" she asked as a single tear trailed down her cheek.

Nodding again, Dylan looked over at her. Tears shimmered in his blue eyes, turning them silver.

"He told me who it was," Dylan told her, his gaze going back to where his hands continued to fidget with her hand. "He had managed to grab the mask from the rebel's face. It was in his hand when I reached him. Holly, it was Jacob."

Time stopped in its tracks.

Jacob.

Jacob had tried to kill Dylan.

Jacob, who she hadn't seen once since his—supposed—abduction.

The message Dean had relayed to her played through Holly's mind as her eyes darted to the clock on the wall.

The crow caws at noon.

It hadn't been more than thirty minutes since she had seen Jay's body in the hall. Everything clicked into place in her mind. The message hadn't been as cryptic as it had sounded.

"Jacob is Crow," she muttered under her breath.

"What?" Dylan snapped up his head and stared at her. "What did you just say?"

Holly met his gaze. "Dean told me they had received a message from G.H.O.S.T., '*The crow caws at noon,*'" she clarified. "It was noon when you were attacked."

"Jacob is Crow," Dylan breathed.

Holly gasped as something else clicked.

"Raven!" she exclaimed. "She has to be Jacob's sister. They have the *exact* same shade of hair."

Dylan's eyes widened. "You're right. How did we not realize?"

Holly shook her head and moved to stand. Dylan tightened his grip on her hand. She looked at him.

"Don't go," he pleaded.

Holly felt a crack in her chest at the pain in his voice, the *fear* in it. She could wait to tell Dean. For now, her friend needed her. Scooting backward on the bed, she laid down, patting the spot beside her. Dylan laid down next to her.

Wrapping her arm around his shoulders as he rested his head on her shoulder, she started playing with his hair, and he laid an arm over her stomach.

"Holly," he muttered. "Will you sing that lullaby for me?"

Holly felt her cheeks flush. "You heard that?"

"Please?"

"Okay," she relented.

Dylan's breathing slowed as she sang softly. Craning her neck, Holly saw that he had fallen asleep. Leaning back on the bed, she closed her eyes. It was nice to just lay there, somewhere between wakefulness and sleep, running her fingers through Dylan's silky black hair while she kept humming the tune of the lullaby. She wasn't sure what they were to each other anymore, but she didn't want to worry about that right now. Right now, she just wanted to enjoy the peaceful moment. There hadn't been enough of those to go around lately—not for her at least.

Holly peeked open an eye as she heard the door open. Dean stood frozen in the doorway. He looked like he was about to leave when he saw them, but Holly opened her eyes fully and motioned him in with her free hand. Dylan buried his face deeper into her shoulder and tightened his grip on her waist as Dean quietly walked over to the bed and sat in the chair next to it.

Leaning forward—hands clasped together in front of him—Dean asked, "Did he tell you anything before he fell asleep?"

"Yes. I know what the message meant. While we were in the compound, we heard a lot about this higher-up called Crow. In the message they said the *crow* caws at noon," Holly replied softly. "Dylan told me that—before he... died—Jay recognized the person who had attacked Dylan."

"I assume this person was part of G.H.O.S.T. and wearing a bird mask to hide their identity," Dean interrupted.

"Hush!" Holly hissed at him, checking on Dylan, who was still sound asleep. "Yes, he was a rebel and he wore one of the masks. Dylan didn't see who it was, but he said Jay had the mask in his hand when he found him."

Holly paused.

"Are you going to keep me in suspense or are you going to tell me who it was?" Dean asked.

"I will if you stop interrupting me. Now be quiet."

"Fine," Dean huffed, leaning back in his chair and crossing his arms.

"It was Jacob. And, before you interrupt me again," she said as Dean opened his mouth to do just that. "You remember Raven?"

Dean nodded. "How could I forget?"

They both knew she had likely been the one to kill the General.

"I met her at the compound—hideout, whatever you want to call it—where they were keeping us. Something about her seemed familiar to me, I just couldn't place what it was, until now. Her hair is the same shade as Jacob's. I think she's his sister. It's not just the hair either, they're so similar in their mannerisms, and I heard one of the rebels saying something about Crow being Raven's brother."

Dean waited for her to say more, but when she didn't, he started speaking. "It makes sense. You're probably right. It also makes sense as to why we haven't been able to find him."

"There's one other thing that's been bothering me," Holly said. "If Jacob has been a high-ranking member of G.H.O.S.T. this entire time, then why did he fight so hard against them when they were taking Dylan and the others?"

"I don't know, Holly," Dean replied, running his fingers through his hair. "It could be that someone moved up their timetable and he wasn't happy about it, or he was just putting up an act to make it seem like he was fighting them."

"To throw me off," Holly finished.

"Exactly, but there could be a million different explanations and the only person who can tell us the truth is Jacob."

Dylan stirred but didn't wake up. Holly glanced at him and then back at Dean.

"I'll leave you alone now," Dean said, his eyes leaving hers as he stood. "You have been through a lot. I've posted two corporals outside the room. Please don't run off anywhere."

Holly nodded and watched him leave. She caught a glimpse of said corporals before the door clicked shut. Turning her attention back to running her fingers through Dylan's hair, she leaned back against the bed and started humming the lullaby again hoping she would be able to sleep.

Chapter 30

Dylan was still sleeping when Holly woke to the silence of the hospital room, her heart pounding from her most recent nightmare. She sighed. Her dreams had gotten better, or so she had thought. Someone—probably Dean—had found her phone where she had left it in her car and had set it on the table next to the bed. Holly reached her arm over to it. Stretching as far as she could without disturbing Dylan, she finally grabbed it and held it up in front of her. The screen lit up as she turned it on. She had texts from Naomi, Zac, Kelly, and an unknown number.

Holly checked the messages from Naomi and Zac first. They were short messages—dating back to right after her abduction—asking where she was and why she wasn't answering the phone. Naomi had called multiple times, leaving a voicemail reminding her that it was graduation day and she would be late. The most recent ones were from the previous day saying they had to leave and that they would see her soon.

Kelly's message was longer than theirs, but it was something Holly knew she needed to read;

Holly, I thought you would like to know

that I contacted Kevin's and Sora's

families. I know you might not see this

for a long while, or maybe not at all,

but I needed to text you anyway.

The Walker brothers contacted

General Falcon. They've been looking

for you guys everywhere they can. They

Already raided seven G.H.O.S.T.

hideouts, but you weren't there.

I was invited to Kevin's funeral,

Sora's too, and I plan on going if I can.

I don't think the Walker brothers have

slept in days. They haven't left the house

much other than to go on the raids.

I'm really worried about you guys,

but I know they're going to find you.

Anyways, I'll, uh, talk later.

Hopefully.

Holly was glad Kelly had contacted Sora's parents. She knew she would have told Kevin's parents, but it was really kind of her to have reached out to Sora's.

Once she finished reading Kelly's message, Holly opened the message from the unknown number. It was dated to yesterday. Right after her escape with Dylan.

I will see you again soon, Dolphin.

Holly immediately blocked the number. Only one person called her that, and she had no inclination to speak to him. He had likely already ditched the phone anyway.

After she blocked the number, she took a deep breath as the events from yesterday slammed into her like a ton of bricks. Someone would have to notify Jay's mom.

As the thought crossed her mind, a soft knock came at the door. Carefully extricating herself from Dylan's arm that was still wrapped around her waist, she stood and walked to the door where the hospital chaplain was waiting patiently in the hallway. Holly left the room, closing the door softly behind herself. The two corporals Dean had assigned to her and Dylan stood guard outside the door—just like he had said. Neither of them moved as Holly stepped away from the room to see what the chaplain wanted.

"Major Walker mentioned that you knew the boy who was killed yesterday," the chaplain said, his voice as tender as it had been the day he had talked to her about the decision for Dustin's body. "Would you happen to have a number I could call for his next of kin?"

Nodding, Holly gave him Jay's name and showed him the number for Jay's mom she had saved in her phone from sophomore year of high school. She watched as, after thanking her, the chaplain went over to the hospital phone and made what was going to be the most devastating call for Mrs. Featherstone. Her feet remained planted in place as her eyes bore holes into the back of his head. It killed her that Jay's mom would have to deal with this. Her divorce had been messy and had left her needing to work two jobs just to earn enough money for rent. And then there was Jay's little sister. Natalie was going to be heartbroken when she found out her big brother was never coming home.

She was still standing there when the chaplain turned and motioned her over to ask if she knew who Jay's girlfriend was. Holly gave him a look of confusion. *When did Jay get a girlfriend?*

The chaplain said something softly into the phone, waited a few seconds, then elaborated, "His mother says her name is Artemis."

Holly blinked. "Oh. Yeah, I have her number too. Would you mind if I called her? I have something else I need to talk to her about."

Giving her a soft, pity-filled, smile, the chaplain nodded then returned to the conversation with Jay's mom.

Letting out a shuddering sigh, Holly wondered if she had just made a monumental mistake. Could she really be the bearer of bad news like this again? She didn't know if she wanted to find out how Artemis would react to this news. She hadn't even known Jay had gathered up the courage to ask Artemis out—then again, it was entirely possible that Artemis had been the one to initiate things.

Not letting herself get psyched out, Holly lifted her phone and clicked on the call button of Artemis' contact.

Artemis picked up on the second ring.

"Sup, Holly," Artemis said, her tone so casual Holly could almost imagine she wasn't calling to tell her that her brother and her boyfriend had been killed. "Heard you and Dylan are back. You guys doing okay?"

"We're fine," Holly replied softly. She cleared her throat. "Listen, Artemis, do you have a second to talk?"

"Yeah, what's up?"

"This has got to be the worst day in history," Holly muttered to herself. Then, to Artemis, she said, "You might want to sit down for this." She waited until Artemis gave her the all-clear before continuing, "I don't know if Dean or Shawn have said anything to you about the whole rescue thing, but I just wanted—*needed* to tell you that... Apollo is gone. I-I'm so sorry. He's dead. I couldn't save him and now..."

Holly trailed off, nearly choking on the words as she tried to get them out. On the other end of the phone, Artemis made a choking sound.

Hating herself for the pain she was about to cause, she said, "There's something else. I hate to dump this on you all at once, but I need to just get it over with. Jay is–he got killed. Yesterday."

Unable to bear listening to the gut-wrenching screams coming from the other side of the phone, Holly hung up and nearly chucked her phone at the floor. It shouldn't be like this. Life shouldn't be filled with this much death. Not like this. Death was a part of life, but this wasn't a fatal car crash or a terminal illness. This was intentional. And she hated that the only way she could think to get justice was starting to look more and more like revenge.

She felt like a bad luck charm. Everyone she loved seemed to be dropping like flies around her. And there was nothing she could do about it.

Glancing at the time on her phone, she realized just how early it was. Eight in the morning. Turning toward the window at the far end of the hall, she walked over to it and looked out. It was a lovely morning to what would most likely be a wonderful day for many people. Holly knew she wouldn't be one of those people—already wasn't. She had gone through so much in the past few months that she wasn't sure she even knew what normal was anymore. Maybe all this—the fighting and the deaths—was her new normal.

Birds chirped outside the window. Their song was so peaceful it made her want to scream. Her eyes found the offending birds and she felt her chest tighten. They were starlings. Images of Apollo's unseeing brown eyes flashed across her mind's eye. Shaking them away, she doubted she would ever think of birds the same after what had happened with G.H.O.S.T.

Turning away from the window, she returned to the room where she had left Dylan, leaving the sound of the chirping starlings behind her. The corporals hadn't moved a muscle as she approached the room. Neither of them so much as glanced at her as she reached for the handle—it was kind of creepy how statuesque they were just standing there staring blankly into space.

Dylan stirred as she opened the door, sitting up and yawning. His body tensed as he realized he was alone, his gaze darted around the room until it came to a stop at the door where she stood, hovering in that space between the room and the hallway. She watched him visibly relax at the sight of her standing there.

"Would you like some food?" she asked, not quite ready to be stuck in another small room. Trying to lighten the mood, she added, "I might consider trying to find you a shirt, but maybe not."

The corner of his mouth twitched but couldn't quite lift into a smile—so much for that. "I wouldn't mind if you didn't find me one, but I'm not sure anyone else would share your sentiment."

Chapter 31

T he food was easy to find, the shirt, on the other hand, proved to be elusive. One of the corporals Dean had assigned followed her everywhere as she tried asking a few nurses, but they were all too busy to give her a full response. Eventually, she told her enormous shadow— whose name tag read *Penhallow*—she was going home. Taking a taxi to get there, she grabbed a few things from Dylan's suitcase and her closet before returning to the hospital. None of her friends had been there, or at least upstairs— something she was grateful for. It was a blessing to just have the house to herself. Aside from her military bodyguard. She didn't think she could face the disappointment or pity in her friends' faces—not yet, at least. Maybe not ever.

Dylan was standing by the window when Holly walked into the room. He turned around when she opened the door, backpack slung over one shoulder. She eyed the scars on his back, opening her mouth to ask about them before deciding not to and closing it again. Making her way over to him, she handed him the clothes she had brought for him.

"I couldn't find a shirt for you here so I went home to grab some things," she told him.

"Thanks, princess," Dylan said, accepting the clothes from her.

"Will you stop calling me that?"

"Hmm." He seemed like he was considering it, his blue eyes glinting in the harsh white light of the hospital light above them. "No."

Holly huffed and stalked over to the chair and sat down. She crossed her legs and pulled out a book she had grabbed from the bookshelf in her room. In her peripheral vision, she saw Dylan frown as she opened the book.

Dylan went into the bathroom, coming out a few minutes later wearing the outfit Holly had grabbed for him. Walking over to her, he snatched the book from her hands.

"Hey! I was reading that." She reached up to grab the book, but he dangled it just out of her reach.

"Not anymore, you're not." Dylan held the book above his head as he spoke.

Holly stood up, eyeing the book as she climbed on top of the chair and reached for it. Dylan tossed the book onto the bed, causing her to lean too far forward and topple off the chair. She crashed into him as the chair tipped over. Dylan collapsed as he tried to catch her, landing on the floor with her on top of him wrapped in his arms.

Her face mere inches from his, she glared at him, the expression diminished by the proximity of his lips. She could feel his heart racing in his chest, a mirror to her own heartbeat.

Clearing her throat, Holly sat up and reached up to grab the book from the bed. "Thanks for catching me. Are you okay?"

Dylan shrugged, the action awkward from his position on the floor. "I'm fine. I would be a lot better if Major Walker wasn't standing in the doorway, though."

Holly looked up to see Dean frozen in the doorway—was that hurt in his eyes—and stumbled to her feet. She cleared her throat again as a blush spread across her cheeks.

Dean coughed, any sign of whatever she had seen in his gaze replaced with second-hand embarrassment—she must have been mistaken.

"I was just coming in to... check up on you. You seem to be fine so I'll just–leave." The words were rushed coming out of his mouth, and he left the room faster than a mouse escaping a cat. As the door shut behind him, Holly covered her face in her hands. She wanted to scream in humiliation—even though nothing had happened. Lowering her hands, she glanced at Dylan. He was still lying on the floor, his head resting on his hands. She gave him a little kick.

"You know you're a pain in the butt, right?" She sat down next to him, his head next to her leg.

He gazed up at her and grinned, his blue eyes sparkling in the light.

"And yet you still play with my hair when I'm sleeping." His grin widened as he reached up and booped her on the nose with his finger.

Holly rolled her eyes at him—pretending the action hadn't sent her stomach swirling with butterflies. As much as she wished she could claim otherwise, she found she couldn't remain annoyed with him. It was part of his charm, she supposed.

"I forgot to grab food," she said. She hadn't, actually, she had simply not wanted hospital food. "I saw the cafeteria, but I'm afraid I've had far too much Jello in this hospital to last a lifetime."

Dylan scrunched up his nose. "I don't like Jello. How about we go to the café across the street and get some sandwiches?"

"You're not supposed to leave the hospital yet," Holly replied, remembering that, technically, she had yet to be discharged as well. "I'm sure we can find something in the cafeteria that's edible."

Rolling his eyes, Dylan said, "Unfortunately, I believe you are right. Not that the hospital staff can keep us locked up here, but I'm sure they would be none too pleased if we just up and left."

Dylan sat up and turned to face her. His eyes darted briefly to her lips before shifting quickly away. Pushing himself to his feet, he cleared his throat and offered a hand to help her stand.

The corporals didn't object when Holly and Dylan left the room and headed toward the cafeteria. She wasn't sure if she was supposed to tell the corporals where they were going, but they hadn't exactly come with an instruction manual and she wasn't used to telling someone everything she was planning on doing so she figured she could just pretend like they weren't there unless she needed something from them.

The hospital cafeteria was mostly empty as they entered. There were a few options for food, but the only thing that looked even remotely edible was the sandwiches.

Both of them grabbed a sandwich then found a place to sit.

They ate in silence, neither of them having much to say as they stuffed their mouths full of the bland sandwiches.

Holly looked up at the holo-screen across the room as it showed footage of the riots in the capital. The Domina had already announced an earlier curfew and more military vehicles were patrolling the streets than there had been months earlier, but it was just a matter of time before she enacted full martial law.

Finishing her sandwich, Holly stood and threw away her garbage. On the holo-screen, the news footage cut out and was replaced with the symbol of G.H.O.S.T. She turned away from the screen, only partially listening as they spewed their manifesto about the corruption of the government and tried to get people to join their so-called revolution. The government was far from perfect, but it was what it was because of countless wars. Just like everything else in nature, the country had adapted to its situation and adjusted to better survive it.

Dylan joined her as she led the way back to the lobby where they could then access the elevators. In the lobby, a dark haired woman was arguing with the nurse at the front desk. Skirting around them, Holly started down the hall toward the elevator, but paused when she noticed Dylan pause.

As she turned to face him, he said, "Mom? What are you doing here?"

The woman at the desk stopped speaking midsentence and spun around. The resemblance was uncanny. Her dark hair, a few shades lighter than Dylan's, was a stark contrast to her fair skin. Dark blue eyes so deep they could swallow the ocean drank in Dylan standing before her.

"I came to see my son," she replied, relief washing over her face.

She reached out for him, but Dylan backed away from her. Holly couldn't read the emotion in his gaze, but she got the sense he wasn't too thrilled to see his mom.

"Why haven't you called?" his mom asked, her tone soft and pleading while her eyes scanned his face. "The military police notified me that they had found you, and I kept expecting to hear from you. I was worried about you."

Dylan didn't respond.

Crossing the short distance back to the front desk, Holly came to a stop next to Dylan. His eyes were glued to his mom, but as soon as Holly approached, those deep blue eyes darted to her, the expression in them darkening while her lips formed a thin line.

"Dylan," Holly started.

He wasn't listening to her though—didn't even seem to notice she was there.

"You shouldn't have come, mom," he told her, his voice flat.

Mrs. Moros reluctantly returned her gaze to her son. "You could have at least called. It's bad enough that you aren't coming home—"

"That is for my protection," Dylan cut her off. "Major Walker called you and explained it to you."

"You're sleeping at a house with no adult supervision with a girl I haven't met," Mrs. Moros retorted. Anger was beginning to fill the lines in her face. "For all I know you've been doing more than sleeping."

"Mom!" Dylan nearly shouted at her. "I'm not sleeping with anyone. Holly is just–a friend. She's just a friend. And I will not have you accusing her of—"

"Of what, taking my son from me?" His mom flicked her eyes back to Holly accusatorily.

Dragging a hand down the side of his face, Dylan blew out a breath. "I didn't call, mom, because the last time we talked you were shouting at me and telling me not to go to the festival."

"That is no excuse not to call me," she said, her scrutinizing gaze finally leaving Holly. "I'm your mother and I care about you."

Fury lit in Dylan's eyes, sparking the blue into a pure silver. "If that's true then maybe you should have *cared* more after dad left. I wish he had taken me with him. Staying with you was more of a mistake than him leaving in the first place."

Grabbing Holly's hand, Dylan pulled her away from his mom. Holly didn't resist. Glancing behind her as they approached the elevator doors, Holly saw his mom staring after them, her shoulders slumped in defeat as Dylan slammed his finger on the button to call the elevator car.

As they entered the elevator a moment later, Holly pressed the button to their floor and asked, "Are you okay?"

He nodded, squeezing his eyes shut for a moment before opening them. "I wasn't expecting to see her so soon."

They didn't speak for the rest of the ride, and it wasn't until the elevator came to a stop that Holly realized Dylan was still holding her hand. As the doors opened, though, any thoughts about what that meant flew out of her mind as she saw Dean pacing the hallway.

Pulling her hand from Dylan's, she hurried over to the Major. "Dean? What's wrong?"

Dean glanced up at her and answered, "Shawn started seizing. They had to take him into surgery. The knife he was stabbed with was coated in some kind of slow-acting poison, but the doctors are hopeful."

"He's going to be okay, Dean. Shawn's tough, he'll be fine." Her voice was strong as she said it, but Holly could feel her stomach churning with worry.

Dean nodded and sat down in a nearby chair. His anxiety evident in his bouncing leg. Holly glanced at Dylan, her gaze asking him for advice, but his eyes had a far off look to them—like he was lost in thought. Sighing, Holly took the seat next to Dean. She hoped that just being there would be enough of a comfort.

Dylan took the seat on Holly's other side, still lost in his head as he stared at his hands in his lap.

The wait for any news on Shawn was excruciatingly long. Holly doubted Dean would last much longer. She hoped the doctors would finish soon before she had to do something to stop him from barging into the operating room to demand answers.

After a long moment, a doctor walked out into the hallway. It was good timing too because Dean had looked like he was one second away from stalking into the operating room.

All three of them stood as the doctor walked over to them to deliver the update.

"Your brother is stable," the doctor said to Dean. "There should be no more complications.

We expect him to make a full recovery in the next week or so."

Tension in Dean's shoulders visibly dissipated at the news. Holly felt herself relax and reached up to squeeze Dean's shoulder. He glanced over at her with an appreciative look.

Before going to check on his brother, Dean said, "You two should sign your discharge papers. Go home. You deserve the rest."

"We will," Holly assured him, watching him walk off before making her way over to the nurses' station where a nurse looked up from the computer she was working on to ask what she could do for her. Holly asked for the discharge papers.

The nurse checked their charts then replied that all they had to do was sign a couple of places and then they would be free to leave as long as Dylan picked up some pain medication before leaving. Thanking her, Holly signed the papers then set the pen down.

Doing the same, Dylan turned to her and said, "You ready to get out of here, princess?"

Holly rolled her eyes and led the way back to the room to grab her things. The corporals, who Holly had almost forgotten were shadowing them, stayed outside the room as she gathered the things she had picked up earlier that morning. They fell into place behind her and Dylan as they made their way to the elevator and clicked the button to the ground floor.

It wasn't until they had picked up Dylan's medication and had walked out of the front doors that Holly realized they didn't have a way back to her house. They had driven there in Dean's car, and she was sure her own car was back at her house after the fight at the warehouse. She had taken a taxi to grab the things from her house, but she doubted that a single cab could fit both her and Dylan as well as the two military police.

"How are we going to get to the hotel?" she asked.

Without missing a beat, Dylan turned around and asked one of the corporals for a ride.

Chapter 32

As Carlton pulled up in front of Holly's house and put the car in park, Dylan thanked him for the ride and they all climbed out and strode up to the front door. Thankfully, the door was still unlocked—which meant that somebody was probably there. Then again their friends were using it as a safehouse so they weren't allowed to leave very often so it shouldn't have been unexpected for someone to be there.

The front room of the house was empty but for Holly and Dylan—accompanied by their glorified bodyguards—as they entered the house. Holly immediately went to her mom's old room, only one thing on her mind. Dumping her things onto the desk, Holly flopped onto her mom's bed and pulled a pillow down to her, pressing her face into it. She heard Dylan laugh from behind her.

"Don't laugh at me," Holly reprimanded into the pillow. "I missed sleeping in a real bed." Lifting her head, she looked back at him.

Dylan was standing in the doorway, a soft smile on his lips. "Are you going to lay there cuddling with the bed all afternoon?"

"Of course not. I've got something important to do, but this bed deserves to be loved right now."

Dylan laughed and walked over to the bed, sitting on its edge. "And what is that important thing you have to do?"

"Not right now," she told him, pressing her face into the pillow again. "I'm not done loving this pillow."

The pillow was yanked out of her arms, leaving a pocket of air in its place. Holly leveled a glare at Dylan. "Fine. I'm done."

Dylan raised an eyebrow, causing her to roll her eyes.

"If you *must* know," she relented, sitting up and dragging her laptop over to her, the device still where she had left it the night they had gone to the park. "Before everything happened, I was doing some research on G.H.O.S.T. Dylan, these people have been around for decades."

Typing in her passcode, she pulled up her notes and turned the screen so he could see it.

"They weren't originally revolutionists either," she continued. "The G.H.O.S.T. initiative was a governmental task force focused on researching and observing genetically altered humans—or something of the sort. The article doesn't go into what they were doing aside from observing and collecting data."

Dylan nodded thoughtfully. "I feel like I've heard of that before. Didn't they get shut down?"

"Yeah." Holly turned her laptop back to face her and clicked through the dozens of open tabs until she found the one she needed. An article on the incident that had led to it being shut down. "Apparently they were doing inhumane experiments on people with Chinese heritage, citizens and immigrants alike, and they ended up killing a lot of people. One of the victim's families sued them and that dominoed until they were forced to shut down all operations."

"Do you think that's where we were?" Dylan perked up. "At one of their old compounds?"

Holly considered it then nodded. "You might be right. The buildings would have been marked as hazardous and not repurposed. Not to mention the layout felt a lot like a lab."

Dylan stood. "I'll be right back."

Her attention focused on her laptop, Holly nodded absentmindedly as she scrolled through the notes she had made prior to their incarceration.

Dylan returned a few minutes later with his own laptop tucked under his arm, along with a notebook and pencil, then sat next to her on the bed. They got lost in the depths of their search while the sun continued to trace its path across the sky out the window. Every so often one of them would share something interesting with the other.

After hours of hunching over her laptop, Holly decided to take a break and stretch her legs. Dylan was still sitting on the bed, pencil tucked behind his ear as he typed on his laptop. Every once in a while he would pause his scrolling and write a note. Holly stretched her arms over her head, leaning to one side then the other before hearing a pop as she cracked her back. Lowering her arms, she glanced at Dylan, a thought coming to her mind.

"Dylan," she said.

"Hm?" He squinted at something on his screen before jotting something down.

"We still need to get our high school diplomas. We kind of missed graduation day."

Dylan groaned, his research momentarily forgotten. "I forgot about that."

Holly laughed softly. "At least we didn't miss any of the actual tests for classes. We just have to pick up our diplomas."

"At least there's that. It can wait though, our top priority right now should probably be staying alive and finding out why G.H.O.S.T. was so interested in us," Dylan reminded her.

"I know that," Holly replied. "I'm just saying, we need to think about the future at some point. Like, going to college and all that. I'm pretty sure we missed orientation."

Dylan sighed. "You make a fair point." He tapped the end of his pencil on his lips. "I've been thinking. How did they know about our powers?"

Holly returned to her spot next to him. "What do you mean?"

"Our powers. You know, water, earth, fire, air? How did G.H.O.S.T. know about them? How did they know it was us who had them? Well, aside from you, of course. I hear you made quite the debut at the warehouse."

"I would assume Jacob told them," she said with a shrug.

Dylan set his laptop on the bed next to him, his eyes meeting hers. "Thay might be true if we had shown our powers before going to the park, but we didn't. Think about it. None of us displayed any sign of having these powers before we all went to that park."

"That's not necessarily true," Holly said, then told him about the night on the roof with Kevin—when she had manifested her powers.

"Okay, but nobody else saw that," Dylan replied.

"What about Apollo? Do you remember our paintball game at the hotel in Visceralis? None of the paintballs touched him. It was like his powers were subconsciously pushing them away."

Dylan tilted his head in consideration. "That would make sense. It would also account for the gust of wind that knocked us all off the tables."

Holly nodded. "Now that you mention it, that does make sense."

"Okay," Dylan said, sitting straighter. "So that accounts for the possibility of them knowing about Apollo in advance, but what about me and Karen? Your powers may have shown earlier, but you literally showed G.H.O.S.T. what you could do. And mine didn't manifest until we were sitting at the fountain in the park."

"Maybe Jacob did call them to tell them while we were there," Holly said slowly, her mind piecing together the sequence of events. "I mean, remember when he said he was going to call Dean? What if, instead of doing that, he called his sister to tell her he had found people with powers?"

"It's possible." Dylan still didn't sound convinced. "Don't you think it's weirdly coincidental though that it just happened to be the four of us who went with him that day?"

She sighed, laying back on the bed. "You're right. It doesn't add up. Unless..." Holly sat up, a crazy thought crossing her mind. "Could they have been the ones to give us the powers in the first place?"

Her gaze locked with Dylan's. His eyes widened. The possibility would account for the holes in the narrative they had cooked up. If G.H.O.S.T. had given them the powers then they had to have put a plan in place to get them before the government could.

"The energy wave." Dylan suddenly jumped to his feet and began pacing. "There were chemicals released into downtown Visceralis while we were at the hotel."

Holly caught on to what he was saying. "G.H.O.S.T.'s main priority before getting shut down was the experimentation of genetically altered humans. No doubt they had access to the chemicals and research needed to create them. You think the chemicals are what gave us our powers?"

Dylan nodded, his feet landing softly on the carpet as he stood and began pacing, leaving his laptop on the bed. "But how would they have known who would get the powers?"

Questions piled up in her mind. There were too many things that didn't make sense. Dylan was right, how did G.H.O.S.T. know who would manifest powers? They couldn't. There was no way for them to even know if people would get powers, let alone who those people were once they did get the powers.

After a few moments of silence, Dylan stopped pacing. He pinched the bridge of his nose.

"I'm getting a headache thinking myself in endless circles, and all I've got are more questions than answers piling up," he said. "I think I'm going to find a place where I can think about this in solitude. I'll write down whatever questions I can think of and we can go over them tomorrow."

"Okay," Holly said as he gathered his things. Before he left, she said, "Dylan, you can use my older brother's room in the basement. It's the room with the acoustic guitar leaning against the wall."

Thanking her, Dylan left, closing the door behind him.

In the wake of his absence, her attention strayed to the notes she had written on her laptop, her eyes going to the section she had highlighted in pale red; *What is Harry's connection to G.H.O.S.T.?*

Her father seemed to have some sort of connection with them. What that connection was, however, Holly had no idea. It was thin, but it was there. The only things she had were the text he had sent her the day of her escape and his invitation to join him back in Visceralis, and those weren't much of anything. It could just be a coincidence.

Shaking her head, Holly closed her laptop and grabbed her wallet and the keys to her car—which she had noticed sitting in the driveway upon their arrival at the house—as she walked out the door. She needed to get some air, and figured she may as well do something productive. Penhallow was waiting by the front door when she reached the main level. Carlton was there too. Both of them were sitting in chairs in the front room facing the front door. While Penhallow followed her out to her car, Carlton remained in the house.

Holly stopped at an all-night diner to grab some food on her way. The plastic bag crinkled as she walked out of the diner and climbed back into her car. It had only been a few hours since she had left the hospital, but it was an hour past sunset—almost curfew—and she doubted Dean had gotten anything to eat.

The luminescent lights in the hospital reflected off the white tiled floor as she made her way to the front desk and signed onto the visitor log. She set down the pen then made her way up the stairs to Shawn's room, Penhallow trailing after her, where she found Dean pacing once again. Shawn wasn't in the room. Dean glanced at Holly and stopped in his tracks.

"What are you doing here?" he asked, his voice tense. "I thought you and Dylan went home."

"We did. A few hours ago." Holly walked over to him as she spoke. "I just thought you might want something to eat. I didn't think you'd eaten anything all day."

"Oh, thanks." Dean took the bag from her and sat down to eat.

Holly sat next to him. "Is Shawn still in surgery?"

"They finished a couple hours ago, but he started bleeding through his stitches about an hour ago and they didn't want to risk giving him any more argenteral than they already had so they took him back in."

"He's going to pull through, Dean. You don't need to worry about him as much as you do," Holly told him. "He probably thinks you're overprotective, you know."

Dean gave her a half smile, one corner of his mouth lifting slightly. "He's told me so himself. On many occasions."

"Have they given you any updates since they took him back into the operating room?"

"Not yet."

"Do you want me to stay until he gets out?" Holly offered.

"That's very kind of you, Holly," he replied. "But I'll be fine. Go home and get some rest. I'll call you in the morning with an update."

"Okay."

Holly stood and left. Penhallow was waiting for her in the hallway when she walked out of the room. He didn't say anything as she walked to the elevator and pressed the ground floor button. The city was quiet, the bioluminescently lit billboards glowing dimly on the side of many buildings.

Her house was quiet when she walked in, most of the lights turned off as she closed and locked the front door before checking that the other exterior-leading doors were locked. Once she had done that, and made sure all the blinds were shut on the windows, she made her way up to her mom's room. Changing her clothes, she turned off the lights and climbed into bed. She did not fall asleep quickly, but when she did, her nightmares were ready to greet her with open arms.

Sunlight was shining through the light gray curtains when Holly woke the next morning. The gentle rays kissed her face as she blearily opened her eyes. Her phone buzzed for a few seconds on the nightstand next to her then fell silent. Pushing herself up onto her elbow, she leaned over and grabbed it. The screen lit up to show she had missed a call from Dean.

Flopping back on the bed, she closed her eyes again. She knew she should be calling him back, but her mind was still fogged over with the remnants of sleep. Her phone started buzzing in her hand, the vibrations flowing up her arm. Lifting it to her ear, she answered.

"Hello?" she slurred.

When she heard nothing, she peeked open an eye and looked at her screen. She had clicked the ignore button. *Oops.*

Setting her phone down, she closed her eyes again. Dean could call back at a more decent time.

A knock on her door jolted her from her meditative state. Holly groaned but got up to answer it.

Dylan stood in the hallway wearing only sweatpants, his black hair mussed. The look in his eyes had Holly stopping herself from scolding him for waking her up—not that she hadn't already been so rudely awoken by Dean's call.

"What is it?" she asked, using all her self-restraint not to snap at him.

"I found something," Dylan told her. "I think I know why we were the ones to get powers."

Chapter 33

Her hair was a mess, and she was in her pajamas, but Holly still let Dylan drag her down to the basement—past their friends who were still asleep on the floor of the theater room—and into the room Adam had occupied for little more than a year before he had left. Despite his absence, her mom had kept the room exactly as he had left it with the hope that someday he would come back. He never did—not while she was alive at least. Now, the space was changed from Dylan's overnight research quest. Papers were scattered on the bed, flowing over to the floor. Holly carefully tiptoed over them as she followed him to the desk where his laptop sat open with an ancient-looking website pulled up on it.

"What is this?" she asked, scrolling through the website. "This looks archaic."

Dylan moved closer to her, his shoulder brushing hers as he navigated the website. "That's because it kind of is."

Holly glanced at him, dark circles had appeared under his eyes. "What time did you go to sleep last night?"

His eyes flicked to hers for a moment before returning to the screen. Next to the laptop sat an empty mug that Holly had a sneaking suspicion had been filled with coffee.

"I didn't," he replied, his hand going to the mug and lifting it to his mouth. He frowned when nothing came out then set it back down. "I stayed up all night searching for answers until I found this about an hour ago. Here, look at this."

Her eyes stayed on him a moment longer before shifting to the screen where she saw a picture of a woman in a forest outlined in fire, the flames harmlessly licking her skin. The image was grainy, the woman's features blurred. Holly squinted her eyes and leaned closer. Her jaw dropped.

"She looks like—"

"You," Dylan finished, his eyes scanning the woman in the photo. "But older."

"But that can't be me," Holly said, her eyes finding the date it was taken. "This was taken in the early twenty-first century. It has to be at least two hundred years old."

Dylan scrolled down a bit further to another grainy photo of a man with a whip of water lashing at another man who hovered at least a foot above the ground. He zoomed in on the photo until the silver of the water wielder's eyes were visible despite the low quality of the image. Holly felt her jaw drop and checked the date of the image. It was from the same day as the one of the fire wielder.

"How is this possible?" she asked as she studied the man in the image. He was practically identical to Dylan, and the other man in the photo was eerily similar to Apollo.

Dylan shook his head. "I don't know how each of us can have a doppelganger from two hundred years ago, but I wanted to show you the main page of this website."

After a few clicks, the home page of the website popped up. Holly leaned closer as she read the story.

Thousands of years ago there were people who were blessed with powerful gifts. Gifts of nature. People around them saw these gifted individuals as gods, naming them elementals. As time went on the powers of these elementals began to frighten the very people who had named them. They were deemed witches and evil sorcerers who had dared to try and control the forces of nature.

The elementals went into hiding. They hid their abilities from the world until their deaths. This was not the end, however, for their powers were reborn in a new generation. Some legends claim this cycle of powers to be reborn through the descendants of the original elementals, but even in the present day, it cannot be known for certain how each new generation of elementals receives its powers. The only thing that is certain is that as each cycle ends, the powers are reborn in a new host who has reached the age of twenty years.

As the centuries have gone by, the legends of the elementals have been all but lost to time. Few stories remain that know the truth of the elementals, but it is suspected that the elementals wander the earth still.

Holly stared at the screen for a moment. "This is..."

"Crazy?" Dylan suggested. "I know. It's a lot to take in, but it would make sense."

"*If* it's true," Holly reminded him. "For all we know, this could be fake. It's a good story, but maybe that's all it is—a story."

"You're right, but then how do you explain the pictures?"

Holly shook her head. "Photoshop?"

The following silence was interrupted by Holly's phone vibrating from where she had set it on the table. Holly picked it up to see Dean calling her.

"I better answer this," she said, answering the phone. "Hello?"

"Holly."

"Hey, what's up?" she asked. "Is Shawn okay?"

"He's fine. I tried calling you this morning, but you didn't answer," Dean said.

"Oh, sorry," Holly said, her eyes scanning the homepage of the website.

"Holly, are you still there?"

"Hmm?" Holly tore her gaze from the screen. "Yeah, I am. Sorry, I'm a bit distracted with something right now. How's Shawn?"

"He's doing good, doctors think he's out of the woods now." Dean paused on the other end of the phone. "I have to go, but I just wanted to check in with you. Call me if you need anything."

"Okay, I will," she assured him. She hung up the phone and set it back on the table.

"Who was that?" Dylan asked, temporarily shifting his attention from his research notes.

"Dean. I asked him to call me in the morning with an update on Shawn."

"I see. How is he doing?"

Holly looked back at the screen, something catching her attention as she said, "He's going to be fine. What's that?"

She pointed to a phone number at the bottom of the screen.

"Looks like a phone number," Dylan said. "Should we call it?"

Holly gave him a pointed look. "Are you sure that's a good idea?"

"Why wouldn't it?" he asked, phone already in hand as he dialed the number.

"I can think of about a dozen reasons why," Holly retorted, but her words fell on deaf ears as Dylan held the phone up to his ear.

The room was silent as he waited for someone to answer. Holly was about to tell him it was pointless when he perked up and said, "Yes, hello. My name is Dylan, I was calling because I wanted to ask you about your elemental website."

There was a pause as the person on the other end spoke.

"No, this isn't a prank call. I want to talk to you about the elemental story." A pause. "Really? Yes, I would love to." Another pause. "Hold on, let me write this down." Holly handed him a pen and paper. "Okay, got it. Can I bring my friend?" He paused again, listening. "Yes, tomorrow works fine. Great, we'll be there. Oh, one more thing, we kind of have a military protection detail right now." Dylan waited for an answer. "I don't think that's such a good idea." More silence followed, Dylan's shoulders were tense as he waited. After another moment, he relaxed. "Yes, that's fine. We'll see you tomorrow then. Great, bye."

Dylan hung up, releasing a breath.

"Well?" Holly urged.

He looked at her. "That was Robert Pendleton, a professor at the University of Sunhaven. He has a PhD in Ancient History and he agreed to meet with us and show us some historical texts on the elementals."

As he talked, Dylan searched up the professor, pulling up his credentials. Holly looked at the page he pulled up from the university's website.

"He looks legit," she muttered under her breath. "That means—"

"That the story on his website is probably true," Dylan interrupted. He was practically bouncing on the balls of his feet. "Do you know what this means, Holly? It means we can finally get some concrete answers on our powers."

Holly watched the sun begin its descent beneath the horizon hours later, replaying her conversation with Dylan in her head. Of course she wanted to know how she got her powers, and why, but it all seemed too good to be true. This mysterious professor with a PhD in Ancient History just happened to create a website on elementals. A website that just so happened to have centuries-old images of people who looked nearly identical to her and her friends. It didn't feel real.

The sky darkened outside her window as her thoughts and worries swirled around her head. When she had left him, Dylan had been at the desk, still in research mode as he prepared a list of questions for the professor. Upon returning to her mom's room—though she supposed she could start calling it her room now, but that felt wrong to her—Holly had dug further into the credentials of the professor and came up with only good things. Despite her reservations for him, she had begrudgingly accepted the fact that Professor Robert Pendleton was a credible source of information.

In her research, she had found his final thesis paper that had gotten him his PhD. The paper had been a comparison of the Japanese internment during World War II in the nineteen-forties and the mass execution and internment of Chinese immigrants and Chinese Americans after the beginning of World War III. It was an interesting read, but it had nothing to do with the elementals.

Her thoughts were interrupted by a soft knock on the door. As she opened the door, she was greeted by Leo standing in the hallway.

"What's up?" she asked.

"Kelly made dinner," Leo said. "Since, you know, we're kind of under house arrest. Care to join us?"

"Sure."

Holly followed them downstairs to the dining room where she was greeted with a massive bowl—likely the largest one in the kitchen—filled with mac and cheese. She wasn't sure what she had expected, but she hadn't realized there was enough mac and cheese in the world to have fit into that bowl.

Artemis, Kelly, and Dylan were already sitting at the table when Holly and Leo came down the stairs and joined them. The corporals, Penhallow and Carlton, had left their positions in the living room and were sitting at the kitchen counter in the adjoining room with their own bowls of mac and cheese.

"We need to talk," Leo said, his usually jovial tone of voice solemn.

Artemis nodded.

Leo swallowed a bite of mac and cheese before continuing, "We need to talk about what to do next. About the rebels."

Kelly opened her mouth to object, but Leo cut her off.

"I know what you're about to say, Kelly," he told her. "I know we're just teenagers and we shouldn't get involved. I also know that you think the Walker brothers should be here, but one of them is currently hospitalized. And, I don't know about you, but I'm pretty sure Holly is sick of the hospital."

"He's right," Holly said, stirring her bowl of noodles with her fork. "I've spent enough time at the hospital to last a lifetime."

"Okay," Kelly conceded. "But we have to tell them about it later. We don't need a repeat of what happened at the warehouse."

"Fine," Leo agreed, his eyes going momentarily vacant as he likely remembered the look on Kevin's face in death.

"What were you thinking, Leo?" Dylan asked, drawing their friend from his thoughts. "You're the one who brought it up, so you must already have a plan."

"Well, not exactly," Leo replied, his mouth still partially full. After swallowing, he said, "I was hoping one of you guys would have an idea."

"You said *not exactly*, which implies that you have at least part of a plan," Artemis pointed out.

"Okay, yes. I do have *part* of a plan, but it's not much," Leo relented. "Holly, Dylan, how panicked was G.H.O.S.T. when the military raided their facilities?"

"Well," Holly started. "From what I heard, the lower-ranking members sounded worried about it, but the higher-ups didn't seem too concerned."

"But you also have to consider the fact that we didn't have much contact with them aside from the occasional training session," Dylan chimed in. "The four of us were in cells for the majority of our time there."

"That's true," Holly said. "They might be worried now that two of us are dead and the other two escaped."

The others shared a look, their eyebrows scrunched in confusion. Right, they didn't know about the elemental powers Dylan, Karen, and Apollo had. Holly glanced at Dylan, who shrugged.

"We need to tell you guys something," Holly started.

"It's going to sound crazy at first," Dylan told them. "But we have a way to prove it."

Leo raised a skeptical eyebrow but didn't object. Artemis nodded to them, her arms crossed.

"Just before we were..."

"Abducted. Kidnapped. Captured," Leo offered.

"Yeah, that. We found out that Karen, Apollo, Dylan, and I have... well we—" Holly cut off. She didn't know how to phrase it so she decided to show them. "You know what, just watch this."

Holly held up her hand and summoned a small flame above her palm. The others gasped as she held it there and turned it into the shape of a dragon then had it fly over the table above their heads. Leo jumped from his chair, the legs scraping on the floor. Artemis pulled him back down a moment later.

"Karen could do that?" Leo exclaimed.

"Hush," Artemis said, smacking him upside the head and shooting a wary glance at the two military police in the other room. "It's time to use your inside voice, Leo."

"Sorry," Leo mumbled.

"No," Dylan replied, answering Leo's question. "Karen could control the earth."

"So you guys are like elementals or something?" Kelly asked, her fingers fidgeting with a napkin.

"Yes," Holly replied.

"Which one was Apollo?" Artemis asked, her eyes downcast.

"Air," Dylan said.

"That means that Dylan controls water, right?" Kelly asked.

Holly nodded. They were taking this much better than she had expected them to.

Artemis tilted her head to the side. "Holly, you used your powers at the warehouse, didn't you?"

"Used is a relative term," Holly replied, remembering the way her powers had torn out of her. How she couldn't truly control them. "It was more like I couldn't contain them. They sort of just... exploded out of me in a moment of high emotion and adrenaline."

Dylan nodded knowingly, his eyes glazed over as a memory replayed in his mind. Holly wondered if that's what he had felt when he had accidentally frozen the water in Merlin's blood.

The group fell silent after that, intent on making it so there would be no leftovers of the enormous bowl of mac and cheese—a feat they were somehow able to accomplish but one that left them with no room for serious discussion.

As they finished eating, Leo said, "We have to discuss this again at some point, guys—come up with a solid plan and not some half-baked idea. G.H.O.S.T. killed our friends. And whether we like it or not, they dragged us into their war, and we need to learn to fight back. No matter the cost."

Chapter 34

Shadows chased Holly through her dreams that night. The faces of those she had lost haunted her until she bolted upright, drenched in a cold sweat, the nightmare fading with the coming light of dawn.

Throwing back the covers, she walked into the bathroom and splashed water on her face. Her heart slowed its pace, her breathing following suit as she leaned on the edge of the sink. Faces of the dead seared the backs of her eyes as she squeezed them shut. She blindly reached for a towel and wiped the water from her face. Not for the first time, she found herself wishing for a way to avoid ever falling asleep again.

Carpet scrunched under her feet as she walked over to the window and fully opened the blinds. Light from the early morning sun glinted through them onto her face. A smattering of clouds rolled sluggishly through the sky, the sun peeking through them in brilliant rays of white.

Holly returned to the bed and grabbed her phone from its place on the nightstand. Unlocking it, her finger hovered over the icon for the camera app. After a moment, she swiftly turned off her phone and tossed it onto the bed, her eyes straying to the door as a knock sounded through her room.

Walking over, she opened the door. Dylan stood in the hallway, already dressed. A soft smile grew on his face, offsetting the dark circles under his eyes—a matching set to the ones that were ever present under her own eyes.

"I had a feeling you would be up already," he said.

"Did you get any sleep last night?" Holly asked, her fingers itching to reach up and brush the bags under his eyes.

"Some," Dylan replied. "It's hard to get any after... well, you know."

Holly nodded. "I do."

Opening the door wider, Holly invited him in. Dylan walked in, his shoulders drooping after the door clicked shut.

"I don't know how you do it," he said. "How do you get any sleep after what you've seen?"

Holly walked over to him, stopping a little ways away.

"How do you sleep after seeing your friends die?" Dylan continued, turning to face her. Tears glistened in his blue eyes, threatening to spill over at any moment. "I didn't even see their faces, and I can't get more than an hour of sleep."

Holly's gaze softened.

"I don't know," she said under her breath. "I've learned to live with it I guess."

Dylan studied her for a moment, then, crossing the distance between them, he wrapped her into a hug, pulling her as close to him as he could. Holly buried her face in his chest.

"I miss them," Dylan whispered into her hair.

"Me too," Holly muttered, her friends' faces flashing in her mind. Her family's faces followed, Andrew's, Dustin's, Eddie's, her mom's. Even Adam's. Holly's eyes snapped open. She pulled back from the embrace, taking a step back.

"He wasn't there," she muttered.

Dylan's eyebrows scrunched together. "What are you talking about?"

Her eyes flicked to him. "Adam. My older brother. He wasn't at the rehearsal dinner when the bomb went off."

Understanding lit in Dylan's eyes. "He's still alive."

Holly rushed to the bed and snatched her phone. Her fingers flew over the screen as she pulled up the contact and pressed the call button. She waited, hope causing her heart to pound in her chest. Adam hadn't answered her mom's calls. He could still be alive, and if he was, then she wasn't alone. She still had family.

Her heart froze when she heard his voicemail, but the hope in her chest didn't disappear. Getting his voicemail didn't mean he was dead, it only meant he didn't answer.

At the tone, Holly left a message. "Adam, it's Holly. Why won't you answer the phone? I need to talk to you. Call me back please."

Holly sighed and tossed her phone back onto the bed.

As she turned to Dylan, he was checking something on his phone. His eyes met hers as she walked back to where he stood, waiting for her.

"He didn't answer," she said, not bothering trying to hide the disappointment in her voice. She shouldn't have expected anything different. It had been years—she shouldn't have expected things to have changed between them now.

"He'll call you back," Dylan reassured her. "Why don't you get dressed? We can go grab some breakfast and go meet up with Professor Pendleton."

Holly nodded. "I'll meet you downstairs in a few minutes."

"How far is the professor's office?" Holly asked as she and Dylan walked out to her car fifteen minutes later, their military shadows following at a distance.

Dylan pulled up the address on his phone. "It's only a short drive from here, but it'll take us a while if we walk."

Holly nodded as she started her car. "Send me the address, would you?"

A ding on her phone indicated the location of the professor's office that Holly put into her car's navigation as Penhallow and Carlton climbed into the back seats.

Seven minutes later she was parking on the street in front of the building, her eyes roving over the towering skyscraper that housed Professor Pendleton's office. Beside her, Dylan's eyes scaled the building.

"You ready?" she asked him.

He nodded, his blue eyes meeting hers. "Are you ready for some answers?"

Holly smiled. "Yes."

The corporals followed them into the building where Dylan asked the receptionist for directions to the professor's office. An elevator ride and a walk down a hallway later, and they were standing outside a solid oak door with a plaque on it that read: *Doctor Robert J. Pendleton, Ancient Historical Studies*.

Dylan knocked on the door. Behind which, there was a shuffling of feet followed by the door being swung open by a middle-aged man with no hair on the top of his head and crow's feet at the corners of his blue eyes. The professor gave them a smile as warm as an early summer sun.

"Good morning! It is so good to meet you in person, Dylan. Is this your girlfriend?" the professor asked.

Holly smiled and extended her hand. "Just a friend. And it's good to meet you, professor. I'm Holly."

The professor took it and shook it gently.

"Would you mind if I asked your military companions to wait in the hall during our discussion?" Professor Pendleton asked. "I wouldn't want to bore them with all my technical talk."

"Of course not," Dylan offered.

"We'll be just outside the door should you need us," Penhallow said, his deep voice all business as he spoke, his eyes inspecting the professor a moment longer before turning to face the hallway.

Holly followed Dylan into the professor's office as he welcomed them in and offered them tea. After accepting the cup, Holly and Dylan each took a seat in front of the professor's desk.

Professor Pendleton sat in his cushioned chair opposite them with a grunt, mumbling something about getting old.

Professor Pendleton laid his forearms on his desk, lacing his fingers together as he leaned forward. "So, what can I tell you about the elementals?"

"We were wondering how it is you know about them," Dylan started. "How do you know that the story you wrote on your website is real? That it's accurate."

The professor tilted his head to the side and leaned back in his chair just enough to grab a book from a pile on his desk and plop the large text in front of Holly and Dylan.

"This," he said, opening the book and slowly turning the pages. "Is an incomplete record of eye-witness accounts regarding sightings of the elementals spanning over the past seven centuries, complete with copies of pictures of each of the elementals for many of the sightings. This book, along with a few other historical texts, details a few versions of the elemental stories. I based my article off of the parts of those texts that told the same story."

Holly leaned closer, her eyes scanning the handwritten pages and the centuries-old pictures that filled the book. The professor stopped at a page about halfway through the massive volume, his brows scrunching together. He pulled the book back towards him and turned it around to study a picture. His eyes darted between the image and Holly.

"You're one of them," he said. "Aren't you?"

Holly blinked. "What—"

Professor Pendleton turned the book back towards them and pointed to the picture he'd been inspecting. Holly stared at the picture, the woman's pixelated features near identical to her own. Next to her, Dylan stood.

"I'm sorry, professor," he said. "But I think it's best if we get going."

"Sit down, boy," Professor Pendleton said. "I'm not going to tell anyone."

Dylan cautiously sat back down, his eyes flicking to Holly's. She nodded to him. The professor didn't seem like the type to lie about something like this.

"What makes you say that?" Holly asked the professor.

The professor gave her a soft smile. "You, my dear, didn't read the full article, did you?"

"I did," Holly said.

"Then you should remember that I theorized the possibility of the elemental powers being passed down to their descendants," the professor stated. "I'm familiar enough with the images in this book to say that you and your friend here are descendants of the elementals. This picture, here is of the fire elemental in the late twentieth century. Have your abilities started showing yet?"

Holly nodded.

Shifting in his seat, the professor tried to suppress his excitement as he asked, "May I see them?"

Shifting her eyes to Dylan, she searched his eyes for an answer. He shrugged ever so slightly. Holly turned her gaze back to the professor.

"Okay," she said. "Here we go."

Holding her hand above the desk, Holly sparked a small flame to life above her palm. The brilliant orange flames tickled the air. Professor Pendleton's eyes widened in amazement. He leaned forward, studying the fire.

"Amazing," he whispered.

Holly doused the fire, closing her fingers around the bright flames. The professor was mumbling to himself under his breath. He checked something on his computer, his eyes roving over the screen intently. Dylan cleared his throat, catching his attention.

Looking up at them, the professor pushed his chair away from his desk and stood. His eyes continued darting to the door, his brow furrowed.

"You two need to leave," he said, his voice grave. "They're here."

"Who?" Dylan asked, sharing a look with Holly. "Who's here?"

Professor Pendleton's blue eyes were hard as he looked at them. "Who do you think? G.H.O.S.T. They've finally found me."

Holly furrowed her brow. "What are you talking about?"

The professor grabbed a notebook from a drawer and thrust it into Holly's hands.

"This has everything you need to know about how to find Volcrum," he said, his blue eyes flitting to the door. Holly's attention shifted to the door at the sound of a loud thud. "If you have any questions, call your brother."

Holly blinked. Her gaze snapped back to the professor. "How do you know my brother?"

"There's no time," the professor said, moving over to the bookshelf behind his desk, his finger skimming over the titles.

"How do you know he'll answer my call?" Holly tried. "I called him this morning and all I got was his voicemail."

Professor Pendleton stopped on a book and pulled it out, a click sounding as the bookshelf swung inward to reveal a hidden stairwell. The professor turned back towards them.

"Adam Carnell is a busy man," he said. "If you want him to return your call, tell him Professor Pendleton told you about the Arvum mission."

"What's the Arvum mission?" Holly asked.

"Don't worry about it. Just tell him you know about it. He'll call you back. Now go." Professor Pendleton herded them into the stairwell and then began to pull the bookcase closed.

Dylan put his hand on it. "Aren't you coming with us?"

The professor smiled sadly. "I've lived a good life, my boy. I would only slow you down. These stairs will take you to a parking garage below the building. Follow the signs to the exit."

"What about the soldiers in the hallway?" Dylan asked.

A rattling sound came from the office door. Holly's stomach dropped.

"They're dead," she said, grabbing Dylan's hand. "Let's go. It was nice to meet you, professor."

"You as well, my dear," he said.

Dylan let the hidden door close, the light disappearing with it. There was a soft click as the bookshelf latched back into place just as they heard the sound of the door crashing open. Holly grasped Dylan's hand tightly, clasping the professor's notebook close to her chest as she pulled Dylan down into the winding darkness.

The only sound in the stairwell was that of their feet against the polished wood of the stairs that eventually turned to soncrete. As they reached the bottom of the stairs, Holly could see a sliver of light from underneath the door before her. Releasing Dylan's hand, she pushed against it and walked out into an underground parking garage, just as the professor had said. Dylan followed her out and closed the door behind them.

Sparsely placed lights illuminated the empty garage. As she scanned the space, Holly spotted a lone car across from her. Dylan started towards an exit sign, leaving her to follow him.

Sunlight gleamed on their faces as they eventually found their way to the exit and wandered onto an empty back road between buildings. It was probably only used to access the garage behind them. Pulling out his phone, Dylan looked up their location. Holly led the way around the corner of the building, freezing in her steps as she saw a black car parked halfway on the sidewalk in front of the building and mere feet from her own car.

"Your house is that way about a half hour walking. We'll have to come back later for your car," Dylan said, pointing in the opposite direction. He lifted his eyes, his gaze locking on the car. "Let's go."

Too late. The front door of the building slammed open and Holly's father walked out, pulling an eagle-shaped bird mask from his face. As he exited the building, he turned, noticing Holly and Dylan standing only a few feet from him. A grin spread across his face as he slipped his mask into the inner pocket of his jacket.

"Hello, dolphin."

Holly paled, watching as her father drew a gun from his waistband and aimed it at Dylan. Her hands shook as Harry took a step towards them. Terror sluiced through her veins as she forced her face to remain neutral.

"I thought I told you not to call me that," Holly said.

Beside her, Dylan clenched his jaw, his eyes focused on the gun pointed at his chest.

Harry rubbed the stubble on his chin. "I vaguely remember you saying something like that."

Holly glared at him, images of suppressed memories fighting their way to the forefront of her mind. Images of her aunt being murdered in front of her. Of her father chasing her with a bloodied knife. She shook her head.

"What are you doing here, Harry?" she asked.

Sorrow filled her father's eyes for a moment but was soon replaced with determination.

"I came to deal with a problem," he said. "I didn't expect to run into you so soon. Come with me, Holly."

Holly scoffed. "Why would I ever go with you? The last time I was alone with you, you tried to kill me and Dustin."

Harry's gaze hardened. "That was a mistake."

"Which part? Me being there, or killing your wife's sister?"

"We can discuss this later," he told her, checking his watch. "I have places to be so I'll ask you one more time. Come with me."

"No."

Fire danced in Holly's veins as she raised her arm, flames beginning to ripple down it. A ball of fire formed on her hand as she drew back her arm and threw it at her father. Harry fired off a shot just before ducking beneath the flaming ball, the bullet piercing Dylan's shoulder. He cried out as the bullet hit him. His hand went to the wound, pain glazing over his eyes.

Holly grabbed his free hand and dragged him with her as she ran. Dylan stumbled after her. She glanced back once, just in time to see her father race after them. Two other rebels walked out of the building and followed him. Her grip tightened on Dylan's hand as she faced forward again and sprinted away from her father. She turned a corner and crossed the street, hoping to lose their pursuers among a series of turns and alleys.

Dylan breathed heavily beside her, his face pale. His pace started dragging the more they ran. No matter how many turns she took, she couldn't shake their tail.

Holly careened down an alley between buildings when Dylan pulled her to a stop. She turned to him, her heart pounding.

"We have to keep going," she said.

Dylan leaned against the wall. Blood oozed from his wound, leaking through the cracks between his fingers. "I know. I just... I need a second."

Her eyes darted in the direction they'd come from. A moment later, the car pulled up, tires screeching to a halt as they were spotted.

"We have to go," Holly said, her eyes shifting to Dylan.

He nodded. "Go. I'm right behind you."

Holly hesitated, but Dylan was shoving her down the alley.

"Run, Holly!"

Grabbing his face in her hands, she planted a kiss on his mouth and said, "You better be right behind me."

Then, without another moment's hesitation, she sprinted down the alley, unable to shake the feeling that she was leaving him behind. When she made it to the end of the alley, she stopped and turned back. Dylan hadn't moved. She took a step toward him, but her father and his men had reached him.

"I will find you," she whispered to him. "I promise."

Before her father could notice her, she spun on her heel and sprinted away. Tears streamed down her face, flying away in the wind as she ran. The sidewalk blurred beneath her, hair whipping around her head as she raced away.

Faces blurred around her as she passed people on the street, swearing at her as she bumped into a few of them. Air burned in her lungs and her feet throbbed, but she ran. Her feet pounded against the sidewalk as she kept running until she barreled into someone walking out of a diner. She almost fell to the ground, dropping the professor's notebook as the man caught her and helped her back to her feet, picking up the notebook and handing it to her.

"Holly?" Her attention snapped to Dean's face. "What's wrong?"

Her shoulders trembled as she held back the sobs that threatened to take over.

"My father. He... damn it!" Her hands shook as she brought them to her head. Holly glanced in the direction she had come from. She had left him. She had just left him and ran away.

"Holly," Dean brought her attention back to him. "Tell me what happened."

"I-I left him. I left him and they took him. How could I leave him?" More tears started falling down her cheeks as she searched Dean's eyes, looking for an answer she knew she wouldn't find. The tears were hot and angry. Grief filled her veins with fire that caused her tears to sizzle before evaporating, but they were quickly replaced.

Dean pulled her into a hug and said, "It's okay, Holly. Everything will be okay."

He released her from the hug and guided her down the street to the hospital. Holly didn't say anything as he led her to Shawn's room and helped her sit. Her hands shook relentlessly as she sat down. She hugged the notebook to her chest to stop them from shaking. Dean started speaking with his brother as soon as she was seated.

After a while, he turned back to her, walking over and crouching in front of her.

"Holly," he said slowly. "I need you to tell me what happened."

Holly nodded but didn't say anything. Dylan had been captured, again, and it was all her fault. She had left him there. She knew he wasn't in any shape to run, and yet she had believed him when he said he would be right behind her.

Finally, she found her voice. "Dylan and I were doing research on our powers and we stumbled upon a website this professor had made so we went to meet him. We talked for a few minutes, but then G.H.O.S.T. showed up. Professor Pendleton, he—he helped me and Dylan escape the building."

"Were you alone?" Dean asked.

Holly shook her head, toying with the notebook in her lap before setting it on the floor. "Those two corporals you assigned to us were there. I think they're dead."

She paused, closing her eyes. After a moment of silence, she took a deep breath and opened them.

"When we were leaving the building, my father saw us. He wanted me to go with him, but I refused. I used my powers as a distraction, but he shot Dylan." Holly stopped, her throat constricting. "We ran... but Dylan was losing a lot of blood. We stopped to take a break, but they caught up to us. Dylan told me to run. He said he'd be right behind me, but he wasn't. I *left* him."

Holly buried her head in her hands. She was so angry. With herself. With her father. She should've gone back for him.

Tears steamed as they landed on her hands. Holly lifted her head, inspecting them. No fire. She sighed.

"Holly, we'll get him back." Dean gave her a reassuring look.

"I know," she replied, but she wasn't sure if she believed it or not. She glanced at Shawn. "How's he doing?"

Dean looked behind him then turned back and said, "He's going to be fine. The doctor said he can leave tomorrow if he doesn't pull his stitches again."

Holly nodded. Her voice cracked as she said, "I don't know what to do."

Dean sighed. "For now, I'm going to take you to my apartment where I can personally keep an eye on you, and you can tell me more about this professor you went to see as well as your powers."

"Okay," Holly said. "Can I get some things from my house first?"

Dean nodded and stood. Holly did the same, grabbing the professor's notebook from off the floor before she followed him out of the room after he said farewell to his brother, promising to update him later when he returned.

The drive to her house was silent.

People and buildings blurred as they drove past. Birds flew above them, soaring on the invisible currents of air. Holly replayed the conversation with Professor Pendleton over in her head. She had yet to open the notebook he had given her, but it didn't feel right to look through it yet.

Dean parked on the street in front of her house. It reminded her of all the times he had dropped her off after their training. If she closed her eyes, she could almost pretend that the past few months had been nothing but a nightmare, but she knew that was only a fantasy she told herself to feel better.

"I'm going in with you," he said, leaving no room for debate. Holly opened her mouth to object anyway. "I'm not leaving you alone."

She closed her mouth and nodded.

Her room was eerily quiet when they walked in. The blankets on the bed were still rumpled from when she had woken up. She hadn't thought to make it before she and Dylan went to meet the professor. Her hands clenched the notebook tightly against her chest.

Holly gathered her things, throwing them into a duffel bag. She bent over to pick up a discarded t-shirt when she paused. Dylan's hoodie he had given her the week of the festival was lying on the floor a mere foot from where she stood. Without hesitation, she picked it up and was out of the room as quickly as she could.

Dean was waiting for her in the hallway. He nodded to her when he saw her bag and walked with her to his car. She was secretly grateful none of her friends had been upstairs to see her in that state. There was no way she could have told them what had happened. She knew they wouldn't blame her—even though they should, she blamed herself after all.

The lights in Dean's apartment were off when they walked in. With a flick of the switch, the dark space was lit.

"I have a spare bedroom you can use," Dean said, leading the way.

Holly walked in behind him and surveyed the small room. She thanked him and he left her to herself, saying something about being back in a few hours.

Setting her duffel bag at the end of the bed, she sat on the edge. Her mind replayed the day over and over again. All she could think about was the look on Dylan's face when he told her to run, the pain in his eyes as she kissed him. Tears welled up in her eyes again as she realized that he had never intended to be right behind her. She rubbed her temples. Her head began pounding with the beginning of a major headache.

Holly slipped off the bed and opened her duffel bag. She grabbed Dylan's hoodie and pulled it over her head, inhaling deeply. After a moment, she climbed onto the bed and curled into a ball in the center. She pulled the hood over her head and closed her eyes, remembering her promise to Dylan. Nothing in the world would stop her from getting him back. She would do anything to save him. Anything.

Chapter 35

Dean's apartment smelled like pasta when Holly woke up hours later. She sat up slowly. Her gaze drifted to the door. Crawling off the bed, she walked into the kitchen where Dean was cooking.

"You're awake," he said.

"What are you making?" she asked, fighting back a yawn.

"Spaghetti."

Holly nodded and sat down at the table. She laid her arms on the table and rested her chin on them as her thoughts drifted to ways she could find Dylan. Thoughts of guilt pushed at the back of her mind, but she shoved them down. They would have to wait their turn.

Only a few minutes later, Dean carried over two plates with spaghetti and apple slices along with cups of water and set them on the table. Holly sat up and thanked him.

"When are we going to talk about how we're going to rescue Dylan?" she asked, the words spilling out of her mouth.

Dean sighed, setting his fork on his plate. "I don't know, Holly. I still need to talk to Shawn about all of this."

"We don't have time," Holly snapped. "It's already been hours since they took him. I have to find him."

"I understand that, Holly," Dean told her. "But we need to come up with a plan. You and your friends didn't exactly think it all through last time, and look what happened. It took us months to find you the first time. Besides, we don't even know where they took him. These things take time."

Holly took a bite of her food as she continued to think. She sighed. He was right, they did take time, but it was time they didn't have. Time Dylan didn't have.

"You're right, but I think we need to involve the rest of my friends."

"No. After what happened last time? Not happening. We are not letting them get involved," Dean said, shaking his head. "I'm only keeping you in the loop because I know you'd do something whether I let you or not and because I need you to tell me more about your powers."

Holly took another bite before saying, "My friends are the same way, you know. They're just going to make their own plan without you."

Dean set down his fork again and rested his head against his hand sighing.

"How much of a plan do they have?" he asked.

"Not much. Leo didn't say much about it, but I know he has an idea," Holly said, swirling her food around her plate. "He only told us about it yesterday."

"Okay," Dean relented, his tone conveying just how much he didn't want to allow this. "They can come, but they have to let me train them in hand-to-hand combat and basic firearms. I know we don't have a lot of time, but I want them to get as much training as I can give them with what time we do have."

Holly nodded. "Okay."

"Holly," he said. Holly looked up at him. "They're going to need at *least* a week of training. Even that's pushing it. It took weeks for me and Shawn to pass our combat training."

Holly's breath caught in her chest, but she forced herself to say, "I understand. What about Shawn? You know he's going to go regardless of what you or the doctors say."

Dean took a bite, then said, "He's getting released from the hospital tomorrow. We'll have to see how much he heals in the time that we need to get your friends some training. That will take a few days, Holly. Don't try and persuade me otherwise. I won't budge on this."

Holly reluctantly nodded and finished her food. It had tasted like ash in her mouth, but she knew she had to keep her strength up so she had forced herself to eat it regardless of how it tasted. Washing it down with water, she stood and went to the sink to clean her plate, returned to the spare bedroom, and lay on the bed staring at the ceiling.

Her mind replayed the events of the day again until her head began to throb. Holly massaged her temples in an attempt to dispel the oncoming headache. When that didn't help, she walked into the kitchen where Dean was loading the dishwasher. He looked up at her as she got closer.

"Do you have anything for a headache?" she asked him.

"Yeah," Dean said, brushing off his hands on his pants. "Follow me."

Holly followed him into his room where he opened a medicine cabinet on the wall. He pulled out an almost empty bottle of small red pills and handed it to her.

"Here. There should be enough for your headache, and then some if it comes back. Go ahead and keep it. I can get more later."

Dean left the room and returned to the kitchen. Dishes clinked as he finished loading the dishwasher. Holly left a moment later and returned to her room. She took two of the round pills and set the bottle on the nightstand.

Pulling the sleeves of Dylan's hoodie over her hands, she laid back on the bed and stared at the ceiling. Eventually, she fell asleep.

Holly went from one nightmare to another as she slept. They chased her through the dark abyss.

Hours.

Days.

Months she spent running through the darkness, sprinting from the shadows of her memories, but they always caught up to her. She didn't know how long she had been asleep before she had started screaming, but it felt like years before she was roused from the black hole of her dreams.

Something jerked her from her nightmares. The sky was dark outside, the moon hanging high in its waning crescent as Dean shook her hard enough to drag her from the depths of agony. Dean pulled her into a tight embrace as she shoved away the remnants of her dreams. She was panting heavily as she clung to Dean's arm and started crying. Her eyes squeezed shut as she sobbed, her lungs constricting so tight she started seeing spots behind her eyes. Dean hugged her tighter and murmured comforting words in her ear.

"It was just a dream. You're okay, sweetheart. You're okay."

Holly's tears slowed with her breathing. She forced down deep breaths of cold air as the seconds ticked by until her breathing had calmed down. Her viselike grip on Dean's arm loosened as she moved her hands to wipe away the tears.

Dean released her and moved so he was sitting in front of her.

"I'm sorry. Did I wake you?" she asked, eyeing his sweatpants and bare chest.

"It's fine, Holly," Dean reassured her. "Are you okay?"

Holly nodded. "Yeah. It was just a bad dream."

Dean moved to stand but hesitated. "Are you sure?"

"I'm fine."

Dean seemed reluctant to leave, but after a moment he got up and left. As the door closed behind him, Holly released a breath and pulled her knees up to her chest. She needed to get Dylan back.

Holly grabbed one of the pillows on the bed and hugged it to her chest as she lay in the stillness. She knew she should try to get more sleep, but the memory of her latest nightmare haunted her as she stared at the wall. Shadows deepened and shifted around the room as the sun rose sluggishly above the horizon outside the window.

She was still awake when she heard Dean get up and walk past her door to the kitchen. Holly stayed in bed for a while longer before she sat up and walked into the kitchen. Dean didn't say anything as she walked in.

He handed her a spoon before pouring her some cereal. Holly accepted the food and sat at the table to eat. Her stomach grumbled at her, begging for food, but she couldn't bring herself to do more than idly push her spoon around the bowl.

Dean sat down across from her. She watched him take a few bites before speaking.

"So," she said. "What are the plans for today?"

"Shawn should be released around eleven," Dean said. "I'm going to pick him up."

"And after that?"

Dean sighed and pinched the bridge of his nose. "I don't know. I haven't thought about it yet."

"What about talking to my friends after you pick him up?" she suggested. "If you want to give them as much training as possible, why not start today?"

"You're right," he said. "Fine. After I pick up Shawn we can gather your friends."

"Okay," she said. "I'm going to take a shower. I'll see you when you get back."

Holly forced down a few bites of food before standing, rinsing off her dishes, and returning to her room, shutting the door behind her.

The water was cold as Holly stepped into the shower. Drops of water pattered softly on her back, the sound of it falling on the shower floor drowning out the noise in her head.

As she had expected, Dean was gone when she exited the bathroom and went back to her room. She sat on the edge of the bed as her mind replayed the events of the previous day in her head for the millionth time since it had happened. Holly leaned her head in her hands and sighed. She dragged her hands down her still-damp face, her eyes going to her suitcase where Professor Pendleton's notebook peeked out from under the shirt she had worn the day before. A single tear dripped down her cheek as her mind replayed Dylan's face as it had been when he had knocked on her door. The way his blue eyes had shone with excitement about what he was about to show her. The dimple in his cheek as he grinned at her.

Holly didn't know how long she had been sitting on the edge of the bed when she was suddenly jolted back to the present as the apartment door slammed shut and two voices entered the kitchen, arguing loudly.

Standing, Holly crept into the hallway, listening to what was being said.

"—just kids Dean." Shawn's tired voice filled the apartment as Holly walked closer to the kitchen.

"Kids who have gone into more danger than we did at their age." Dean's voice was soft as he spoke. Almost as if he thought Holly had fallen asleep again and didn't want to wake her. "And if that doesn't tell you something about how strong they are—"

"I'm not saying they aren't strong, Dean. I'm saying that it's crazy to think that we should be allowing them to go on a mission this insane. Especially with only a *week* of training. You know how long it took us to pass combat training and we had *dad*." Holly paused around the corner to listen.

"I understand your concerns," Dean said. "And I agree, but Holly was right; those kids are going to create their own half-cocked plan and go after G.H.O.S.T. with or without us, and they're going to get themselves killed. She told me herself that they've already started. How are you going to explain that to Adam? He's already stressed enough with General Falcon's death."

Holly barely heard Shawn's exasperated sigh, her mind reeling. They knew Adam. Dean *personally* knew her brother.

"So you think that a few days of combat training is going to be any better? Have you forgotten what happened in Denver? What happened to Angela? Adam went berserk when she almost died."

"Of course, I haven't forgotten. Atlas saved our lives that day. A week is better than nothing, Shawn. If they're going to go anyways, better to have them at least somewhat prepared."

"They're going to get themselves killed!" Shawn bellowed. "They have no idea what Volcrum has risked to keep them out of this fight. Atlas would have our heads if we let his brother get killed by the same people who killed his father not too long ago. Not to mention how pissed Adam was when they took Holly."

Holly stepped around the corner. "How do you know my brother?"

Both of them turned to look at her.

"Holly," Shawn started.

"How do you *know* him?" she asked, over-enunciating each word.

"We can't tell you that, Holly. Adam would want to—"

"Adam can't be bothered to answer my calls!" Holly glared at him. Her mind flashed back to what Professor Pendleton had said would get Adam's attention. "What happened in Arvum? With Professor Pendleton and my brother?"

Dean shared a look with Shawn who said, "That's not for us to say."

"I don't care," Holly retorted, feeling her skin get warm as her powers rose to the surface. "What happened in Arvum?"

"Look, Holly," Dean said. "We can talk about this later. Right now, we need to focus on getting Dylan back."

Holly narrowed her eyes but relented, letting her powers sink below the surface once again. "Fine, but I expect a full explanation."

"How soon can you get your friends to the gym I took you to?" he asked her.

"Whenever you need me to. I can get them there," she replied.

"Okay. Text them the address and tell them to be there in an hour."

Holly nodded and walked back to the room she was staying in. She closed the door, careful not to slam it in her subdued anger, and grabbed her phone from its place on the nightstand. The screen lit up with a picture of Holly and Dylan at the lake with the rest of their new friends on the day of the volleyball game. Her breath hitched as she took in all their smiling faces and the joy that had yet to be destroyed.

Shaking herself from her thoughts, she unlocked her phone and opened the group chat Kevin had started all those months ago.

Hey guys, I'm going to send you an address. Meet me there in an hour. The Walker brothers are going to give us some combat training over the next couple of days. Please come, there's something we need to talk about.

Holly typed in the address, sent the same text to Naomi and Zac, then heaved a sigh and tossed her phone onto the bed. She wanted to flop onto the bed next to it, but she knew if she did she wouldn't get back up. Instead, she changed into more suitable clothes for training.

Dean knocked on the door as she was finishing braiding her waist-length hair. Holly glanced at him as he walked in, flipping the braid over her shoulder.

"I'm leaving to grab some lunch for everyone," he told her.

"Okay," she replied. "I can go with you if you want."

"No, that's alright. I just wanted to let you know in case you needed anything."

"Okay."

He moved to leave but hesitated, like he was about to offer an explanation, or an apology, for their argument earlier. There were a thousand things that he could say in that moment, but he said none of them. After a short pause, he left without another word.

Holly sat on the edge of the bed, leaving her feet hovering a few inches above the floor, and picked up her phone. She knew she would regret it, but she opened the photo album anyway and began scrolling. There were dozens of photos from the activities with her friends. From images of the aftermath of the food fight to pictures of the group jumping into the pool at the hotel. So many happy memories. The tears she expected to well in her eyes never came. Instead, resolve hardened in her chest. G.H.O.S.T. would pay for what they'd done to her and her friends. Holly would make sure of that.

First things first, though, she had to get Dylan back, and to do that, she had to face her friends and rebuild her strength. The past week had been one disaster after another. Holly was determined to prevent any more from happening.

Dean returned a while later with enough sandwiches to feed an army packed into the backseat of his car.

"I don't think you brought enough sandwiches," Holly remarked sardonically. "Maybe we should go back and get more."

"Ha, ha," Dean said. "I don't think you understand how hungry teenagers get after extreme exercising."

"Don't I?"

Dean shrugged and said, "Okay. If you're ready to go now, I'll take you and you can get an early warm-up before your friends show up."

"Sounds good to me."

"Great. Hop in."

The ride to the warehouse was silent, an unbearable fifteen minutes of tormenting thoughts thundering through her mind before they finally made it to the warehouse gym she had trained at shortly after Dustin had died. It had been months since Dean had first taken her there and she felt a sense of familiarity as she walked through the doors. The growing anticipation crowded in the back of her mind as she took the first few steps into the building.

Holly didn't wait for Dean before she started going through the warm-up routine he had drilled into her. He came in a moment later hauling in the sandwiches, setting them next to the wall before leaving again. She was just finishing when Dean walked back in carrying a box of water bottles. Walking over to him, she took the box from him.

"Thanks," he said. "There's another box in the car. I'll be right back, Shawn said he'll get here soon."

"Okay," Holly replied, setting the box on the floor next to the sandwiches as he left.

Holly went back to stretching out her muscles for the next few minutes as Shawn arrived—his arm in a sling—followed by Dean and all of Holly's friends.

Standing up, Holly walked over to them and was immediately wrapped in a hug by Zac and Naomi.

"Did Jay's mom tell you?" she asked.

"Yeah," Naomi whispered. "They won't get away with his death, Holly. We won't let them."

Holly stepped back and nodded, then said to the rest of them, "Thanks for coming."

"You know we're always here for you, Holly," Kelly told her.

"Yeah," Leo chimed in. "I'm ready to kick some rebel butt."

"Holly," Artemis said, her blue eyes rimmed with red. "You said you had something to tell us. Can we hear it before we start?"

Holly swallowed, her eyes fixed on her feet. She didn't know how she was supposed to tell them about Jacob. About Dylan. A lot had happened since she had last spoken to them. So much so that she didn't know where to start.

Taking a deep breath, Holly took a step back and looked around at her gathered friends. Shawn and Dean busied themselves with setting out sparring mats as she began telling her friends everything that had happened since the escape from G.H.O.S.T. She watched the expressions on their faces as she revealed Jacob's betrayal. Kelly's eyes welled with tears. Leo's jaw clenched as she relived the visit to Professor Pendleton. As she finished her story, she had to clench and release her fists as a reminder. This was real. It wasn't a dream. Not a dream. Not a dream.

Holly couldn't look her friends in the eye any longer so she glared at the floor, waiting for someone to say something. Nobody did. There was a rustle of clothes and the shuffling of feet and then she was wrapped in a tight hug.

"It wasn't your fault, Holly," Naomi whispered. "None of it was. We'll get him back."

Her shoulders relaxed. "I know."

Holly took a step back and looked at the rest of her friends. She was taken aback by the mixture of anger and determination on all of their faces. Nodding to them, Holly glanced over at

Shawn and Dean, who had finished setting up the room.

"Listen up," Dean said, stepping forward. "You all better be ready for this. We only have a week to train you, and we're not going to go easy on you."

Shawn looked each of them in the eye. "If you're going to be fighting for your lives, you're going to train like your life—and that of your friends—depends on it, because it will. I don't want to see any more of you lose your lives because you weren't prepared."

"So stop giving us crappy pep talks and start teaching," Leo smirked, cracking his knuckles. "Those douchebags aren't going to see us coming."

A smile spread across Shawn's still-pale features as he said, "You're going to be eating your words in a few minutes."

Chapter 36

Hours later they were all lying on the floor covered in sweat. Holly was sitting against the wall, a bottle of water in her hand as she stared at the ceiling trying to catch her breath. Somebody groaned from their spot on the floor.

"Who's ready for another round?" Leo laughed mirthlessly, his voice muffled against the sparring mat.

Kelly groaned. "Don't let Shawn hear you say that. He'll actually take you up on it."

They were all silent for a moment. Someone shifted their position, the movement followed by a low groan.

"I think their training broke my ability to move without being in pain." Zac groaned as he tried to move again.

"Maybe they're hoping we'll give up if we're too sore," Artemis muttered.

Holly sat there listening to her friends talk, her thoughts wandering. She wondered how Jay would have reacted to their situation. Whether he would have agreed with what they were doing or whether he would have argued against it as Shawn had.

Turning her head, she watched the Walker brothers talking just outside the glass doors of the gym. They both had grim expressions on their faces, it looked like they were arguing again. She continued watching them until Dean shouted something at Shawn and spun on his heel before walking back inside. Shawn remained outside.

Any sign that he'd just been arguing was not visible on Dean's face as he strode over to the group sprawled out in various positions on the floor.

"You all look like crap. Don't tell me a few hours of easy training has already got you beat."

"Screw you and your *easy training*," Leo snapped. "No normal person can spend that much time doing hundreds of pushups and running five miles and *not* collapse on the ground."

"If I could move my body I would stand and punch you in the face," Zac said.

"If you so much as *tried* you would find yourself slammed to the mat in a matter of seconds, but go ahead, I dare you. At least be sure to have good technique if you have the balls to try." Dean and Zac glared at each other.

Holly knew she should try to stop them from arguing—tensions were running high for all of them—but something in her was too tired. Tired of watching brothers argue. Tired of friends dying. Of losing. The list of people she had lost was growing exponentially and she was so *tired* of it. Her mom used to tell her that the grief of losing someone you love was powerful enough to rattle the heavens. Those words held true. Holly's world had crumbled when G.H.O.S.T. had killed her family. Her friends. And she was sick of watching herself fail.

Lost in thought, she had tuned out the argument long enough for Zac and Dean to be standing toe-to-toe shouting at each other.

With half a thought and a flick of her fingers, Holly sent a tiny spark of flame in the space between the two. Both of them whirled to face her as she struggled to her feet, setting down the bottle of water she had been holding. Her other friends had shifted to sitting positions, all except for Leo. He was still lying facedown on the mat. Nobody said anything as she sauntered over to where Dean stood next to Zac. She could see frustration and anger reflected in both of their eyes as she came to a stop before them and slapped them both upside the head.

"Stop it," she hissed. "Stop arguing. I know you're frustrated. I know we're all pissed right now, but that does not give you the right to start fighting with each other."

Zac opened his mouth, but Holly spoke before he could utter a word. "Don't bother telling me you weren't considering throwing a punch despite how sore you are."

She gave him a hard look and he closed his mouth.

"If we start fighting ourselves, then they win. They're going to win because you're too busy with your crap to realize it. We're all here to save Dylan and get justice for the friends we lost. Our friends are dead, or have you forgotten?" Holly paused. "We can't let them win. We can't."

She didn't give them a chance to reply before she stalked past them, passing Shawn, and exiting the building to get some fresh air. Let them think about what she had said. If she was lucky they would even apologize. Cool air filled her lungs as she breathed deeply.

As she stood there in the parking lot, a summer breeze blowing loose strands of hair across her face, she wished she could wake up to the sound of chirping birds. She wished for it all to have been a bad dream. What she wouldn't have done to go back to the day she had been chosen for the festival. Holly held up her hand in front of her and lit a small flame in the center. She didn't want this. Didn't want the powers, the pain, and tragedy they came with.

Holly let the wind extinguish her little fire. Watched as it winked out of existence. Gone on a breeze that would carry with it any lasting doubts. The world was a cruel place that didn't allow for any mistakes or second chances. Once you'd shot your shot that was it. The end of the line. You either made do with the hand you were dealt or you live a miserably wretched life, unable to escape the shadows of the past.

She didn't know how long she had been standing there, listening to the wind before she heard someone walk up behind her.

"Shawn and Dean want to talk to us," Artemis said.

Holly nodded.

"Do you think he's dead?" She asked, watching a sparrow flutter from one tree to the next.

Silence. Artemis' voice was soft as she spoke. "No. I think he's too valuable to them right now. I think your father wants to use him as bait. For whatever reason, he wants you to join him, and for that purpose, he will keep him alive."

"You're probably right."

"Do you—do you think it's possible that Apollo is alive?" Artemis asked, her voice quavering.

Holly loosed a breath and looked at Artemis from the corner of her eye. "I want to tell you that it's possible. I want to tell you that he could be alive, but I can't. I saw his body, Artemis. His eyes were empty. He's gone."

Artemis choked on her breath, closing her blue eyes as a tear rolled down her cheek. "Thank you, Holly. I know you could have lied and said it was possible, but somehow hearing the truth makes it easier, you know?"

She nodded. "Let's go in and hear what they have to say."

Holly turned and followed Artemis back into the warehouse where the rest of their friends were waiting. Seeing the girls walking over, Shawn started speaking.

"I know you all worked hard today, and you're definitely going to feel it tomorrow, but you all came here of your own volition. I know you think you have a plan to get back at G.H.O.S.T. don't try to deny it," he said pointedly as Leo opened his mouth to do just that. "Which is why we offered to train you guys for the next couple of days while we plan our next move. I don't want any of you to be a part of this, but I'd rather be there to help you than let you get yourselves killed based on a half-cocked plan you pulled from nowhere.

"So, for the next week or so until we have a plan, all of you are going to come here and train as hard as you can, for as long as you can, while Dean and I continue to search for Dylan and plan what to do next."

"Wrong," Holly interrupted. "You're going to let me help. I was there, it's my fault they have Dylan. I have a right to be a part of the planning to get him back."

"Fine," Dean replied, a muscle ticking in his jaw.

"That being said," Shawn continued. "I don't care what you originally had planned. Forget it. As of right now, our top priority is getting Dylan back safely. Any arguments?"

"I hate to be the one to say it, but what if he's already dead?" Leo asked with a glance at Holly. "Will it all have been for nothing if we make this big plan, and possibly lose someone, only to find out that he's dead?

Holly glared at him. She knew he had a point, but she couldn't think about it.

"It's worth the risk," she growled. "If any of you have a problem with that, then you can leave."

"Nobody has a problem with it, Holly," Kelly told her. "But Leo has a point. We need a backup plan in case something goes wrong or Dylan *is* dead."

"He's not dead. Dylan is not dead. Do you hear me? I don't want any of you to even *think* that he might be," Holly snarled. Flames writhed up her arms, her anger releasing whatever hold she had had on her power.

Holly met each one of their gazes. The only thing she saw there was the determination to get him back. She looked back at Shawn, pulling back on the thread of power she had released.

"Now that that's settled, would you like to go back to the hotel now, or would you like to stay and get in another hour or two of training?" Shawn asked the group.

They all shared a look.

"Give us your worst," Naomi smirked, throwing her curls over her shoulder.

"You're going to regret saying that," Dean told her.

They spent the next couple of hours practicing hand-to-hand combat against each other. Sweat dripped down Holly's temple as she sparred. It was nearly sunset by the time Dean called for them to stop. Holly was breathing heavily as she took a long swig from a water bottle.

"Okay, everyone. Good job today. We'll see you all tomorrow at nine," Shawn announced.

Holly followed him and Dean out to their cars. The drive back to Dean's apartment was quiet, their minds all focused on the days ahead and the plans they were making.

Buildings blended together out Holly's window as they drove past. The people walking nothing more than blurs. The brothers walked into the apartment and went straight to the kitchen for a drink. Holly closed the door behind her and went to her room, their quiet conversation becoming nothing more than ambient noise behind her door.

Holly lay down on the bed and stared at the ceiling. She lay in the silence, watching the remnants of sunlight travel across the wall until it eventually faded to darkness. The sound of knocking on the apartment door stirred her from her thoughts. She walked over to her door and opened it a crack. Voices filled the corridor. Dean was talking to someone, likely a neighbor. Holly closed the door and walked back to the bed.

A wave of exhaustion hit her as she plopped onto it. She was asleep before her head hit the pillow, her nightmares waiting for her as she fell into the darkness.

Chapter 37

The sound of shouting woke Holly hours later. She groaned. Knowing she wouldn't be able to go back to sleep, she got up and walked into the front room. Holly rubbed the sleep from her eyes as she came to a stop.

"Do you mind?" Holly asked, yawning.

Dean and Shawn turned to face her, each of them shooting the other a pointed look.

"Sorry, Holly. We didn't mean to wake you," Dean said. "You can go back to bed."

Holly glared at both of them for a moment before sighing and flopping down in the nearest chair.

"What happened?"

The brothers shared an exasperated look.

"It's nothing," Shawn said. "Go back to bed."

"If it were nothing you two wouldn't be arguing about it," she snapped. "I'm not going anywhere until you tell me."

Shawn sighed. "It's nothing you need to worry about, Holly."

"I don't care."

Shawn shared another look with his brother.

"Don't even think about it. I am not moving from this spot until one of you says something."

"We found a note from your father in the mail," Dean relented. Next to him, Shawn held the aforementioned note.

Holly waited for him to say more. When he didn't, she said, "And? What did it say?"

Dean hesitated and spared a glance at Shawn, who gave him a look that said *you got yourself into this, you have to get yourself out.*

"All it said was to meet him at an abandoned church two days from now... to talk," Dean explained.

"Okay. How do you know it's from him?"

Again, Dean hesitated. Holly sighed, rolled her eyes, and moved to stand.

"If you're going to be like this all night I'm just going to take it from you."

"See for yourself," Shawn told her. "It's definitely from him."

Standing, Holly took the letter from him and scanned it; nothing. She looked up, raising an eyebrow.

"There's nothing here to indicate that it's from my father," she said.

Shawn wordlessly handed her the envelope. At the bottom of the envelope... Holly froze. The necklace Dylan had worn every day since she had met him was sitting in the bottom with a newly added dolphin charm attached to it. Shawn and Dean seemed to shrink under her glare.

"How long ago did you find this?" She snarled.

"Holly," Dean started.

"How long?" She snapped.

"Since we got back from the gym," Shawn told her.

Holly's vision went red, her breaths quickening. She dropped the envelope and the letter as sparks began to dance at her fingertips. Fear flashed in Dean's eyes as he watched them ignite and grow. He took half a step away from her.

"Holly, calm down," Shawn pleaded. Holly's eyes snapped to him.

"Dylan's life is at stake and you took it upon yourselves to hide something this important from me, *after* promising to keep me in the loop, and you expect me to be calm?" Holly's hands were engulfed in flames. "I lost my entire family to these people. I will *not* lose him too."

"Why do you think we were arguing?" Dean asked, his eyes focused on her hands.

Her attention flicked back to his face. His eyes met hers.

"I wanted to tell you sooner," Dean told her. "I'm sorry."

Her fire blinked out.

"If you ever keep something like this from me again, I will not hesitate to end you."

Their faces paled. Holly looked back and forth between them before picking up the envelope.

"I'm going back to bed," she said, picking up Dylan's necklace and tossing the empty envelope back onto the floor.

Neither of the brothers said anything as she turned and walked back to her room.

Holly pulled the necklace over her head before flopping onto the bed. She fidgeted with the pearl, trying to fall back asleep, knowing it was unlikely to return. Sleep still hadn't found her by the time dawn approached outside her window. Sighing, Holly sat up. She glanced at the window, walked over to it, and opened the blinds.

The chirping of birds was muffled through the glass as Holly leaned against it, surveying the waking city beneath her window. Car horns blared in the distance as her thoughts wandered. She knew she had to figure something out for the meeting with her father, but she couldn't bring herself to think about it. Her fingers fiddled with Dylan's necklace. Faint sounds of clinking dishes came from the kitchen. Dean must have stayed up the rest of the night as well.

Dean was eating breakfast when Holly walked in. They didn't say anything to each other as Holly poured herself some cereal and began eating.

"You have to tell your friends, Holly," Dean said, breaking the silence.

Holly grimaced, that was another thing she had been avoiding.

"Do I?" she retorted. "The last time I told them something like this, three of them died. I can't see another person I love die, Dean. I just can't."

"They're going to find out regardless of whether you're the one to tell them or not," Dean reminded her. "They have a knack for knowing things they shouldn't."

"I can't just give him leverage to use against me."

"You don't need to, he already has it," Dean replied bluntly.

Holly glanced at him, too tired to properly glare. "You don't need to remind me."

"You're right, I don't. But remember, Holly, this is what they signed up for. Whether you like it or not, your friends want to be a part of this."

Sighing, Holly gave in and said, "Fine. I'll text them after breakfast."

Dean nodded and returned to his food. Holly was still eating when he got up and went to his room.

As she finished eating, she got up and returned to her room. She sent a text to Naomi, asking her to gather everyone in the living room of Holly's house.

After sending the message, she quickly got dressed and knocked on Dean's door.

"What's up?" he asked, straightening his uniform.

"I'm going home to talk to my friends," she told him.

"I'll drop you off." Holly opened her mouth to object, but Dean held up his hand. "I don't want you alone in the open."

Holly nodded. "When are you leaving?"

Dean checked his watch. "Give me five minutes."

"Okay." Holly turned and went to her room, sitting down on the bed to wait.

She was lying on her back when Dean knocked on the door and opened it. Holly lifted her head.

"Are you ready to go?" he asked her.

Holly nodded as she stood and made her way out the door after him.

"Good luck," Dean said as she got out.

"Thanks," she replied, then said under her breath, "I'm going to need it."

Taking a steadying breath, Holly opened the front door and found her friends waiting in the living room just inside. Her breaths were shaky in her chest as she met their expectant gazes. All of them were seated on the chairs and the couch as she stopped just inside the house and closed the door behind her. She took a sweeping glance at them, her heart pounding in her chest. Her fingers found the pearl at the hollow of her neck. She opened her mouth to say something but stopped when her throat constricted. She couldn't do this.

Holly didn't realize she was shaking until she felt Naomi's hand on her arm. Turning her head, Holly gave her an attempt at a smile before turning back to face the rest of her friends. Then she told them about the note, and what it meant.

"Okay," Kelly took a deep breath. "So what do you want us to do?"

"I *want* you to stay out of this," Holly told them, holding up her hand when Leo began to object.

"Would the risks be higher if we went with you?" Naomi asked.

Holly considered for a moment. She knew the scales could tip either way if she brought her friends. They could be the determining factor between failure and success. But she didn't want to risk their lives if she didn't have to. Sometimes taking the risk, no matter how big, was necessary, but was it worth the risk this time?

"I don't know. You guys being there could be the deciding factor for getting Dylan back, but at the same time we might have a better chance of getting out alive without having you all there."

Her friends were quiet, waiting for someone to say something.

"I want to risk it," Artemis said at last. "I can't just sit around waiting."

The rest of them nodded in agreement and turned their heads to Holly. She nodded and pulled out her phone. Dean didn't reply to the text she sent, but she knew he'd seen it.

"I hope you realize the training tomorrow is going to be on a whole other level of pain," Holly said.

"Anything they put us through tomorrow or the day after will be nothing once we get Dylan back," Leo stated.

Holly nodded in appreciation then walked over to the window and stared out at the horizon, her friends starting quiet conversations behind her. She stood there staring at nothing for a few moments before turning and sitting on the ground next to the couch between Artemis and Kelly.

The two girls were discussing the policies the Domina had put in place to stop the rioting as Holly laid her head back against the couch. Kelly spared her a glance, but she waved her off and studied the ceiling as she listened halfheartedly to the conversation.

After a few moments like that, Holly sat up as her phone vibrated. Dean had replied to her text.

She got up, telling the girls that she was leaving. Without another word, Holly left the house. She had mentioned to Dean that her car was still at the building, and he had apparently found the time to drop it back off at her house, so she climbed into that. There was just one stop she had to make on the way to her destination.

Holly stopped when she reached the entrance of the cemetery. There was a slight moment of hesitation before she began making her way down the path and stopped when she reached the headstones she was looking for.

Anger boiled in her stomach, mixing with the guilt and sadness already there as she read the name engraved on the headstone closest to her: *Andrew Carnell.*

Holly wanted to scream and rage at the world for taking her family from her, but she stood there like a statue for a moment before she placed one of the flowers she had bought next to each of the five headstones. Then she sank to her knees in front of her mom's headstone and started talking.

She told her everything that had happened since she had left for the festival. At some point she started crying, thinking there hadn't been any more tears left to cry, but there she was, practically sobbing by the time she reached the meeting with Professor Pendleton and everything that followed.

"I'm so scared, mom. I don't know what to do anymore. I wish you were here to help me. You always knew what to do. I wish I had some of your strength right now because I could really use it."

Holly sat there in silence for a while, her tears having long since dried when she heard footsteps behind her. She turned her head as she heard Dean say, "It's late. Do you want a ride back to my apartment?"

Holly thought about walking, but instead, she stood—brushing grass from her legs—and turned to face him as she said, "No thanks."

The walk out of the cemetery was near silent. Only the whistling of the wind through the trees disturbed the stillness. Holly couldn't help but think of it as the calm before the storm.

Chapter 38

The next day and a half were full of hardcore training for Holly and her friends, and not much sleep. When they weren't training, Dean and Shawn were arguing about every little thing. How long they would focus on teaching one concept or another, and whether Shawn would be joining them or not were frequent topics.

Holly had finally had enough of it on the second day. She was trying to relax in her room before the meeting the next day when she heard them yelling at each other. Storming out of her room, Holly walked into the kitchen—their regular place for their fights.

"Would you both just *shut up?*" She yelled over them. "I swear you two argue more than a married couple. Don't you know how to talk without everything turning into an argument?"

Shawn opened his mouth.

"Don't even think about it. I've heard enough come out of your mouth over the past two days."

Holly shifted her gaze between the brothers.

"What is wrong with you? It's not your decision anymore on whether or not my friends and I are going. We made that choice, and we're not turning back now so don't get your boxers in a twist arguing about it.

"Yes, you could tell your commanding officer about this. Yes, it would be nice to have professional backup to help, but did you ever stop to think that maybe they wouldn't help? Isn't it against government policy not to negotiate with kidnappers? Don't answer that." She paused, taking a breath. "I know this isn't the best situation to be in—in fact, it's probably the worst-case scenario. But we already discussed this. I will stop at nothing to get Dylan back, and my friends will do anything to get justice for our friends who were killed."

Neither of them said anything for a moment.

"I'm sorry, Holly," Shawn said at last.

"It doesn't matter anymore," Holly told them. "The meeting is tomorrow. You're adults— soldiers—so act like it. Stop your bickering and get over it."

Holly turned on her heel to leave when she heard Dean mutter, "Did we just get scolded by a teenager?"

Shawn coughed. "She's right, Dean."

"I know."

The next morning was spent going over the plan again and again until it was drilled into their minds.

After an hour of it, everybody was about ready to pummel the Walker brothers just to shut them up. Then, it was time.

There would be no more waiting. Holly was fidgeting in anticipation of what was going to happen. As everyone piled into the same cars they had driven to the last meeting, Holly began to, once again, question whether she should have told her friends about the meeting. She knew they would have been pissed about her not telling them, but they would have been safer.

Shaking her head, Holly told herself that what was done was done, and there was nothing she could do about it now. All she could think about after that was hoping this meeting would end better than the last one, and how relieved she would be when she got Dylan back.

The church where the meeting would take place was only a thirty-minute drive from the gym where they had gone over the plan. Overgrown plants surrounded the church, turning yellow as summer came to an end. A few wildflowers were growing in sparse patches in the grass around the building. A few lone trees rustled their branches in the breeze.

Clouds covered the sun, leaving the sky slightly overcast as Holly pulled up next to the church and parked. Dean parked his car next to her and got out, Shawn climbed out as well. Holly did the same, her eyes squinting in the temporary rays of sunlight before adjusting to the brightness.

Walking up to Dean, she asked, "Do you think this will work?"

Dean looked her in the eye as she handed him the keys to her car and said, "If it doesn't, most of us won't live to regret it."

Holly felt her heart pick up its pace. She knew why he had said it, but that didn't make things any easier.

"Thanks," she muttered. Dean nodded to her. She knew he understood that nothing but the truth would be helpful to her at that moment.

Holly took a deep breath before nodding to Kelly, who had climbed into the driver's seat of her car. Kelly waited for Dean to hand her the keys before she began pulling away to park the car at a charging station down the road.

Alone, Holly walked up to the front of the church and gazed up at its towering form. The sun was reaching its zenith causing Holly to squint as its light peaked over the point of the church's steeple before a small cloud drifted over it. Returning her focus to the wide French-style doors, Holly took in the church once more. The walls were an off-white color that had dark spots of mold near the base. All of the windows were broken, letting the bright noon sunlight into the building as the cloud blocking the sun moved on.

The door creaked as Holly pushed it open and coughed as her feet stirred up decades-old dust on the floor. Shawn had said he had come and scouted out the building the day before, but maybe he hadn't gone inside. Holly looked around her as she walked down the aisle toward the altar. There were holes in the roof letting in beams of sunlight, dust dancing in the rays. The rows upon rows of pews were falling apart as she walked past them.

Holly wondered how old the church was to have been in such a sorry state. Plants were growing around the base of the altar as she came to a stop before it. The vines looked like ivy, but Holly couldn't tell for sure.

Pulling out her phone, Holly checked the time. He was late. That didn't surprise her, Harry was always late, but it made her feel more on edge. She sat on the altar, waiting anxiously for her father to show up. His letter hadn't specified what he wanted aside from talking to her.

Her leg began restlessly bouncing up and down. Where was he? He was supposed to be there. She was about to get up and go searching through the building when the doors she had just entered were thrown open and her father walked through them, alone.

"Where is he?" she demanded.

"Holly," her father started.

"Where is he? You want to talk? Let me see him first."

"I can't do that."

"Why not?"

"Because he's not here yet."

Holly stiffened.

"If he's not here, then this meeting isn't happening."

Holly stood and stalked past the rows of pews. She was halfway down the aisle when Harry spoke again.

"They won't bring him until they're finished."

Her whole body tensed.

"What is that supposed to mean?" she snarled.

"He's on his way, Holly," Harry told her, his gaze darkening. "Let's just talk until he gets here, okay?"

Holly glared at him. The man who was supposed to be her father. She growled but turned on her heels and stalked back to the altar. Hopping up, she sat cross-legged on top of it.

"This used to be a place of worship. I'd think you would show more respect."

"Are you talking about God or yourself?"

Harry was silent.

"For someone who went through all of this just to get a face-to-face, you sure aren't saying a whole lot," Holly said to him.

"It's because I'm trying to figure out who your mother let you become while I was gone."

Holly snorted and rolled her eyes. "Mom didn't *let* me become anyone. I am who I am because it's who *I* want to be. Not Mom, not Nathan, and most certainly not *you*."

Harry cautiously took a few steps forward, then continued down the aisle until he was standing in the second row. He sat down in the seat next to him as he asked, "Who's Nathan?"

"My ex."

"You had a boyfriend before Dylan."

Holly didn't bother correcting him. "What's with you wanting to know about my love life? You haven't seen me in years and this is what you want to waste your time asking about?"

"I'm not wasting my time. As you said, I haven't seen you in years. I want to know what I missed, and what I need to make up for." Harry rested his forearms on the pew in front of him, his gaze focused solely on her.

Holly shifted her gaze as she replied. "It doesn't matter. You were sent to prison because of the choices *you* made. Now you have to live with the consequences."

"That doesn't mean I don't regret them, dolphin. Let me make up for them. Let me be a part of your life again. We're the only family we both have left."

Holly's gaze snapped back to him, anger burning in her eyes.

"You stopped being my family the day you made your first kill," she snarled.

"How would that be possible if you weren't even born?" Harry smirked.

Her gut tightened, rage hollowing it out, but she shoved it down with the embers beginning to spark along her skin.

"I guess that means you were never my family to begin with, doesn't it?" she droned, her voice devoid of emotions. "If you wanted to have a family, you should have started trying to mend things long before now. I might have even considered forgiving you if your cult hadn't murdered my *actual* family. But I guess that wasn't meant to be."

They stared at each other in silence, both of them waiting for the other to say something. Holly knew Harry would break first, she had nothing to say to him unless it was regarding him rotting in Hell.

"How long have you been on the swim team?" he asked.

"Seven years," Holly answered. She only answered to stall for time, she just hoped he wouldn't catch on until it was too late. He seemed to think she might open up to him before whoever it was got there with Dylan.

Harry smiled. "I remember the first time your mother and I brought you to the pool for swim lessons, and you had your hair in those little braids. You had such a big smile on your face, and you were begging, just begging us to let you get in the water. You used to spend hours telling me about how much fun you had."

Holly remained silent. She had pieces of memories like that with her father. Happy memories that she had treasured until they had been tainted with the blood of his victims.

"Was that the day you decided to kidnap and murder my swim instructor, or did you wait until the last day of lessons to decide she was to be your next victim?"

Harry flinched. Holly knew she had hit her mark with that comment. He didn't think she would find out about that one, but Holly had researched the entire case against him, and in doing so had learned just how little he truly cared about human life. It's the reason Shawn's plan wouldn't end the way the brothers wanted it to.

"What?" Holly asked, venom coating her tongue like honey. "Didn't expect me to know about sweet little Millie? Poor Millie who had just told her class that she was ten weeks pregnant when she disappeared, only for her dismembered body to be found three months later in the very pool she had taught swimming lessons, her engagement ring nowhere to be found.

"Or how about Penelope? You remember her, don't you? You spent six months raping and torturing her before you decided to dismember her too."

"That's enough."

"Is it?" Holly retorted. "I think you should keep listening. You wanted to talk to me again, didn't you?"

"Not about this," Harry said.

"Of course not. You probably want to talk about your favorite one, don't you? Beautiful, darling Catherine. She was your first victim. I've heard they're always a serial killer's favorite, but you would know that for sure. You probably picked her out as an easy target, but your ruse worked a little too well. Not only did she fall in love with the person you pretended to be, but you fell in love with her. You couldn't kill her now, so you married her, had kids with her, and then murdered her sister when you couldn't suppress your urges anymore.

"This story sounds familiar, doesn't it? Do you want to finish it or should I?"

"Holly, stop," Harry tried again.

"No. I spent so much time afraid of you and what you did. I'm not afraid anymore, *Dad*. I know what you've done. I know *exactly* how despicable you truly are!"

"I said *enough*!" he yelled, jumping to his feet.

Holly smirked. Harry looked like he was about to say more when the doors behind him opened and two men walked in. The one on the left Holly didn't recognize, but the one on the right...

"Dylan," she muttered.

Holly hopped off the altar and leveled a glare at her father. "This meeting is over. You got what you wanted, now let him go."

Harry's composure had changed dramatically in the seconds Holly had been distracted by Dylan's entrance.

"I don't think so," Harry told her. Then to Shawn and Dean, who were hiding behind the altar—having come in through the back door and hidden there before Harry had entered—he said, "Why don't you two boys come out from your hiding place? I don't know how you managed to get there without me noticing, but my associates have informed me of your position."

Clothing rustled as the brothers stood and stepped up beside her, but she kept her gaze on the man dragging a half-conscious Dylan down the aisle and dropping him at his feet. She stared at his motionless form, her pulse racing, holding her breath until she saw his chest rise shakily as he breathed.

"We had a deal, Harry," Holly growled. "You got an hour of talking with me. Now let Dylan go, and leave."

"Did you really think you could surround me without me noticing?" Harry changed the topic. "Besides, it hasn't even been an hour. Not yet."

"What are you talking about?" Holly asked.

"Your friends have slowly been moving in closer during our conversation. Tell them to come out."

Holly stood still, waiting for him to call his bluff. He couldn't possibly know her friends were there.

"I saw the two cars pull up, Holly." At the flicker of surprise on her face, he said, "Did you really think I would be late? I was here the whole time. I watched you pull up from inside the building."

Holly glanced at Shawn and nodded. Shawn whistled, calling her friends out of their various spots throughout the chapel. They didn't bother staying where they were, not when each of them had a rebel aiming a gun at their heads.

Holly's eyes returned to her father, his blue eyes had never left her face.

"What now?" she asked. "I assume backup is already on its way if it's not here already. So what do you want?"

"I want you, Holly. I've always wanted you. You were one of the only things I thought about during those long years in prison."

"Clearly it wasn't enough time for everything you did," Dean mumbled next to her.

"Do be quiet, Major. You'll get your turn." Harry didn't even shift his gaze as he said it. "Holly, I know we've had our differences, but I truly believe that the best thing for you right now is to come with me."

"Go with you?" she asked in disbelief. He couldn't possibly believe she would go with him. "Why would I ever go with you? You're the reason my friends are dead. The reason my *family* is dead."

"I might have a high standing with G.H.O.S.T., but their plans do not stem from my goals. The deaths of our family and your friends are on their shoulders, not mine."

As he spoke, Holly noticed movements in the shadows just before a tall blonde woman strode through the open doors.

"Oh, good. Everyone's here. Thank you for keeping them busy, Eagle," Raven said. "I think it's time we all had a good heart-to-heart."

Chapter 39

Holly's hands began to shake as she held back from throwing a fireball at Raven and burning her to a crisp. That wouldn't help the situation, however, so she clenched her hands into fists and did nothing as Raven gave them a victorious smile.

Dean put his hand on her shoulder and squeezed. She appreciated the gesture, but she shrugged him off. Nothing could distract her. There were only two things on her mind at that moment and nothing anyone said or did would stop her.

Raven pouted as she took in Holly's expression.

"No fight from you today little firebird?" She teased.

Holly didn't respond. She wouldn't let herself be goaded into saying anything that could make matters worse.

"Fair enough. I guess having your entire family killed and all your friends leaving or being killed as well has taken its toll on your fiery spirit. Jacob sends his regards, by the way. I'm afraid he's a bit preoccupied at the moment. I think your friend's blood may have stained his favorite shirt."

Holly gritted her teeth. Nothing Raven said would get her to risk the lives of her friends beside her.

"Oh, did you spoil the surprise?" Raven asked, looking at Dylan. "And to think my brother was all worried about you figuring out it was him who tried to kill you. I think he grew quite fond of your little group during his time with you all."

"That's funny," Holly couldn't stop herself from saying. "I didn't think traitors could feel anything for the people they lied to. But who am I to talk, my father is an infamous serial killer."

Raven smiled. "There she is. That's the little firebird I remember."

Holly scowled at her and took a step away from the altar behind her.

"I would stop calling me that if you want to keep that tongue of yours attached to your head," Holly told her.

"Holly." The warning in Dean's voice almost gave her pause as she took two steps further from him.

She knew what he was trying to tell her, but she wasn't listening. All she could think about was Dylan and getting him and the rest of her friends away without any of them getting killed.

"You're here for a reason, Raven. Stop talking in circles and spit it out." Holly took another step forward. Somewhere amongst the gathered rebels, a gun was cocked. Holly stopped moving.

"Where would the fun be in that?" Raven mused, taking a few steps down the aisle.

Holly's friends were motionless behind her. She kept her eyes on Raven but didn't miss it when Harry slid out of his seat and disappeared into the shadows.

"Who said anything about fun?" Holly replied, walking down the steps of the altar. "I thought you were here on a serious matter."

Holly wasn't sure any of her friends were breathing as she continued walking down the aisle—Raven matching her step for step—until she was just out of arm's reach of the woman.

"Of course I am, but that doesn't mean I can't have a bit of fun while I'm at it."

Holly's hand twitched at her side. "What do you want?"

"What *I* want isn't important. What *he* wants, however," Raven pointed to the man behind her, the one who had come in with Dylan. "Is a whole other matter entirely."

Raven took a step back. Holly looked back and forth between her and the man she had indicated to.

"Hello, Holly," the man said, his deep voice resonating in the stillness of the chapel. "I am Hawk. It's nice to finally meet you in person."

"Who are you, and what do you want?" Holly demanded, her eyes momentarily going to Dylan, who lay almost motionless on the ground a few feet from her. She was tired of beating around the bush, she needed to get her friends out.

"I'm the leader of G.H.O.S.T.," Hawk stated. "And, to put it simply, I came to clean up Eagle's mess. If you would like to join us, that is your decision and we would welcome you, but I would think very carefully before you decide."

Holly opened her mouth to reply, but stopped, as though she were contemplating the offer.

"Don't do it, Holly," Leo said from somewhere behind her.

"Shut up," she told him.

"Before you decide, there is something I must tell you," Hawk said. "There are bombs planted in various locations around this building. They are set to go off any minute. You better make your decision quickly."

Hawk grinned, triumph glimmering in his eyes behind his mask. Holly returned the smile, her left hand inching to the waistband of her pants as she took a step forward and stuck her right hand out to him.

As soon as Hawk took her hand, Holly pulled the gun from her waistband and aimed it at his heart.

"You're going to let my friends take Dylan and leave here, unharmed. Then, and only then will we talk about your offer," Holly said.

"Holly, I know what you're thinking. Don't do it." Dean was starting to get on her nerves, she had to get him to go along with her plan, but she knew he wouldn't understand.

"Shut up and let me handle this," she told him. To Hawk, she said, "Do we have a deal?"

Hawk scanned her eyes and said, "Raven, if you would."

Holly spared half a glance at Raven to see her pull Dylan to his feet and shove him toward Hawk. This close, Holly could see that his hands were bound, but she still tightened her grip on the gun as Hawk released her hand and slowly pulled out a hunting knife and grabbed Dylan's wrists.

"Go say goodbye to your girlfriend, it might be a while before you see her again," Hawk said, then he cut through Dylan's bonds and took a step back.

Holly rushed to Dylan and pulled him into a hug. She kept her gun on Hawk for a moment before sliding it back into her waistband.

"Are you okay?" she whispered in Dylan's ear.

"Holly," he rasped. "What are you doing?"

"Don't worry about it."

She felt Dylan huff a laugh against her neck.

"I'm sorry," he murmured. "I can't believe I got caught, again."

"It's not your fault. Okay? It's not." Holly pulled him closer. "Just go with Shawn and Dean. They'll take you somewhere safe. Don't worry about me, I'll be fine."

Holly pulled back and leaned her forehead against his, closing her eyes.

"Holly—" Dylan stopped short. A choking sound came out of his mouth.

Holly opened her eyes and scanned his face. A trickle of blood dripped from the corner of his mouth.

"Dylan? Dylan!" she cried.

"I-I love you." Dylan smiled and fell out of Holly's arms.

Holly screamed, taking a step back. Hawk sighed and wiped the blood from the knife on his pants.

"So messy," he said. "I hate cleaning up after other people's messes."

Holly stared at Dylan, willing him to get up. She couldn't move. Someone said her name. Hands were on her shoulders, but she shoved them off and fell to her knees, pulling Dylan to her chest. No tears fell from her eyes. It felt like her whole world was caving in on itself.

In a matter of seconds, the mind-numbing grief turned into an icy rage, and she focused on that rage, she honed it into a weapon—a promise for vengeance.

Holly stood and stared at Hawk, gave him a look that promised death, and he laughed. He. Laughed. At her. At what he had done.

"I will end you," she promised.

"I look forward to seeing you try," Hawk said. "If you make it out alive that is. You have roughly two minutes before you're all blown sky high."

With that, Hawk turned on his heel and began walking swiftly toward the exit.

Holly pulled the gun from her waistband, about to pull the trigger when she heard a gunshot. Blinding pain caused her to cry out. Dropping the gun, she clutched her shoulder.

"Everybody out!" Shawn yelled.

"Holly we have to go," Dean was telling her. "We have to go *now*."

Holly shook her head. "Not without Dylan."

"I'll grab him. You go."

"I'm not leaving without him!"

Dean forced her to look at him.

"Trust me. I promise I will get him out. Now run!"

Holly stared into his eyes as he pulled her to her feet.

"I will hold you to that," she said.

Then she was running. Once she was out the doors, she was jumping down the stairs and sprinting as fast as her legs could carry her to where Shawn stood with her friends. Adrenaline blocked the pain in her shoulder as she ran. As she came to a stop in front of them, she spun around, clutching her shoulder and staring at the doors of the church.

A gunshot came from the direction of the church, but Shawn grabbed her arm, stopping her from running back. After another moment, Dean was running from the building, no, limping from the building. One moment Shawn was holding

Holly back from rushing back in, the next he was sprinting to his injured brother and half carrying him back to Holly and her friends.

The Walker brothers were only halfway there when the church behind them exploded, sending them crashing to the ground. Holly's friends cried out behind her and fell to the ground covering their ears, but all she could do was stand there and watch as the church went up in smoke and flames, with Dylan's body still inside.

Chapter 40

The drive to the hospital was a blur. Holly only remembered bits and pieces of what had happened after the church exploded. Scenes would come back in flashes, and then they would be gone. The one thing she could remember clear as day was the fact that Dylan was gone.

Gone. The word rang in her head the entire drive to the hospital. It was the only thing she could recall clearly. Dylan was gone.

As she sat on the hospital bed hours later, the word still rang through her head. Even as she was released from the hospital, gone. Dylan was gone.

Holly spent days on end just sitting in the spare bedroom of Dean's apartment staring, at the wall, at the ceiling, at her hands. She was wearing Dylan's favorite hoodie and his necklace. Naomi had brought over his things from his hotel room the day Holly had been released from the hospital and had stayed with her for the next couple of days just so she wouldn't be alone.

Eventually, Naomi had to stop visiting. Dean had told her to let Holly be alone for a while. Dean wasn't ever at his apartment in those days, so she was completely alone. She made herself get up and eat once a day, but she was glad for the solitude.

Holly had blacked out at some point on the ride to the hospital, but when she had awoken, Naomi had told her everything. The blast from the explosion had put Shawn in a coma. He had used his body to cover Dean and had taken the brunt of the explosive force. Holly had stood there staring at the church as her friends called for ambulances. Scrapes from the flying debris littered Holly's cheeks in the aftermath, but she wouldn't move an inch. The paramedic had to drag her into the ambulance where she blacked out from blood loss.

"Police searched the wreckage," Naomi had said. *"Dylan's body wasn't there."*

Holly would never be able to forgive Dean for leaving Dylan there. Left him. She had left him too, but he was still alive then. Still alive. Still—gone.

Dylan was gone.

Gone.

He was gone.

She couldn't forgive him.

She was still sitting on her bed, staring at the wall when she heard the apartment door click shut. Her attention snapped to the closed door to her left. She stood up. It had been a couple of weeks since the explosion, and she was done sitting around with nothing but her thoughts and her phone. Holly stormed into the front room and glared at Dean.

Dean looked exhausted. He probably hadn't slept much in the past week, but neither had Holly. Most of his time had been spent sitting at his brother's bedside, and this was the first time he had been back in days.

Surprise alighted in Dean's eyes as he took in Holly standing before him.

"Holly," he said. "You're up!"

"How could you do that?" she asked him. "How could you leave him?"

"Holly." Pain filled Dean's eyes as she spoke. "I couldn't carry him."

"I don't care!" She shouted. "You should have dragged him out if you had to."

"I didn't have a choice, Holly."

"Of course you did. You just picked the easier option."

"I tried to get him out of there," Dean told her. "I did."

"You promised!" She yelled. "You promised me you would get him out! You lied to me!"

"I didn't lie to you. I tried my best to get him out. If I had stayed I would have died!"

"Better you than him," Holly said with deadly calm. "Go rot in Hell, Dean Walker."

She didn't let him say another word before she shoved past him and left the apartment. There was nowhere specific on her mind, but she was done sitting back and doing nothing.

Holly walked for an hour before she hailed a taxi. Once the taxi had dropped her off, she kept walking until she was standing among the ruins of the building that was supposed to be where the wedding reception was held. She checked the time on her phone and then scanned the debris around her.

"I know you're here," she said. "I came alone, just like you asked. You can come out."

She stood there in silence, waiting. The shifting of rubble to her right alerted her to his position.

"Are you finally ready to hear me out?" Hawk asked.

Holly nodded. All those hours alone with her thoughts she had contemplated whether or not she would accept his offer. It wasn't until she had seen Dean that she made her decision.

"I'm ready to listen," she told him. He walked closer and stopped within arm's reach of her.

"I had hoped you would say that." Hawk smiled at her, but it turned to a frown when she pulled the gun from the pocket of Dylan's hoodie and aimed it at his head.

"Now, now, Holly. Let's not repeat the past. I thought you learned from our last encounter that I don't take kindly to having a gun pointed at me."

"This isn't a bluff anymore. I have nothing left to lose." Holly pulled the trigger.

A deafening crack sounded through the ruins, almost like the sound of thunder, as the bullet zipped through the air. Hawk's head snapped back as it entered his brain, and his body collapsed to the ground.

The ruins were disturbingly quiet for a moment before Holly heard clapping coming from her left. Lowering her gun, Holly turned to the newcomer.

She was short, with wavy shoulder length, hazelnut hair, and electric blue eyes. A bird mask was fixed on her face.

"Hello, Owl," Holly greeted her. "I upheld my end of the bargain, now it's your turn."

Owl smiled and nodded. Her impressive owl imitation call brought forth Harry. He stopped next to Owl and Holly walked up to him, looking him dead in the eyes.

"Last week you told me my family's deaths had nothing to do with your goals," she said. "I know the truth now. I know it was your scheming that led to this building being a target for the bombing all those months ago."

"I'm sorry, dolphin," Harry said.

"No you're not," Holly muttered under her breath at the same time Owl said, "You don't get to be sorry. I am the leader of this organization. You do not get to put your own agenda above that of our rebellion."

"What are you saying?" Harry asked, taking half a step away from them.

"I'm saying," Holly told him. "It's your turn. Karma's a bitch, isn't it?"

Holly aimed her gun at his head.

"What, not going to use your powers?" Harry mocked, fear making his voice shake as he tried to regain the upper hand he hadn't had since Dylan's death.

Despite knowing that he was goading her, Holly couldn't stop the feeling of dread in her stomach at the thought of using her powers again. All they ever caused was pain and destruction. And maybe he deserved that. But she had to do this her way. Had to do it without the help of something he gave her.

She met his green eyes with a hard look and... hesitated. Her father didn't have green eyes.

Thunder cracked through the ruins, and Harry fell forward, landing face-first in the rubble.

Holly stared at his motionless form, her finger still hovering over the trigger that she hadn't pulled, before lifting her gaze to Dean as he lowered his gun.

"What did you do?!" She screamed at him. "He was *mine*! You had no right!"

"Holly. It's time to leave," Owl told her.

Holly blinked, turning her head to the woman. The sound of helicopter blades in the distance was getting closer. Holly's clothes blew in the wind as the chopper flew over them and began landing in the street.

"Let's go," Holly said, tossing aside her gun.

"Holly!" Dean shouted. "Don't do it! Holly!"

Holly didn't spare him another look as she and Owl picked their way through the rubble and climbed into the helicopter. As the chopper lifted off the ground, Holly, at last, spared one more glance at Dean's shrinking form as she adjusted the headset Owl had handed her.

Holly looked back at Owl as she removed her mask.

"Welcome to the G.H.O.S.T. initiative," Selena said.

"Glad to be here, Secretary Garcia," Holly replied. "When do I get my first assignment?"

"You can call me Selena when we're alone," Selena told her. "And your first mission starts now. How do you feel about assassinating the Domina?"

"You don't have to do this," Domina Garner pleaded.

"No. I don't," Holly told her. "But I want to."

The blood was hot on her hand as Holly slid the sword across the Domina's throat. Her body fell to the floor as Holly wiped the blade of the sword in her hand on her uniform and turned her gaze to the camera before her.

"Your domina is dead. G.H.O.S.T. has taken complete control of the government. As of today, this country is no longer a republic. This is an empire, and this is your empress. Her majesty Selena Rosé Garcia," Holly announced as Selena walked up next to her and smiled for the camera, her owl mask hanging around her neck. "Broadcasts will be made over the next week of how the country will transition, and any citizen found resisting will be executed."

The broadcast ended. Holly adjusted her mask as she turned to her empress.

"You did well, Phoenix. I hope to see more success like this in the future."

"Of course, Your Majesty," Holly bowed.

"Thank you, Phoenix. You have the rest of the day off. Be back tomorrow morning for your next assignment. It's time this country learned to fear my general."

Chapter 41

He didn't know where he was, all he knew was that he was running. Running to her, but she was always just out of reach. He ran as fast as he could, but something was keeping him from her.

Sometimes he would get within arm's reach of her, but then she would start wailing. He couldn't discern what it was she was saying, but it sounded familiar. Like a name. A name he couldn't quite grasp its familiarity.

Then, as she stopped, her voice going silent, he would ask her why she was screaming, and she wouldn't answer. She would erupt into flames and disappear in a cloud of ash. He would panic and spin around in the darkness calling for her, but her name sounded fuzzy in his mouth and he couldn't remember what he was saying, or why he was calling out for someone. Ashes filled his lungs causing him to choke, but in an instant, they would dissipate. Panic and fear gripped his heart as he tried to see or hear anything but everything was clouded and muffled. Anything he touched dissolved into dust.

But then he would see her again, her green eyes haunting him as he tried to run to her. If only he could reach her. If only he could just...

His body jerked. He sat up gasping for air. Where was he? He looked around him, frantically searching for something familiar. Everything was strange to him.

He tried to get out of the chamber he was in and fell to the ground. There was a liquid coating his skin making it hard for him to stand, but suddenly someone was kneeling in front of him trying to get his attention.

He lifted his gaze and stared into the eyes of someone familiar—not the girl from his dreams, someone else—but he couldn't place how he knew them. He paused his frantic movements as he tried to place where he knew this person, and then he remembered.

Where was she? He had to find her. He had to get to her. She was hurt. He tried to stand again.

"Calm down," they were saying. "You're okay. You're safe."

He licked his lips and asked in a husky voice, "Where am I? Where's Holly?"

Just then another familiar face floated into his vision.

"Naomi?" he rasped, his throat was so dry. He cleared his throat. "Where's Holly?"

"You're awake," Naomi breathed. "You've been in a coma. We didn't know if you would wake up. How do you feel?"

His reply was interrupted by a man who walked in behind her—Dean.

Dean stared at him in disbelief.

"Dylan?"

Acknowledgments

I want to thank me, myself, and I for not giving up on this book that I started seven years ago in the middle of seventh grade. I had no plan for where it was going to end up, but after all these years I have finally finished it.

Ok, but for real now.

Thank you to my brother in law for being the beta reader of all beta readers. You've been here since the first draft—disaster that it was—and you still stuck around. I am so grateful for all of your notes and comments, even when the only thing you would compare this to was *The Hunger Games*. It means so much to me that, even with your busy schedule, you took time out of your day to read this so critically and give harsh critiques—I know I certainly needed them.

This book wouldn't have happened without the continuous support of all my amazing friends—you know who you are. Even if none of you really knew what my plan was for this book—

don't worry, I didn't know for a long time either—
you were so supportive and encouraging. You
gave me the strength to push through and to keep
working on it. And to my best friend, you were
there for so many of those late night writing
sessions and for every random idea that came into
my head during our workouts at the gym. Your
constant hype over these characters that I have
known for years has not gone unnoticed, nor
unappreciated, so thank you.

I want to give special thanks to my cats for
their endless "help" in writing this. Every button
sat on, every time you sat on my keyboard—
making it impossible to write— has led to this
moment. I know one of you is gone, but your
legacy lives on in the tiny paws that threaten to
accidentally press the power button on my laptop
when I don't give her the attention she desires.

Last but not least, thank you to all past, present,
and future readers who are the ones I wrote this
for. Stay tuned for book two.

About the Author

Morgan Summers is a reader and writer with a love for swimming. She is entering her senior year of college, pursuing a bachelor's degree in English with an emphasis in creative writing. *Shadows of the Past* is her debut novel, and she hopes to keep sharing her stories with the world until she greets the grave. When she's not writing, she's experimenting with other art forms—such as songwriting—pets her cats, or lifts weights at the gym with her best friend. You can find Morgan on Instagram **@golden.ink.of.summers** for updates on her future projects.